THE JUDGE

Highland Heroes
Book Three

by Maeve Greyson

ARE YOU SIGNED UP FOR DRAGONBLADE'S BLOG?

You'll get the latest news and information on exclusive giveaways, exclusive excerpts, coming releases, sales, free books, cover reveals and more.

Check out our complete list of authors, too!

No spam, no junk. That's a promise!

Sign Up Here

www.dragonbladepublishing.com

⟫⟫⟫⟪⟪⟪

Dearest Reader;

Thank you for your support of a small press. At Dragonblade Publishing, we strive to bring you the highest quality Historical Romance from the some of the best authors in the business. Without your support, there is no 'us', so we sincerely hope you adore these stories and find some new favorite authors along the way.

Happy Reading!

CEO, Dragonblade Publishing

Additional Dragonblade books by Author Maeve Greyson

Highland Heroes Series
The Guardian
The Warrior
The Judge
The Dreamer

CHAPTER ONE

Edinburgh, Scotland
Spring 1698

"THOSE MEN ARE here again. At the service door." An irritated huff seasoned the announcement. "And it's not even midday yet. Shameful, I tell ye. Utterly shameful."

Alasdair Cameron didn't bother to look up from the document on his desk. His prim housekeeper, Mrs. Aggie, made it clear with her tone that she expected him to call down a shower of hellfire and damnation on the two unexpected, yet familiar, guests at the rear entrance to the kitchen.

A pert stomp of a heel and a growling *ahem* stressed her desire for immediate action.

Hungry for a bit of levity to brighten the dreary morning, he couldn't resist teasing her a wee bit. He looked her in the eyes and winked. "I dinna suppose ye'd be good enough to see them to the study?"

"I would not!" The door banged shut as cold and final as the sealing of a tomb.

"I thought not." He pushed up from his chair and stretched before scrubbing both hands across his face. He hadn't realized Ian had returned to Edinburgh so soon. When he got hold of his younger brother, he'd be kicking his arse for him. How dare the wee rascal visit Château Delatate before letting his only brother know he'd survived his latest mercenary campaign.

Damn, Ian. Ever since the lad had discovered Lettie, one of Madam Georgianna's harlots, who possessed a disturbing resemblance to his dead wife, the heartsick fool spent all his coin and quite a bit of Alasdair's at the elite establishment renowned for satisfying a gentleman's every whim. Whenever Ian passed out drunk and ran out of money, Madam Georgianna sent for Alasdair to come and collect him. Said she pitied Ian. What with losing his wife and unborn child the way he had at the massacre at Glencoe, she couldn't bear to treat him ill.

The brothers considered it an act of kindness on Madam Georgianna's part. Any of the establishment's other clients discovered penniless and pickled in one of the boudoirs, found themselves charged fourfold the usual rate while they sobered up. After all, 'twas a brothel, not an inn.

Alasdair strode down the long narrow hallway leading to the manor's kitchen. This house was a far cry from a drafty stone keep hidden in the unbridled wilderness of the Highlands. Part of him hated the tamed air of the place, but the part of him growing accustomed to the conveniences and comforts of higher class living in Edinburgh liked it just fine.

He shoved through the swinging door of the kitchen and came up short as every servant froze, faced him, then stood as though holding their breath so as not to miss a single word that fell from his lips. He wasn't particularly fond of that either. Hell, he was just a man. No better or worse than the lot of them. Fate had just been kinder, and he'd prospered. Well…in some ways he had. He pushed away the long-ago memories threatening to surface. Now was not the time to ruminate over regrets and past mistakes.

He headed toward the duo standing just inside the service entrance. Twins. Identical mountains of blonde-haired brawn except for the color of their eyes. It was the only way Alasdair could tell apart Château Delatate's armed *keepers of the peace*, as Madam Georgianna had fondly dubbed them. Alasdair pulled his wallet from the inside pocket of his waistcoat as he addressed the closest giant. "How long this time, Einrich?"

He flashed a brilliant smile, his perfect teeth gleaming. "Master Ian arrived early," he said in a heavy German accent. He turned to his brother. "Delatate's *erster kunde* for today. *Ja*, Adalbert?"

"*Ja*," Adalbert said as he stepped forward with a flawless smile of his own. "Said for you to come at once. Said very important."

After several *fetchings* of Ian, Alasdair had learned more German than he had ever thought to encounter in Scotland. *Erster kunde* meant Ian was Delatate's first client or customer of the day, and *ja* was German for *yes*. But from the way the Friedrich brothers acted, his brother was not drunk, passed out, nor out of funds—yet. It appeared Ian had sent the pair.

Mrs. Aggie interrupted with another shrill clearing of her throat. "Edinburgh's finest solicitor should nay be seen traipsing into a common brothel this early in the day."

"So, ye'd have no issue if I waited 'til after midday, aye?" He did so love nettling poor Mrs. Aggie. She acted more mother than housekeeper and, on most days, he didn't mind. Her meddling grew a bit thorny at times, but for the most part, her caring ways brought a nice bit of comfort to the house.

"Ye know verra well that is not what I meant!" She puffed up like an angry hen, her white starched apron nearly popping free of its pins at her rounded shoulders. She shook a finger at the twins. "Ye canna go with them. Ye've always fetched Master Ian in the dead of night before. Ye've appearances to think of."

"We bring him in the back way," Adalbert offered. "Just like always."

Einrich nodded and gave Mrs. Aggie a kindly smile. "No one see. *Das verspreche ich.*"

"What did ye just call me?" The sputtering woman stomped closer to Einrich with fists trembling as though readying for a fight.

Einrich held up both hands and shook his head faster. "*Nein. Nein.*" He frowned down at the furious housekeeper for a moment, then brightened with a smile meant to charm. "I said I *promise* no one see him."

Time to take control before Einrich got hurt. Alasdair edged his way around Mrs. Aggie. "We'll exit the gardens by the back gate, and go through the alleyway, aye?"

"I'll be having a stern word with Master Ian. I promise ye that." She clasped her hands and twitched with a haughty sniff. "Shame on him for risking such disrespect to his brother's name."

Deciding it best not to comment, Alasdair gave the housekeeper a kindly nod, then herded the Friedrich brothers out the door ahead of him. Mrs. Aggie had no idea of Alasdair and Ian's past, and her ignorance was for the best. Life could be a cruel taskmaster and force a man to do many a regrettable thing at times.

"What is so important, Einrich? Why did Master Ian send for me?" Alasdair took the lead as they wound their way through the private gardens at the rear of the manor. In all the months since Ian had discovered Château Delatate, this was the first time he had sent for Alasdair. Always before, he'd been too drunk.

Einrich just shook his head and increased the length of his stride.

They rounded the final hedgerow and exited the gardens. A private, cobblestoned alleyway separated the exclusive gentleman's club from Alasdair's property. Little had he known when he'd purchased the land that it abutted the morally questionable establishment. It mattered not, though. It made fetching Ian easier.

Château Delatate maintained a respectable facade while catering to the baser needs of Edinburgh's elite. According to Ian, the upper-class brothel also serviced several visitors from London's royal court on a regular basis.

The pair ushered Alasdair toward the steps leading up to the first floor's back entrance rather than the servant entrance at the cellar level. Einrich held the door open and stepped back. "Master Ian waits in Madam Georgianna's parlor."

So, Ian had fully endeared himself to the indomitable French businesswoman? Madam Georgianna's most experienced harlot and longtime business partner, Fanny McGraw, had succumbed to Ian's charms on his first visit to the establishment. It had taken his brother a little longer to soften Madam Georgianna. Alasdair snorted out a laugh. Ian had always possessed the rare gift of making women yearn to take care of him.

He paused in the hallway, waiting for Adalbert and Einrich to direct him. Heaven forbid a man open the wrong door in Château Delatate. Some things could not be unseen.

"Here, Master Alasdair." Adalbert opened the first door on the right and gave a polite nod.

Alasdair strode into the room, old warrior instincts tensing him as the door clicked shut behind him.

Ian turned from the window, allowing the sumptuous, floor-length cascade of burgundy velvet to fall back in place in front of the glass. "Took ye long enough."

"What have ye done, Ian? It must be dire since ye're not drunk on yer arse, and the Friedrich brothers demanded no coin for yer stay."

"I only arrived this morning, but soon as I saw what I saw, I had to send for ye." Ian hooked his thumbs into his belt. "I've not even seen Lettie yet. That's how important the matter."

Alasdair studied his brother, searching for guile in the gray eyes that Mam had always sworn matched his own. None existed. Ian spoke the truth. His unkempt, curly mop of hair had partially escaped its ties, and his kilt, waistcoat, and jacket appeared a bit dusty from his travels. Grime smudged his knuckles and smeared down one side of his leg. Madam Georgianna's ladies always bathed with their clients before seeing to any other *requests*. Lettie had not yet bathed Ian.

Uneasiness tingling across his nape, Alasdair braced himself. "Out with it, man. What did ye see?"

Ian gave him a blood-chilling look, then moved to the gilded cabinet beside the fancy, tile-inlaid hearth. He uncorked a crystal decanter of golden liquid and filled a pair of glasses with the whisky. He proffered one and nodded for Alasdair to take a drink.

The burning swallow almost cut off his air as Ian uttered the only word powerful enough to bring him to his knees.

"Isobel."

The delicate glass shattered in his hand. Memories, painful ones, hammered through him. A vicious roaring across his senses drowned out all else.

"Isobel," he choked out in a whisper. Her name caught in his throat, cleaving his heart in two.

"Take care, man!" Ian hurried forward, pried open Alasdair's fist, and plucked the shards of glass out of his palm. He tossed them into a porcelain bowl perched on a small pedestal table nearby. "Ye get blood on Madam Georgianna's fine new rug, and she'll have yer arse." He yanked free his neckcloth and wound the linen around Alasdair's bleeding hand.

He pulled his hand free of his brother's grasp. "Explain. Now." He couldn't form complete sentences through the ripping storm of emotions.

"Isobel is here." Ian took a step back and gave an apologetic shrug. "Working."

"*My* Isobel?" Alasdair clenched his teeth. "Ye're saying my Isobel has become one of Madam Georgianna's whores?" He surged forward and grabbed hold of Ian by the throat of his shirt. Rage out-roared reason, possessing him like a thunderous, unrelenting demon. He gave him a hard shake. "Ye lie."

Ian shook his head as he pried Alasdair's fingers open and freed himself. "I swear it. Isobel is here. She greeted me in the entry hall. Soon as she saw it was me, she ran upstairs quick as a minute."

The regret and sympathy flashing in his brother's eyes burned like salt in a fresh wound. Alasdair strode to the door and yanked it open. He'd find her. By all that was holy, this time, he wouldn't fail. He'd find her and explain. He'd not miss this second chance.

Madam Georgianna, older but still a flaxen-haired beauty that looked more queen than harlot, appeared in the doorway. "One does not ascend the stairs without the escort of a lady, Monsieur Alasdair." Her sharp, blue-eyed gaze slid past Alasdair and settled on Ian. "You promised no incidents, Monsieur Ian."

"Take me to her. Now." Alasdair had no time for niceties or brothel rules. He'd borne this pain and guilt for ten years. Ten painful years. Now was the time to confess his soul to the only woman possessing the power and the right to forgive him.

The madam gave him a chiding look and blew out a heavy sigh. "It is my understanding that Isobel has fallen ill and finds herself unable to fulfill her duties. She retired upstairs for a brief rest before leaving for the day."

"Leaving for the day?" Madam Georgianna's words made no sense. All the whores of Château Delatate resided on site. Alasdair pushed past her and stepped out into the hall.

She snatched hold of his arm and held fast. The woman was stouter than she looked. "*Non*, Monsieur Alasdair."

He'd not treat the madam ill, but he'd not tolerate any ruses either. Not this time. Too much was at stake. "I will see her. *Now*."

"Do not make the mistake of thinking Einrich and Adalbert will not restrain you if I order it, monsieur." She shifted to stand in front of him, blocking his way to the set of stairs down the hall. "Their employment always takes priority over any possible friendships." The faintest smile curled her heavily painted lips. "Even though you and Monsieur Ian are two of our favorite people, the brothers will still do as I instruct them."

He didn't give a whit if she called the entirety of His Majesty's regiment. He'd easily best them all. But what she'd said about Isobel leaving for the day nettled him still. She hadn't given him a proper answer. "What did ye mean when ye said Isobel would leave for the day?"

A woman with plentiful, bouncing curves descended the stairs and ambled toward them. Flaming red hair piled high in loose ringlets and a silk dressing gown flapping in her wake like a pair of wings, Fanny McGraw shook a bejeweled finger in Alasdair's direction. "She's locked the door. Said she canna bear to see our Master Ian here. Reminds her too much of yerself. Said she'd be going home soon but was sure to return tomorrow." Huffing to a stop, she shoved both hands up under her abundant bosoms and adjusted their bulging situation above the neckline of her straining corset. Her crookedly penciled brows drew together as she scowled at Alasdair. "She talked like she thought ye dead. Why is that?"

With a growling roar, he punched the wall, then shot back around and faced Madam Georgianna. "Answer me, damn ye! Since when do ye allow yer whores to live elsewhere?"

Fanny gasped, and Madam Georgianna's eyes flared. The madam returned her hand to Alasdair's arm and attempted to steer him back inside her sitting room. "If you would be so kind as to lower your voice and have a seat, Fanny and I will be more than happy to explain Isobel's situation here at Château Delatate. Since you have helped us on more than one occasion with legal issues, I shall afford you that courtesy. But I do insist you calm yourself, or we will tell you nothing and will do our best to conceal the girl. The choice is yours, Monsieur Alasdair."

"Give over, Alasdair. Ye know they can hide the girl where ye'd never find her." Ian took hold of his other arm and pulled. "Calm down, man, and have a drink. She's locked herself upstairs and is not going anywhere."

He stomped into the sitting room, fighting to regain a bit of composure. *Damn them all.* They couldn't possibly understand. He sucked in a deep breath and groaned. He'd always prided himself on remaining calm. Clear-headed and logical. It was how he'd earned his nickname, *The Judge.* Only Isobel had the power to render him so crazed. Over the last ten years, he'd conquered his past, controlled the memories, and overcome how they twisted him. Within a heartbeat of hearing her name, he'd lost the ability to rise above the pain and function with any civility.

Ian held out a generous glass of whisky. "Sit and drink, man. This isna like ye."

Alasdair emptied the glass in a single, fiery gulp and held it out for another. He lowered himself into the only chair in the room sturdy enough to support him. The salon was filled with delicate upholstered furniture better suited to the female form. Damned French and their gaudy designs.

Ian handed him another drink and took a seat on the matching couch in front of an ornate hearth of ceramic and copper tiles. Fanny and Madam Georgianna seated themselves across from Alasdair. Both of them folded their hands in their laps, sitting stiff and straight as though in a church pew.

"Well?" Alasdair tossed back the second glass of whisky and held out his glass for more.

"Perhaps it would help your composure to learn that Isobel is not a *lady* of Château Delatate." Madam Georgianna cast a glance over at Ian. "Do be a gentleman and pour Fanny and me a glass of port. *Oui?*"

Ian hurried to do her bidding.

"In what capacity is she in yer employ?" Alasdair tensed to the edge of his seat, hands fisted atop his knees. The madam had no reason to lie, but he had a hard time believing her. Isobel had been a rare beauty ten years ago, and more than likely had only improved with age. A beautiful whore, especially in a brothel with such elite clientele, would bring in a great deal of coin. Her indulgence of Ian aside, Madam Georgianna was a businesswoman first.

"She cleans up a bit here on the first floor and is also our hostess," Fanny said as she accepted her glass of port from Ian. "Greets our customers in the hall. Seats them in the smoking room and finds out which lady they're here to see. Keeps'm happy whilst they wait."

"Keeps them happy how?" He downed his refill. The neckcloth wound around his hand reminded him to watch his grip and not allow his temper to shatter a second glass. "Another."

"Pleasant conversation. Drinks. Tobacco. A bit of food." Madam Georgianna gave him a perturbed look, then shifted a sideways glance in Fanny's direction. "She does nothing more, Master Alasdair. As per the agreement Fanny made with Isobel due to her unfortunate circumstances."

"Poor thing," Fanny said before he could respond. "Penniless. Wandering the streets with a bairn at her knee and her aged auntie at her side." Fanny leaned forward and shook her head. "Her auntie looks older than Moses himself."

"Bairn?" The word made Alasdair's blood run cold. He swallowed hard and stared down at the floor. *Fool. She's been married ten years. Of course, she has a child by now. Probably, more than one.*

"Aye," Fanny answered, then beamed with an indulgent smile. "Young Connor. Five summer's old, he is, and full of piss and vinegar."

A son. Isobel had a son. A duke's son. Alasdair lifted his head and locked eyes with Fanny. "How the hell did the Duchess of Temsworth end up in Edinburgh penniless and looking for a means to support her son?"

Lord Archibald Cuthbarten, Duke of Temsworth, was known as

one of the more affluent of the peerage, well-landed, and unfortunately, still very much alive—at least the last Alasdair had heard.

Fanny leaned forward and made to speak again, but Madam Georgianna held up a hand and stayed her. "It is our understanding that Isobel wished to separate herself and her son from the duke for her own safety as well as her child's." The madam's regal composure shifted to a repulsed look as though she'd been offended by a stench. "We have no doubt she speaks the truth. The Duke of Temsworth is no longer on the exclusive clientele list of Château Delatate after his behavior here last summer."

"Sick, cruel bastard, that one is," Fanny said as though she couldn't bear remaining silent any longer. She shook her head. "Poor Daisy. Lass has never been the same since that man did what he did to her."

"Why the hell did she not come to me?" Alasdair turned and asked Ian, "Why?"

"I told ye, she talked like she thought ye dead," Fanny interrupted. She pointed at Ian. "Told me she grew up with that one there and had loved his brother, meaning yerself, of course. When I asked her what happened, she said fate took ye away. She didna know ye still lived and breathed."

"The only fate that took me away was her avaricious father selling her to that damned duke." He stared down at the floor, wringing his hands. "I meant to stop the wedding. Steal her away." He turned to Ian, his anguish reflected in his brother's gaze. "Then the morbid sore throat swept through our clan and took down the lot of us."

"Alasdair and I were among the few who survived, but ye dinna recover from such an ailment with haste." Ian rose, went to Alasdair's side, and rested a hand on his shoulder. "Took us months to get back on our feet and pull together the few of us who lived." He shook his head. "There were nay enough left to even see to the burying of all the dead. We had to beg help from clans farther afield that had nay been stricken with the disease."

"And after that, it was too late. She was married." Alasdair rose, crossed the room, and refilled his glass. He moved to the window and swept aside the heavy curtains. He stared out the pane, but all he saw was the memory of what he'd seen the day he'd gone to London to fetch Isobel back. The aching pain in his heart burned all the fiercer. "I meant to steal her back from him. Get the marriage annulled. I went to his estate in London, and I waited."

"And?" Fanny prompted, scooting to the edge of her seat.

"And I saw her smiling up into that bastard's eyes as the two of them strolled arm in arm through their gardens, laughing together at the secrets only lovers share." Alasdair let the curtain drop back in place and returned to his seat. "So, I left her there to enjoy the life I could never hope to give her. A life of ease. Of riches. Of status." He shook his head, the knots of his pain tightening. "But I always wished her to know that I had kept my word. I *had* come for her. Just like I said I would." He looked at the two women staring back at him. "I still love Isobel. Love her as strong as ever." The barest glimmer of hope flickered within him. Isobel had left the duke. Willingly. Was fate offering him a small crumb of recompense? "Fetch her. I beg ye. Fetch her down, and let me speak with her."

Fanny and Madam Georgianna's gazes met as though reading each other's thoughts. Madam Georgianna finally nodded, and Fanny rose and hurried out the door. Turning back to Alasdair, the madam fixed him with a concerned look that struck him as almost tender. "You understand, she may refuse to see you?"

"She has to see me. I have to make her understand what happened all those years ago." He took a step closer to the door, itching to chase after Fanny but knowing that would be rash. He had to wait. Be patient. He couldn't fail again. Not when he'd been given this second chance. "I can help her now that she's in need. I can take care of her—and her child."

"And if she does not wish for your care?" Madam Georgianna

stood and positioned herself between Alasdair and the door as though sensing his urge to follow Fanny. "The Isobel here at Château Delatate is not the Isobel you knew ten years ago. This woman has endured much, monsieur. She trusts no one and is as protective of her son as a wild animal protecting its young."

"That sounds verra much like the Isobel I have always loved."

Fanny reappeared at the door of the sitting room. The downcast look on her face told all. She gave a sad shake of her head. "I am sorry, Master Alasdair. She willna see ye nor Master Ian." She threw both hands in the air. "I thought she'd at least see Master Ian once she knew ye to be alive. Everybody loves Master Ian." She clasped her hands tight. "But she said no. Said ye abandoned her to Satan himself, and she'll never forgive ye." Fanny cocked a brow at Madam Georgianna. "And she said all this through a locked door. I doubt she'll be coming out anytime soon. She knows well enough her aunt will take good care of the lad and keep him hidden."

"Where are they?" Alasdair moved closer to the door. He knew Isobel's aunt from childhood. Clan MacNaughton and Clan MacCoinnich had been close on the Isle of Skye. Their lands bordered one another, long ago before the dreaded illness hit. If he could get Isobel's aunt to remember him, mayhap she could convince Isobel to see him. "Are they near?"

Madam Georgianna rose from the velvet sofa. "We promised Isobel our protection. That protection extends to her family. I shall intercede on your behalf and attempt to convince her to see you. Grant her some time, Monsieur Alasdair. As I said earlier, she has been through much. Give her the time and understanding she so badly needs."

"Swear to me, ye willna allow her to leave without my seeing her." That was Alasdair's greatest fear. If he did as the madam suggested, he might never see Isobel again. She might slip out of his life once more.

Madam Georgianna's mouth tightened. After a nod in Fanny's direction, she turned back to Alasdair. "I shall place her under the protection of the Friedrich brothers. It's the least I can offer after your handling of the rather delicate matter of Lord Dunfold for us." She fluttered a hand in the air. "But I can promise no more." Motioning for both Ian and Alasdair to exit the room, she held the door wide. "I will do my best, Monsieur Alasdair. Now, return to your home. I shall send for you if she changes her mind."

"*When*," Alasdair corrected. "*When* she changes her mind—because I promise ye, I'll not be losing her again."

CHAPTER TWO

A LASDAIR LIVED.

Eyes shut tight against the sting of unshed tears, Isobel held her churning middle. A sob almost escaped her. *Nay!* She would not give in to weeping. Weeping showed loss of control, and she'd never lose control again. She forced her eyes open and paced across the length of the room. A single word, that once precious name, whipped her into a panic. It played over and over in her mind. *Alasdair.*

He'd been alive all this time. Her dearest love. Or he had been once. A lifetime ago. Her Alasdair. The man who'd sworn upon all that was holy, he'd never let another take her. Sworn he would come for her no matter what. Steal her away even if it meant rushing the altar on her wedding day and fighting off any who dared to thwart them.

But now she knew the truth. Alasdair had lied.

She pressed trembling fingers across her mouth, fighting the need to keen out her rage along with all the other agonizing emotions she'd contained for the last ten years. He'd lied. He'd never come for her. Instead, he'd left her to a horrendous fate and gone on to enjoy life without her.

The muffled thump of footsteps echoed out in the hallway, followed by the rattle of keys. She jerked around and stared at the door.

Surely, they would not bring him up here. Fanny had promised. She forced down the bile churning in the back of her throat as metal on metal clicked. The key turned in the lock. The door swung open.

"Breathe, Isobel." Madam Georgianna handed the ring of keys back to Fanny as the two entered the room. She motioned toward the upholstered bench at the foot of the bed. "Sit, child, before you faint away. We've no time for that. There is much to discuss here."

"I'll be going to fetch us some biscuits and ale," Fanny said. "Or maybe something stronger. Me thinks we'll be needing it."

"Thank you." The madam seated herself atop the stool in front of a small dressing table. With a graceful flip of one hand, she settled her swirl of skirts around her. A sense of peaceful composure emanated from the woman as her delicate brows drew together. Lips pursed, she tilted her head to one side and studied Isobel.

"I canna speak with him." Isobel lifted her chin. Her voice quivered against her will. "I will surely kill him if I do."

"And why would you wish to kill Monsieur Alasdair? I assume you *are* referring to Monsieur Alasdair Cameron?"

How could she put into words all she felt? All that had happened? Isobel rose from the bench. She couldn't sit. Somehow, pacing gave her strength. Perhaps it was because when she walked, she felt free and unshackled. A feeling she hadn't known for ten long years.

"Alasdair swore he loved me so much he'd never let another man have me. No matter what." She brought her troubled steps to a halt and met Madam Georgianna's gaze. "He lied." She thumped a fist to her chest and choked back a sob. "I lost ten years of my life. I suffered unspeakable things because he lied and never came."

Madam's gaze dropped to her hands folded in her lap. "I have no doubt you suffered, *ma chère*. Knowledge of the duke's proclivities is the very reason I granted you sanctuary here at Château Delatate without requiring you to…" She gave a subtle shrug of a shoulder. "How shall I put it?" Her voice sank to a conspiratorial tone. "Earn

16

your living the usual way? And I hope you appreciate the risk of my even allowing you here. A duchess? In a brothel?" She brushed her fingertips across the base of her throat. "I could lose my head for such."

"And I am forever grateful," Isobel hurried to say. "But now that Alasdair has found me, I fear my plans must change."

Anxiousness filled her. She needed time and money. Time to save money to reach the Highlands and approach one of the old allied clans about granting her shelter. Maybe the MacDonells or the Macleods. Both those clans had been on good enough terms with the MacNaughtons. She needed little and could earn her way with her knowledge of herbs and healing. She wouldn't be a burden on any clan willing to take in her odd little family. A tiny croft would do them just fine. A wee house where she and Auntie Yeva could raise Connor safe and hidden from his diabolical father.

She swallowed hard and composed herself. If she had learned anything during her short stay at Château Delatate, it was that Madam Georgianna admired strength. "I must leave Edinburgh as soon as I can. Alasdair was once a verra determined man. I doubt the years have changed that."

"They have not." Madam rose from the stool as Fanny returned, bearing a tray with a bottle of dark ruby liquid and a trio of glasses. "No ale?"

"I felt we needed something stronger than ale." Fanny slid the tray to the dressing table, uncorked the bottle, and poured. "I wouldha brought whisky if they had brought some up from cellar and restocked the cabinet already."

Isobel agreed with Fanny. She needed the stoutest drink they had. This situation also called for drastic measures to ensure the new life for which she had planned so carefully and risked so much wasn't ended before it ever started. She'd already had to amend her plans once due to lack of funds. She had never thought to find herself working at a brothel. Mama had surely turned in her grave the day Isobel had begged for a job as a cook or a seamstress at Château Delatate. But everything had cost so much. Food. Lodging. Transportation. Ten years of imprisonment at Temsworth's isolated country estate had left her ill-prepared for what to expect when it came to the financial side of escaping and building a better life. She wished Temsworth had been foolish enough to leave more money accessible for her to take.

She accepted the goblet Fanny offered and sniffed it. She wished the whisky had been ready. This was the fancy port reserved for the clients waiting in the sitting room.

"Do ye not think ye should at least give the man a chance to explain himself?" Fanny toddled over to the bench at the foot of the bed and lowered herself to it with a weary huff. "He seems a good man, lass, and good men be scarce as hen's teeth."

"He seemed quite genuine when he explained the circumstances," Madam Georgianna said. She took a delicate sip of her port and gave a decided nod. "I trust both the Cameron Messieurs."

Trust. Such a dangerous word. Isobel rolled the stem of her goblet between her fingers. "I can no longer afford the luxury of trust." She had trusted Alasdair once. He had lied. She had also trusted her father to never put her in harm's way. That, too, had been a lie. Her arranged marriage to the Duke of Temsworth had turned into an inescapable nightmare within days.

"Why did ye think Master Alasdair dead?" Fanny shifted as though settling in for a good story.

"Because I was foolish enough to believe he would never let another take me. I believed only the finality of death would keep him from my side." Isobel washed the bitter taste of the words away with another sip of the sweet wine. A sour laugh escaped her. "That and the fact that Temsworth took great delight in reminding me at every opportunity that the entirety of Alasdair's clan, as well as my own, had succumbed to the morbid sore throat." She cradled the glass to her chest. "He enjoyed telling me on a daily basis that he was my only means of survival since all I had ever loved was gone." Temsworth's cruel laugh echoed through her mind. "I thought myself alone," she whispered. "The only reason the duke allowed me the company of my aunt was to have yet another threat with which to torment me."

"Monsieur Alasdair told us he did come for you in London." Madam looked to Fanny for reinforcement. "Did he not?"

She nodded. "That he did. Spied on ye, in fact. Said ye looked to have fallen in love with yer new husband, so he left ye to what he thought was a better life than he could ever afford to give ye."

Isobel nearly snapped the stem of the goblet between her fingers. "He came for me?"

"Aye." Fanny nodded. "Said he showed up at Temsworth's estate in London and saw ye walking in the gardens with yer duke. Arm in arm. All laughing and close and such."

"When?"

"From the way Monsieur spoke," the madam said, "it sounded as though you had been married but a little while. A matter of weeks, perhaps. He talked of a plan to steal you away and have the marriage annulled but then cast it aside when he witnessed your happiness."

"Married a matter of weeks." The memories of how Temsworth had brutally *trained* her to behave those first few months of marriage almost made her retch. "By the time Alasdair spied me in the gardens, I had already been well disciplined on maintaining the appearance of a delighted, adoring wife whenever others happened to be around, or I suffered the consequences. Temsworth and I never walked in the gardens alone—nor was I ever allowed in the gardens without him. Only during dinner parties or when guests visited. It was one of his games to break me and show me any attempts to escape were futile."

Fanny snorted out a disgusted huff. "Why did ye not kill that bastard in his sleep? Poison him or something?"

"*Merde!*" Madam Georgianna made the clucking sound of an indignant bird. "Fanny!"

A sly look arched the redhead's brow as she shook a finger in Madam's direction. "Dinna *Fanny* me. Ye were thinking it same as I."

"We were never alone." Those dark memories plagued Isobel as well. The duke's perversion of performing in front of others was but one of the many degradations she had endured.

"Never?" Madam repeated, leaning forward with an incredulous scowl.

"*Never.*" Isobel took another sip of wine, then pulled in a deep breath. "One of his *proclivities.*"

"Proclivities, my arse. The bastard knew he deserved a long, slow killing." Fanny shook her head as she rose from the bench, toddled over to the bureau, and poured herself another. She turned and lifted her glass in the air. "Coward was afeared ye'd kill him for sure if ye had the chance."

"Be that as it may…" Madam Georgianna interjected with a delicate flutter of her hand to end Fanny's rant. "You are here now. A roof. Food. Safety. Perhaps fate brought you here for a second chance at life." She fixed Isobel with an indulgent look. "Talk with the man, *ma chère.* Give both him and fate a chance to make amends for your years of suffering."

What could she say to make them understand? These two women, who should better understand life and men more than anyone she had ever met. Why could they not see? A disturbing thought came to her. Would they turn her over to Alasdair? Would they betray her? "Ye promised me safety, aye?"

Fanny and Madam shared a knowing look, then nodded in unison.

"Ye swear ye willna tell him of my wee apartment in the corner of the alley?" Connor and Auntie Yeva's safety came first.

"'Course not," Fanny said. "He already asked about yer auntie and the boy, and we told him we wouldna say."

Madam Georgianna bowed her head.

"Guess I should not ha' said that." Fanny shrugged. "Sorry."

It was just as she feared. Alasdair would stop at nothing now that he'd found her and knew she had left the duke. "Ye must ban him from the premises, or I willna feel safe." She stepped closer. "I beg ye. Blacklist him and Ian. At least until I've saved enough to travel north and settle, then ye can lift the ban and allow them back inside."

Madam held up a hand. "*Non*, we will not block them. Monsieur Alasdair has been of great legal aid to us, and Monsieur Ian is a regular client who has never given us any reason to deny his visits with Lettie."

"Aye," Fanny agreed. "And now that Lettie's feeling so poorly, the man's been nothing but kindness itself. Helps her bring in enough to pay for her tonics when all the rest of her men have switched to other girls."

Isobel had no doubt Ian possessed genuine feelings for the ailing woman who had been moved to the most remote room in the château to prevent her bouts of consumptive coughing from disturbing others. Isobel had known Janet, Ian's deceased wife. Lettie could pass for her twin. "Please…I dinna have enough saved to set out for the Highlands. I canna leave, yet I canna stay here."

A knock on the door interrupted them. Fanny ambled over and cracked it open. "Have Marjie sort out the sitting room, Del, and tend it for Isobel, aye? Ye get too many requests to cover it yerself. Ye'd lose a lion's share of money. Besides—I think yer London earl is still in town."

Isobel strained to make out the conversation on the other side of the door. Del had one of those deep, sultry voices made for keeping secrets.

"Absolutely not. Call Einrich and Adalbert," Fanny said. "No admittance to the likes of him no matter how much gold he waves in yer face." Fanny shut the door and pressed her back to it. "Temsworth's carriage is here. Parked 'round front. Right at the end of the lane. He sent his valet to the door."

Terror surged through Isobel, more for Connor and Auntie Yeva than for herself. What if her husband or his footman entered the close? What if they caught sight of Connor playing outside in the alleyway?

Madam Georgianna gave Isobel a serious look. "Fate again, *ma chére*? If not for Monsieur Alasdair's arrival this morning, you would have answered the door to your husband's valet. Methinks you have much to consider and should grant Monsieur Alasdair a short audience—if only to appease fate itself."

"Speaking with Alasdair is the least of my worries. I fear Temsworth or one of his servants will discover Connor. Please send Adalbert to warn Auntie and guard them. Please, I beg ye."

Madam shooed Fanny toward the door. "Send Rosie to warn Yeva to keep the boy inside and the curtains drawn until we say otherwise. Have both Adalbert and Einrich lock the gate to the alleyway, then flank both the front and rear doors, *oui*?"

With a bob of her head, Fanny shot out the door.

The madam turned back to Isobel. "If you were to accept Monsieur Alasdair's protection, your son would be safe within a gated estate. Secure and guarded rather than hidden in an apartment in an alley."

"I promised when I escaped that I would only move forward. Alasdair is my past." Isobel refused to back down. If the woman forced her hand, she would do whatever it took to protect Connor and get him to the Highlands. It had taken her ten years to recover her strength and take action. She'd allow nothing to stand in her way now.

"There are times when the past bears revisiting, child." Sadness and knowing showed in the depths of the madam's eyes.

"Not my past," Isobel whispered. The only way she had survived—then and now, was by never looking back. To remember the past held the danger of madness. *Nay.* She needed enough money to make it to the Highlands. There was only one type of employment that would render her access to enough funding in a short amount of time. *Forgive me, Mama.*

She straightened her shoulders. The madam was the first woman she had ever met who was as tall as her. "I want to start receiving clients like the rest of the girls."

Madam Georgianna's dark lashes fluttered. "What?"

Isobel cleared her throat. "I need money, Madam Georgianna." She lifted her chin. "Ye said a woman with looks such as mine could earn her weight in gold in no time—especially with yer clientele."

She shook her head. "I think not. You are overwrought and would regret such a decision."

The door flew open, and Fanny blew into the room, a hand pressed to her heaving bosom. "Adalbert says the duke's valet left without a fuss, and the carriage drove away."

"That was too easy." A sense of doom tightened in the pit of Isobel's stomach. "Temsworth never gives over that easy." She turned back to Madam. "I canna stay here, and I need more money before I can move Connor and Auntie to the Highlands. Make me one of yer girls. Please. I swear I willna hold ye responsible for this decision. It is my choice alone."

"What?" Fanny clicked the door shut and slumped back against it. "Nay, lass. Talk with Master Alasdair first. This is not an easy path ye're thinking to take."

"I have had no easy path since I was a lass, Fanny. This is but another stepping stone in my effort to secure a better life for my son. I feel certain it canna be any worse than what I endured with Temsworth." Isobel turned back to Madam. "If ye're not going to loan me the money outright, then I ask ye do this for me. Allow me to earn the high wages ye mentioned when ye first met me." Isobel smiled. Madam Georgianna never loaned money. Considered it poor business and didn't hesitate to inform those asking that she wasn't the Bank of Scotland.

Madam's gaze slid to Fanny, and the women shared their often-seen look of silent communication. She rose from her seat and shifted with a deep intake of breath. "I see you have made up your mind and refuse to be dissuaded?"

Isobel nodded, not trusting herself to speak.

"Very well." With a dramatic resettling of her trailing skirts behind her, she gave a single, imperious nod. "You will start tomorrow evening. Go home today and spend time with your son." She ushered Fanny out the door and followed. "I pray you do not regret this decision, *ma chére.*" Then she closed the door behind them.

"I shan't." Isobel prayed for the strength to do whatever life required for the safety of her family. She closed her eyes and swallowed hard, flinching against what Alasdair would think when he found out. What did it matter how he felt? He had given up that right long ago.

She drew in a deep breath, yanked open the door, and hurried down the hall to the back staircase. She couldn't hold Connor safe in her arms fast enough. Retrieving her *arisaid* from the peg beside the rear door, she wrapped the plaid about her shoulders but didn't bother belting it. There was no need. The living space she shared with Connor and Auntie Yeva was but a few steps across the alley. The irony of the small flat's location brought a bitter smile. Alasdair had walked right past it if he had entered through the back entrance.

She hooded the shawl up over her head and shielded her face as she exited the building. She still didn't believe Temsworth had left the premises so easily. The man thought the world belonged to him, and others had been put there for his pleasure alone. To make the duke want something even more, one only had to refuse him. And then there was Alasdair. She wouldn't put it past him to lay in wait either.

A glance around the private alleyway assured her no one lurked. She hurried to the shuttered lean-to attached to the rear of the brothel. Thankfully, the place looked more like a gardener's shed than living quarters. Isobel tried the door, then smiled. Locked. *Just as it should be.*

She rapped on the door, then placed her mouth close to a crack in the wood patched with a remnant of dark cloth stuffed into it. "Auntie, it's me."

Wood thumped against the opposite side of the door, then it creaked open a bit. "It is safe now?"

"Aye, Auntie. For now."

The door opened wide enough to allow Isobel inside.

"Mama!"

She glanced around the dirt-floored room. The dim interior was lit by a single candle sputtering inside a dented lantern on the table in the center. Threadbare plaids draped across a rope partitioned off the sleeping area at the far end of the small space. She pushed the makeshift curtains aside, but the straw-filled pallet where they all slept was empty. "Connor?"

"Can I come out now, Auntie? Please?"

"Yes." Auntie fumbled with the wooden latch on the tall cupboard beside the single window of the room. The wizened old woman smiled as she bent and peered under the lowest shelf. "You are a good boy, Connor. You listen fine to Auntie."

Connor rolled out of the cabinet, sprang to his feet, and charged into his mother's arms. "Did Einrich kill the bad men, Mama? I wanted to help fight, but Auntie made me hide."

Isobel pressed a kiss to the top of her son's head. She breathed in the familiar, little-boy scent of him and tightened her hold. "Einrich didna kill the bad men, but he did scare them away." Connor idolized both Einrich and Adalbert. She hugged her son closer. "And I'm verra proud of ye for obeying Auntie Yeva."

"I canna breave, Mama." The boy wriggled free of her grasp and stepped back. "Can I go outside now?"

The thought of Connor out in the open, vulnerable as an unsuspecting rabbit beneath a sky filled with hawks, struck fear to the bottom of her soul. Isobel shook her head. "Wait a bit, aye?" She took hold of his small shoulders and steered him to one of the three rickety chairs around the table. "Let's have a bit of bread and milk first. I've not seen ye since yesterday eve. Ye hadna risen before I left this morning." She tousled his hair, his tangled locks as black as her own. Isobel found comfort in the fact that the Armenian side of her ancestry appeared strong in Connor. Thanks be to God, he looked nothing like his father. Mama would have been so pleased.

"I dinna want milk and bread." Connor gave her a dark-eyed scowl as he crossed his arms over his chest. "I wanna go play with Jemmy. His mam lets him outside whenever it's not raining, and Auntie said it's not raining."

She pointed at the table and gave a warning look. "I dinna care what Jemmy's mam allows him. Ye will do as ye're told, or rue the day, aye?"

Connor dropped his gaze to the floor and kicked at the dirt with the toe of his boot. "Aye, Mama."

"Nice bowl of milk. Fresh today. Mistress Rosie brought it," Auntie said as she placed a small, chipped bowl filled with the creamy liquid on the table. She shook a finger at Connor. "Should be thankful. We could be hungry today rather than blessed with food."

Isobel fetched the crusts of bread left from the day before, motioning for Connor to sit as she placed the board of leftover bread on the table. "Sit."

"Ladies first." Connor held tight to the back of her chair and lifted his chin.

Pride filled her. "There's a good lad. Minding yer manners. Well done, Connor." She nodded for Auntie to sit opposite her, then took her seat and smiled at Connor.

"Wish we had some jam," Connor said as he climbed into his chair.

"Someday, Connor." Isobel held out her hands for them to take. "Say the blessing now, aye?"

Connor took her hand and bowed his head. "Thank ye, Lord, for food, a place to sleep, clothes, and my best friend, Jemmy. Amen." He lifted his head, then grabbed hold of their hands again and jerked his head back down. "And thank ye for Auntie and Mama. Amen for certain this time."

Isobel bit the inside of her cheek to keep from smiling. "Thank ye, Connor. Well done." She tore a crust of the stale bread into bite-sized pieces and added them to Connor's bowl. "Eat yer fill, son. There's more if ye wish it."

Auntie shook her head as she dipped a crust into her own bowl of milk. "Is all we have here on this table."

Isobel pushed her bowl to the center of the table. "He can have mine if he's still hungry when he finishes that bowl."

"You must eat." Auntie pointed a dripping crust of bread in Isobel's direction.

She willed her aunt to understand. "I have little appetite after this morning."

Auntie shrugged and continued with her meal.

"Tomorrow, I will nay go to work until later than usual." A sense of dread filled Isobel. Auntie had not approved of Isobel's employment arrangements but had grudgingly come to accept the situation as the only means to keep Connor fed.

"Who is to clean the parlor before visitors arrive?" Auntie's dark eyes narrowed. The dear old woman was not a fool.

Isobel laced her fingers together and placed her hands on the table. Courage almost left her when it came to meeting her aunt's sharp-eyed gaze. "I do not know. All I know is that within a few days, I hope to have enough money to get us out of Edinburgh and to the High-lands."

Auntie smacked a hand down on the table, rattling the spoons and bowls. She fired off a stream of Armenian as she rose from the table and bore down on Isobel, shaking a finger in her face.

"Ye're in trouble now, Mama," Connor said out of the side of his mouth as he nudged her under the table.

It was at times like this that she was thankful Temsworth had forbidden Connor be taught Armenian. His lessons in the language from that side of her heritage hadn't begun until they'd escaped the duke's vile clutches. However, anyone, whether they spoke Armenian or not, would understand Auntie Yeva's irritation. Isobel held up a hand to stave off the verbal onslaught. "I have no choice. Ye know as well as I that he'll be back. We must leave soon, and that's the only way I can get the money."

"The bad men will be back?" Connor stared at her, fear shining in his brown eyes and milk dribbling down his chin.

Isobel snatched up a rag from beside the washbasin on the stand and wiped Connor's face. "Dinna fash yerself, son. We'll be long gone before the bad men return." She turned and gave a cold look to her aunt, willing her to understand and say no more in any language. "Mama will see to it. I promise ye."

CHAPTER THREE

"ND WHAT WILL ye do when that limb breaks and yer arse hits the ground?"

Alasdair ignored Ian and shifted to what he hoped was a sturdier branch. The sprawling oak next to the back wall of the garden was his best hope for watching Château Delatate's side of the alley during the day. He couldn't see the entire area between his estate and the brothel, but at least he could watch the main gate leading to the street on this side of the alleyway. The fact that he couldn't spy the exit at the other end worried him something fierce. He pointed in that direction. "Dinna ye worry about my arse. Go to the far end of the alley and watch the south gate, aye?"

Ian shook his head. "This be a fool's game, Alasdair. Ye spent the entirety of last night propped against the gate, and now ye've taken to perching in a tree like the devil's own raven. This isna like ye. Climb down and act like the level-headed man ye've always been."

Alasdair dug his fingers deeper into the rough bark of the trunk and kept his focus locked on the brothel. His brother didn't understand. Isobel robbed him of logic. She left him with nothing but raw need to set things right.

"Do ye know where Master Alasdair is, sir?"

The familiar voice, cracking, then pitching high with the throes of becoming a young man, drew Alasdair's attention downward. "What is it, Lachie?"

Mrs. Aggie's favorite kitchen boy stood beside Ian. Tall, lanky, his skinny arms too long for his sleeves, the lad shaded his eyes and peered upward. "Mrs. Aggie says come quick. She's fair beside herself." He stole a glance around the garden, took a step closer to the tree, and lowered his voice. "'Cause of them there women, if ye ask me. I never seen Mrs. Aggie get in the state she does when them women come 'round."

Them women. Alasdair had an inkling of who the women might be, but he had to be certain before he abandoned his post. "What women?"

Lachie's fair skin flashed a bright red from the neckline of his tunic to his unkempt brown hair. He jerked his head toward the house of ill repute. "*Them* women. Mrs. Aggie calls them the head trollops over yonder. The ones what come by here before."

"Since it seems ye've got company, brother, I'm off to see Lettie." Ian gave a back-handed salute and was out the gate before Alasdair could respond.

An ominous sense of something about to go very wrong hurried him out of the tree. A visit from the esteemed ladies of Château Delatate could mean only one thing; Isobel had escaped. He hit the ground with a hard, determined stride. Lachie scrambled to catch up.

"Shall I ask Mrs. Aggie to make up a tray?" The boy hopped along sideways like a devoted dog trotting beside its master. "She put them women in yer study 'til I could find ye."

"*Ladies*, Lachie. Not *them women.*" He strode along. The house-keeper's tainting of the boy's regard toward Fanny and Madam Georgianna grated on his nerves. The ladies' chosen profession didn't warrant mistreatment. Prostitution might be immoral, but the service didn't prosper in isolation. Many a self-righteous, dubiously *moral* client contributed to the business's survival. "And yes, ask Mrs. Aggie to make up a tray to offer the ladies." Although, if what Alasdair feared was true, their visit would not be a pleasant chat over a cup of honeyed wine and biscuits.

"Yes, sir." The lad took off at a fast lope.

Alasdair rounded the corner of the house, heading for the side entrance. He was not in the mood to enter the service door and go through the kitchen. His housekeeper's opinions wouldn't be received well today, and he couldn't guarantee a civil response. He pushed inside, blinking to hurry the adjustment from the spring day's bright sunlight to the manor's dim interior. The door to his study was closed. Mrs. Aggie had probably also drawn the curtains to ensure no one espied his visitors.

Alasdair sucked in a deep breath and opened the door. "Ladies."

Fanny and Madam Georgianna sat in the armchairs angled in front of his desk. They each gave a polite nod as he rounded the room and took a stance behind the sprawling piece of furniture buried beneath stacks of books and scattered papers. He preferred to stand until the ladies shared their reason for the unexpected visit. "Isobel is gone. Isn't she?"

"*Non.*" Madam gave a quick shake of her head. "But her situation has changed, and after much discussion, Fanny and I felt you must be told."

"Aye." Fanny bobbed her head so hard, her feathered hat slid to one side. "That husband of hers showed up and tried to buy his way back into the Château. Gave us all a scare, I grant ye that."

"When?" Protectiveness flared hot and fierce. He'd not abandon Isobel to that bastard again.

"Yesterday. Right after you and Monsieur Ian departed." The madam shifted and resettled her red skirts in a neat circle of silken folds around her ankles.

A light pecking rapped on the other side of the door.

"What?" Alasdair demanded. The need to gather up sword and

pistols was fierce. Precious time, time to save Isobel, slipped through his fingers while they sat here making idle chatter and observing social niceties.

The study door eased open. Maggie, the most timid of the household's maids, peeped around its edge. "Begging yer pardon, sir. Biscuits and mead?"

He waved the girl inside. "Leave it here by the desk. Quickly, aye?"

Maggie hurried to comply, scurrying so fast, the cart's contents rattled and sloshed. Focus locked on the floor, she made a quick curtsey, then turned and ran from the room, closing the door softly behind her.

"Have ye ill-treated that girl?" Fanny scowled at him with a judgmental set to her jaw.

"I willna grace that insult with an answer." Alasdair strode to the sidebar beside the bookcase and poured himself a glass of whisky. He shot a glance back at the ladies. "Help yerselves to the cart. I fear I dinna possess the manners of a parlor matron." He downed the drink, then poured another before taking a stance between his chair and his desk. "What happened with Temsworth yesterday?"

Fanny rose and circled the cart of treats with the interest of a bird of prey about to pounce on a juicy carcass. She glanced over at Madam Georgianna. "Ye want I should fix ye a plate, lovie?"

Madam held up a hand and shook her head. "*Non, merci.*" She returned her attention to Alasdair with a delicate sigh. "The duke left without incident, but Isobel feels certain he will return." Her mouth, painted the same bright red as her dress, tightened into a worried line as she clasped her hands in a prim pose atop her knees. "His appearance, as well as your own, has filled her with fear about remaining in Edinburgh any longer."

"I can protect her." Alasdair set aside his empty glass. Every muscle tensed, and he leaned forward. "Ye must convince her to see me. Force her to do so. Her life depends on it."

"Oh, ye havena heard the worst of it yet." Balancing a plate laden with honey-drizzled biscuits and dried fruits, Fanny toddled back to her chair and eased down into it.

Madam released another delicate sigh. "That is why we are here, monsieur. Isobel refuses help from anyone. She has chosen a different course, of which we felt we should make you aware."

"What course?"

"To secure the funding she requires in a timelier manner, Isobel has requested to become a *lady* of Château Delatate." The madam shifted in her seat and rested her hands atop the arms of the chair as though bracing for Alasdair's response. "She is prepared to receive gentlemen."

"Like hell she is." Alasdair leaned farther over the desk and stabbed the air, pointing at Madam Georgianna. "Ye will take me to her now. Enough of this foolishness." A blinding haze of emotions roared through him. He barely contained the urge to tear the brothel to bits until he found Isobel and made her see sense.

Fanny stretched to slide her plate onto the corner of the desk and held up a hand. "Steady now, Master Alasdair. That's why we've come." She paused and nodded toward Madam Georgianna. "We thought ye might wish to be Isobel's first client." Her lips curled into a conspiratorial smile. "If ye purchase Isobel's time for a night, ye'd have an entire evening to talk sense into the girl. She's no more suited to our profession than I'm suited to be queen." She let out a wicked chuckle. "And whilst I might enjoy setting the country on its ear, we both know I'm not suited for such a life."

"What do you say, Monsieur Alasdair?" Madam rose from her seat. "Would such an arrangement be suitable? We will make Isobel understand that when a gentleman purchases her evening, it belongs to him." She gave a light shrug. "Unless the gentleman threatens harm, of course, but I am certain such a thing would not be a concern with you."

For the first time since he'd learned of Isobel's current situation, the logical, plotting side of him regained control. What the ladies suggested made sense. Damn good sense. He reached into the inner pocket of his waistcoat and retrieved the small key to the desk drawer he kept locked at all times. Clans MacCoinnich and Mackenzie paid for his services in gold. Gold was the securest form of currency. He selected three doubloons and thumped them down atop the pile of books closest to the madam. "I am the only one Isobel is to receive. *Ever.*"

One of the madam's brows ratcheted upward, and Fanny's painted mouth formed an awestruck *o*. Madam gifted him with a regal nod as she stepped forward, plucked up the coins, and tucked them into the draw-stringed silk purse hanging from her wrist. "You have my word, Monsieur Alasdair."

"Mine as well," Fanny added as she pushed up from her seat whilst brushing biscuit crumbs from her dress.

Madam gave a gracious nod. "We shall take our leave now. When might we expect your first rendezvous with our Isobel?"

"Today."

If not for the fact he'd slept in his clothes, he'd escort the ladies back to the brothel and see her now. But no. He wouldn't present himself in such a light to Isobel. Clean clothes and a bit of scrubbing came first. He would have her see him after all this time as the proper gentleman he had become. Rounding the desk, he strode across the study and opened the door. A sense of gratitude and hope lightened the pressure inside him for the first time since yesterday. "I am grateful to ye both. More than ye will ever know."

"We are happy to help such a fine gentleman," Madam said as she and Fanny swept from the room. She paused in the hallway and gifted him with a wistful smile. "We truly hope to see Isobel find genuine happiness for herself and her son."

"Aye," Fanny said. "And that happiness willna be found in a brothel. Not even one as fine as ours."

"I shall do my best, ladies," Alasdair promised as he walked them out. "Once again, I thank ye."

"Good day, Monsieur Alasdair," Madam Georgianna floated down the steps of the front stoop with the grace of society's noblest lady. Fanny gave him a wink and a cheery wave as they turned up the street and sashayed home.

Alasdair closed the door. Anticipation and resolve banished the gritty weariness of his sleepless night. "Mrs. Aggie!"

The rapid staccato of sturdy heels clacking against hardwood floors greeted his bellow. "Aye, Master Alasdair?" The housekeeper hurried around the corner, hands fisted in midair as though willing to hop at his slightest command. Lachie must have warned the woman of his dark mood.

"I require a bath. In my room. Quick as the boys can fetch the tub and water." He tugged at the knot of his neckcloth as he strode toward the steps leading to the second floor of the manor.

"Aye, sir. 'Twill be done." Mrs. Aggie sounded dubious, but she spun about and barked out the orders as she headed toward the kitchen. "Lachie! Fetch Rob and Hugh. Master wishes a bath drawn. In his rooms. Hie yerselves now!" Still within earshot, she continued in a low grumble loud enough for Alasdair to hear, "And it not even June yet. He'll catch his death taking a full bath this early on in the year."

He snorted out a laugh as he took the steps two at a time, stripping off the neckcloth and unbuttoning his waistcoat in the process. The untimely bath would take a bit of effort to achieve, but he distinctly remembered a much happier time during his youth when Isobel had wrinkled her nose and informed him as long as he smelled like a Highland goat, he'd be getting no kisses from her. He didn't know if this particular meeting would end in kisses, but he'd damn sure make certain he'd not give her any reason to refuse him. He hurried to his bedchamber and tossed his clothes aside as quickly as he peeled them off.

A loud clunking behind him in the sitting room announced the arrival of the tub. "We gots four boiling kettles, Master Alasdair," Lachie called out. "Cook's set more to the fire, and we'll fetch them up soon as they're ready."

"They dinna have to be boiling. Bring them straight up. I can wash in cold water, aye?" Four kettles of boiling water were plenty. He grabbed the pitcher of cool water off the washstand, a cake of soap, and an armload of linens. Hugh and Rob emptied the kettles into the oblong copper tub, then all three boys hurried out to fetch the rest.

Adding the pitcher's cooler water to one end of the tub, he eased in a toe to test the heat, then stepped in the rest of the way. With a quick sousing of the rag into the water, he lathered it up. While scrubbing, he ruminated about what he would say when he faced Isobel. Ever since he could remember, she'd had a temper, and if yesterday was any sign, still possessed it. He prayed God would grant him the words to make her understand.

The boys bumped back into the room, bearing a kettle of water in each hand.

Alasdair directed them to empty one kettle over his head and down his back. He braced for whatever temperature, hot or cold, might hit.

"Mrs. Aggie says ye must be going to an important meeting to warrant taking a bath before June," Lachie said as he handed his empty kettle to Rob and took the next full one from Hugh.

Alasdair was not a fool. The housekeeper had instructed the boys to fish for information. The nosy woman was probably beside herself with curiosity, especially since she knew who his visitors had been. "I'm headed to Château Delatate," he said as he scrubbed his head. He jabbed a thumb toward his soapy hair. "Rinse."

Lachie complied, then cleared his throat. "Master Ian says he takes his bath with the ladies there."

"Aye, well…those ladies do not wish to string Master Ian up by his bollocks." He'd not be making his man parts vulnerable to Isobel until he knew her frame of mind was a bit kinder toward him.

The boy gave him a shocked look and held up the empty kettles. "Ye want we should fetch more?"

"Nay, lad." Alasdair stepped out of the tub, scooped up a folded linen from a nearby chair, and slaked away the wetness with a hurried swiping. He squeezed the water from his shoulder-length hair and slid the drying cloth back and forth across his back. The quicker he finished and dressed, the quicker he saw Isobel. "Thank ye, boys. That'll be all for now."

The trio trooped out, their shoulders slumping at being dismissed, and conversation about the brothel ended.

Alasdair donned fresh clothes. His best waistcoat, jacket, and shirt. A new neckcloth. Polished boots usually reserved for Sundays or important meetings. He belted his kilt, then slicked back his damp hair, and secured it into a tidy queue with a leather tie. He slid his *sgian dhu* into his boot and patted it for good measure. Some might think it odd, taking a knife to meet a long-lost love. But if Temsworth reappeared, Alasdair would not be ill-prepared.

He cast a glance at his reflection in the standing frame of polished metal that had come with the purchase of the manor and been considered quite the selling point with the previous owner. Alasdair didn't give a damn about the thing. If it had not come with the house, he would have been fine without it. Although, at least now, he could ensure Isobel wouldn't find him lacking. He straightened the knot of his neckcloth and smoothed down the lines of his waistcoat. He was not a vain man, but today's reunion meant more to him than anything he'd ever risked before. He was ready.

Charging out the door and down the stairs, he headed toward the kitchens. Mrs. Aggie looked up from her mending as he stormed through the door. "I willna be home this evening. Enjoy the night off, aye?"

"No supper?" Her piercing scowl gave him a good up and down.

"No supper." He exited through the service door before she added any additional comments that might force him to reconsider his wisdom in hiring her. This was not the day to try his patience.

He strode across the gardens, pushed through the gate, and crossed the alley. He paused with his hand on the cool metal of the ornate black iron latch of Château Delatate's gate to the small enclosure leading to its rear entrance. An eerie sense of being watched tingled across his nape, standing every hair on end. He looked up and down the way. Not a soul present other than the black and white stray cat that often showed up in his gardens. Old mercenary senses died hard. Something ill was afoot. He felt it.

"Keep watch, aye?" he advised the cat before proceeding. He closed the gate behind him, then vaulted up the steps to the rear door. As soon as he entered, he found his way blocked by an immoveable wall of muscle.

"You should enter by the front door, Master Alasdair." Adalbert assumed a stern look as he settled his feet farther apart and flexed his arms. "Madam Georgianna will not be pleased."

"It is all right, Adalbert," Madam said from farther down the hallway. "I am expecting Monsieur Alasdair. You may return to your post."

Adalbert made a half bow, then resumed his stance with his back against the door.

Madam Georgianna waved Alasdair forward and held out a key by its dark green ribbon. "Third floor, monsieur. End of the hall. The door to the green suite matches this ribbon. Your lady awaits."

He accepted the key with a curt nod, then climbed the stairs. The closer he drew to the third floor, the harder his heart pounded, and the more difficult it became to breathe. The moment was at hand. The moment he'd never dreamed of receiving.

The gentle, golden glow from the sconces beside each door washed the hallway in a seductive light. The very air of the place thrummed with the excitement of the forbidden. Upon reaching the dark green door at the end of the corridor, he hurried the key into the lock. A belayed thought stilled his hand. His conscience warned him to tread through this portal to his hopes and dreams with utmost care. He rapped his knuckles against the frame.

"Ye may enter."

Alasdair closed his eyes. He'd never thought to hear the sweetness of that voice ever again. He turned the key and walked through the door, taking care to close it behind him and lock it. Neither of them would leave this room until he'd had his say.

Isobel stood with her back to him, gazing out the open window. The evening breeze riffled the lacy gauze of her thin chemise, outlining her lean, lithe form. How thin she'd grown. Gone were the plentiful curves of years past, the curves that had made his mouth water and his body beg for relief. Her waist-length hair was the lush ebony he remembered, tresses fluttering like a river, set aglow with amber and copper highlights in the candlelight.

"Isobel."

A sharp gasp escaped her as she turned. Her dark eyes, the deepest, richest brown and framed in thick black lashes, flared wide. Fear. Anger. Sorrow. Hatred. All shone in her face. Shouted at him. Accused him. She recoiled a step.

God help me make her understand. He swallowed hard, struggling to find the right words. If possible, her loveliness had increased over the course of the past ten years. But his beloved Isobel had lost the soft innocence of her youth. She had hardened, become a vision of feral grace. An angry leeriness tightened her stance. His lost love bore the look of a beast escaped from a snare and willing to fight to the death before being trapped again.

"Isobel," he repeated in a softer tone. He longed to close the distance between them and gather her into his arms, but instinct warned him to hold fast.

She bared her teeth and pointed a trembling finger at the door. "Get out." Stomping forward, she shook a finger at the door again. "Ye've no business here. Get out before I ring for Einrich and have ye thrown out."

Gut wrenching at her reaction, Alasdair held the key aloft with the green ribbon. "I am yer gentleman for the evening."

She lowered her hand and fisted it at her side. Her eyes shimmered with unshed tears as she jutted her chin upward. "A shameful ploy. Even for ye, Alasdair." She clutched her arms across her body and made a jerking nod in his direction. "Was it not enough that ye lied to me all those years ago? Deserted me? Left me with a cruel, perverted man? Do ye now pay to see the depths ye've forced me to sink to?" The purest hatred shown in her face. "Are ye satisfied now?" She flipped a hand in his direction. "Go ahead. Laugh all ye like. Ye always accused me of putting on airs. Well done, Master Cameron. Ye knocked me from my pedestal."

He tucked the key into the inside pocket of his waistcoat, then scrubbed both hands down his face. Her words cut him worse than any dagger. How could he make her understand? "I never meant to hurt ye, *mo chridhe*."

"Dinna call me that!" She stormed back to the window and threw herself down on the pillowed couch in front of it. "Ye have no right to call me that. I am not *yer heart*. Not anymore."

So much loss. So much pain. The suffering he heard in her voice ripped him in two.

She shot a hard look in his direction. "Ye gave up yer right to say such to me when ye forgot I existed. Understand?"

"I never forgot ye existed. Ye looked happy when last I saw ye." His voice broke against his will. He swallowed hard and tried again. "I came for ye, Isobel. I swear I did. I saw ye there with him. In the gardens. Smiling. Laughing. Looking up at the fool as though he was all ye ever wanted." He shook his head, wishing he could travel back in time and make a different choice. "Ye looked settled. Contented. Well suited to a life I could never hope to offer ye."

She rocked forward, cupping her face in her hands. "Looks deceive." She straightened and combed her fingers back through her hair. Hopelessness painted shadows under her eyes and in the hollows of her cheeks. She fixed her gaze upon him, unblinking. "Why did ye not come to the chapel? Ye promised me, Alasdair. Ye swore on yer mam's grave."

"Morbid sore throat took out most of the clan. Few of us survived, and it took us weeks to regain enough strength to put one foot in front of the other." Alasdair cringed. The excuse sounded lame even to him. Isobel thought the same. He saw it in her eyes. He swayed a step forward. "I came here to beg yer forgiveness."

"Well, ye canna have it," she spit out the words as though they tasted of poison. "I wouldha gladly returned to Skye with ye, had ye but asked. We couldha rebuilt the clan. Ye had a croft. Land. What more would we have needed?"

"I had nothing." He risked another step forward. "I lost it all. Without the protection of the MacCoinnich Clan, with our people all but wiped out, Campbells took control of our land with the crown's blessing. The handful of us that lived through the sickness only survived by leaving Skye and becoming mercenaries."

"I wouldha happily lived with nothing but yer plaid to shield me from the weather." She scooted back against the cushions, drawing her knees to her chest, and wrapping her arms around them. "Ye didna even give me the chance to decide, Alasdair. Ye denied me the choice that was rightfully mine to make—not yers!"

She was right. How could he argue with the truth? He pulled an armchair out of the corner of the room, angled it in front of her, and lowered himself into it. He'd rather sit closer, share the couch with her. But to approach her now would be a mistake. "I was wrong, Isobel, and dinna think I havena suffered with the foolishness of my decision."

"Ye suffered?" She huffed out a bitter laugh. "Ye have no idea about suffering." She flipped a hand toward the window. "I suppose ye left yer wife for the evening. Does she know ye spent her household money on a harlot?"

"I have no wife." He clenched the wooden arms of the chair, digging his fingers into the grain of the wood. "Ye were the only woman I ever wished to marry. The only woman of my heart."

Her soulful eyes flashed with fury. "Dinna insult me with more lies. I am no longer the naïve lass who once believed every word that fell from yer lips."

Someone knocked softly on the door.

Heart heavy, Alasdair went to the door but didn't open it. Instead, he held the latch and leaned close. "Aye?"

"Madam and I thought ye might need some refreshments to get through the night. I've brought a tray for ye." Fanny's voice held a note of expectancy laced with worry.

They must think him a fool. The women were checking on Isobel's welfare. The harlots had taken her in and considered her one of their own. He unlocked the door, opened it, and stepped aside, all the while keeping an eye on Isobel. He'd not be surprised if the woman attempted to bolt.

Holding an overflowing tray of bread, cheese, and dried fruit piled around several bottles of wine and a pair of glasses, Fanny stepped into the room. "There now. Here be a fine lovely repast to get ye through the night."

"I will never forgive ye," Isobel snapped, her venomous glare locked on Fanny.

Fanny gave her an apologetic smile. "I know, lass. I know." Without another word, she deposited the tray on top of the low dresser against the wall and left the room.

Alasdair closed the door behind her and locked it. This evening was far from over.

CHAPTER FOUR

HOW DARE HE come here and witness her shame. Isobel clutched a hand to her throat as she stared out the window. *Nay.* This was not shame. She was not ashamed of anything she had done to keep Connor safe from his wicked father's influence. A deep breath failed at calming her.

And how dare he look at her that way. How dare he stir the long-buried memories of her heart. The hopeless love she had locked away and done her best to forget. By the saints above, how could he still have such power over her after all that had come to pass?

"Would ye rather port or whisky?"

"I'd rather ye left." The words slipped out with little effort. She prayed Alasdair would heed the acidic hate laced in them and give up this cruel farce. She needed him to leave. Every time he spoke, the treacherous memories of all they had once hoped to share threatened to surface and cloud her judgment. The mere sight of him had rendered her weak. *Damn him. Damn him straight to hell.*

"Port, it is." The soft shushing of liquid gurgling into a glass broke the strained silence between them. Floorboards creaked. Boots thumped dangerously close. "Isobel."

Even before she faced him, the heat of him touched her, making her wish she could shy away. She daren't allow herself any closer. It would be like a midge risking a spider's deadly web. She shifted on the couch, scooting as far back in the corner as she could. A glance up at him almost choked her. She had forgotten how much his eyes reminded her of storm clouds one minute and soft morning mist the next. Avoiding the slightest brush of his fingers, she accepted the goblet of port. "Thank ye."

He gave her a polite nod that didn't mask the fact he'd noticed she'd done her best not to touch him. He returned to his seat in the center of the room. With elbows propped on his knees, he rolled the glass of whisky between his palms, staring into it as if in a trance. "I am sorry, Isobel," he said soft and low. "Sorrier than ye shall ever know."

She sipped at the port to keep from blurting out her pain and sounding like some hysterical, empty-headed lass. She had shared enough for one day. He'd caught her off guard. She wouldn't give him that satisfaction again. Rubbing a fingertip around the rim of her goblet, she allowed herself a bitter smile. Her reflection in the drink looked quite the sullen shrew, and she felt it to her bones. 'Twas easy to embrace the part. "Aye. Ye said that a'ready."

"And I shall keep saying it until ye believe the truth of it." He sipped at his whisky, but she could tell he longed to toss it back and pour himself another. Alasdair had always loved his whisky and handled it well.

"The sickness took my clan, too," she volunteered. She didn't know why she said it. The words seemed to surface of their own accord. "Temsworth informed me—daily, in fact—that all I had ever known or loved was dead, and I was alone in this world."

He studied her, a pained frown knotting his dark brows. "I had heard of yer father's death. I am sorry."

"Dinna be. Father turned out to be a self-serving, greedy man who cared for nothing other than gaining enough gold to fund his travels."

She shifted on the seat, rearranging her chemise to cover herself as best she could. It was bad enough having her feelings exposed to

Alasdair much less her body. She took another sip as she allowed herself to look over this man who had once held the key to all her hopes and dreams.

He was still the strong, muscular Highlander who made a lass's heart beat faster. But the longer she watched him, the more she realized he had changed. Hardened. Seasoned. Less the arrogant, self-assured youth she had once known. He seemed almost humbled. A strained weariness tensed his broad shoulders, and the little finger on his left hand appeared permanently bent at an odd angle. It must have been broken and poorly set. "Ye've gone a bit gray at the temples, Alasdair."

He touched a hand to the side of his dark hair slicked back in a queue. "Aye. I suppose I have." He locked eyes with her. "Ye're as lovely as ye ever were. Even more so if that's possible."

He shouldn't look at her like that. She cleared her throat. "If I am to understand ye correctly, ye came here this evening to confess yer sins and beg forgiveness from me, aye?" If forgiveness would rid her of him, perhaps she should feign it, so he'd be gone from her.

"In part."

"In part?" She drained her glass, unsure whether she wished him to continue. Surely, he didn't suggest... She swallowed hard. When she had told Madam and Fanny, she wished to become one of their ladies, she had felt certain she could follow through and do whatever it took—as long as she kept the thought of securing funding for the Highlands firm in her mind. But with Alasdair? The courage required for that fled her. "Am I to understand, ye're a regular here at Château Delatate then? Like yer brother?"

He scowled at her with the same perturbed look he'd often given her when they were young. "I am not a regular here." He rose and held out his hand for her glass. "I came here to beg yer forgiveness and offer my help. Madam and Fanny informed me about Temsworth sniffing about and yer fear of discovery."

She'd not be bullied with the mention of Temsworth. "Ye know I have a son." That should run him off quick enough. What man wished to offer protection for another man's child? Especially when that child was a duke's only heir.

Alasdair handed her the refilled glass, this time taking care to brush his fingertips across hers. "Madam and Fanny told me of yer son. Young Connor." He gave her a smile, but sorrow darkened his eyes. "Full of piss and vinegar, Fanny said."

His touch addled her more than she cared to admit. She switched her glass to the other hand and tucked the fingers he'd touched under her arm as though to warm them. "Aye," she agreed softly, then took a quick drink to steady her inner storm.

"Tell me of him." He had the audacity to seat himself beside her. Granted, he sat on the other end of the long couch but was still beside her just the same.

If she rose and paced about the room, the infernal chemise she'd allowed Fanny to convince her to wear would leave nothing to the imagination. Every dimpled dip and scar showed through the gauzy material. So, she tucked herself even tighter against the rolled arm of the couch and leaned away, putting as much distance as possible between them.

"Tell me of yer Connor, Isobel. Please?"

She was not a fool. She knew what he played at, but if he wished to perpetuate this laughable game, she'd play along. After all, he'd paid for the entire night, and Fanny had stressed several times that clients of Château Delatate always got their money's worth. Isobel could only assume that rule included Alasdair.

"Connor is my dearest heart." She allowed herself a faint smile. "Braw, courageous wee lad, he is. Five years old this month." She eased out the softest sigh. "He is my only joy." A long drink of the port sobered her. She turned and glared at Alasdair, willing him to understand. "I will do anything to protect him."

"Spoken like the fine mother I always knew ye'd be."

They needed to change the subject. He had learned enough about her. Isobel shifted her gaze back to the faded wine stain on the golden damask of the sofa. "Madam and Fanny said Ian lost Janet in the massacre at Glencoe."

Alasdair frowned down at his whisky. "Aye. A Campbell bastard slit her throat, and Ian held her in his arms as she died." His fingers flexed around the glass, his knuckles whitening. "She had just told him the night before that she carried his child." He slowly shook his head. "For a while, I feared he'd take his own life—or fight with such abandon, his enemies would take it for him."

Sadness for Ian and all he had lost filled her. Alasdair's only brother had always been such a dear soul. "God bless him," she whispered.

"Aye," Alasdair said. "God bless him, indeed." Silence once more settled between them, but it seemed softer, less threatening.

With an impatient shifting on the couch, he faced her. "Allow me to help ye, Isobel. I can help ye, yer aunt, and Connor. Ye need safety. I can offer it. A young lad Connor's age needs room to stretch his legs. My home has that both inside and out. Halls made for a boy's running and a walled-in garden made for exploring. I know ye may never forgive me, but at least allow me to pay for my poor judgment by doing this for yerself and yer son."

"Do ye not realize once Temsworth discovers ye live in Edinburgh, he'll turn up at yer home, too?" She stood. The sheer chemise be damned. She couldn't sit still any longer. "He knew I loved ye when we married. Da told him all about ye. Even how ye offered for my hand after we made our promise in the caves. That's one reason he taunted me with the lie about yer death for years. Every time he forced me to…" She refused to speak the rest of the despicable words. Instead, she hurried to refill her glass. "He is a powerful, heartless man, Alasdair. And he has a long reach that crushes his enemies. My only hope lies in the Highlands with whatever clan I can convince to take us in." She took a deep drink. "We can hide there. Connor will be safe."

"Ye mean to go begging?" He stared at her as though she'd lost her mind. "Begging yer way through the Highlands 'til ye find a clan willing to take ye in after I've offered ye safe haven here?"

"I would nay be begging." She tightened her hold on her glass, fighting the urge to throw it in his face. "I can sew. Cook. I know the healing arts and herbs." She stormed closer. "How do ye think I prevented myself from getting with child for the first five years of my hideous marriage?"

He rose from his seat. A head taller, he had always been one of the few men who towered over her. His scowl grew dangerously dark as he lunged a step closer. "Ye must not have been verra good at yer healing arts. Ye have a son, do ye not?"

"Temsworth took away my herbs when he discovered them. That's when he imprisoned me in the tower!" She shuddered, biting the inside of her cheek to keep from sobbing. Damn him for tricking her into speaking her mind. Ten years of pent-up rage threatened to explode. *Nay.* He would not be allowed to make her guilt any worse. She regretted so much. Regretted that she hadn't left Temsworth sooner. "I *am* a good healer. Auntie Yeva taught me well." She stood prouder. "And I love my son. I dinna regret having him."

"Imprisoned ye?" Alasdair reached out to her.

Ingrained reflexes from past beatings took over. Isobel flinched and shied away, lifting both hands to fend off the strike. Too late, she realized her error. She stared at him for a long moment, then hugged herself and turned away.

"Isobel?" he whispered. His tone made her want to retch.

"Dinna pity me," she warned in a low, growling sob. She fought away the dark memories. "I survived. I finally found my courage and escaped." She faced him and lifted her chin. "And I saved my son and Auntie."

"Aye." Alasdair eased closer. "That ye did, lass. Ye've more courage than most men I know."

"Dinna be condescending, either." She couldn't bear his kindness any more than she could bear his pity. And his kindness was far more dangerous. It risked eroding her defenses. She turned and busied herself at the tray of food beside the bottles, rearranging the bannocks and cheeses into orderly stacks. "Tell me of the MacCoinnichs. Did all the brothers survive?"

"Aye." Alasdair drew closer still. "All four."

Isobel closed her eyes against the feel of him so near. Would this accursed night never end?

The lightest touch brushed her arm. She stiffened, hands fisting on either side of the tray atop the dresser.

"Isobel." His deep voice rumbled through her like the grumbling of a summer storm. "I know perhaps ye'll never forgive me." He paused and pulled in a deep breath, then blew it out. His air tickled across the bare skin of her shoulders. "I pray ye will someday, but I understand how ye might not do so. But I..."

She flattened her hands on the dresser and stared straight ahead. Surely, he wasn't about to ask for more than she could give. Didn't expect her to honor her part of the night's transaction. Merciful heavens, she couldn't bear it if he did. Not now. She had hungered for his touch so long. Still did, if truth be told. But she daren't sate that hunger. Not ever. They had lost their opportunity to the past. Lost it when he'd chosen to leave her in hell.

"But at least let me help ye." His hand fell away from her arm, and he retreated a step. "As a...friend."

A friend. Of all the things she had thought about Alasdair over the years, *friend* was not one of them. She turned to find him standing in the center of the room. Wide stance. Fierce look. He appeared ready to go to war. Perhaps, he was. This night definitely felt like a battle.

If she had learned anything over the last decade, it was that nothing in life came free. She folded her arms across her breasts and held herself together. "And in return?"

"In return?" he repeated, then the gist of what she asked triggered a dark scowl. He snapped, "In return *nothing*. Since ye refuse to forgive me, helping ye will ease my conscience for all the pain I caused ye."

A sliver of remorse pricked at her heart. Alasdair *had* behaved the perfect gentleman since even before entering the room. He had knocked. Had made no advances on her person even though he had wished to do so. The yearning had shown in his eyes. She gave an apologetic nod. "Forgive me. I find kindness a rare commodity of late."

"I intend to change that." He bowed with the respect of one addressing the queen. "What say ye?"

A wild thumping rattled the door. "Isobel! Master Alasdair! Forgive me, but it's urgent!"

Alasdair strode to the door, unlatched it, and hurled it open.

Fanny blew in like a red-headed windstorm and slammed it shut behind her. "The duke's men found the apartment."

"Connor!" An anguished cry ripped from Isobel. Her son. Her precious son. Auntie Yeva. Her aunt would die protecting Connor. She shot to the door, but Alasdair caught her back.

"Nay, love. Stay here. I'll save yer son and aunt." He pushed her into Fanny's arms. "Keep her here, and get Einrich to stand guard. Roust Ian from Lettie's bed. I'll be taking him and Adalbert with me."

"I will not say here!" She wrenched herself away. "I'm going to save my son!"

"Both of ye *haud yer wheesht!*" Fanny clapped her hands, rattling the bracelets on both wrists. "Ye didna let me finish. The men found the rooms, but Yeva and young Connor hid in a wee space between the shed and the château." The woman shook her head and held up her forefinger and thumb, displaying the tiniest of spaces between them. "Lordy me, I dinna know how they squeezed into it. Einrich said it's narrower than a midge's arse."

If the harlot continued babbling, Isobel would either scream or slap the woman—or mayhap both. She took hold of Fanny's shoulders and gave her a hard shake. "Where are they now?"

"In the main kitchen." Fanny jerked her head toward the hall. "But I came to warn ye because we fear the duke's men still lurk about. Einrich and Adalbert search for them now."

"Lord Almighty, woman. Ye couldha handled yer warning a damn sight better. What the hell is wrong wi' ye?" Alasdair glared at Fanny, then motioned at Isobel. "Fetch her a robe, aye?"

"A robe?" Fanny repeated. "Why?"

He shoved his face to within inches of the woman's nose. "Because I'm sure Isobel needs to go to her son, and I daresay she willna wish him to see her so attired."

Self-conscious all over again, Isobel hugged herself. He read her true. She needed to hold Connor in her arms and feel him safe. A tendril of gratitude, the subtlest warmth coaxed at the hardened walls around her heart. Alasdair understood and even cared. She turned to Fanny. "Aye, Fanny. Please?"

Her scowl still locked on Alasdair, Fanny slipped her silk dressing gown from around her shoulders and held it out. "Here, lass. Wear this." She nodded toward the ribbon of a belt dangling from the loops in the sides of the robe. "Tie the wee belt tight. I know ye're swimming in it, but at least ye'll have some covering."

Isobel slipped it on and tied the belt. She cast a glance back at Alasdair as she headed into the hall. "Forgive me for cutting yer evening short." Gentlemen who purchased an entire night enjoyed the pleasures of their lady until dawn—or so had stressed Madam and Fanny. "I shall ask Madam to return yer money." Although she could think of many better ways she would have ended this hellish night, at least her forced attendance with Alasdair was finally over.

He shook his head. "Oh no, lass. My evening is nay over yet. I'm coming with ye. I think it's time I met yer son."

She shot a glance at Fanny, who responded with a firm nod, then rubbed her thumb across her fingertips in a silent reminder that Alasdair had paid for her time. Isobel forced a graceful look in Alasdair's direction. "Very well. Follow me."

She pushed through the narrow door to the back staircase leading to the main kitchen. Racing down the stairs, she steadied herself, sliding her hands along the walls of the narrow passage. Alasdair kept pace behind her. His boots filled the tight space with the sound of galloping thunder. The noise jarred her nerves, triggering memories of the duke's visits to the tower. His boots had sounded just as loud and ominous each time he had approached her rooms, like the tolling of a death knell. She shook herself free of the nightmarish feeling and picked up the pace. She shot through the last door with such fervor, it bounced against the wall.

"Mama!" Connor sat perched on the end of the worktable, swinging his feet as he munched on a biscuit and basked in the attention of Marjie, Rew, and Rosie, three of Madam Georgianna's ladies.

"Connor!" Isobel rushed to him, gathered him up, and hugged him tight.

"I'm fine, Mama." He squirmed in her arms. "Ye're crumbling my biscuit."

She allowed herself one more hug, then resettled him back on the table. She pecked a kiss to his tousled head and brushed his hair out of his eyes. "I feared for ye, son, but ye did well making it here to safety." She'd always told the boy if anything happened to run to the château. Madam and Fanny had granted her permission to do so.

"He's a fine, brave lad, this one is," bragged Rew as she handed Connor a small tin cup of milk.

"That he is," chimed in Marjie as she set a fresh plate of biscuits and a crock of jam beside him. "Said he hasna had jam in forever." Margie winked. "I reckon we can fix that!"

"And who might ye be, sir?" Rosie asked Alasdair as she sidled closer with a suggestive wiggle.

Alasdair gave a polite nod. "Alasdair Cameron."

Isobel nearly laughed aloud at Alasdair's strained expression. "He is my assigned gentleman, Rosie." She glanced around the kitchen. "Where's Auntie Yeva?"

The Delatate ladies parted and pointed to the far corner beside the hearth. "We offered her food and drink, but she doesna seem to understand what we're saying," Rosie said. She gave a sad shake of her curly blonde head. "Poor thing. Seems fair addled, she does."

Auntie was not addled. Auntie was enraged. Isobel could tell by the way the old woman had drawn herself up into a knot and sat glaring at all around her. At any moment, an explosion of Armenian curses and predictions of dire moral consequences would surely ensue.

She made her way over and knelt in front of her. Taking hold of her aunt's calloused hands, she held them tight and whispered, "This is but a temporary situation. Please, Auntie, bear with me. We will get through this."

Auntie's mouth tightened, the twitching corners drawing down even more. Her dark eyes narrowed as her gaze swept across Isobel's attire. She jerked her hands free and tucked them tight against her body as she turned aside.

Isobel's heart sank. She hated disappointing the dear woman who had raised her since her mother had died, but it couldn't be helped. She pushed up from the floor and returned to stand beside Connor.

"What did ye say yer name was again?" Connor asked Alasdair between bites of biscuits, his small cheeks bulging.

Alasdair bowed. "Alasdair Cameron, at yer service." He held out his hand. "I'm an old friend of yer mother's."

Connor switched his biscuit from his right hand to his left, wiped his jam-covered fingers across the front of his shirt, then took Alasdair's extended hand and shook it up and down. "Peezed to meet ye, Master Cameron."

Isobel's heart swelled with protective pride. Now and then, Connor still had trouble saying certain words, but the more time that elapsed from the last time his father had belittled him, the more sure of himself he became.

Connor released Alasdair's hand and held out his plate of treats. "Wanna biscuit?"

"I thank ye, m'lord." Alasdair helped himself and downed the morsel in one bite.

The boy held a hand to his mouth and leaned forward. "Ye dinna have to call me that," he whispered, then stole a glance at Isobel. "Nobody's 'posed to know I'm a marqest. Just call me *Connor*, aye?"

"Marquess," Isobel gently corrected. She pecked another kiss to his temple. "Finish yer biscuits," she urged with a hug.

The lad nodded and happily complied.

Madam Georgianna appeared in the doorway. "Rew, Rosie, Marjie." She cast a glance in Connor's direction and shooed the ladies out into the hallway.

"Where they going?" Connor asked, his disappointment at the loss of his admirers evident.

"Their friends have arrived for a visit," Alasdair volunteered. He cast a devilish look in Isobel's direction, a look that made her stomach tighten with dread. "Tell me, Connor, do ye like dogs?"

The boy brightened and bobbed his head. "Aye, I do."

"My stable master's dog, Toaty, had six pups. Wiggly wee things they are. Would ye like to see them?" Alasdair beamed at Isobel with a smug, self-satisfied smile.

"Can we, Mama?" Connor kicked his feet faster at the prospect. "Can we?"

"I shall think about it. Such a visit would be for another time. It is too late today. As soon as ye finish yer biscuit, we must see to getting ye to bed." Isobel shot Alasdair a warning glare. The man best keep his mouth shut. She knew well enough his sly game. Befriending her son.

Indeed. She was not dull-witted.

Armenian mutterings came from the corner.

Isobel turned to find Auntie Yeva on her feet, shaking her kerchief-wrapped head and jabbing a bent finger in the air. She vehemently refused to spend the night under the brothel's roof. Said she'd rather be dead, and Isobel should be ashamed to have her son sleep in such a place. She went on to remark on the cleanliness of anywhere Connor might lay his head, but after that, her rant increased to such a fast stream, Isobel couldn't understand her.

"My manor has bedrooms aplenty." Alasdair rested a hand on Connor's shoulder. "And in the morning, after ye've had a fine breakfast, we could go to the stables and see the pups."

"Aye, Mama! That would be finer than fine, do ye not think so?" Connor bounced in place, making the worktable creak with all his wiggling.

Irritation simmering, Isobel pointed at the cup of milk and plate of biscuits. "Sit still, and finish yer treats whilst Master Cameron and I step into the hall and have a wee chat, aye?"

"Peeze?" Her son folded his hands and gave her a dangerously angelic look.

"What did I say?" She pointed at the cup of milk again.

"Aye, Mama," Connor said, his small shoulders slumping in a show of mock obedience.

She fixed a meaningful scowl on Alasdair as she headed toward the hall. "Master Cameron."

The man followed with a smile that irritated her even more. "Aye?" he responded as he folded his arms across his broad chest and leaned back against the wall.

One thing hadn't changed about Alasdair. He still possessed the power to enrage her with that smug look of his. "Dinna use my son against me!" she warned through clenched teeth. "We will stay here and be fine as long as Madam and Fanny allow it."

"Shall I ask yer auntie her opinion on the matter? I dinna understand Armenian, but she made her meaning clear enough. Or shall I ask Madam Georgianna or Fanny? Ye know as well as I that giving ye an apartment on the property is one thing, but having a child running about the brothel is a different matter entirely." Alasdair leaned forward and lowered his voice. "Dinna let yer stubbornness rule ye, Isobel. Ye're cutting off yer nose to spite yer face."

"What do ye know about it?" she snapped. She massaged her throbbing temples, wishing she'd chosen somewhere besides Edinburgh to run out of money.

"I know well enough that a child doesna belong in a brothel, and neither do ye." Alasdair glanced down the hallway toward the sound of females laughing, followed by a loud male guffaw. "My home. A safe haven as long as ye need it." He lifted his chin. "I offer it as a friend and as an atonement for my sins against ye. It's a damned sight better payment to ye than reciting a stream of Hail Marys."

"Fanny said they believed the men to still be about. How will we get there without being seen?" Isobel glared at him. Alasdair thought himself so smart. How would he manage their escape without discovery?

His victorious look made her wish to smack him all the harder. "One of my clients, Clan Mackenzie, might be of some assistance. I believe Madam Georgianna warehouses a good bit of their Edinburgh stock in her cellar."

"Their stock?" All she knew for certain was she wished this worrisome night would come to an end.

Alasdair eased a hand under her arm and urged her farther down the hallway toward Madam Georgianna's sitting room. "Whisky. Port. Rum." He glanced around as they walked and kept his voice low. "Regular deliveries come and go. Wagon loads of the goods. Tied and covered from prying eyes. I'm certain we could spirit the three of ye out amongst the barrels." A half-smile lifted one corner of his mouth. "In fact, I'm due a delivery of whisky. Perfect timing, methinks."

CHAPTER FIVE

THE CRAMPED, DARK space between the barrels in the wagon made her mouth go dry and her palms bead with sweat. The canvas and rope piled next to the cart, waiting to cover the cargo, caused her stomach to lurch. *Nay.* She couldn't do it. She couldn't bear the thought of being trapped again. Isobel gasped in a deep, desperate breath, blew it out, then pulled in another. She shook her head and backed away. "I canna do it."

"It's the safest way." Alasdair pointed at the narrow opening between the casks. "The three of ye tucked in cozy as peas in a pod." He patted the lowered footboard. "It's but a short distance. We'll cut through the far alleyway and round the square to come out on the other side of my property. Those watching the château will nay suspect a thing."

Without hesitation, Auntie Yeva snatched hold of Alasdair's extended hand, scrambled up into the wagon, and crawled into the opening. Connor climbed up next, snuggling up against the old woman like a wee mousie in a nest.

Memories of Temsworth's stone closet crashed in all around her. Visions so real, she smelled the place, relived its terror. Dank. Dark. Barely big enough to stand upright. Too narrow to sit. Too tight to lift her arms. The cold rear wall had pressed against her backside whilst the iron door had shoved against her front. Turning her head had been almost impossible. An upright tomb, Temsworth had called it. He'd laughed and sworn that someday he would leave her there to rot. He had locked her within, trapping her for hours whenever she displeased him. Isobel had learned quickly how to behave.

She dug at her arisaid, pulling it away from her throat and fighting the smothering sensation. "I canna do it." She waved away the wagon and retreated another step. "Take Connor and Auntie. I'll take my chances on foot. Fanny told me where ye live. I've but to cross the close to reach yer back garden. They'll never see me in the darkness. I can sneak well enough."

"All is loaded. We can cover it now," Einrich called out from the other side of the wagon.

Alasdair held up a hand. "Give us a moment, aye? I'll call out when we're ready."

"*Ja.*" Einrich dipped his chin, then disappeared deeper into the storage cellar.

"What do ye fear, Isobel?" Alasdair's piercing glare troubled her. It was as though he looked into her soul and saw all her weaknesses. He gave a perplexed shake of his head. "I remember when we used to race and hide in the darkest, tightest caves along the beach. Many a time. We risked drowning a time or two because of the tide. Remember? Scared our kin to death."

She swallowed hard. The dear memories made her yearn for those carefree days again, yearn so badly she wanted to weep. "I remember the time yer da tanned yer arse for scaring him so, and I had to stay inside and empty all the chamber pots for a sennight."

"Aye." Alasdair grinned. "I got off better than ye did. I'll take an arse whipping over tending chamber pots any day."

She resettled her arisaid around her shoulders and hooded it over her head. "Take them on now. I'll be fine on the streets."

How could she tell him her fears? Fears that wouldn't exist if he had but kept his word and stolen her away. She struggled to fan the dying embers of her anger against him. Anger gave her strength. But those emotions faltered with every kindness he offered. He had given good reasons for all that had happened. Reasons that made sense. Reasons which, even in her fury, she could nay find fault.

She tried to harden her heart. Fanny had said he was now the finest solicitor in all Edinburgh. Solicitors excelled in polishing lies until they sparkled like the truth. Perhaps his reasonings were nothing more than falsehoods. It didn't matter how much he lied as long as he kept Connor safe.

She turned to go. "On wi' ye now. I'll see ye there."

Strong fingers closed around her upper arm, shooting panic through her. Isobel yanked away and stumbled to one side. Alasdair caught her, then blocked the wide ramp leading up from the cellar to the street. "Ye canna walk the back alleyways of Edinburgh alone. Not at night. Not when murderous bastards are hunting ye." He drew close until his nose nearly touched hers. "Tell me what ye fear so I can help ye. I owe ye that. I know this is my fault. Every last bit of it. I beg ye, allow me my penance. Allow me to help ye." The sorrow and pain in his eyes reached out to her, threatened to melt her defenses completely. "Please, Isobel."

"I can no longer stand cramped places." She pulled in another deep, shuddering breath. "I canna breathe in them." She would rather not explain why. To speak of the darkness gave it more power over her.

Alasdair's jaw tightened, and his eyes turned into angry slits. "I see."

His low tone struck a chord of fear through her. Did he? Did he truly see? She gave a sharp nod. No more would be said. She wouldn't give him the details of her fears, no matter how long they stood there.

He rubbed his chin as he studied her, walked a circle around her, making her more nervous by the minute. He held up a finger and gave her a gallant smile. "I have an idea." Stepping aside, he looked up and down the shadowy aisles of the cellar. "Einrich!"

"*Ja?*" Einrich stepped out from behind a stack of additional cargo.

"Would ye fetch Mistress Fanny?"

Einrich nodded and took off at a loping stride.

Alasdair chuckled and pointed at the wagon. "Look. They're fair worn out."

She leaned to one side, looking around Alasdair. Auntie and Connor had already fallen fast asleep between the barrels. The sight eased some of the tension from her shoulders. "It's been a wearisome day," she admitted.

"Aye." All mirth left Alasdair, and he stared downward. "The three of ye have suffered more than yer fair share." He lifted his head, a combination of regret and determination tightening his jaw. "But I mean to change that. Things will be different from now on. Better for ye. Easier. Ye dinna fight alone anymore. I swear it."

He had no idea how much she longed to believe him. Alasdair had always been an honorable man. At least, until he'd proven himself otherwise by failing his oath. But he'd told her his reasons, and she knew well enough the truth of the morbid sore throat. In her heart, she also believed his tale of seeing her in the garden with Temsworth and thinking to sacrifice his own love to leave her to a better life. That act was something the Alasdair of ten years ago would have done.

She closed her eyes and rubbed her fingers hard against her throbbing temples. She didn't know what to believe anymore. Dare she risk trusting him again? So much more was at stake. It wasn't just her life anymore. Her son's life hung in the balance.

Hurried steps echoed through the cave-like cellar. Fanny ambled into view. "Business hours, Master Alasdair."

"Ye've been well compensated for this night, madam. Ye know that as well as I." He gave Fanny a look that silenced any further comment. "Isobel and I shall be on our way as soon as ye provide her with a pair of trews, a tunic, a jacket, waistcoat if ye have it, and a hat. Boots, too, if ye've got them. She needs to dress as a man."

"What?" Fanny and Isobel asked in unison.

"Dress as a man," Alasdair repeated, directing his response to Isobel. He jerked a thumb in the wagon's direction. "In a man's attire, ye can ride beside me as I drive."

Fanny stared at Isobel, then Alasdair. She rolled her eyes and shook her head. "Einrich!" she bellowed in a curt, unladylike tone.

"*Ja?*" Einrich rounded the wagon and came to a halt in front of the harlot.

"Take Isobel to the costume room." Fanny spun around with a fluttering of her fingers and scuttled back across the cobblestones toward the door. "Take whatever ye need, lass. I've a caller waiting. Deep pockets, this one has. Money to be made for sure."

"This way, Mistress Isobel." Einrich extended a hand for Isobel to take the lead.

Unable to find the words to thank Alasdair for the way he had reacted to her inability to hide among the barrels, Isobel ducked her head and hurried after Fanny. She knew the costume room. She'd helped Rew sort through the apparel and organize it to help the ladies when their clients made requests for more whimsical attire. She nodded at Einrich. "I know where to go. Ye can stay here and help Master Alasdair, aye?"

Einrich gave a polite bob of his head and headed back across the cellar.

She paused long enough to admire Alasdair from afar. The man had always worn his colors well, and the fine suit coat, fitted to his warrior's form, made him look all the better. She pulled in a shaky breath. He hadn't judged her nor belittled her for her fears. That fact raced through her mind over and over as she shook free of her reverie and hurried down the hall. She pushed into the room and opened the cabinet containing the clothes she needed.

Thankfully, she found a tunic and breeches that fit a shade loose. She shoved the neckcloth in the jacket pocket, swallowing hard as she envisioned the thing wrapped around her throat. *Nay.* Temsworth had strangled her once until she'd fainted. She could bear nothing close about her throat ever again. Waistcoat, jacket, stockings, and boots. She snugged the belt tighter as she dug through the assortment of items for a wide-brimmed hat to hide her face. Urgency made her hands shake as she pulled back her hair and cinched it in place. She wouldn't wear a plaid. If anyone stopped them, she'd feign being French rather than a Scot. Tucking her long hair up under the hat, she pulled it snug and low across her brow. With an unusual feeling of unencumbered freedom, she strode down the hall, the clumping of her boots making her cringe. Merciful heavens, no wonder men sounded like clod-footed beasts.

Alasdair drew his pistol as she descended the steps into the dimly lit cellar. "Halt! Ye've come the wrong way, sir. I suggest ye go back the way ye came."

His words took her aback but gave her hope. She'd chosen her costume well. "Alasdair. It's me."

His brows shot up, and he shoved the weapon back in his belt. "Well, I'll be damned." He waved her forward. "Let's have a look at ye then. Ye fooled me in the shadows. Let's see how ye fare if ye're looked upon closer."

She approached the wagon, doing her best to move with as little femininity as possible. The closer she came to Alasdair, the darker his scowl became. She held out her hands and looked down at herself. "What's amiss? What did I forget?"

"Nothing." Alasdair's jaw flexed. "To the wagon, aye? Einrich just finished securing the ropes."

Isobel scrambled up on to the seat. "Alasdair? Tell me what's amiss? If ye see somewhere I erred, someone else might as well. I dinna wish to endanger Connor over a poorly assembled disguise."

He settled himself down beside her, clenching the reins. "If ye must know," he forced out between gritted teeth, "I dinna like the cleft of yer behind showing to all and sundry." An irritated growl escaped him as he urged the pair of horses up the ramp and out into the street at a fast pace.

Isobel held tight to the iron railing on her side of the bench, not risking another glance in his direction. His protective jealousy warmed through her with a giddiness she hadn't felt in years. It made her want to smile, but she daren't do so. Instead, she forced herself to brush the feeling aside and concentrate on watching the shadows for those wishing to do them harm.

"Are ye still able to shoot as well as ye used to?" he asked over the rattling of the wagon.

"I've not done it in quite a while, but I'm sure I still can." She prayed she could. Many a time, she'd envisioned putting a bullet through Temsworth's heart, but she'd never had the opportunity.

Without taking his eyes from the road, Alasdair handed over one of his pistols. "There's one dark turn that concerns me, and we're coming up on it. After that, it's but a little distance to the far side gate leading to the cellar of the manor house."

She took the pistol, then leaned forward and inched to the edge of the seat, watching the shadows up ahead. The lane into the alley narrowed, forcing Alasdair to slow the horses for the turn. He transferred the reins to one hand and readied his second pistol in the other. No sooner had the wagon fully entered the shadowed path than three men jumped in front of the horses, blocking the way with swords raised.

"Nobody passes without paying the toll," said the shadowy figure in the middle.

Isobel clicked back the hammer and leveled the flint-lock pistol at the man. She'd pay their toll.

Alasdair did the same. "Let us pass, gentlemen, or die."

"Three of us. Naught but two pistols." The man in the center, taller than his mates and the obvious leader, edged closer. "Odds be in our favor, methinks."

"What if they gots good aim, Hays?" asked the man on the right. "That means two of us shot dead."

"*Oui, messieurs,*" Isobel interjected in a deep-voiced snarl.

"What shall it be, gentleman? Go yer way, and all three live, or two of ye die, and I leave one to bury the others?" Alasdair trained his pistol on the man in the middle. "Hurry now. When my arm tires, I risk maiming ye instead of killing ye."

"I'll not be getting shot." The man on the left turned and ran down the alleyway.

"Ahh," Alasdair purred. "My odds just improved."

"Leave off, Hays." The man on the right nudged his companion. "We done good enough tonight, and with Brooks done turned tail and run, we can split our take even. No time for us to be getting greedy."

"What say ye, Hays?" Alasdair urged the horses forward. "Live to rob another day or bleed to death in the alley?"

Hays jerked his head at the other thief and motioned to the far wall of one of the buildings lining the lane. "We'll stand here all peaceful like and let ye pass." He lowered his sword. "This time."

Alasdair shook his head. "Nay, friend. I'll not be played for a dullard." With his pistol, he motioned toward the direction the third miscreant had taken. "Off wi' ye down the lane and to the left. Follow yer wise friend, aye?"

"Come on, Hays." The third criminal waved Hays forward as he took off at a fast trot. "Hurry up before he decides to shoot."

"Bastard," Hays mumbled, then spit on the ground beside the wagon. He sheathed his sword and hurried after his comrades.

Isobel blew out the breath she hadn't realized she held. "Thank God above."

"Aye." Alasdair set the horses at the fastest clip the dark alley allowed and kept his pistol raised. "Dinna lower yer weapon, and be sure to watch behind us. I willna breathe easy until we get into the light."

She turned and knelt beside Alasdair, hanging on and resting her arm atop the iron bar running along the back of the seat. As she swayed back and forth, her rump bumped against Alasdair with every sway of the wagon. If anyone gave chase, she doubted her aim would be true. "I'll waste my shot with all this rocking."

He draped his arm across her backside and held her tight against him. "Hold fast, lass, the thieves' cutoff is up ahead."

Too unsettled by his hold of her, Isobel didn't argue. She steadied the butt of her pistol in her left palm and sighted it in just as the thieves exploded from their lair, running to catch up with the wagon. She pulled in a deep breath, aligned the pistol with one man's broad chest, and squeezed the trigger. He dropped to the ground, clutching his midsection, and the other two men dove into the shadows. Isobel twisted around. "Give me yer other pistol in case the others give chase."

Alasdair took her spent weapon, shoved it in his belt, and pressed the other gun into her hand. "Well done, love. Well done." He returned his arm tight around her rump as the wagon roared into the street lit by the candle lanterns of the barbers, apothecaries, and taverners along the way. His secure hold of her remained as the wagon careened to the right, and the horses came to a halt in front of a large double gate of wide thick planks of weathered wood.

"*Je ressuscite!*"

Alasdair's roar of Clan MacCoinnich's battle cry brought an unbidden smile to her lips. How often had he shouted those words when they had been nothing more than wee bairns playing along the shoreline?

The double gates swung inward, and Alasdair urged the horses through them.

Two young men hurried to close the gates and secure the heavy beam down across it. "I heard a shot, Master Alasdair," one of them said. "Be ye hurt?"

"Nay, Lachie." Alasdair leaned forward and peered under the brim of Isobel's hat. "My fine guard protected me well."

She brushed aside the warm rush of emotions his words triggered. *Nay time for such foolishness,* she scolded herself. "Connor and Auntie will be afraid. Help me get to them." She scrambled down from the wagon and yanked loose the ropes. "Connor! All is well. Dinna be afraid." She'd heard nary a peep from either of them. She prayed the barrels and crates hadn't tipped over and crushed them.

"I'm not afeared, Mama." Connor popped out from under the folds of canvas, brandishing a jagged slat of wood as if it were a sword. "I canna be afeared when I have to protect Auntie."

"Ye are a brave lad, son, and I'm so verra proud of ye." The band of tension squeezing her lessened a notch. She pointed toward the center of the wagon. "Be a gentleman now and help Auntie get to the end of the wagon, so ye can both climb down, aye?"

Connor disappeared behind the pile of canvas, then reappeared with his scowling aunt. The sour-faced woman fixed her glare on Isobel, daggers flashing in her eyes as she grumbled a stream of swear words. "Auntie!"

"At least I say it in my language." Auntie gave her a look that dared her to argue. She shook her hand. "Black and blue, I will be from all this. I am too old. You should have left me to die at Hestlemoor."

"Nay, Auntie." Connor wrapped his arms around the old woman's tiny waist and buried his face against her middle. "Ye canna die. I love ye."

"Are ye happy now?" Isobel fixed her aunt with a stern look. "Shame on ye for saying such in front of Connor."

Alasdair rounded the wagon, flipping the rest of the canvas and ropes out of the way. His glance settled first on Yeva, then Connor.

"What's wrong?"

"Nothing is wrong," Auntie said in a loud voice as she hugged the boy, then patted his back. She urged him toward the end of the wagon. "Come. Is late. Time for you to be abed."

"I'm hungry," Connor said as he took hold of Alasdair's hands and swung down with a delighted squeal.

"Ye just ate not long ago." Isobel held out a hand for her son to take. "Time for bed now."

The lad cocked his head to one side. "Why ye dressed like that?"

"Never ye mind." She scooped up Connor's hand and tugged him over to stand at her side. Turning to Alasdair, she removed her hat. "I'm grateful to ye. More than ye'll ever know." She swallowed hard, the victorious spark glinting in Alasdair's eyes, making her wonder at the wisdom of accepting his help. "If ye could have one of yer servants show us to our room, we'll be out of yer hair for the evening so ye might seek yer own rest."

"Lachie!"

"Aye, Master Alasdair?" The boy came around the wagon at an awkward gallop and careened to a halt a few feet in front of Alasdair.

Alasdair nodded toward the horses. "Ye know what to do. If Hugh's not enough help to ye, roust Rob out of his bed, aye?"

"I be more help than Rob ever thought of being," Hugh argued as he labored and grunted with winding up the ropes and stacking them in the back of the wagon. He treated Isobel to a gap-toothed grin. "I be better than Rob any day."

Alasdair eased Auntie down from the wagon, then extended his arm to the elderly woman. "Allow me to escort ye to yer suite, ladies." He nodded at Connor. "Offer yer arm to yer mother, lad. It's the proper way to treat a lady with respect."

"When Mama takes ahold of my elbow like that, I'm about to get me arse smacked," the boy said with such sincerity that Isobel had to bite her lip to keep from laughing.

Even in the flickering torchlight of the cobblestoned path between the stable and the main house, she could tell that Alasdair's face had gone several shades ruddier as he struggled to keep from laughing, too.

"Aye. Well. Be that as it may, when escorting a lady, ye always offer her yer arm, aye? 'Tis proper."

With a dubious look, Connor pulled his hand free of his mother's grasp and held up his elbow.

Isobel rested her fingers on his extended arm and gave him an encouraging nod. "I thank ye, son."

He bobbed his head, then marched forward until they drew up even with Alasdair and Auntie. "I still be hungry. Reckon there be any leftover biscuits in yer kitchens?"

"Connor!" Isobel squeezed his arm, praying the silent admonition wouldn't go unheeded. The child was a bottomless pit of late. She feared it was because they'd gone hungry a time or two whilst escaping Hestlemoor.

As Alasdair held open the door to the house, he pointed down the hallway. "I'm sure of it, lad. Once ye're settled in, I'll see if Maggie's gone through the house to check the fires yet. If she's not abed, I'll have her fetch ye a biscuit and a cup of milk, aye?"

"And jam?" Connor asked, snatching his arm out of Isobel's grasp and scooting forward out of her reach. He cut a look back at her, the sly proof of his sins gleaming in his cherubic smile.

"Connor William…" She clenched her teeth and stopped mid-reprimand, reminding herself that all that mattered was the fact they were temporarily safe. Mannerly behaviors could be reinforced once they'd all had a bit of rest.

Alasdair winked at Isobel as he bent down to look Connor in the eye. "Jam, too. Now, let's get ye settled. The ladies are weary, and tired ladies smack bums a lot harder." He led them up the stairs, down the hall, and opened the door to a sprawling sitting room filled with plump, overstuffed chairs and couches laden with pillows and throws. His gentle smile sought out Isobel. "Mrs. Aggie keeps these rooms at the ready." He pointed at two closed doors on the other side. "The bedchambers are yon. I believe the one on the left has two beds. The one on the right is considered the master." He made an up and down wave toward her apparel. "I'm certain there are pitchers for washing. Mrs. Aggie is always after Maggie and Rob to keep the ewers freshened."

The sight of the comfortable rooms threatened to take her to her knees. It was a far cry from the stark room she'd rented from Madam Georgianna. Warmth and safety emanated from these rooms. A warmth and safety she'd not felt in ten years. She clenched her hands together, struggling to settle herself enough to speak.

"Ye are safe here, Isobel," Alasdair whispered as he eased a step closer. "And I hope ye'll stay...for quite a while."

Auntie cleared her throat, fixing Isobel with a stern glare, then shifting it to Alasdair. She took hold of Connor and steered the boy through the door of the room on the left. "We wash, then you in bed."

"But my biscuits!"

"You will wait in bed for biscuits." Auntie gave her one last meaningful look, then closed the door behind them.

"Thank ye for all ye've done." Isobel stared down at her hands, worrying her thumb across the black powder marks from firing the pistol. A pricking uneasiness, a frustrated struggling between the past and the present, churned inside her. It was so much easier to feel only rage and betrayal when it came to Alasdair, but her wall of rage and betrayal was crumbling.

Nay. She couldn't allow feelings of warmth toward him. She lifted her chin, met Alasdair's gaze, and took shelter behind the facade of the emotionless, detached smile she'd mastered to survive in her husband's harsh world. "Ye've been most kind. But once I get us on our feet, we'll be moving on. We dinna wish to be a burden."

His mouth tightened. As his broad shoulders slumped, he looked away and scrubbed a hand across his face. "I best go down and see about Connor's biscuits. I wouldna wish the lad to think I forgot about him." He took hold of the door latch, then stopped and stared down at the floor for a long moment. "The only way I'll fail ye this time is if I cease to draw breath. I swear it." He yanked open the door, strode through it, then clicked it shut behind him.

"That is exactly what I fear," she whispered. The last thing she wanted was Alasdair dead.

CHAPTER SIX

ONNOR'S INFECTIOUS PEALS of laughter filled the stable. Excited
yips and barks and the boisterous rustling of fresh hay rose from
one of the stalls.

Alasdair couldn't resist a wide grin, and he'd challenge anyone to
remain sour-faced at the sound of such pure joy.

"Those pups love that boy as much as he loves them," observed
Jock, the stable master who seemed as old and solid as stone. The
talented horseman had come with the manor. He scrubbed his knobby
fingers through his scraggly beard that was white as his hair. "Good
lad, that one there." With a shake of his head, he hitched down the
aisle with a saddle thrown over one arm. "Endless havering, though.
Wears a body's ears clean off with all his chatter."

"He is a fine lad," Alasdair agreed. With each passing day, he liked
Connor more and more. It made him wonder what life would have
been like if he and Isobel had married and had bairns of their own. The
wondering pained him, festered inside like a wound refusing to heal. It
was a deadly game of *what if* he played. It poisoned the joy he found in
Isobel and Connor's presence at the manor.

Of the three, only the lad had seamlessly adapted into the household. Yeva and Mrs. Aggie never agreed on anything, constantly
bickering like wild animals fighting for territory. Isobel had warmed

71

toward him, but for the most part, she remained withdrawn and kept to her rooms when not chasing after her son.

At least she lived in his home now. It was a step forward. Eventually, he would wear her down and make her forgive him. It was his greatest hope that she would someday realize how much he still loved her. Even if it took him the rest of his days. He was a patient man. *Well, to a point.* He had to admit the nights plagued him something fierce.

The scent of her lingered in the halls and haunted his every waking hour. She had always smelled sweet as the Highlands, and that hadn't changed. Then there was the agony of remembering how she had looked in that sheer chemise at Château Delatate. His man parts ached with the need to make her his. He shifted his stance, moving to stand behind one of the half-walls of the stable and prop his arms atop it. That's all he needed. A tenting of his kilt to show all and sundry just how little control he possessed when it came to Isobel.

"Connor!" Isobel's call came from across the cobblestone courtyard, separating the stable from the main house. The property was a rarity in Edinburgh. Broad and sprawling within its gated boundaries, it seemed out of place inside the borders of the crowded city.

"Lad!" Alasdair adjusted the front of his kilt and stepped away from the wall. "Yer mother calls."

"Dinna tell her I'm here," Connor pleaded, peeping out of the stall, a fuzzy black and white pup tucked in the crook of each arm. "It be time for my lessons, and they're nothing but a waste a time." His eyes rounded with the seriousness of the situation. "I'm bound to be a pirate, I am, and pirates dinna speak Latin or Ar-ar-meanun."

"Aye, but the richest pirates study their history to learn of lost treasures. Learn their sums, too. How will ye know if one of yer crew is cheating ye?" Alasdair pointed toward the house. "Out wi' ye now. There'll be no hiding or lying to yer mother. She'll skin us both, ye ken?"

"Aye." With a dejected huff, Connor lowered the pups to the ground and tromped over to Alasdair's side.

"Connor William James Cuthbarten!"

"Ye best run to her, lad. Yer full Christian name means ye're spoiling for a smack on yer arse." Alasdair nudged him to move at a faster pace than that of a salted slug.

The sight of Isobel standing with her arms crossed and a toe tapping gave Alasdair pause. She wore one of the revealing gowns Fanny had sent over. Dresses commissioned for the brothel's hostess to wear as she tended men in the smoking room waiting for their ladies. Some might consider them modest compared to the revealing apparel of the harlots, but he deemed them the sort of garment no proper lady would wear in the presence of anyone but her husband. Too low a neckline. Shoulders exposed. An overtight bodice that forced her breasts upward until they threatened to spill out. The lacy hem on one side of her skirts was pinned clean up to her knee, revealing her ruffled petticoats and even part of her ankle. She had swept her dark hair into a cascade of ringlets at the back of her head and brought down teasing strands to frame her high cheekbones.

"Why are ye dressed like that?" He already knew the answer, but it was the best way he could think of to start what he felt certain would become an argument.

Isobel's eyes flashed, then narrowed. She held up a silencing hand as Connor came to a halt in front of her. Ignoring Alasdair, she focused her attention on her son. "From now on, ye dinna visit the stable until ye've finished *all* yer lessons. Do ye hear? Auntie Yeva is beside herself."

"But—"

She caught hold of Connor's chin and bent to level her gaze with his. "Do ye wish to lose the privilege of playing with the pups completely?"

"Nay, Mama." Connor squirmed, his chin caught in his mother's firm hold. "I am verra sorry I made Auntie Yeva fret by slipping out when she went to use the chamber pot."

"Do better." She fixed him with a stern look that softened as she pecked a quick kiss to his forehead, then released him. "I love ye, Connor. Now, off wi' ye."

"Love ye too, Mama," Connor said in a sullen tone as he stomped off toward the house.

"And mind the pouting, or there'll be no jam and butter on yer bread this afternoon, ye ken?" Isobel shook her head, scowling after her son, as she watched him disappear through the side door. "That lad."

"Stubborn as his mother." Alasdair took the spot Connor had just vacated, the space directly in front of Isobel. "Now, I would appreciate an answer." He nodded toward her displayed cleavage. "Why are ye wearing that infernal gown?"

She squared her shoulders and lifted her chin. "This is my work attire. I'm returning to the château this evening."

"Like hell, ye are." He widened his stance, struggling to keep his tone civil. "Ye are not going back there, Isobel."

"I dinna believe ye have a say in it, *Alasdair*." Color riding high on her cheeks, she resettled her full skirts around her. "I shan't allow us to be a burden on yer hospitality forever."

"Ye are not a burden." Without thinking, he took hold of her upper arms and pulled her close, so close, she bumped into his chest. The thought of losing her again drove him beyond reason. He had to make her understand. "I need ye safe, m'love, which means I need ye here." The temptation of her mouth was right there. He swallowed hard, holding back a groan, then bent closer. Unbearable longing filled him. Just one wee sampling. Surely, she would allow—

"Unhand me!" Isobel shoved at his shoulders, pushing away. "Unhand me, now." A panicked cry escaped her.

He recognized her fear for what it was. Those damnable memories held her prisoner. The bastard had left his scars upon her, and they ran deep. He released her and stepped an arm's length back. "Forgive me," he said as he retreated another step to give her even more space and hopefully, the certainty that he'd never hurt her. "I should nay have touched ye without yer permission."

Teeth clenched, he struggled to find the words to put her at ease and also make her abandon her foolish plan to return to the brothel. "Please, Isobel, I beg ye. Dinna go back to the château. And please know, I would never hurt ye, nor ever force ye to do anything ye nay wished to do." Guilt and anger at his own stupidity filled him. How could he have acted in such a way? He was worse than a stag in rut. "Forgive me. Please. It's just…"

"*This* is why I must return to work." She stood with a hand pressed to her throat, taking in deep breaths. "*We*…ye and I, what we had before, it belongs in the past, and there it shall stay. It is too late, Alasdair. I willna risk yer life any more than I have already." Her voice dropped so low, he strained to hear her. "I canna bear to hear of yer death a second time, and this time, know it to be true." Smoothing her hands down her bodice, she composed herself into a vision of grace. "Connor, Auntie, and I still plan to build a simple life in the Highlands." She managed a strained smile. "We are grateful for all ye have done for us, truly we are, but we will nay interrupt yer life here in Edinburgh any longer than necessary."

Her words fed the hope that had sprouted and grown ever stronger with each passing day since they had taken up residence in his home. The hope that he might not only win her forgiveness but reclaim her heart as well. She sounded as though she might still care for him just a wee bit. A plan, a logical plan, formed in his mind, falling in place like the meticulous strategy for a victorious battle. He resolved she would remain in his life forever.

"First, ye are nay a burden nor an interruption." He chose his words with care. "And neither is Connor nor yer aunt." He tossed a glance at the manor, the truth of what he was about to say, tugging the corners of his mouth into a sad smile. "This is the first time since I've lived here that the place has felt like a home." He shrugged. "Ye brought light into my darkness, and wee Connor fills the lonely silence with laughter." He shook his head, praying she'd truly hear his words. "How could anyone think that a burden or an interruption?"

Brows drawn together and eyes shimmering with emotion, Isobel looked away, hugging herself as she turned. "I promised myself if I was successful in my escape, I'd spend the rest of my life devoted to the raising of my son—nothing else." Her lips trembled as she glanced skyward. "I promised God, as well." Her gaze sank to the ground. "We canna stay here indefinitely. I fear neither of us could..." Her voice trailed off as though she hadn't meant to say the words aloud. She turned and faced him, sadness etched in her features. "We are a danger to ye here. Temsworth will surely find ye and discover ye've helped me. I canna bear to be the reason ye come to harm."

The more she talked, the more his spirits lifted. Aye, she still had feelings for him, feelings he could nurture and feed. He could win her trust—if he tended her with care. A monumental task but well worth it. She was a wounded soul in dire need of healing, and he relished the opportunity.

"Since ye no longer feel safe here in Edinburgh, allow me to take ye to *Tor Ruadh*. I feel certain Clan MacCoinnich will take ye in. Alexander is their chief. Ye remember, Alexander?"

Isobel frowned and stepped closer. Suspicion hardened her features. "Ye told me our clans were no more. Ye said the Campbells seized MacCoinnich and MacNaughton lands."

"Alexander's wife was a Neal. She saved his life after Glencoe. Saved all of us, in fact." A shiver ran across him at the memory. Seven of them had escaped the February 1692 massacre at Glencoe by fleeing north into the mountains. Wounded. No supplies. They'd taken shelter in a cave, trying to escape the cruel clutches of the bitter

Highland winter. Clan Neal's hunters had come upon them and carried them to their keep, *Tor Ruadh*.

"After Alexander married Catriona, the Neal clan took the MacCoinnich name as their own. It's a twisted tale. One I'll leave for Catriona and Alexander to share with ye." He shifted in place, fisting his hands at his sides. He wanted so much to hold her, reassure her, make her know he'd never deceive her. "*Tor Ruadh* is their stronghold. Built into the side of Ben Nevis. Nearly impenetrable."

"Nearly?" She arched a brow and gave him the same look he'd seen her give Connor when catching the boy in a lie.

"There was a wee difference of opinion before Alexander and Catriona married. We had to break in." He risked moving a step closer. She hadn't refused his suggestion, but she still hadn't agreed. "But it was the seven of us. The four MacCoinnichs. Magnus de Gray. Ian and I." He allowed himself a proud smile. "No fortress can withstand us."

Isobel rolled her eyes, but he spotted the hint of a smile tickling across her mouth and was glad of it. "What say ye? Ye know as well as I that Alexander will nay refuse ye sanctuary."

"I had thought to go farther north than Ben Nevis. Closer to Skye. Seek shelter from the clans once allied with the MacNaughtons." She dropped her gaze again, tracing the toe of her shoe along the edge of a cobblestone. "Think ye Ben Nevis would truly be safe from Temsworth?"

His heart soared, but he kept his voice calm and without emotion. He didn't wish to frighten her now. She was as delicate and skittish as an orphaned colt. "Aye, I do. And my taking ye to *Tor Ruadh* will be a damn sight safer than yer traveling into the Highlands with only Connor and yer aunt. Temsworth will have his men looking for two women and a boy. They willna be watching for a group."

"A group?"

"Aye." Alasdair nodded and eased even closer. "I'll have two of the lads come along to drive the wagon and help me keep an eye out."

She fixed him with an unreadable look. A troubled squint crinkled the corners of her eyes as she swiped a stray curl back behind her ear. "Ye would do all this even though ye understand well enough we shall never be as we once were? I canna break my promise. Connor is my life's purpose now." She looked away, scowling, then turned back to him. "And ye know Temsworth is sure to have ye watched whilst trying to find me. I've endangered ye enough as it is. Ye would still make such a trip knowing all this?"

He held out both hands and waited. "Aye, *mo chridhe*. I do it because I love ye and always will no matter our situation." He held his breath, praying he hadn't overplayed his hand. "I shall be whatever ye wish me to be in yer life. Trusted friend. Ally. Protector. The choice will always be yers, Isobel. Never again will I make the mistake of choosing for ye."

"*Mo chridhe*, my heart. Ye always used to call me that." She visibly swallowed hard and he spotted the sheen of tears in her eyes. She inched a step forward and rested her hands atop his. A weak smile trembled across her lips. "I accept yer offer to escort us to *Tor Ruadh*." She glanced down at her breasts, then lifted her head, fixing a shy look upon him. "I shall return this dress to Fanny with a note that says I'll not be working any longer at Château Delatate." Her smile steadied. "Thank ye, Alasdair. Truly." She pecked a quick kiss to his cheek, then fled up the path leading to the house.

Alasdair pressed a hand to his cheek, cherishing her kiss more than any amount of gold. He'd meant what he said. The choice was hers. He just prayed he could convince her to give their love another chance. He understood the promise she'd made to herself and God. A desperate bargain made during a desperate time. But surely, the Almighty would understand and smile upon them. He intended to convince her of such.

"Why are ye standing there holding yer face?" Ian followed the question with a jaw-cracking yawn as he entered the courtyard and meandered up the cobblestoned path.

Alasdair glanced up at the sun. "Lettie let ye sleep later than usual."

His brother's face darkened. With a sad shake of his head, he scratched at the dusting of stubble along his jaw. "Lettie sent me away. Refuses to see me again. She's worse. Ye should see the blood when she coughs." He clenched his bared teeth and stared down at the ground, kicking aside a loose rock in his path. "Says she willna have me sit there and watch her die. Said she'd rather die alone knowing that I'd remember her as she once was."

Ian didn't handle loss well, and fate had cursed the poor man with more than his share of painful situations. Alasdair's heart went out to his brother. "I am sorry."

Ian shrugged, closed his eyes, and pinched the bridge of his nose. "I have news for ye. News ye need to hear." He rolled his shoulders, sucked in a deep breath, and did his best to stand taller. "The duke's offered a reward for the lad. Enough gold to make it dangerous. He's reported him kidnapped. Says he'll pay double to any man ensuring Isobel dies during the boy's recovery."

"Bastard." It was the nicest title Alasdair could use for the devil. "Where did ye hear this?"

"Every pub I visited." His brother gave him a grim look and drew a folded bit of parchment from his waistcoat and held it out. "Two men are covering Edinburgh with these. Probably the same two from a week ago that flushed her aunt and the boy out of the apartment."

Alasdair unfolded the yellowed paper and scanned the print. The duke had spared no expense, even commissioned an artist's rendering of the boy, Isobel, and Yeva. Thankfully, the likenesses were terrible. Unfortunately, the detailed description of their persons was not. He refolded the notice and shoved it in his pocket. He'd not have the servants see it and succumb to temptation. "I'm taking them to *Tor*

Ruadh."

Ian nodded, hooking his thumbs in his belt. "The quicker she's shed of Edinburgh, the safer she'll be." He glanced toward the house. "How much do ye trust yer people?"

The question tightened Alasdair's gut. Since he'd purchased the manor a year ago, he'd never had issues with any of them, but there also had never been such an opportunity laid out to test them either. Could he trust them? Any of them? "I dinna ken whether they can be trusted or not." He patted the pocket holding the paper. "Gold changes many a man's morals."

"Last I saw Sutherland, he mentioned a visit to Edinburgh. Should pass through here any day now." Ian yawned again. "With the three of us, the journey to *Tor Ruadh* should be safe enough."

Alasdair trusted his brother and his cousin, Sutherland MacCoinnich, a damn sight more than he trusted anyone else. He nodded. "Aye. We'll prepare to leave, and hopefully, Sutherland will arrive soon. I'll give him a week. I'm not comfortable waiting any longer." He motioned for Ian to join him as he turned toward the house. "Come. We'll get ye fed before ye seek yer rest." He clapped a hand to his brother's shoulder as he fell in step beside him. "Not a word of this to anyone, aye?"

"So, ye dinna trust them?" Ian gave a sad shake of his head as they entered through the side door and turned down the hall toward the kitchen. "I told ye living in the city rather than the Highlands was not the best for yer health."

"What does that mean? Ian? Alasdair? What has happened?" Isobel hurried down the remaining steps of the back stairs and rounded the corner. She had changed into the sober skirts and matching bodice of a modest Scottish woman. Her hair was pulled back in a braided bun, and the creamy white ruffles of her chemise peeped up around her proper neckline. She gathered the folds of her belted arisaid closer about her shoulders. "Alasdair? What did he mean by saying such?"

"I leave ye to explain it to her, brother." Ian ducked aside and retreated into the kitchen.

"Coward," Alasdair muttered under his breath before turning back to Isobel. He forced a smile and offered his arm. "I feel we would be better served discussing this matter in my office, aye?"

She stared at him as though trying to read his mind. A frown puckering her brow, she gave a gracious nod and slid her hand into the crook of his elbow. "Verra well."

They made their way to his office without speaking. Alasdair opened the door and motioned toward the pair of cushioned chairs angled in front of the wide bay window at the other end of the room. "Have a seat beside the window. I'll push open the panes for a bit of fresh air as soon as I've ensured we're not interrupted."

While she seated herself, he closed the office door and locked it. He wished no intrusions, and eavesdropping would prove more than a little difficult with them sitting at the far end of the room. He strode across the study and pushed open a pane, then seated himself opposite Isobel as he withdrew the folded parchment from his inner pocket. The last thing he wished was for her to read the paper that amounted to a death warrant. But he had sworn he would never lie to her. "Ian gave me this."

With a quizzical look, she took the missive and opened it. The longer she stared at the paper, the paler she grew. She pressed trembling fingers to the base of her throat. "Where did he get this?"

"In a pub. Here in Edinburgh." Alasdair leaned forward, aching to console her but struggling not to make the same mistake he'd made earlier. "Sutherland is due here anytime. We shall give him a week. I feel it would be prudent to have him and Ian both on the journey to *Tor Ruadh*. But in one week, we leave, whether or not he has arrived. We dare not wait any longer."

"I see." She refolded the paper with slow, careful movements, staring down at it as though fearing it would sprout teeth and attack her at any moment. She huffed out a humorless laugh and attempted a tremulous smile. "I canna say that I'm surprised. Temsworth threatened to end me numerous times after Connor was born." She smoothed a thumb along a fold of the paper, and her jaw tightened. "The only reason I'm still alive is that I convinced him of what a chore it would be to entrust Connor's care to a reliable maid since he was too young to send off to foster." Her voice took on a bitter tone. "Temsworth loathed female servants and refused to hire any. Not that any woman knowing of the rumors would ever risk working for him." Her eyes took on a cold, hopeless look. "He had women brought to Hestlemoor for his inner circle's amusement." She paused, her voice dropped to barely above a whisper. "It is my understanding that many were never seen again."

"The man deserves a slow, painful death for all he did to ye." Alasdair slid out of his chair and knelt in front of her. "I would never have burdened ye with this, but I felt ye should know. I willna lie to ye. Not ever, Isobel." He slid his hand under hers and lifted it for a tender kiss. Peering into her eyes, he willed her to trust him. "Keep yerself and Connor away from the garden walls and gates, aye? Better yet, the two of ye would do well to stay at my side whenever outside of the house. No matter where I may be, if ye wish to go outside, fetch me. The two of ye are more important to me than anything else. Understand?"

She leaned forward and trailed a trembling fingertip along the edge of his jaw. "Always the protector," she whispered. "What would I do without ye?"

He reveled in her touch, praying it would never end. "If I have my way about it, ye will never have to find out."

"Remember the promise I made." Regret and sadness laced her words. "To God and myself." Tears welled in her eyes. "And I canna risk yer life, my long-lost love. I canna be the reason ye die." She pulled her hands away and turned aside. "If I had any decency in my bones, I'd gather up Connor and Auntie and run away from this place as fast as I could to save ye from this danger." She bowed her head and closed her eyes. "But I am a selfish coward. I fear I couldna keep my son safe without ye."

"Ye are nay a selfish coward, *mo chridhe*." He remained kneeling in front of her but refrained from touching her. "Ye've battled evil all alone for so verra long, ye're weary and feel as though ye're up against a wall of stone."

Isobel nodded. "Aye," she whispered, swiping tears from her cheeks. "I am weary."

"Let me be yer strength." He leaned closer and held out his hand. "Let me keep ye safe and protect yer son as though he were my own."

Her eyes widened, but she avoided meeting his gaze. Instead, she stared down at his hands. After another shuddering breath, she slid her fingers across his and squeezed. She lifted her head and gave him the saddest smile. "There will never be another love for me. I swore it to myself and God Almighty. But know this—ye will be in my heart forever. And please know ye will always have my gratitude, aye?"

"Aye, my love." Alasdair bent and brushed a kiss across her fingers, her words filling his heart with bittersweet emotions. He would accept whatever she was prepared to give for now, but that didn't mean he'd relinquish his fight to change her mind and make her truly his.

CHAPTER SEVEN

"THIS ONE'S NAMED Posy 'cause Master Jock says the white around her nose looks like flower petals." Connor kissed the wiggling puppy's head, returned her to the ground, and picked up another. He made a face, going all squinty-eyed and talking fast. "Dis one's Haggis." Haggis received a fierce hug and a kiss and was set back down among his siblings.

"What is that smell?" Isobel pressed the backs of her fingers across the end of her nose. The air suddenly reeked of rotted eggs, rancid meat, and fresh dog shite.

"Haggis," supplied old Jock with a scowl directed at the guilty pup. "Fearsome stench when he breaks wind, and he does it all the time." The stablemaster's stern look shifted to Connor. "I thought I told ye not to pick him up? He's worse when ye squeeze his belly."

"Oh, Connor." Isobel fanned to clear the air. "Hurry and tell us the rest of their names so we might catch our breath outside." She didn't wish to hurt her son's feelings, but it was all she could do to keep from gagging. How could such a cute little puppy create such an enormous stink?

Alasdair fisted a hand in front of his mouth and coughed. "Aye, lad. Be quick about it."

Nose wrinkled, Connor pointed at the puppies squirming around his feet, naming them off. "That one's Bonnie 'cause she's verra pretty. Tags 'cause he's always biting at the other's ears, then taking off. Nipper 'cause he's a biter, too, and then Laddie, 'cause he's the runt and needs a good name to grow into."

"Fine names all, lad. Well done." Alasdair gave an impatient nod toward the door. "Let's get a bit a fresh air now, shall we?"

"He canna help it." Connor squatted back down and scooped up Haggis, hugging him close. The pup yipped and squirmed with tiny, playful growls, all the while licking and nipping at the boy's chin. "He's my favorite. I love him even if he does stink something fierce."

Love for her soft-hearted son filled her soul near to bursting. Isobel knelt beside Connor and waved Alasdair on. "Ye go ahead. Connor and I need to visit with wee Haggis for a bit since we're leaving him in a few days."

Alasdair stared down at them, then shook his head, and joined them on the ground. "Nay. I'll not be outdone by the two of ye when it comes to bearing a pup's case of belly gas." He reached across and tousled Connor's already mussed hair. "Soon as yer friend here is old enough to leave his mam, what say ye we have Ian bring him to us at *Tor Ruadh*? He can be yer verra own dog. Plenty of room to run and play there."

Connor beamed as he hugged the puppy tighter and rubbed his floppy little ears. "Ye hear that Haggis? Ye get to be mine!" He placed the tiny dog back in the hay and clapped his hands.

Haggis romped about even faster, twirling his plump black body in circles.

Isobel pressed a hand to her chest. Alasdair played her weaknesses well, knowing the surest path to her heart was through her son. As if the man needed a path at all. Saints have mercy, how she loved him still. She'd grudgingly realized that fate and ill luck had separated them rather than the lies and cowardice she'd blamed on Alasdair. Her past wasn't his fault. And with that revelation, the floodgates of her heart had burst open wide. All the memories, all the emotions, all they had shared before life had turned so sour had rushed back to her with a vengeance. God forgive her, she loved him true.

But circumstances stained that love with hopelessness. Her head told her such a love could never be no matter what her heart demanded. She blinked away the threat of tears. While she no longer blamed Alasdair for their separation, they still couldn't be together. Her promise was not the worst of the problems standing in their way. She felt sure she could figure a way around her panicked oath to God. The Almighty always forgave. *Nay.* There was but one reason remaining why they could never be together. A reason she saw no way around. The duke would never grant her a divorce, and to even request one would endanger Alasdair's life. That, she could never do. She would spend the rest of her days devoted to her son and thankful to at least have Alasdair back in her life as a friend.

"With any luck, he'll outgrow his belly troubles," she observed as another wave of choking puppy gas wafted up around them and rudely brought her back to the matter at hand.

"Lore a'mighty, boy!" Jock rounded the stall, slid his hands under Connor's armpits, and yanked the boy to his feet. "Leave him be awhile, and let the air clear. Ye'll put the horses off their feed."

Alasdair wasted no time in rising and held down a hand to Isobel. "M'lady," he said with a smile that made her heart beat faster.

She slid her hand into his, standing with little effort as he took the opportunity to pull her upward so quickly, she stumbled into his arms.

"Oh, dear!" She steadied herself against his muscled chest. "Forgive me." Cheeks aflame, she eased a step away and busied herself with brushing strands of hay from her skirts, anything to keep from looking him in the eyes.

He closed the distance between them and leaned in even closer. "Nothing to forgive, *mo chridhe.* Unless it would be yer haste to leave my embrace." His hushed voice, his tone meant for her alone, swept across her like the softest caress.

"Can I ride Flossy now?" Connor tugged on her sleeve as he shoved to stand in between them. "Peeze? I need the practice. Lots a horses at *Tor Ruadh*. Aye, Master Alasdair?"

She gave Alasdair an apologetic smile but was secretly grateful for the inability to have a private moment in the presence of a five-year-old. Her son had saved her from melting into a babbling fool. She pulled in a steadying breath and stood taller. She had to remain strong.

Alasdair seemed unperturbed as he gave the boy a serious nod. "Aye, lad. Verra true. Many a horse at *Tor Ruadh*." He offered his arm to Isobel and smiled down at Connor. "I think old Jock has Flossy waiting for ye in the paddock. He knew ye'd want to practice yer skills on such a fair day as this. Yer mother and I shall watch ye from the gate. Run and tell the man ye're ready."

Connor shot off across the stables, bellowing for Jock's attention. The man set his rake aside with a slow shake of his white head and a disgruntled look in Alasdair's direction. He clapped a hand on the boy's shoulder and steered him toward the door leading to the small, fenced-in area beside the stable.

"I believe Master Jock will be more than happy to regain the peace and quiet of days free of inquisitive young children." Isobel pulled her light, knitted shawl tighter about her shoulders and breathed in the floral fragrance of the warm spring breeze as they exited the stable and took their post beside the gate. It was the first time in a long time she had allowed herself to hope that life had finally taken a turn for the better. "Poor man. If Connor's not pestering him about playing with the pups, he's nettling him about riding the horses."

"Dinna let the old goat fool ye." Alasdair patted her hand in the crook of his elbow and winked. "There's been more spring in his step since Connor arrived." He smiled down at her fingers resting atop his arm as his thumb tickled back and forth across her hand. "There's been more spring in my step as well with the two of ye in my life."

She squeezed his arm, rallying all the composure she possessed to say what her conscience had been badgering her to say for days. "I understand now that...the past...all that went wrong, I know it was nay yer fault." She pulled her gaze from his and focused her attention on an industrious beetle creeping up the gray, weathered post of the gate. "Ye've been so kind and helpful." Pride and gratitude warmed her as her son appeared, riding the small mare Alasdair had just purchased for him. "Ye've been so good to Connor." She rested a hand atop the gate and watched her lad beaming with more joy to be alive than she had ever seen in him before. "I know now that ye wouldha done anything in yer power to save me if ye had only known." She blinked against the misting of tears. "Fate deemed us to never be. None of it was yer fault. I dinna place the blame at yer feet any longer."

"I've yearned to hear those words for ten years." He turned her toward him. "And we can still *be*, my love." He lifted her hand from his arm and pressed a lingering kiss to it. "Bad luck, a curse, evil itself, tore us apart. I prefer to believe fate brought us back together."

She lost herself in the safe, compassionate depths of his gaze. So many things flickered in his eyes. Love. Yearning. Loneliness. She felt certain her eyes reflected the same. How could they not? All those things and more churned inside her. But she couldn't allow emotion to rule her. Not with so much at stake. "I know God would forgive my rash oath, but we can still never be more than friends. I am the wife of another man. A devil of a man who will never grant me freedom." She struggled to make him understand. "He'll hunt us down. Hurt ye. I canna bear that."

With the gentlest of touches, he slid his fingers along her jaw and cupped her face with his palm. "Ye forget I am a stubborn man, *mo chridhe*. Once we get ye safe and settled at *Tor Ruadh*, ye will be mine." He teased a kiss across her mouth, the sweetest and most endearing kiss she could ever imagine. A kiss filled with promise and hope.

She closed her eyes as he pressed his forehead to hers and clasped both her hands between them. "I daren't wish," she whispered. "Ye canna imagine how crazed he is."

"Are ye gonna be my new da, Master Alasdair?" Connor called out as he urged Flossy toward them. "Auntie Yeva says ye be a damn fine man. Way better than that cruel bastard who sired me."

"Connor!" Isobel jerked a step back and placed her full attention on her son. "Such language! I should wash out yer mouth with Mrs. Aggie's strongest soap to rid ye of those filthy words!"

Alasdair's amusement escaped him in short, huffing snorts.

Isobel turned back to him. "Ye are nay helping. Dinna encourage him!" She returned her attention to Connor, sitting taller in the saddle, a triumphant grin on his rosy-cheeked face. "Ye are not to repeat such ever again, or I'll tan yer tail for ye, wash out yer mouth, and forbid ye to do anything ye enjoy for a month a Sundays. Do ye understand me?"

Connor's grin disappeared, and his little chin hit his chest. "Auntie Yeva said it."

Isobel had no doubt she had. The woman had been known to use coarse language, and the older she got, the less inclined she was to curb her tongue on all subjects. At least most of the time when her aunt chose to express herself, she did so in her native tongue that Connor was just now learning.

"Dinna be so hard on the lad," Alasdair whispered with a nudge. "After all, everything he said was true."

"It was nay what he said," Isobel whispered back, praying Connor wouldn't overhear. "It was how he said it."

"So, will ye be my new da then?" Connor repeated with a daring, side-eyed glance in his mother's direction before edging his mare closer to Alasdair.

"Halt, ye bastards!" Ian's roar ripped through the balmy spring day, echoing across the courtyard. The jarring crack of gunfire split the air.

Alasdair grabbed Isobel around her waist, kicked open the paddock gate, and scooped Connor down from the saddle. "Into the stable. Both of ye. Dinna come out 'til I come for ye."

She grabbed her son and dashed to shelter. Hugging him tight, she ran down the aisle, feet pounding on the soft earthen floor. She careened into a center stall and crouched against the rear wall. Heart pounding, gasping for breath, she clutched the boy to her chest. With a back-and-forth rocking as though he was still a babe, she sent up a silent, fervent prayer. *Please God. Protect us. Protect us all. Please, keep Alasdair safe, too.*

Connor clutched at her. Arms and legs wrapped around her, he burrowed his face harder into the crook of her neck. She had to be brave for him. She had to show him how to get through this. "Ian and Alasdair will keep us safe, son. We must have faith," she whispered as she rubbed his back and kissed his head. "We're safe here, aye? None can harm us, and here we shall stay 'til Alasdair returns. All will be well."

Connor remained silent except for shuddering out a sniff and butting his head up tighter under her chin.

Isobel found solace in the fact she hadn't heard any additional gunfire. She settled lower into the pile of clean hay against the wall and situated Connor on her lap. They would stay put until Alasdair came for them. Aye. That's what they would do. She continued rubbing her hand up and down her son's back. "I feel sure ye will like *Tor Ruadh.* All those horses. Fresh air. Lots of room to run and play. And soon enough, Haggis will be there to join ye. Ye can run through the fields and explore the land together. Ye'll have a grand time."

"Isobel!"

Alasdair's deep voice was surely the sweetest music she had ever heard. Isobel closed her eyes and blew out a relieved sigh. *Thank ye, Lord, for protecting him.* "Here!" She patted Connor's back and gently pried him away. "Come, son. Stand on yer own so I can get up. Alasdair has returned just as he said he would. All is well, see?"

Connor allowed her to slide him from her lap but maintained a tight hold on her hand and the fold of her skirts once she'd risen to her feet. Isobel struggled to refrain from gathering him up into her arms again. He was not a baby, and she shouldn't treat him as such. But the poor lad. He had endured so much for one so young. She kept an arm around his shoulders and held him close to her side.

Alasdair rounded the side of the stall, scooped up Connor, then pulled her into his arms. He held them both close, hugging them with fierce urgency. Then he lowered Connor to the ground and nodded toward Jock standing behind him. "I need ye to go with Jock. He'll take ye to the kitchen for a treat from Mrs. Aggie, aye?"

The lad scuttled back to his frantic hold of Isobel's skirts. "I dinna wanna leave Mama. I be afeared for her." He sniffed and scrubbed the back of one hand across his little nose, red and runny from his tears. "I be afeared for me, too," he added in a quivering whisper. "Father said I am the biggest sort of coward, but I canna help it. I am what I am."

Every fiber in Isobel's being filled with a fresh surge of pure hatred for her cruel husband. She hugged Connor closer. "Ye're nay a coward, my son. Ye're the bravest boy I know."

Alasdair crouched beside Connor and patted the little boy's shoulder. "There is no shame in being afeared, Connor. Fear keeps a wise man safe and ready." Ever so gently, he drew the boy away from his mother's skirts and into the curve of his arm. "Do ye know what the true meaning of courage is, lad? Real and for certain bravery such as that of a warrior?"

Connor shook his head.

"It is nay the absence of fear or worry. Every man, no matter how fierce, fears something. True courage is having the strength and stubbornness to push through whatever that something is. Face yer fears head-on, and do yer best to conquer them. That is true courage."

"Were ye afeared when Master Ian shouted, and the guns went off?" Connor chewed on his bottom lip, his tender face pulled into a worried scowl.

"Aye. Verra much so." Alasdair rose to his feet and held out his hand for Connor to take. "I was frightened because I care for ye and for yer mother. I couldna bear it if anything happened, and ye werena safe."

"But ye ran to help him anyway." Connor took Alasdair's hand, then gave a half-hearted shrug and peered around at Jock. "I shall go with Jock now if ye swear to keep Mama safe and bring her inside soon, aye?"

"Aye." Alasdair gave the boy a solemn nod and thumped his fist on his chest. "I swear it."

"Come along, boy." Jock waved him forward. "Baking day in the house. Bound to be something good for us to eat in old Aggie's kitchen."

Connor took Jock's hand, gave his mother a shy wave, then headed out of the stable, passing Ian and another man as they entered.

Isobel peered closer at the man walking beside Ian, leading the largest horse she had seen in a while. Recognition clicked. "Sutherland MacCoinnich, as I live and breathe." A profound sense of relief lightened the chokehold of worry cutting off her air. She held out her hands. Alasdair would be so much safer with both his brother and his cousin at his side.

Sutherland, the youngest of the MacCoinnichs but just as braw and fierce, strode forward, his light blue eyes sparkling. "Isobel. It's finer than fine to see ye here with Alasdair." He squeezed her hands, then grazed a polite kiss across her knuckles. "Dinna fret, my fair lass. We shall get ye and yer son safe to *Tor Ruadh*."

"We leave tomorrow night," Alasdair said as he shot Sutherland a jealous look and pulled Isobel's hands out of his grasp. He sidled closer and turned her to face him. "Ye can be packed and ready, aye?"

Alasdair had nothing to worry about regarding Sutherland, but she wasn't about to let him in on that fact. A wee taste of jealousy wouldn't hurt him, and she rather enjoyed watching him react. She knew the MacCoinnich cousin for the incorrigible womanizer he was, had always known him to be such and never taken his antics seriously. She liked the lad, though, in spite of his reputation. He had a good heart. Someday the right woman would tame him. She gave Alasdair a solemn nod. "Auntie and I shall see to it that we're ready. We've not that much to pull together."

"I wounded one of the two blackguards spying over the wall but not enough to keep them both from slipping away," Ian said. "Ye're no longer hidden here. Word will spread fast."

"If word spreads and we're watched, will they not follow us into the Highlands?" Hope for the future seemed to be slipping out of her grasp. Isobel lowered her voice and glanced around the courtyard, struggling to keep the distant light of a better life burning bright. "Should we leave tonight instead? Slip away when even the household nay suspects?"

Alasdair's eyes narrowed to a plotting squint. He rubbed his chin, scratching his fingers through the dark stubble. "It might be prudent to do so."

"From the notices I saw tacked in every pub, it would be more than prudent to do so," Sutherland observed as he scanned their surroundings. He gave Alasdair a meaningful nod. "Dinna tell yer staff. Leave a vague note of an extended absence or provide them with some such excuse for the journey, but dinna give them a clue as to where ye're going or how long ye'll be gone. The gold offered for the boy would tempt the most loyal of servants."

"I had thought to bring Lachie with us, but now I'm nay so sure." Alasdair stared off into the distance. His worries made his scowl all the fiercer and struck an ominous sense of doom deep in Isobel's heart.

"I can drive the wagon," Isobel said. "Connor could make the trip on horseback, but I fear Auntie couldna survive it." Her poor aunt had been through so much, and whilst the proud old woman never complained about her ailments brought on by advancing years, Isobel noticed her slowing down just the same.

Alasdair gave a curt nod, then spurred into action. He motioned toward Ian and Sutherland, and then toward the stable. "The two of ye ready the wagon and the horses. Ye can tell Jock it's for an extended trip, and he'll help ye without question. I'm off to the kitchen to arrange for supplies, and I'll send them out here to ye." Turning back to Isobel, he took hold of her hands and squeezed. "Gather yer things and try to convince Connor that he's not to tell anyone of the trip. I'll be telling the servants as little as possible just to ensure we've all the supplies we need."

She didn't trust herself to speak, whether from the protective urgency of Alasdair's touch or the pending escape into the night she had no clue. All she knew for certain was it took all her strength to hold together for yet another battle to secure them a better life.

"All will be well, *mo ghràdh*," Alasdair said softly. He touched her cheek with the gentlest caress. "I will see to it."

Although she knew she shouldn't, she found comfort in the thunderous storm of emotions flashing in his eyes. Alasdair would wade through the fires of hell for her and Connor, and that knowledge made her feel all the worse for putting him in such danger. He didn't deserve it, didn't deserve one as damaged as her, one tainted from years of unspeakable mistreatment. He deserved a great deal more than a woman on the run from a madman who would stop at nothing to punish her for having the audacity to defy him. "Promise me when we get to *Tor Ruadh*, ye will distance yerself from me—for yer own safety. I beg ye. Swear it."

"I will never swear to that," Alasdair said quietly as he cradled her face in his palm. "Not ever."

His mouth was so close. The yearning to melt into his embrace and forget all her fears, to lay the complicated weight of her life upon his shoulders, tempted her. *Nay.* She couldn't weaken. It wouldn't be fair to give him such hope. She spun away, biting the inside of her cheek to keep from crying out at denying herself his touch. She gathered up her skirts and raced across the cobblestones toward the house. There was much to do. This was not the time to wallow in what could never be. She burst into the kitchen in search of her son.

Connor looked up from his cup, a milky mustache spread across his upper lip. His brows knotted together in a serious little scowl. "Why are ye crying, Mama? Did the bad men come back?"

Isobel touched her cheeks, surprised at the wetness. She swiped at the tears and shook her head. "Nay, lad. Just dust in my eyes." She hated lying to Connor, but there was no way she could tell him the truth. It was not something in her eyes that brought on the tears, but something in her heart.

CHAPTER EIGHT

"THEY LAID LETTIE to rest yesterday."

Alasdair glanced over at his brother as they rode through the darkness. The crowded streets and wide, hard-packed roadways leading out of Edinburgh had faded to nothing more than a dry, rutted path bordered by tufts of sedge and rolling countryside. Even in the eerie blue-white light of the waxing moon, the pain on Ian's face was clear. "I am sorry, brother." And he was. His brother's poor heart had suffered much.

Ian shrugged. "I dinna know if I loved Lettie or just Janet's memory 'cause she looked so much like her." He shifted in the saddle, then met Alasdair's gaze. "I didna do Lettie justice. I shouldha made her feel like I loved her for herself. She deserved better, ye ken? She was a kind lass. A bigger hearted, more loving woman, ye'd be hard-pressed to find."

"She knew ye loved her," Alasdair lied.

Anyone who had known his brother's late wife, Janet, knew why Ian had been so attracted to Lettie. He stole a look back at the wagon. Isobel sat alone on the bench seat, controlling the team as though born to it. Yeva and Connor had succumbed to weariness hours earlier and bedded down among the bundles of supplies in the back. Sutherland rode behind them, lagging back, ever vigilant.

Alasdair righted himself in the saddle, consoled somewhat that nothing ill had beset the start of their journey, but wishing he could ease his brother's pain. "Ye gave her happiness for a time and eased her lot in life. Enabled her to claim ye as her only client so she could rest when ye were nay in Edinburgh."

"I think it best I steer clear of women for a while." Ian blew out a heavy sigh. "Cursed when it comes to the lasses. First Janet. Then Lettie." He turned a bitter smile on Alasdair. "The lot falls to ye, brother. Marry Isobel so ye can sire a son to carry on the Cameron name, aye?"

"Once I rid her of that bastard she married, I will." He squeezed the worn leather reins tighter, wishing his hands were wrapped around Temsworth's neck instead.

"And if he refuses to grant her a divorce?"

Alasdair nudged his mount to a faster clip, a sense of urgency nagging him to get Isobel to safety as quickly as possible. He gave his brother a look that wouldn't be mistaken. "I will do whatever it takes to make Isobel mine."

Ian agreed with a dip of his chin.

The faster rhythm of the clattering wheels of the wagon behind them assured him that Isobel had noticed the change of pace and increased the team's speed. They maintained the rate for the better part of an hour. The horses' ground-eating trot carried them far enough from Edinburgh's dangers to earn Alasdair a bit of peace. He held up a hand and stopped as Stirling came into view, pondering the choices of resting the remaining few hours before dawn at an inn or pushing onward and skirting any potential problems.

"Why are we stopping?" Isobel brought the wagon to a halt beside him. She stretched to sit taller, craning her neck to take in the view ahead. "What town is that?"

"Stirling." Alasdair resettled himself in the saddle. "We made good time for the first bit of our journey. We could find an inn up ahead.

Hot food. Beds. Care for the horses. Such a stop could make the rest of our trip easier." Even in the poor lighting, he noticed her weariness and the strained set of her shoulders. She needed rest. At least for what remained of the night, and mayhap even a few hours into the morning. The rest of the journey would be in the wild. They'd best make use of whatever comforts they found now. "What say ye, lass?"

"I shouldha known that was Stirling. I see the castle now." Isobel leaned back and peered down into the wagon. As she turned back to him, she rubbed at the corners of her eyes. "It would be nice to rest a bit." She nodded toward the pale flicker of scattered torchlight winking among the buildings. Stirling Castle rose in the distance like a great hulking beast standing guard over the populace below. "If ye feel certain it would be safe."

"I will make it safe." He would see that Isobel got her rest if he had to stand guard at her bedside. He waved Sutherland forward. "Ride close to their side, aye? We'll be finding an inn to seek some rest."

Sutherland nodded and pointed toward the western side of town. "Old Guntie MacPherson runs a clean enough place. Far enough from the castle and barracks to suit my liking, if ye get my meaning."

"I get it." Alasdair took the lead, heading his horse in the direction Sutherland had suggested.

If Temsworth had gone so far as to place a bounty on his own son and wife's head, the man would have also alerted the military. They needed to avoid any interactions with soldiers. The duke had powerful connections and never hesitated to use them. Everyone feared the man. Alasdair snorted. He didn't fear the bastard. He looked forward to the day he could snap the man's neck.

The silence of the hours just before dawn cast a chill to the air as they entered the deserted streets of Stirling. Every move, every rattle of their gear, and clop of the horses' hooves echoed. The buildings resembled tall, grim sentries, scowling down with their dark windows watching like wide, sightless eyes.

"There," Sutherland called out in a hushed voice as he pointed to the sparsely windowed, stone building on the corner. "MacPherson's stable is across the way. See it?"

"Aye." Alasdair brought them to a halt in front of the inn. He dismounted and held up a hand to assist Isobel in clambering down from the wagon. "Ian and Sutherland will stand watch whilst we arrange for rooms."

Isobel paused beside the wagon, reaching over to tuck the blanket higher around Connor's shoulders. She looked up at Sutherland. "If he wakes, be sure and tell him all is well, aye?"

"I will, m'lady. Ne'er ye fret." Sutherland edged his horse closer, all the while continuing to scan the surrounding area.

Ian dismounted, led his mount to the rear of the cart, and tied it off. He climbed up into the wagon seat and settled down, his pistol resting in the crook of his elbow. He gave Alasdair a solemn nod.

"Come, Isobel." Alasdair held out his arm. The sooner they got rooms, the sooner they wouldn't be out in the open. As near as he could tell, no one noticed nor cared about their untimely arrival, but one never knew who or what lurked in the shadows.

With Isobel tucked close to his side, they entered the inn. The place reeked of spilled ale, roasted meat, and a hint of smokiness from the dwindling fire glowing in the hearth. Good enough. He had been in worse. Mounds of plaid-draped bodies lay scattered across the floor, rumbling with loud snores. Slumbering patrons were everywhere, some even propped in chairs around the edges of the room. The sight of so many sleeping in the general area of the inn concerned him. The number seemed in excess of those who couldn't usually scrape up enough coin to pay for a private room.

"Looks to be full," Isobel whispered, drawing even closer as she peered through the room lit only by the dying embers in the hearth and a lone lantern flickering on the mantel.

"We shall see." He maneuvered around bodies, tables, and chairs to the closed door at the end of the bar. The word *Owner* was painted across it. He rapped on the door, listened for any sound of movement beyond the portal, then knocked again with a bit more force.

"Aye, I'm coming," a weary voice growled from within. Latches clicked and rattled, then the door swung open. The owner of the tired voice, gray hair tangled and wearing nothing but a dingy léine that covered his round body to just below the knees, squinted up at Alasdair. "Aye?"

"Rooms. A pair of them." Alasdair cast a glance back at those sleeping around the tables and added, "If ye have them."

The old man hitched out a jaw-cracking yawn as he scratched his arse. "I dinna have but one room left." He gave Isobel a rude up and down ogle, then winked at Alasdair. "Looks like ye'll have to share a room wif yer lady here, eh?" He made a lascivious clicking sound and wheezed out a rumbling chortle. "Room's got two beds in it, though. She still might refuse ye."

In one swift motion, Alasdair drew his *sgian dhu* and tucked it's point up under the innkeeper's double chin. "Insult my wife again, and yer barmaids will have to mop yer blood before they serve yer guests their breakfast."

The man gasped, his skin taking on a nervous, eerie sheen in the dim light of the room. He held up both hands as he stammered and sputtered, "Begging yer pardon, sir. Only spoke in jest. Meant no harm to ye or yer lady."

"We shall take the room." Alasdair kept the dagger in place, nicking the tip tighter into the fold of the man's fleshy jowls. "I've a wagon. Four horses. My two men will take their ease down here." Alasdair leaned in close. "Their humor and skill with weapons match my own. Do ye understand?"

"Aye." MacPherson bobbed his head and pointed a shaking finger toward the door. "Lagger." He paused and swallowed hard, stretching his neck away from the pricking point of the dagger. "Me boy, Lagger.

He be over at the stable. He'll settle yer horses and wagon. I'll fetch the key and take ye to yer room, aye?"

"Fetch the key and tell me which room. I'll find it m'self." Alasdair withdrew the dagger and glared at the man.

The blade finally away from his throat, MacPherson skittered back behind the bar and scooped up the lone key hanging from a wall of hooks. He shoved it across the bar to Alasdair and nodded toward the set of stairs in the corner. "End of the hall. Last room on the right. Like I said. Two beds if yer men dinna wish to sleep down here."

"I'll let them choose for themselves." Alasdair scooped up the key and nodded. "I thank ye."

"T-think nothing of it," the innkeeper stuttered as he raked a shaking hand through his wild tufts of hair. Inch by inch, he backed farther behind the bar, putting more distance between himself and Alasdair.

"Come, wife." By the saints, how he loved the sound of that. He led Isobel back through the maze of chairs and sleeping bodies. Once outside, he waved Ian and Sutherland over. "One room with two beds. I'll nay be leaving Isobel unguarded, so I'll stay with her, Connor, and Yeva."

"Oh, ye will, will ye?"

Alasdair braced himself for the battle he had hoped wouldn't come. Isobel had never worn weariness well. "Aye. I will." He refused to let her out of his sight until he knew her to be safe, and if she didn't like it, she could just go whistle in the wind. "Connor and yerself in one bed. Yeva in the other. I'll find my rest propped in a chair against the door."

His argument struck her mute, and for that, he was glad. It was late, and truth be told, he had never worn weariness all that well himself.

Isobel bowed her head and rubbed her eyes. With a sigh, she shrugged. "Whatever ye think best, Alasdair."

Praise God above, she'd chosen not to argue. Every moment they stood in the street fussing, was time that could be better spent resting. He held out his arms as Ian straddled the supplies, scooped up Connor, then handed over the limp, sleeping lad.

Alasdair settled the boy against his chest, then turned to catch Isobel's wide-eyed stare. A satisfied warmth filled him. It was plain to see that the sight of him holding her son as if the boy was his own touched Isobel's heart. *Good.* She needed to realize this was how it would be from now on. She, Connor, and Yeva were his family and under his protection.

"I walk myself," Yeva warned, hands slapping and pushing at Ian and Sutherland. "You help me get to the ground. That is all!"

"Aye, m'lady," Sutherland assured with a laugh as he and Ian stood on either side of her and waited for her to stop batting them away.

Yeva gave them both a stern look, then cocked her elbows for them to take. Ever so gently, they lifted the tiny woman and lowered her to the ground, steadying her until she was able to force her stiffened joints to move.

Isobel hurried to Yeva's side, wrapped an arm around the old woman's waist, and supported her. "Come, Auntie, we've a bed waiting."

"We'll see to the horses," Ian assured as he jumped from the wagon. "We'll bed down with the wagon until ye're ready to leave." He glanced back at the load of supplies. "I dinna depend overly much on the honesty of my fellow man whilst in a crowded city."

Alasdair agreed. "Aye. Lagger MacPherson tends the stable. I was nay impressed by his father's manners. I doubt the son's are any better." He glanced down at Connor's peaceful expression and smiled. "We'll sleep a few hours and then be on our way. I dinna wish to tarry long."

He trailed along behind Isobel and her aunt, following them into the inn, up the stairs, and down the hall to the room. Isobel fished the key out of his jacket pocket, unlocked the door, and pushed it open.

"I light the lantern. Keeps evil at bay." Yeva trundled over to the small table between the two beds. She fiddled with the tinderbox for a brief moment, then the soft glow of the candle inside the dingy glass lantern filled the room.

Alasdair remembered Isobel's aunt had always had an uncanny ability to coax a quick flame. The old woman turned, scrubbing her arms. "Cold in here." She climbed into the bed and held out her arms. "Give my boy to me. I need his warmth."

Alasdair glanced over at Isobel, standing beside the other bed, hugging herself against the chill of the room.

"Aye." She gave a quick nod. "Settle him in with her. She needs his warmth more than I."

Alasdair tucked the lad under the blanket with Yeva. The boy immediately rolled and curled up against her. The smiling old crone pulled the blanket higher about them and closed her eyes.

When Alasdair turned, he found Isobel staring at him with an odd expression. Eyes wide, mouth in a tensed line, even in the candlelight, Isobel had gone a bit pale. Her appearance alarmed him. "Are ye unwell, love?"

"There's nay a chair," she whispered.

"What?"

She made a sweeping look around the small room. "There's nay a chair for ye."

Her meaning dawned on him, and her panicked state at the obvious alternative caused him no small amount of dismay. Did she truly find the thought of sharing a bed with him that repulsive? Surely, she didn't think him so low as to attempt to take advantage of her in the presence of her son and aunt? Her reactions on past occasions came back to him, actions triggered by abuse and humiliation. Who knew what had been done to her? Her trust would be hard-won.

Alasdair shucked off his jacket, rolled it up, and stretched out on the floor in front of the door. Folding his arms over his chest, he rested his head on the jacket and gave Isobel his most reassuring smile. "Lie down, my love. Seek yer rest. We willna be here long."

"I canna seek my rest while ye sleep on that hard, filthy floor." She looked back at the empty bed. "It's not right."

She had to make a choice. He wouldn't make it for her "What do ye suggest?"

"Ye know damn well what I suggest, ye stubborn arse!" She pointed at the bed. "If ye're determined to make me say it, then say it I will. I'll share the bed with ye—just this once!"

Alasdair clenched his teeth to keep from laughing aloud. She wore the colors of her fiery side well. Always had. It was one of the many things he loved about her.

"Stop arguing and sleep!" Yeva commanded from the other bed.

Alasdair stood up from the floor, dusted himself off, and shook out his jacket. He held out a hand toward the empty bed against the wall. "After ye, m'lady."

She stared at the bed and shook her head. "Nay. Ye sleep next to the wall. I need to be able to get to Connor should he need me."

Alasdair knew that was nay the reason, but he wouldn't shame her by calling her on her lie. She feared being cornered. A heavy sigh escaped him. His poor, sweet love. Someday, she'd trust him. "I understand yer need to tend to the lad, but I can better protect ye by sleeping on the outside."

"Ye dinna think we're safe here in the room?" She cast a worried glance at the door.

"I dinna wish to let down my guard until we reach *Tor Ruadh*, love." He eased a step closer. "My cargo is too precious to risk."

She wet her lips and gave him a long look. "If Connor calls out, ye'll move aside, quick as a minute, aye?"

"I swear it." He hoped she'd overcome her doubts soon, so they might at least get a few hours' sleep.

Her arisaid wrapped tight about her, she climbed under the covers and scooted back against the wall. She held up the blanket and looked up at him. The sight of her waiting for him to join her in the bed nearly undid him. After giving her a strained smile, he turned away to hide the tenting of his kilt as he lowered himself to sit on the edge of the bed. His poor, long-suffering cock couldn't take much more. He laid on his side, his back to Isobel.

"Are ye not chilled? Do ye not want any of the blanket?"

"Nay, love. I dinna need it. I've my kilt to keep me warm." And the perpetual burn of wanting the woman beside him.

"Rest ye well then." Isobel settled in, her sweet scent a source of torture.

"Aye, love. Rest well, too." Alasdair pinned his gaze on the shadows cast by the flickering flame of the candle. He could tell by Isobel's breathing that slumber escaped her as well.

"Alasdair." Her whisper made his heart pound.

"Aye?"

"Ye are a good man."

Whilst her words warmed his soul, it was not exactly what he had hoped to hear. He risked rolling on to his back, hoping she would think the rise in his kilt just a bunching of the plaid. She faced him. Her eyes glistened in the shadows, blacker than the finest obsidian. "I am not a good man, Isobel. I am a man who loves ye."

"Why?" she asked in a breathy voice filled with such hopelessness, it twisted his heart. "After all these years and all that has happened, why?"

He mulled over the question, choosing his reply with care. "When I lost ye, I lost a part of myself. Call it what ye will. A part of my soul. A part of my heart. All I know for certain is a part of me was gone." He studied the precious curve of her high cheekbones, the dimple in her chin, and the fullness of her sweet lips. "But with ye here at my side, my soul has regained hope for the future."

She brushed the back of her fingers across the stubble on his cheek.

"Ye know we can never be together—"

He pressed a finger to her lips and silenced her. "Nay. We can be, and we shall be. When will ye stop coming up with reasons to deny me? To deny us? Have faith in me, love. The only way we shall cease to be is if ye tell me ye no longer love me." He slid his fingers along her jawline, cradling her face. "Would ye ever say such a thing to me? Truly? Are ye tellin' me ye love me no more?" He held his breath, praying she'd gift him with the words he longed to hear, praying she'd found the courage to give their future together a chance.

A tear slipped out of the corner of her eye. "Ye know verra well, I have always loved ye, Alasdair." A quivering smile teased across her mouth. "I always will. 'Til the day I cease to draw breath."

Moving ever so slowly, he brushed a chaste kiss across her lips. He longed for a more impassioned kiss but didn't want to frighten her. "Find yer rest in the curve of my arm, love. Let me feel the beat of yer heart while I dream."

Without a word, she snuggled up against him and rested her head on his shoulder.

"I still say ye're a good man," she whispered. Her warm breath tickling against his throat stoked his need for her even more. "Why are ye holding yer breath? Does my hair smell of smoke?"

"Nay." He pecked a kiss to the top of her head and hugged her closer. Staring up at the cracked ceiling, he willed himself to remain strong. "I felt the threat of a sneeze. I didna wish to wake the others." God forgive him for the lie. Loving Isobel was a delicate matter, a fragile thing that required gentle tending to help her overcome her past and embrace the joy and passion of the future.

She nestled her head deeper into the crook of his shoulder. He returned to watching the dance of the shadows on the ceiling from the candlelight. *Aye.* This was true contentment—holding his dear one in his arms. He wouldn't sleep, couldn't even if he wanted to. Missing a moment of closeness with her was worth staying awake all night.

CHAPTER NINE

"DINNA DISTURB YER mother."

Alasdair's deep rumbling vibrated against her cheek, pulling her from the depths of the most peaceful slumber she'd experienced in a long while. She struggled not to smile and kept her eyes closed.

"But I need ta take a piss, and Auntie is nay awake," Connor said in a loud whisper.

"The chamber pot is there under yer bed. I see it from here."

Isobel held her breath, determined to feign sleep to witness Alasdair's reasoning skills with a five-year-old who was more than likely tired of being the only one awake. Her son knew well enough how to tend to his own needs. He'd slept his fill, was ready to be up, and didn't wish to be up alone.

"I saw a spider. I dinna want to reach for it."

She could stand it no longer. She lifted her head and gave her son a look he knew all too well.

The boy's eyes widened at her unspoken message. He turned and scampered across the room, pulled the chamber pot out from under the bed, and commenced to using it.

Pushing herself to a sitting position, she turned to Alasdair. "Children can smell indecision and fear."

"And what is that supposed to mean?" he asked as he lowered his feet to the floor, stretching as he rolled his shoulders.

"It means dinna argue with a child. It is a waste of breath." She stood and shook out her skirts. She could use time with the chamber pot herself. "Would ye mind taking Connor downstairs whilst I rouse Auntie, and we tend to our needs?" With the size of the room, the only possibility for privacy was for the males to leave.

"Aye," Alasdair said. He pinpointed the lad with a stern look. "Connor and I shall fetch Ian and Sutherland to join us for breakfast. We shall also have a long discussion about listening to yer elders, not telling tales, and the virtues of behaving like a young man rather than a wee arse."

Connor looked up from buttoning the front of his trews. He brightened with a wide grin. "I am ready to eat. Reckon they have jam?"

Alasdair turned and gave Isobel a look of disbelief. "He didna hear a word I said."

"Aye." She smiled. "He's a male. The lot of ye oft appear deaf at times."

Alasdair scrubbed a hand across his face. "Aye. Well then." With a loud snort, he latched hold of Connor's shoulder and steered the lad toward the door. As he herded the boy out into the hall, he cast a look back at her. "Dinna tarry long, aye?"

"Aye." It was all she could do to keep from laughing aloud. The poor man had no idea how deceptive Connor could be, but she'd show him some sympathy for all his efforts. She wouldn't leave him at the mercy of her son overlong.

She bolted the door and hurried over to the chamber pot. As she finished, she gave a gentle shake of the bed frame beside her. "Auntie. Time to rise."

"I am awake."

There was nothing in the room but the two beds, a tiny table between them, a lantern, and the chamber pot. She wished there was fresh water for washing. *It could always be worse*, she reminded herself. *Aye. That it could.* She and Connor could still be Temsworth's prisoners.

She moved to the side of the bed and helped Auntie to her feet. "Did ye sleep well?"

Fluttering Isobel's hands away, Auntie made her way to the chamber pot. "Yes. Once you and your man stopped talking."

Isobel's face flushed hot from the scolding. "Forgive me, Auntie. I'm sorry we disturbed ye." Even though she feared the answer, she had to ask the question burning in her heart. "Did ye…were ye able to…"

"I hear everything." Auntie snatched hold of Isobel's hand and pinned her with a sharp-eyed glare. "God will forgive you, Isobel. Almighty knows how you have suffered. Knows how you fight to protect yer son." She tilted her head. Silvery white wisps of hair peeped out from under the folds of the brightly colored kerchief she always wore to secure her long braid out of the way. "Be with Alasdair Cameron. Be his wife in all ways except taking his name. Leave the demon bastard you married alone. Do not beg a release from him. You cannot reason with a madman. Pain is the only reward for poking a bear."

Auntie's words brought the threat of tears. Tears of relief. Tears of joy. Tears of worry. "I fear Alasdair will never agree to such." She squeezed her aunt's hand. "He is a proud man, and I fear his pride will be his undoing."

Auntie, weathered and wrinkled with years of laughter and tears, gave a slow shake of her head. "Men do not listen." Her thin lips curled with a knowing smirk as she patted Isobel's hand. "Persuade him. There are ways to convince men other than with words."

"Auntie!"

"What?" Yeva lifted her chin. "I was young once. I have loved."

The thought of her aunt as a vibrant young woman came easily to Isobel. She hugged her tight. "I'd be so lost without ye."

She gave Isobel another affectionate pat and pulled away. "Come. We go now. Yer Cameron say not to tarry." She winked. "Connor slept well. He will be worrisome."

"He will at that." Isobel held tight to Auntie's arm as they made their way downstairs.

She easily spotted Alasdair at a table in the corner of the crowded room that was hazy with smoke from the kitchen and the poorly tended hearth. The unmistakable aromas of sizzling meat, bread baked a tad too long, and several bodies in dire need of a good scrubbing rendered the air thick enough to slice. The place overflowed with hungry patrons seeking to break their fast. With as much haste as possible, she pushed their way to the back of the room. Merciful heavens, she didn't know if she'd rather eat or slip outside and fill her lungs with fresh air.

"They didna have jam, but they had honey!" Connor announced with evidence of said sticky sweetness shining on his cheeks and chin.

After seating Auntie beside Sutherland, Isobel sidled around the table and took the chair between Connor and Alasdair. A harried barmaid reached between them and plopped down a tankard of ale and another platter of fried meats and bread on the table. She pulled a rag from her belt and handed it to Isobel. "For the boy. He's like my wee Remmy. Canna eat his food without rolling in it first." She nodded toward Connor. "Midges'll fair eat him up with all that on his face."

"I thank ye." Isobel gladly accepted the cloth, dipped a corner of it in her water, and set to ridding her son's face of his breakfast. "Why must ye always smear it from ear to ear? Take wee bites," she admonished as she scrubbed.

"Mamaaaa," Connor attempted to twist away, but she held him tight, not releasing until his face was clean.

"Ye're struggling in vain, boy," Sutherland observed with a chuckle as he shoved an oversized chunk of blood sausage into his mouth. "A mam is fiercer than any warrior."

"Especially this mam," Alasdair said as he rested a possessive hand on her shoulder.

A comforting warmth surged through her, a precious sense of being protected. "No more bread and honey 'til ye finish yer parritch, aye?" She tapped a finger beside Connor's untouched bowl of oats.

"Eat up, Connor, we need t'be leaving soon," Ian said, then lowered his voice as he leaned toward Alasdair. "I noticed several of His Majesty's dogs outside. Did ye see them?"

"I didna see any dogs," Connor said around a mouthful of parritch.

"Hush, son." Isobel returned the chunk of bread she was about to bite back to the plate. Any contact with soldiers could be a problem.

Alasdair nodded, then drained his tankard. "Aye. I saw them."

"They appeared to be in search of someone," Sutherland said. "Stopped several passersby and asked questions. Showed them some sort of paper."

Isobel's stomach clenched. Had Temsworth's bounty notices made it to Stirling as well? "We should go now."

Alasdair covered her hand with his. "Nay, love. Remain calm. We must not raise suspicions by appearing over-anxious to be shed of Stirling."

"Of course." She swallowed hard. Alasdair spoke a wise truth, no matter how hard it might be to carry out. She hazarded a sip of ale. She could do this. This was no different from the first time they had run for their lives.

"Ye need to eat if ye can," Alasdair advised with a gentle urging as he slid the platter of sausages closer to her.

"Aye," she whispered.

She would eat to gain the strength she needed to protect her son. She bit into her bread. Mouth dry, the longer she chewed, the larger the bite seemed. A trio of redcoats entering the inn almost caused her to choke.

"Steady, lass," Alasdair intoned with a reassuring squeeze of her hand.

The men separated and meandered through the crowd, stopping at tables and discussing the tattered papers they showed to each of the patrons. Most shoved the papers aside and ignored the soldiers. Some shook their heads. Others shrugged and turned away. The barmaid who had handed Isobel the rag for Connor's face pointed the redcoats in their direction.

Isobel turned to Connor and whispered, "Dinna say a word. Our lives depend on it. Understand?"

Eyes wide, Connor gave a quick nod and shrank back against the curve of his chair.

The soldiers approached the table. The man in the center, tall and hawk-nosed with cold, predatory eyes to match, appeared to be the leader since the other two stayed a step behind him. He came to a halt beside Alasdair. "Your name, sir?"

Alasdair leaned back in the chair and flexed his hands as he looked up at the man. "State yer business, and I'll decide if ye need my name or not."

The soldier's glare grew icier. "I am Captain Reginald Montpoy, and I have been charged with investigating the abduction of the Duchess of Temsworth and her son." His scowl slid to Connor. "Young man. What is your name?"

Connor sat taller in his chair and squared his tiny shoulders. "Fergus MacCoinnich," he said, then pointed at Alasdair. "And if ye dinna leave us alone, my da will thrash yer arse for ye."

"Son!" Alasdair gave Connor what appeared to be a stern look. "Mind yer manners, aye?"

Under the table, Isobel reached over and squeezed Connor's leg, the pride and relief coursing through her threatened to make her swoon. She had nary a clue where Connor had come up with the fictitious name, but she thanked the Lord above that he had.

"Fergus MacCoinnich," Captain Montpoy repeated in a dangerous tone. He turned to Alasdair. "I would suggest you teach your son to respect His Majesty's guard, else he runs into trouble when he's older."

"Be that all?" Alasdair's voice thundered with defiance.

Isobel closed her eyes and prayed the soldiers would move on. They didn't need to provoke the captain.

"Actually..." The captain paused, his gaze settling on Auntie Yeva. "No. That is not all. Along with the Duchess and her son, the abductors took the duchess's aged, Armenian aunt. All three were kidnapped from the duke's summer home at Hestlemoor Estate." He tapped the corner of the folded parchment beside Auntie's cup. "Your name, madam?"

Auntie scowled up at him, bit a chunk out of a steaming bannock, then snarled, *"Je ne parle pas anglais."*

Isobel held her breath and clenched her teeth, hoping the captain understood French and would be thoroughly convinced her aunt could not speak English and was most definitely not Armenian.

"Votre nom?" he asked, his utter contempt obvious.

"Célia Marchand," Auntie answered, then pushed the captain's paper aside with a disgusted huff.

The captain's face grew red. He turned to Isobel. "Your name?"

"Camille MacCoinnich," Isobel replied with a French accent. She'd always liked that name. She nodded toward Auntie. "My *maman.*"

"I see." The captain shoved the paper back inside his coat, then turned to Alasdair. "Where are you and your family headed, sir?"

"I dinna see how that's any of yer business, Captain." Alasdair pushed back his chair and stood, rising to stand a full head taller than the scowling captain.

Ian and Sutherland followed suit. The three Scots dwarfed the trio of Englishmen in both stature and muscle.

"We received word of highwaymen between here and Fort William." The captain gave a noncommittal shrug. "I merely thought to warn you."

"Ach." Alasdair smiled. "I thank ye for yer kind words, but we're headed to Inverness. We should nay be troubled by them." He pulled back the flap of his jacket and patted the handle of the pistol stuck in his belt. "My men and I are fine shots. We can protect our own."

"So, I see," the captain replied. He gave a condescending nod. "Just so you are aware."

"I am," Alasdair said in a tone that left no doubt he understood the captain's insinuations and was prepared to make a few of his own. "Now, if ye dinna mind, I'd like to finish my meal before it grows any colder."

The captain responded with a rude nod, then turned and motioned for his men to follow. They vacated the inn.

Alasdair, Ian, and Sutherland returned to their seats. Alasdair waved over the barmaid. "More ale and fill a basket with oatcakes, bread, and a crock of honey for us to take, aye?"

Isobel breathed a bit easier as the woman walked away. She didn't trust that wench as far as she could throw her. Not after she had pointed them out to the soldiers. "I dinna like that woman. I wouldna be surprised if she spits in our food."

"She had to answer whatever the soldiers asked, love." Alasdair scraped his bowl clean, then shoved it aside. "She lives here. We're merely passing through." He winked at Connor. "Well done, my boy, well done indeed."

Connor beamed under Alasdair's praise, took one last, overlarge bite of parritch, then pushed his bowl away. "I'm done."

"I willna breathe easy until we're well away from here." Isobel stretched to peer out the dingy panes of the window at the front of the room. She swore she'd spotted another flash of red. Several, in fact. "I fear they're outside. Waiting."

"They probably are," Alasdair observed as he stood up. "Let's be about it, shall we?"

"Our food." Connor pointed at the barmaid headed toward them holding the basket high as she wound her way around the other diners.

She smiled as she reached them and handed the basket to Connor. "Here ye go, me fine lad. Mind ye hold it tight. Ye've two crocks of honey inside."

"Two? Thank ye verra much!" Connor hugged the basket to his chest and fell in step between Ian and Sutherland as they headed outside.

Alasdair dropped a few coins in the barmaid's hand, then stepped back for Yeva and Isobel to take the lead.

"A word, Yer Grace?" the barmaid called out as Isobel took hold of Auntie Yeva's arm and turned to go.

Yer Grace? The formal address to a duchess shot a chill down Isobel's spine. No one had called her *Yer Grace* since her escape. Struggling to maintain a calm facade, she faced the barmaid and smiled. "*Yer Grace?* Surely, ye're not addressing me?"

"Ye dinna recall me, do ye?" The round-cheeked maid's eyes narrowed. Her gap-toothed smile took on a malicious curve. "I knew it was ye as soon as I saw ye."

Isobel swallowed hard, thankful for the reassuring weight of Alasdair's hand pressing against her back. "Ye must be mistaken. This be my first visit to Stirling." That was a lie, but the girl need not know. She studied the young woman's face. The barmaid seemed vaguely familiar, but no immediate recollection came to mind.

"Perhaps so," observed the wench with a chuckle that raked across Isobel's nerves. "But ye spent quite a bit of time at Hestlemoor with yer husband, did ye no'?" Her gaze snaked over to Alasdair, and she huffed out a snort. "Not that husband, o' course. The Sassenach devil."

She winked. "Worked at Hestlemoor, I did, 'til that sorry bastard's games got too rough. I was one o' his women for at least a sennight. Hurts me pride something fierce that ye dinna remember me. 'Course, it could be 'cause I've got me clothes on now."

Alasdair pushed his way between Isobel and the conniving girl. "How much?"

The barmaid planted a hand on her hip and wiggled back and forth. "How much ye got?"

"Dinna overplay yer lot, woman," Alasdair warned, baring his teeth as he took another step forward. "Ye threaten my dear one again, and I'll see that yer bones are never found to pray over. Do ye understand my meaning?"

The barmaid backed up a step and wet her lips, her self-assured air slipping. She jerked a nod toward the leather pouch cradled in Alasdair's hand. "A guinea'll do."

Alasdair fished out the gold coin and pressed it into her palm, leaning in close as he did so. "This be yer only payment. If ye demand more or speak of this to anyone, ye'll be paid in lead, aye?"

The woman paled a shade, gave a nervous nod, then scuttled back across the room.

With a tight hold on Auntie's arm, Isobel shoved their way to the door. She needed air before she retched, and couldn't be shed of this place fast enough. Recall of the barmaid still hadn't come. Temsworth had brought far too many men and women into their bedchamber over the years for her to remember all of them. Sanity and survival depended on blocking those humiliating memories from ever resurfacing. "Hurry, Auntie. Please," she whispered as they moved toward the wagon.

Auntie squinted against the morning sun as she glanced up and down the street. "More soldiers have gathered."

Bile burned at the back of Isobel's throat, and her stomach clenched. Auntie was right. Soldiers were at the head of the alleys and street corners. The trio they'd encountered inside stood within a few yards of the wagon. The bloody Sassenachs had them surrounded. Praise God above that all the soldiers appeared to be on foot. Not a horse stood near any of them. They needed to get moving and start their journey at a breakneck pace.

Ian and Sutherland helped Yeva into the back of the wagon. Connor waited on the wagon's seat. Alasdair helped Isobel up beside Connor, giving her hand a reassuring squeeze as he did so. She took up the reins, staring straight ahead as she warned her son under her breath, "Dinna speak nor pay them any mind, son. Just keep yer eyes on the road, aye?"

With Alasdair and his mount to her left and Ian and Sutherland riding behind the wagon, she coaxed the team into motion, steering them at a fast clip into the center of the busy thoroughfare.

"Lord Temsworth!"

She cringed as Connor shifted beside her, turning to see who had shouted his name. She wrapped an arm around him and gave a hard flip of the reins, urging the pair of horses into a full gallop. Out of the corner of her eye, she noted Alasdair had pulled his pistol before falling back to join Ian and Sutherland.

Isobel stole a glance backward. The redcoats had mobilized, streaming into the street as they dashed forward with pistols and muskets raised. Shots rang out, and puffs of white smoke filled the air.

She pushed Connor onto the floor beside her feet. "Stay down!"

"I'm sorry, Mama!" His face streaked with tears, he hugged tight to her ankle.

Her heart went out to her son, but there was no time to console the poor lad now. They had to put as much distance as they could between themselves and Stirling before the soldiers mounted and gave chase.

They careened through the alleyways, turning toward the freedom of the Highlands. She kept the team at a hard gallop, urging them onward as the clattering rattle of the wagon jarred her nerves raw. It would be a miracle if the thing didn't shake to pieces. As they left the cobblestoned streets to a hard-packed dirt roadway, Alasdair galloped up beside her. He motioned toward a thick grove of trees quite a way off the road. "Over there," he shouted. "Stop there."

Bracing herself for the even rougher ride of open country, Isobel steered the wagon off the road. "Hold fast," she called out to Auntie, praying the harrowing ride hadn't already battered the poor woman to death. Connor still crouched at her feet.

The horses charged forward, weaving their way around the trees, and worked ever deeper to the center of the secluded woods. She pulled the horses to a stop, lifted her face to the leafy canopy overhead, and pulled in a deep breath. If she didn't calm her pounding heart, she'd be of no use to anyone.

Connor jumped up and threw himself into her arms. "I so sorry, Mama. They tricked me."

She hugged him tight, rubbing a hand up and down his back. "It's all right, son. They didna fight fair. It was nay yer fault." He was just a wee lad. How dare they play such a cruel game on an innocent.

"We must rid ourselves of the wagon," Alasdair announced as he thundered up and dismounted. "Can ye ride a horse, Yeva?"

"'Course I can," Auntie replied with an insulted huff. She clamped her gnarled hands onto the side of the wagon and pulled herself to her feet. "Put me on a horse, and I show you."

Alasdair pointed at the team as Ian and Sutherland joined them. "Unharness them. We've nay got saddles for them, but we can put the extra blankets across their backs. Parse out the supplies amongst the horses. We'll take what we can and leave the rest."

Ian and Sutherland sprang into action as Alasdair helped Isobel down from the wagon. "Are ye all right, *mo ghràdh?*" He pulled her into his arms and held her so close his heartbeat pounded against hers.

If only she could close her eyes and melt into his embrace forever.

But there wasn't the time for such. The redcoats couldn't be that far behind. "I'm fine," she assured as she took a step back and gently extricated herself from his hold. "Please dinna be cross with Connor."

Alasdair smiled down at the lad as he did his best to remain hidden behind Isobel's skirts. "Dinna fash yerself, boy. Those bloody bastards have no morals or honor. They dinna fight as a Scot fights. They did ye dirty. Preyed upon yer youth and trust."

Connor eased out from behind Isobel but remained quiet. It was more than apparent the lad blamed himself no matter what anyone else said.

Alasdair turned back to her. "Connor and yer aunt can ride the one horse, and ye can ride the other." He patted the rump of the nearest animal. "Shire's from Clan MacCoinnich's stables. As good with riders as pulling a wagon."

"We should hurry," Isobel said.

Every moment they waited, the closer the British drew. A sense of urgency stole her breath. She glanced into the back of the nearly empty wagon. All that remained was a small crate and a pair of barrels. Every rope, blanket, and bundle had been parsed out and lashed to the horses. She turned as Alasdair placed Connor in front of Auntie on one of the horses.

With a stern look, Alasdair handed the reins to Connor. "Ye are one of us now, Connor. A man sworn to protect his women. A warrior and a mercenary." He thumped his fist on his chest. "Guard them well, aye?"

Connor thumped his little fist to his chest and dipped his chin in a solemn nod. "Aye."

Isobel blinked hard and fast, tears of love and pride threatening to overflow. *Protect him*, she prayed. The same prayer she'd sent up with every beat of her heart since the day of Connor's birth. Her gaze shifted to Alasdair. *And him, as well. I beg ye*, she added.

CHAPTER TEN

ALASDAIR FLEXED HIS right hand and worked his arm back and forth. That blasted burning grated on him, and worst of all, the bullet had ripped his favorite jacket. His bloody shirt stuck to the upper portion of his chest. It was naught but a graze wound. Damned worrisome but not too painful. He still couldn't believe the fool Sassenach had pulled off the shot.

"Ye're bleeding!" Isobel's exclamation as her horse came abreast with his shattered the peacefulness of the quiet glade, bringing everyone in the group to an abrupt halt. Her mount bumped against his as she stretched over and yanked his jacket aside. She peered at his chest with a sharp-eyed scowl. "How bad are ye hurt?"

"Less than a wee scratch." He moved out of her reach and waved for the others to follow. "Come. We need miles betwixt us and Stirling. As many as possible."

She rounded her mount in front of his and blocked the narrow path threading between a cluster of gnarled oaks. "Ye will stop this instant, and let me see to yer injury."

"Ye can tend it later." He nudged his horse forward. "Miles. Now, Isobel."

She squared her horse in front of him again and brought him to a halt. "So, ye're damned and determined to leave a trail of blood all across the Highlands so they can track us with ease?"

"She makes a fair point, cousin," Sutherland observed as he leaned forward and propped both hands on the lip of his saddle. "Why not stop for a bit? It's been quiet since we rid ourselves of the wagon, and there's at least an hour betwixt us and Stirling."

"Aye, brother," Ian chimed in. "Let her clean ye up. Yeva and the boy can stretch their legs whilst Isobel staunches yer wound. Ye forget, they're not used to hours on the back of a horse like we are. It would be a kindness to let them walk about for a while."

He bit back the words he longed to hurl at both his cousin and brother. It would be rude to say such in front of the women. "As soon as we come upon a burn, we'll stop, aye? The two of ye can see to the watering of the horses whilst the others tend to the stretching of their legs, and Isobel cleans up this pitiful scrape that appears to be nettling the lot of ye." He glared at her, daring her to argue. As a wee lass, she'd been stubborn as hell, and it appeared the trait had only strengthened with age.

"Agreed." She rode ahead, leading her horse for higher ground beyond the oaks.

He snorted when she brought them all to a stop mere moments later. The wily woman had always possessed the ability to find water. It was as though her soul was attuned to the soft gurgling of a woodland spring no matter how hard the Highlands attempted to hide it. She slid to the ground and handed her reins to Sutherland before Alasdair could protest.

"I shouldha known water was near when ye agreed so readily." He dismounted, another hitching pain a bit higher along the ridge of his shoulder, making itself known. He flexed his arm, rotating it back and forth. Sure enough, the bastards had nicked him twice.

Isobel nodded toward his chest, then bent and ripped several long strips from the bottom of her chemise. "Off with yer things, aye? Once I get ye bandaged, I'll rinse the blood and mend the tears in yer clothes before we continue on."

"We've no time for anything other than a quick bandage. I'll tend to the rest once we reach *Tor Ruadh*." Granted, the English didn't know the Highlands, but that didn't mean they needed to tarry and make it easy for the damned redcoats to find them.

"There's nay a need to be surly," she said in the same scolding tone he'd heard her use with Connor.

Alasdair yanked off his jacket, waistcoat, neckcloth, and léine, then strode forward, bare-chested with his kilt belted around his waist. "I've had no sleep and been shot twice. I believe I've earned the right to be a mite surly, ye ken?"

Isobel's eyes widened as she took in the sight of him. Twin patches of scarlet highlighted her cheeks. "Uhm…twice shot?" She cleared her throat and appeared to shake herself free of the dazed state. "I thought ye said they'd grazed ye but once?"

Alasdair twisted to peer at his shoulder. Aye, they'd gotten him twice, but both shots had merely ripped open the skin as the bullets missed their mark. "Twice. But both appear to be clean cuts. They'll not trouble me any worse than scratches."

"I'll be the judge of that." She hurried to the nearby burn cascading down a small rise of stones in the hillside. She tore free another strip of cloth from her chemise and wet it.

"Ye keep that up, and ye'll have no chemise left. It's foolish to ruin yer clothes over nothing more than a few wee scrapes."

She ignored him, continuing with the chore of wringing out the material and draping them over her arm.

He seated himself on a downed tree and propped his hands on his knees. Connor and Yeva meandered along the mossy embankment. Sutherland and Ian stood with the horses farther downstream. It was a peaceful enough place, he supposed. At least it was until he'd allowed weariness and a bit of nagging pain blacken his mood.

He pulled in a deep breath and blew it out, a sense of guilt stinging his conscience. They had made it this far. He should not let the enemy taint his outlook on the success of spiriting Isobel away and securing a future with her. She was back in his life. That was reason enough for nothing less than pure joy.

He scrubbed the scowl from his face and forced a more pleasant demeanor. "Forgive my surliness, *mo ghràdh*. I know ye're trying to help."

She dabbed the cool cloth across his flesh, her touch light and tantalizing. She stood so close. The scent of her wrapped around him like a lover's embrace, the subtle, inviting warmth of her as tempting as a siren's song. The way the front of her bodice brushed against his arm as she stretched around him to wipe the blood from his back drove him mad. Lord Almighty, he could hardly draw breath without groaning.

"I dinna blame ye for being cross," she said quietly. Her hands settled softly atop his shoulder, and she bowed her head. "They nearly killed ye today because of me. It is I who should beg forgiveness." She frowned as she touched the cloth to the oozing cut on his shoulder. "I am so verra sorry. Does it pain ye much?"

It didn't hurt him nearly as much as his poor throbbing cock, but he couldn't very well share that. He shook his head. "Nay, love. The pain is nothing. Dinna fash yerself, aye?" He caught hold of her hand and brushed a kiss to it, then peered up into her face. "Our future is nearly secured, *mo chridhe*." He kissed her hand again and smiled. "We'll reach *Tor Ruadh* in a few days' time. Once there, I'll draw up the divorce agreement. Alexander can send for a courier from Fort William. I'll petition the courts for yer freedom on the grounds of desertion and cruelty."

"All know about Temsworth's cruelty, but none will ever admit it." She pulled her hand out of his and stared down at the bloodied rag in her other hand. "Ye know as well as I the courts willna find in our favor. He is a duke, Alasdair. A man of power feared by his peers." Her gaze lifted to his. The storm of suffering in her eyes tore at his soul. "Such a petition will only stir his ire against us even more. He'll hunt down all who dare help me. He's a vicious man who thrives on the blood of his enemies, and he willna rest until he's tracked us down and had his revenge." She shook her head. "We must hide until someone else draws his attention away." She returned to tending his minor wound. "We must hide to keep ye safe."

"I dinna hide." He pulled her to stand between his knees and prayed she wouldn't pull away. "I willna rest until I make ye my wife good and proper—as I shouldha done ten years ago." He smoothed an errant curl from her face and tucked it behind her ear. "I willna rest until ye bear my name, dear one."

"And if he kills ye?" she whispered, allowing the cloth to drop from his shoulder, then framed his face between her hands. "Ye would risk leaving me unprotected and shattered with the loss of ye?" Her frantic gaze searched his face as she leaned closer, pressing her sweet softness against him. "I canna bear the thought of living without ye." She surprised him with a frantic kiss. "I beg ye, m'love, dinna leave me alone."

"Have ye so little faith in me?" He hadn't meant to say it aloud. She eased away.

"I have faith in yer heart and the goodness of yer soul." She laced her fingers in his hair and pressed her forehead to his. "But I know the extent of the evil he is capable of. Ye do not understand the darkness within that man."

"Someone approaches!" Ian called out from farther down the hillside.

Alasdair snatched her up by the waist and sat her over on the other side of the downed tree. He pointed to a trench left from the tree's roots. "Stay down there. I'll fetch Connor and Auntie." He bounded across the stream and grabbed them up, toting one under each arm as though they weighed nothing more than sacks of grain. He lowered them to the ground beside Isobel. "Crouch down. Stay hidden until we discover what's about, aye?"

"Dinna leave me here without a weapon." Isobel held out a hand, her look determined yet pleading. She clutched Connor close, and Auntie huddled behind her.

He understood and wished he could deny her, but he couldn't find it in his heart to do so. He handed her his *sgian dhu* but held tight to the blade until she looked him in the eyes. "Dinna use it unless there's no doubt we have all fallen, aye?"

She nodded, her eyes gleaming with unshed tears. "Swear to me ye willna fall. Swear it."

"I willna fall, my love." He reached down and lifted her up by the shoulders. Covering her mouth with his, he kissed her with a thoroughness that fueled his determination. He tore away, bounding down the hillside to join Ian and Sutherland, where they crouched behind an outcropping of moss-covered boulders overlooking the worn path winding up the hillside.

"I saw a glimmer of red through yon trees. Farther to the south, but I am certain of what I saw," Sutherland whispered. "Appears to be a lone rider."

"A single rider?" Alasdair squinted, straining to see through the thick stand of trees. "That makes no sense. Why would they send a lone rider after us? That's not the Sassenach way." The only movement he detected was the subtle breeze setting the lush greenery of the forest dancing. He stared harder, easing his way to a standing position behind the boulder. He balanced his pistol atop the rock and pulled back the hammer. As soon as the rider passed through the trees, whoever it was, would find himself the proud recipient of a lead ball between the eyes.

"Hold fast, Alasdair," Ian hissed as he rose to stand beside him. "Listen."

The softest whistling filtered through the woods, a lilting Scottish tune Alasdair recognized from his youth. The rider had to be a Scot. Mayhap, even a MacCoinnich. Alasdair lowered his pistol and shoved it back in his belt whilst keeping his focus where the rider would eventually appear.

"Well, I'll be damned," Ian said as he pushed off the boulder and straightened. "It's Crestshire."

Lord Edward John Cunningham, second earl of Crestshire, commander of Fort William, and the childhood best friend to clan chieftain, Alexander MacCoinnich, because the man's wise father had seen fit to take the unorthodox approach of having his Sassenach son foster with a Scottish clan. Lord Crestshire was one of their few allies among the English, an ally who might help with this rather difficult situation.

Alasdair moved out from behind the safety of the boulders and waited.

With a grin and a shake of his head, Crestshire brought his horse to a halt. He dismounted and held out his hand. "Alasdair Cameron. Bare-chested and bloody as the wildest Highland Scot. What would the esteemed courts of Edinburgh say about their favorite solicitor if they saw you now, my friend?"

"They'd say I needed a drink." Alasdair closed the distance between them and took Crestshire's forearm in the firm grip of friendship.

"I should say so." The commander peered at the wound on Alasdair's shoulder, his eyes narrowing. "Might I ask who shot you?" He nodded at the bloody scratch. "Or should I say, attempted to shoot you."

"His Majesty's finest in Stirling." Alasdair watched Crestshire close, waiting for the man's reaction. Crestshire had always been a good friend but was still loyal to king and country.

Crestshire made a noncommittal tilt of his head. "I see." He locked eyes with Alasdair. "And how, pray tell, were His Majesty's finest provoked to fire upon you?"

"A false accusation of kidnapping," Sutherland supplied as he joined them with Isobel on his arm. "Might I present the Duchess of Temsworth?"

"Just Isobel, please," she corrected as she slid her hand free of Sutherland's arm and took her place at Alasdair's side.

Lord Crestshire stiffened, staring at Isobel for an overlong moment before recovering from his surprise. With a proper bow, he remembered his manners. "Commander Crestshire at your service, Your Grace." His jaw tightened as his attention turned to Alasdair. "An explanation would be most welcome since my office recently received notice of not only the duchess's abduction but also that of her son, the young marquess."

"Oh, he's here as well." Alasdair turned in the direction of the uprooted tree. "Come out, lad. Help yer auntie out of the ditch, too. It's safe."

Crestshire raked a hand across his wavy blonde hair. With a roll of his shoulders, he jerked his crimson jacket back in place, then hooked his hands onto his lapels. "I am quite interested in hearing this story."

Before Alasdair could speak, Isobel stepped forward. "My husband, the Duke of Temsworth, is a cruel man, Commander. After ten years of imprisonment and torture, I managed to escape and save my aunt and son as well."

Crestshire pursed his lips, staring downward as though gathering his thoughts, then slowly lifted his head. "Forgive me, Your Grace, but why did you tolerate the man for ten years if he was as cruel as you say?"

Alasdair pushed forward, stepping between Isobel and Crestshire. "How dare ye ask her such a thing!"

Crestshire stood his ground. "I am only asking what the courts will ask if the lot of you are ever taken into custody."

Crestshire's answer sat well—especially the way the man worded it. He was right. Alasdair nodded and returned to Isobel's side.

"I loved Alasdair before my father sold me to Temsworth. The duke needed a wife and heir, and no Sassenach lady of noble blood would ever agree to marry him." Isobel swallowed and wet her lips before continuing. "I could nay understand why all those English fathers denied him one of their daughters until after I married the evil brute."

She swayed to one side, and Alasdair sprang to hold her steady. She held up a hand and shook her head. "I'm all right, love." With a lifting of her chin, she locked eyes with Crestshire. "Temsworth informed me that all I had ever loved was dead and gone, and I believed him. He offered proof of the plague that had swept through our clans. I thought both Alasdair and my family lost to me. So, I resigned myself to my fate." With a deep breath, she hugged Connor to her side and smiled down at him. "That was until Temsworth told me of his plan to take my son from me."

A cold fierceness settled across her features, and hatred flashed in her eyes. "It was then I decided to make my escape. To protect my son from that monstrous bastard." She grabbed hold of Alasdair's hand and clutched it to her chest. "And then I discovered my true love lived." She smiled up at him. "Alasdair is my protector. Without him, Temsworth would surely have already murdered me and set to torturing my son until my sweet lad became as cruel and wicked as he." She turned back to Crestshire. "I assure ye, I was nay abducted or kidnapped, Commander. I liberated myself, my aunt, and my son of my own free will."

Crestshire nodded, then managed a polite but obviously strained smile. "I do not doubt yer explanation. Your husband's dark reputation is well known." He turned to Alasdair, his forced smile dissolving into a concerned frown. "This will not go away easily. Do you truly understand the nature of the man you are dealing with?"

"I will stop at nothing to protect her from that bastard." Alasdair wrapped a shielding arm around Isobel's shoulders.

"Of that, I have no doubt." Lord Crestshire stared down at the ground, then lifted his head. "I assume you are headed for *Tor Ruadh*?"

"It's best ye dinna ask things ye're better off not knowing for certain." Alasdair bent and took hold of Connor by the shoulder. "Run and fetch my clothes, aye? We need to be on our way."

Connor took off like a shot.

Crestshire went to his saddlebag, untied the flap, and extricated a folded linen. He tossed it at Alasdair's chest. "Here. A fresh tunic free of blood and bullet holes."

Alasdair shook out the shirt, then pulled it over his head. "I thank ye."

"Since the abduction notice did not mention you or your kin by name, I can bid you farewell without compunction." He mounted and studied his reins, worrying the strips of leather through his hand. "But if you are ever named, I will be hard-pressed to obey the writ of any command given me. You understand?"

Alasdair nodded. "I understand." He stepped forward. "But ye understand all that I must do as well, aye?"

Lord Crestshire nodded. "I do, my friend." He maneuvered his horse back to the trail, then paused to look back. "I shall return to Fort William by the southern pass. Just so you know."

Alasdair lifted a hand in farewell. "Thank ye, m'friend."

With a curt nod, the commander urged his horse into a canter and rode away.

CHAPTER ELEVEN

ISOBEL EASED AROUND the roots of the ancient tree, then knelt down and peeped over the high embankment. There. Deeper in the ravine and downstream a bit was exactly what she sought. Well-hidden and comfortably cradled behind the mossy rise above the burn, she stretched out on her belly and propped her chin in her hand. Loving contentment flowed through her as sure and fast as the swift-moving water.

Naked as could be, Alasdair and Connor stood in the stream. Both eased their way through the water at a snail's pace. Arms extended, Connor looked to Alasdair for approval before moving forward with each slow step. Their target lay ahead. A formation of rocks hanging over the burn, forming ledges and pools of water.

Alasdair had not only promised fish for supper but had also pro-claimed it was high time Connor learned the fine art of guddling. If he managed to curb the five-year-old's exuberance long enough to tickle a fish free of the stream, the man deserved sainthood. Isobel had sworn to clean and cook the fish for them.

And then after supper, she would seduce him. It was time to take Auntie's wise advice. Seduction was the only way to convince Alasdair to forget about challenging Temsworth.

Isobel's breath caught as she allowed her gaze to rake across

Alasdair's body. What a fine, sculpted arse he had, and the play of his muscles when he moved made her ache. Bitterness soured the view. She didn't even know what she ached for. Submission to Temsworth's twisted demands surely couldn't begin to touch what a man and woman in love might discover in each other's embrace.

She pushed away the thought and concentrated on the tempting spectacle in front of her. *Aye.* Alasdair was a fine man. She loved the way the wet, dark hair sleeked across his chest and legs, accentuating the outline of his hardened muscles even more. She bit the inside of her cheek. A man's member usually shrank from the cold. Not Alasdair's. Even with the water's chill, he was a sight to behold. Saints a mercy, how large might he get with some encouragement?

Alasdair pointed at the slippery gray surface of the rocks peeping just above the waterline. Anticipation tickled a smile from her. She'd lay odds that one or both would end up thoroughly doused before this fishing lesson ended. At least they'd had the foresight to keep their clothes dry by leaving them on the bank.

As the two reached the ledge of stone, she gave the barest shake of her head. Merciful heavens, the boy would surely catch his death from the icy water and cool breeze. His teeth were chattering.

Motioning the lad forward, Alasdair knelt down and stretched over the ledge. Intense concentration hardened his features as he inched forward, running his hand under the ledge until the rushing water frothed against his shoulder. Connor crouched at his side, his tiny face aglow with awe and anticipation.

Isobel prayed Alasdair would be successful. She didn't care over-much for the taste of trout but didn't wish Connor disappointed. She cringed as her son flopped down on his belly alongside Alasdair.

The longer Alasdair lay with his hand shoved under the rock, the deeper his brow furrowed. His face hardened into a predatory grimace, then he bared his teeth and shifted to reach deeper under the water. Just as Isobel had lost all hope, he let out a victorious roar and yanked a hefty, wriggling fish out of the water and tossed it high upon the bank. Connor crowed with excitement, scampering up the embankment.

"What a fine fish!" he proclaimed as he squatted down beside their flopping dinner and poked it with a finger. He hurried back to Alasdair, picking his way down the bank, flinching as his bare feet found sharp bits of rock. "Reckon there's more?" he asked, shivering.

"We'll have to go farther upstream, lad." Alasdair rose from the rock. "If any others shared that one's hidey-hole, we've frightened them away."

Without a sound, Isobel retreated, crawling backward until she felt certain that when she stood, they wouldn't spot her.

She busied herself gathering more fuel for the fire and kept it well fed. The sight of Auntie curled deep in the woolen folds of a plaid at the base of a tree, snoring softly, made her smile. Poor Auntie. This trip through the Highlands was a strain on her.

This was the first day that Alasdair had relaxed enough to permit a fire, and Isobel was glad of it. Ian and Sutherland had gone hunting in case no fish were caught. She pulled her knitted shawl close. As the shadows of the waning day lengthened, the thick woodlands grew chillier.

Isobel nudged the pot of water deeper into the coals and added the seeds and greens she'd foraged. She crumbled a chunk of dried venison into the mix, then sprinkled the steaming liquid with a few ashes from the fire for a nice, salty seasoning. A hot broth to go along with the fish wouldn't go amiss on an evening such as this. Alasdair and Connor would surely be chilled to the bone.

"We've naught but a pair of hares to add to the fire," Ian announced as he and Sutherland entered camp. "Best get the remaining oatcakes and bread to fill our bellies."

"They be cleaned and on a spit already," Sutherland said as he held up the pair of skinned carcasses skewered on a long stick stripped of its bark.

"We caught three fish!" Connor shouted as he burst through the trees. "I caught one of'm m'self, I truly did. All by m'self! And Alasdair let me gut the one I caught!" He hopped along beside Alasdair, hoisting his end of the stick even higher. Three good-sized trout dangled from it. "I did, didn't I? All by m'self?" He beamed up at Alasdair.

"Aye, that ye did, lad." Alasdair gave Isobel a subtle nod as he patted Connor's shoulder. "He's quite the fisherman."

She couldn't remember the last time she had felt such joy and contentment. If only life could stay like this. She rose from beside the fire and waved them forward. "Come to the fire. Warm yerselves whilst I finish cooking this fine supper ye've all provided." She gave Connor a quick hug, her heart hitching as he pulled away and scampered over to the other men. It was obvious the lad was too excited over the fish to be bothered with a hug from his mother. He was growing up too fast.

Alasdair caught hold of her arm and kissed her cheek. He held her close long enough to brush his lips across the tender skin of her temple. "I saw ye watching us," he whispered. His knowing look made her limbs weak.

She recovered quickly and gave a nonchalant shrug. "I was merely ensuring Connor was safe and behaving himself. I know how reckless men can be when excited by the hunt. The both of ye will be lucky if ye dinna catch yer death from that cold water."

"After the papers are sorted, and we're married, 'twill be up to ye to warm me." Alasdair winked, then strode across the camp and pulled a leather flask from one of the saddlebags draped across a stump. With a sorrowful look at the vessel, he blew out a heavy sigh. "For now, I'll have to rely on the *uisge beatha* and the fire." He caressed her with another searing glance, then took a hearty swig.

Auntie Yeva crawled from her nest of plaids and hobbled over to

Isobel. She gave a scowl as she took the fish. "I prepare supper. You plan."

"Plan?" Isobel repeated.

"It is time you make him realize no good comes from trying to reason with a demon." Her aunt paused and glanced back over her shoulder at the men. "You two can live as man and wife in the eyes of God. Does not matter what some paper says." She pinned Isobel with a sly look. "Convince him. A child would help even more."

"Connor?"

Auntie rolled her eyes as she cut the head from the largest fish. "His child, girl. A man like Cameron will listen to the woman carrying his child. Will do anything to protect her and the babe."

Isobel decided not to share she'd already decided seduction was the only way. She took the knife from her Auntie and cut the heads off the other two fish, then handed them to the old woman. "Here. For the soup. Rake the coals higher around the pot, aye? And I'll thank ye to hush. Yer voice travels, ye ken?"

"You know I am right," Auntie grumbled as she took the fish heads and headed for the pot.

Isobel wiped the knife on the ragged length of linen she'd knotted around her waist to shield the front of her dress. *Aye.* Auntie was right. If bedding Alasdair didn't convince him to give up the foolish idea of petitioning the duke for a divorce, would his child?

She turned and watched him as he sat with Ian, Sutherland, and Connor around the fire. A tender wish filled with hope unfurled deep inside her. Alasdair's child. What a joy it would be to have a babe with the man she had always loved.

Alasdair paused and turned to her as though she'd spoken the thoughts aloud. He smiled. A loving smile. A grin that sent a surge of heat flashing through her. Aye, she burned for him and didn't possess the power to hide it.

She broke away from his attention and busied herself with skewering the fish and propping them to roast over the fire. She struggled to keep her mind from wandering as she turned the hares on the spit and stirred the bubbling soup. She had no thought for food. What might happen after supper was foremost in her mind.

"How much longer, Mama?" Connor's impatience yanked her back to the present as he squatted beside her and reached out to poke one of the fish.

Isobel smacked his hand away and carefully turned the fish, their skins charring nicely. "A bit longer. Run and fetch those slabs of bark for the meat and the cups for the broth, aye?"

"Be there fried bread, too?" Connor circled the large fire, inspecting all that was cooking.

"Do as Mama said," Auntie ordered with a shooing of both hands. "I fry the bread now."

The old woman hefted an ancient cast iron griddle out of a cloth sack. The pan's handle was broken, and its surface was blackened from years of use. She placed it dead center atop the chunks of glowing embers she'd raked into a pile. As she knelt beside the fire, she pulled a small cloth-covered crock from the deepest pocket of her skirt and scooped out a finger of a white paste. The fat slid across the surface of the pan, liquifying as it heated. Without looking up, she motioned to a rock behind her. "Fetch dough."

Isobel hurried to comply, then crouched down and held out the bark with the mound of pale white dough. "I canna believe ye kept hold of yer wee pan all this way." As far back as she could remember, Auntie had used the same pan for frying food. It had also come in quite handy when they'd made their escape from Hestlemoor—served as a good weapon, knocking the unsuspecting guard of the tower firmly into his dreams.

"Was my mother's and grandmother's and so on. I could never leave it behind." Auntie pulled off sticky gobs of dough and dropped them on the sizzling surface of the pan. She gave Isobel an affectionate nod. "Will be yours someday."

Isobel placed an arm around her aunt's shoulders. "I shall treasure it."

Alasdair approached, squatted down beside them, and leaned toward the pan. A look of sheer bliss settled across his features as he closed his eyes and inhaled. "Lord Almighty. It's been ages since I've had yer fried bread. If I'd known ye had yer wee pan, I wouldha let us have a fire sooner. Tonight's meal will be a true feast. A damned site better than dried meat and oatcakes."

Auntie nodded. "I teach Isobel. She knows how to fry the bread. When you two have a daughter, I teach her, too."

"I hope we'll be blessed with many bairns," Alasdair said.

"Me, too," Isobel said, her mind made up at that exact moment on what she had to do. Auntie was right. Their only hope for a happy life was to live as man and wife. The rest of the world be damned. Nothing but sorrow would come from challenging the duke. She would do whatever it took to convince Alasdair of such. "Fetch yer board and cup from Connor. Supper's ready."

Alasdair rose but hung back as Ian, Sutherland, and Connor lined up for the meal. Isobel felt his gaze as she parsed out the food.

"Ye saved little for yerself," Alasdair said as she placed the last of the fish and rabbit on his board and filled his cup with the choicest bits of the stew.

"I have all I need." She couldn't keep from smiling as she held up her half-filled cup and small chunk of fried bread. Well...she would have all she needed soon.

He followed her to a moss-covered hillock. "We should reach *Tor Ruadh* tomorrow, late." He settled down beside her and tore into his food like a man starved.

Isobel nibbled at the savory edges of the browned bread and sipped her broth. She had no appetite for the meal. Her entire being was too caught up in how she should put her plan into play. She hadn't realized they would arrive home so soon. That left her but one night. A bairn might come from one joining, but such odds were slim. Once they reached *Tor Ruadh*, sleeping with Alasdair would become a great deal more complicated. She was not so sure he'd be willing to share her bed—at least not without a great deal of coercing. She knew he wouldn't want to risk opening her to ridicule or disrespect. After all, she was married to someone else.

Rage at the injustice of her past nearly choked her. *Nay.* She had never been married. Not in the real sense of the word. She had been enslaved for breeding purposes to give the duke an heir. Temsworth had extended no kindness toward her. She crumbled her bread into her cup, struggling to rise above the hatred threatening to drown her. She focused on tomorrow's reunion with the rest of the MacCoinnich clan. "It will be good to see the MacCoinnichs after all this time. Do all the brothers live at *Tor Ruadh*?"

"All but Duncan." Alasdair sopped his bread into his cup, popped the bite into his mouth, then licked the rich gravy from his fingers. "He and his wife live on an island far from here." He stared off into the distance and smiled. "A warm place. Beaches of the whitest sand surrounded by the sea. Jungles filled with all manner of strange animals." Somberness clouded his features. "It's a fine place, but it's not our beloved Scotland."

"Ye miss him." Isobel set aside her cup. Alasdair had always been closest to Duncan. The two had been thick as thieves when they were lads.

"Aye." He rose and stretched, rubbing his stomach with one hand, then smiled down at Isobel. "But I see him now and again." He thumped his taut middle. "Lord Almighty, woman. Ye've stuffed me full."

She stood and gave a graceful sweep of her hand. "I merely helped prepare what these fine hunters and fishermen provided." She feigned a look at the sky and held out a hand for his cup. "I've little light left to rinse the cups and pans in the burn. I best hurry."

"Connor and I will do." Auntie toddled over to the boy, took hold of his collar, and pulled him to his feet.

"Auntie!" The lad made the mistake of attempting escape, but she latched onto his ear. "Ow! Leave go! Please!"

"Chores make a good man." Auntie shook a finger within inches of the boy's nose, then pointed around the camp. "Gather cups and pot while I get the griddle."

"Dinna argue with Auntie," Isobel warned, doing her best to keep a level tone. She knew exactly what Auntie was about. It was time to convince Alasdair to take a walk. She turned to him and smiled before her courage waned. "Care to join me for a walk? 'Tis good for settlin' the meal."

Suspicion flashed in Alasdair's eyes. After a moment's hesitation, he held out his arm to her. "It would be my pleasure, m'lady."

Her hand firm in the crook of his elbow, she pointed toward a path leading deeper into the woods. With her most beguiling smile, she hugged closer to his side. "We shan't stray far. With night coming, I fear we might lose our way without the fire."

"I've just the thing." He strode back to the saplings, hacked one free, and stripped it of its leaves. He pointed to the linen rag serving as her apron. "Ye dinna mind parting with yer fine covering, do ye?"

"Nay." She untied it and handed it over. "What have ye in mind?"

Alasdair wrapped the linen tight around one end of the stick, then took Auntie's small crock of cooking fat and smeared a healthy amount all around the material. "And a bit of fat to light our way."

"Auntie will have yer arse for using that."

He dipped the rag into the fire and ignited the torch. Turning to Isobel, he gave her a sly smile as he held out his arm again. "Ye'll be good enough to protect me from her, aye?"

She shook her head as she took his arm. "From Auntie? Nay, my brave torchbearer, ye must battle that fearsome dragon alone."

Alasdair laughed, then paused before exiting the camp. "I know yer bellies are full, but see that the boy and Auntie make it back safe, aye?"

Sutherland waved them on with a knowing grin. "On wi' ye, man. We'll tend to the safety of camp, and see ye in the morning, aye?"

"Dinna mind him," Alasdair cleared his throat. He held the torch higher as they left the clearing and pushed deeper into the woods.

They strolled along the winding path in silence, the rising breeze riffling through the leaves. Something skittered across the forest floor.

"A pine marten after his supper," Isobel said. "Or a female marten in search of food to fetch back to her babies."

He glanced down at her. "Ye always amazed me. Ye werena like the other girls only interested in cooking or sewing. I remember yer auntie and da both scolding ye more than once about acting like a laddie."

"That seems so long ago." The torchlight flickered across what looked like the perfect place for all she hoped would happen. She pointed at the mossy ground surrounded by oak trees. "Would ye mind if we rested over there? It looks like such an inviting place to ease away the weariness of the day."

Alasdair abruptly halted and faced her. He gave her a narrow-eyed look. "Isobel."

The man's talent for saying her name in a tone that said he wasn't fooled by her had always infuriated her. *Damn him.*

"We are married in the eyes of God," she defended. "We've loved each other since we were bairns. Even promised ourselves to each other back in those caves we used to play in." Another thought came to her. "We are also married in the eyes of Scotland. Back at the inn. Ye claimed me as yer wife in a public place. And I nay denied it."

He shook his head. "Yer marriage to the duke is recorded in the Church."

If he thought she'd surrender so easily, he was sorely mistaken. Too much was at stake. She gathered up her skirts and picked her way to the trees. Removing her shoes, she slid her skirts high above her knees to untie the ribbons holding her stockings.

"Isobel!" He strode to the edge of the nest and held the torch higher. "I demand ye stop this and...and come up here this instant." He scrubbed his face and gave a frantic look around. "Come now, Isobel."

His faltering encouraged her. *Aye.* She'd win this yet. With a slow, seductive stretch of her leg, she slid off her first stocking and smiled. "I demand ye come down here and consummate our union from long ago. Now."

CHAPTER TWELVE

A STRAINED GROAN escaped Alasdair. God help him, this woman would surely be his death. The torchlight flickered across the satin of her exposed leg. He swallowed hard. Throbbing in his bollocks along with the rigid ache in his cock, threatened to turn him into a mindless idiot. His body raged to partake of the bliss she offered. *Nay.* He would not do this.

"Isobel," he pleaded. "Ye know as well as I that this isna right."

"Ye're saying ye dinna love me?" She rolled her other stocking down until it bunched around her ankle. "Ye refuse to honor our vow?" She fixed him with a look that nearly undid him. "My marriage to the duke is invalid. Do ye not remember that day in the cave all those years ago? The vows we spoke to one another before my father sold me to that brute?" She gave the softest shake of her head. "We planned to run away. Have ye forgotten?"

Forgotten? Nay. He'd never forget that day. After sealing their vows with a passionate kiss, they had both nearly drowned in the rising tide. Caught up in their love, they had sorely misjudged the time they should have fled the cave. "Ye know I have nay forgotten."

He risked a step forward. She had to understand he didn't wish to dishonor her. His love was that pure. "It was after that day yer da locked ye away, and mine berated me for being a lovesick fool for a lass who could never be mine."

She freed her bound hair, allowing the dark river of silk to cascade down around her shoulders. "So, ye see? We are man and wife. My imprisonment with Temsworth was just that." She slid a finger under the ties of her bodice and toyed with the laces, loosening the garment in the process. "It was never a consensual marriage."

He passed the torch from hand to hand, struggling to reason when all he wanted was to cast everything aside and go to her. "Our vows…" He lost the ability to speak as she slipped off the rest of her clothes, leaving only her chemise.

Alasdair wet his lips. The outline of her hardened nipples drew him. "Our vows," he repeated. "No witnesses."

"God was our witness," she whispered as she reached him and slid her hands up his chest. "The land, the sea, and the wind heard our words." She yanked his tunic upward and teased a nibbling kiss above his heart.

All that separated them was his léine, his kilt, and her threadbare chemise. God have mercy on his soul. How could he not surrender to this woman? He stabbed the torch into the ground and took hold of her wrists, fighting for control. "Isobel."

"Aye?" She leaned into him, adding to his agony with a trail of kisses along his throat.

"Those witnesses," he groaned.

"Aye?" She wiggled against him, imprisoning his poor aching cock between them.

He released her wrists, smoothed his hands down her back, then ran them up under the luscious curves of her arse and pulled her hard against him. "Our vows wouldna stand in court."

"Court doesna matter," she reasoned as she slid his kilt upward and wrapped a leg around his bare thigh. "We know. God knows. All who matter know." She slid her arms around his neck and molded her softness to him. "Love me, dear one. Love me, I beg ye." She pulled back a bit and cupped his face in her hands. Her dark, longing gaze searched his face. "Yers is the purest love I have ever known. We *are* man and wife. This is not just some weak argument to justify sleeping with ye. Search yer heart, my love, and ye'll see the truth of it. I swear ye will."

"*Mo ghràdh.*" He could bear it no longer. Sweeping her up into his arms, he lowered her to the soft ground. "Such beauty," he whispered.

A sad smile teased across her lips, a smile that didn't reach her eyes as she trailed a fingertip along his jaw. "The shadows hide the cruelty of the years. I'm no longer the woman ye once loved."

"Nay. Ye are not. Ye're better." He silenced any chance of further argument with the kiss he'd longed for since rediscovering her. Heart and soul poured into it. All his hunger. The years of loneliness. The nights of unquenched need. His dearest lady love responded in full.

He raked endless kisses across the satin of her skin. No amount would ever be enough. Desire raged, surged into torment. He forced himself to slow down, to savor every bit of her. Lips, sweet as rare wine. Breasts, a wondrous delight. The mewling gasps for more. Her fierce urgency as she wrapped her legs around him and arched against him.

Plunging into her ecstasy, he thundered with a claiming growl. He buried to the hilt and held still, ready to pound his way to oblivion. *Nay. Not yet.* Not until she found her pleasure first. He rolled over and held her tight as she straddled him. He slid her chemise off over her head. "Glorious," he whispered as he cupped a breast in each hand.

She smiled down at him, then started rocking. Leaning over him, she brushed her nipples across his mouth and continued her slow ride. With a purr, she intensified her movements. Alasdair drove his hips upward, harder and faster. He clutched her tight as she spasmed and cried out, her fingers raking down his chest. He rolled atop her again and drove inside, hard and deep, thrusting with the fury of endless longing. Isobel clutched at his buttocks, yanking him into her. "Aye, m'love, aye!" She let out another piercing cry and shuddered.

The world ceased to exist as he reeled into her ecstasy and found his release. He collapsed atop her, his forearms resting on either side of her to keep from crushing her. Forehead pressed to hers, he gasped out another groan as he struggled to regain his senses. *"Mo ghràdh. Mo chridhe,"* he whispered between tender kisses. He felt her smile against his mouth.

"Ye own me heart and soul," she murmured as she held him tight.

"Nay, love." Alasdair eased over to one side, pulling her into the curve of his body and covering her with his plaid. He stared up into the darkness. "Our hearts and souls intertwine. Neither owns the other, but each is needed to make a whole."

"Ye've grown quite eloquent with age, Master Solicitor." She settled her head more comfortably in the dip of his shoulder. A deeper, less contented sigh shifted her against him.

"What troubles ye, love?" He thanked God above that his ability to read Isobel's moods had finally returned, as sharp as though nary a year had passed from the days of their youth. He kissed the top of her head and nuzzled his cheek into the silkiness of her hair. She smelled of wood smoke, fried bread, and a woman well-loved. Utterly intoxicating.

"Do ye regret giving yerself to me?" He had feared she would. No matter what she said. He'd recognized her thinly veiled ploy for what it was. "Speak yer heart, love. I would know yer thoughts, good or ill."

"Will ye grow to resent me because we canna reside at yer fine house in Edinburgh?"

Such an idea had never occurred to him, but now that he thought about it, Isobel was right. As long as the duke hunted them, they couldn't return to Edinburgh. He hugged her close and kissed her again. "Ye're worth more to me than any house. I dinna care where we live, as long as we're together."

"I wish we could stay like this forever," she whispered. "Nary a worry in the world."

A snort escaped him. He couldn't help it.

"Young Connor would nay tolerate such lazing about. Ye know that as well as I." A genuine fondness for the lad triggered a deeper concern. "I must file the papers with even more haste so we might make our union legal. I will nay have the boy ashamed of us."

She pushed up from his chest, clutching his kilt across her breasts. "Our union *is* legal. It was first. Remember?"

"Isobel."

"Dinna say *Isobel* in that tone." She yanked the plaid free and jerked to her feet. "I'm not a fool, and I didna use that argument merely to seduce ye, ye stubborn arse."

"We have no witnesses to testify to the oath we made in that cave." How could he make her understand? Unless God sent a lightning bolt into the middle of court, one that engraved the Almighty's testimony in stone, they had no one to testify to the promise they had sworn. "We can prove nothing, and since we can't, yer reputation is in danger."

"And if ye file those papers, yer life is in danger!" Isobel snatched up her scattered articles of clothing.

"The bastard willna kill me." He sat up, raking his hair back from his face. "We shall stay in the safety of *Tor Ruadh* until everything is finalized." He thumped his chest. "I swear it."

"Dinna swear when ye know as well as I do it willna come true." She tossed his kilt to the ground and yanked on her chemise. Her skirt came next and then her stockings. "How do ye propose to get the papers filed?"

"I shall send them by messenger to my contact in Edinburgh. A man I trust. He'll see to the filing." Alasdair sat up and leaned to one side, recovering Isobel's bodice out from under his arse. He held it out to her. "Thomas Abernathy would file papers with Satan himself if I asked him. The man is above reproach."

"No man is above reproach once Temsworth finishes with them." She snatched the bodice out of his hand and threaded her arms through the garment. Fingers fumbling with the laces, her face darkened with sheer misery. She stomped a stockinged foot and aimed her suffering at him. "How could ye ruin our first time in such a cruel way, Alasdair? How could ye?"

"But…" He caught the words before they escaped. He was not that large of an idiot. Far be it from him to point out that it was she and not himself who had complained about what they faced.

He swallowed the argument, then bowed his head, and sent up a silent prayer. *Give me the words, Lord.* With a deep, settling inhale, he retrieved his kilt and knotted it around his waist. He moved forward and took a knee at her feet. "Forgive me, m'love. Tell me what ye wish of me."

Bottom lip quivering, she stared down at him for the span of several exasperated sighs. "Accept that we are man and wife and leave Temsworth to Satan."

Alasdair bowed his head and scrubbed a hand across his jaw. He rose and took her hands in his. "The man will not forget he has a son. His only heir. Ye know that as well as I. We must file the papers and come to an understanding about the lad. For Connor's sake."

"I will never give up my son." She yanked her hands away and retreated a step. "How could ye suggest such?"

"I suggested no such thing." He staunched the urge to reach out. *Nay.* She was about to bolt—either that or club him with a branch. "Yer husband is a cruel, heartless bastard. I'd never condemn the boy to such a fate." He hurried to continue before she could interrupt. "But the duke is also a shrewd businessman drunk on power, wealth, and political maneuvering. I intend to offer him something he'll value even more than an heir."

"Such as?" Her narrowed eyes glittered. She was not the fool either. She knew as well as he that it would take something extraordinary to take the duke's heir.

"I prefer to speak with Graham before I attempt to explain fully." Mercy, Graham MacCoinnich's wife, was goddaughter to King William. It was Alasdair's sincerest hope that such a powerful alliance could serve them well in the permanent separation of Connor from his despicable father.

"Graham is nay the chieftain. Why not Alexander?" She plainly believed him stalling for time.

"Graham's wife is goddaughter to the king." He waited for the weight of his words to hit.

Her immediate shift in demeanor gave him hope. That hope gained strength when she moved a step closer. "Truly?" she asked.

"Truly." He held out a hand. "Will ye trust me now? Ye know in yer heart there's no escaping what must be done. I refuse to spend the rest of our lives on the run and constantly looking over our shoulders."

Scowl still in place, she finally placed her hand in his. He pulled her into his arms and tilted her face upward. "I am nay a coward, and I promise ye, we shall have the life we once dreamed of, aye?" She didn't believe him. He had lost this argument. Badly.

She proved that fact even more when she pulled herself out of his arms, bent to shove her feet into her shoes, and yanked their laces tight. "We best get back to camp, aye? I am weary and need to check on Connor before I seek my rest."

Alasdair gritted his teeth. How had they gone from heated passion to icy separation in the span of a few moments? He swallowed a groan, wishing he could have avoided the conversation. Maybe he was a damned fool after all. He retrieved her shawl from the ground and wrapped it about her. He squeezed her shoulders and hugged her back against him. "*Tha gaol gam ort,*" he whispered, then kissed her neck.

His heart lurched as she stared down at the forest floor and remained silent. "Isobel?"

"I love ye as well," she snapped, then jerked away and wrapped her shawl tighter about her. Without a look back, she hurried toward camp.

"Yer tone denies it." He snatched up the torch and trudged after her.

She didn't respond.

Hell's fire and demon's balls. May God deliver him from an angry, unreasonable woman. He lengthened his stride until he caught up with her. "Isobel—ye must see reason."

She came to an abrupt halt and turned on him like an enraged beast. "I must do nothing other than protect my son and the man I love. That is *all* I must do in this life, and I willna have ye nor anyone else preaching at me otherwise." She poked a finger into his chest. "Ye be a damned fool if ye think ye can outwit Temsworth or out-bargain him. He's not a man of his word. He'll play at taking yer deal and then still hunt ye down and slit yer throat—even if the king himself has a part in the agreement." She jabbed him again. "Ye canna deal with the devil and not get burned by the fires of hell!"

He took hold of her hand before she could hit him again. "The man will not stop trying to recover his son, and I'm damned sick and tired of ye thinking I'm some helpless fool that needs yer protection. I can care for my own, Isobel, and ye and Connor are most certainly mine. Trust me, dammit!"

She exploded with a hissing growl and yanked free of him. Fists filled with her skirts, she stormed away, plowing into the quiet camp and not coming to a halt until she stood beside her son's sleeping form. She knelt and pulled his blanket higher as she kissed his cheek. The firelight flooded Connor's face with a golden glow as she brushed his dark curls aside. Hands folded in her lap, she sat staring down at him.

Alasdair tossed the torch into the fire. He glanced around, noting that Sutherland slept wrapped in his plaid, not a pace away from where Yeva had placed their pallets close to the fire. Ian was missing, but that didn't surprise Alasdair. The man hadn't slept well since the massacre at Glencoe. He probably stood guard out in the woods and had overheard all that had taken place. It mattered not. Ian would understand.

Alasdair rubbed at the burning corners of his eyes. Sleep would not come easy this night. Not until he found a way to cool her anger. *Never let the sun set on yer wrath.* His da had preached those words many a time, but he'd not really understood their meaning 'til now. Aye, well, it was well past sunset. In fact, the wrath hadn't occurred until stars covered the sky. What proverb applied then?

Decision made, he spread a blanket across a layer of pine boughs that someone had supplied for just that purpose. Once the pallet suited him, he went to Isobel and crouched beside her but refrained from touching her. "Come, dear one. Grant me forgiveness by sleeping in my arms, aye?"

She lifted a sorrowful gaze to him. "I do love ye," she whispered. "And it is because of that love that I fear losing ye—not because I think ye're less a man or cowardly." Her unshed tears reflected in the firelight. "I canna bear losing ye again." She pulled in a hitching breath, then released it. "Not now." A tear slipped down her cheek. "Not ever."

He scooped her up into his arms and cradled her like the precious treasure she was. Carrying her to the pallet, he laid beside her, holding her as though he feared she'd disappear into the night like smoke rising from the fire.

She curled deeper into his embrace, burrowing hard against his chest. He smiled as she wrapped a fist in his shirt and brushed a quick kiss to his throat. Her soft, deep breathing soon assured him she had at last found her rest.

Watching the flames tickle through the logs, arms wrapped tight around his woman, Alasdair played out every possible scenario to free Isobel and Connor from their past. Every plan ended the same, leading him to a sobering conclusion. If the duke turned out to be as underhanded as Isobel swore, the man had to die. It was the only way.

CHAPTER THIRTEEN

"IN MY DAY—"

"Auntie!" Isobel looked at the old woman. "Not in front of Connor, aye?"

The failing of her plan still grated on her nerves, tainting her frame of mind against the brightness of the balmy day. She gritted her teeth. Last night's battle may have been lost, but she had not surrendered. Somehow, she would convince Alasdair of the error in his thinking.

"If it's about last night," the lad piped up, sitting taller in the saddle and brightening with a prideful smirk. "I already know what happened. Sutherland told me all about it."

This announcement gave Isobel pause. She turned in the saddle and scowled at Sutherland, threatening the grinning man with a scowl he'd be wise to heed. "Oh, he did, did he?"

Sutherland nodded and made a clicking sound to speed up his mount. "Aye. I did. Tell her what I told ye, lad."

"He said when ye cried out it was because ye twisted yer ankle whilst running from a wolf. Then when Alasdair hollered, it was because he was saving ye by scaring the beast away." Connor beamed. He pointed to a stain on her stocking just above the ankle of her boot. "Is it better this morning, Mama? Ye dinna seem to be favoring it."

"Aye, son. Much better," she assured him, ignoring Sutherland's snorting laughter as he rode on ahead and joined Ian and Alasdair.

"I should be riding wi' the men," Connor said in a serious tone.

"Aye, that ye should." She urged her horse forward and caught up with the men. "Which of ye fine gentlemen shall Connor share a saddle with on this last leg of our journey while I ride alongside Alasdair?" Their wary expressions filled her with satisfaction. *Good.* They'd do well to fear her.

Both Sutherland and Ian fell back and brought their steeds to a halt.

"The lad can ride with me," Sutherland invited with a smile.

"And when he tires of Sutherland's stench, he can ride with me," Ian said with a wink.

Isobel didn't miss Alasdair's low-throated groan. The man sounded like a frustrated stag in rut. "It appears yer men have turned tail and run. Left ye to face yer troubles alone, have they not?"

"I dinna blame them," he muttered. "Cowards. Both of them." He pointed toward the distant horizon as they continued on their way. Dusky, blue-gray peaks dominated the skyline, stretching toward the clouds. "Ben Nevis. *Tor Ruadh* lies a way up from the base of the mountainside, overlooking the glen."

She ignored his unnecessary chatter. She knew the Highlands as well as he did. "I nay yielded last night. I still maintain we be man and wife." His tightening hold on the reins brought her no small amount of satisfaction. *Good.* One way or another, she would make him see sense. She glanced back at the others riding a safe distance behind them. "I know Temsworth and the depths he'll sink to. Ye dinna know him."

Alasdair's eyes narrowed as he stared straight ahead. "We will never agree on this." He looked her way then, the wind whipping a loosened strand of dark hair across his face, making his glare even more devilish. "I will handle this as I see fit. For yer sake, and for Connor's. Understood?"

His bullish attitude both thrilled and enraged her. *Damn him and his power over her.* How she could both love and hate the man baffled her to no end. Last night, he made her scream with bliss, and this morning, the damned fool made her wish to scream in fury. She spurred her horse into a full gallop across the glen. *Damn Alasdair and his useless, noble morals. Damn him straight to hell and back.*

"Isobel!"

His shout reached her, barely audible over the wind whipping past her. She ignored him, riding on. She clung to her mount as the horse flew across the land and jumped across a small stream. Up ahead, at the base of the mountain, stood a smattering of thatch-roofed dwellings. The villagers were more than likely Clan MacCoinnich's crofters. The sight of the small community convinced her to slow. It was unwise to thunder into a village where she was unknown. *Unknown.* The word brought a smile as she lifted her face to the warm sunshine and brushed her windswept hair back in place. Unknown meant safety. Security. Peace.

Alasdair's mount pounded up beside her, then came to a halt with an abrupt bump against hers. "Woman!" he growled. He reached across, looped an arm around her waist, and dragged her over to his saddle.

She squirmed in his grasp and thumped a fist against him. "How dare ye!"

"How dare I?" He repeated, eyes storming as he jerked her more firmly in place. He locked an arm around her. "How dare ye take off like a demon escaped from hell and risk either breaking yer fool neck or being shot by MacCoinnich guards! Are ye daft?"

"No dafter than yerself." She shoved him, struggling to slide to the ground. "I demand ye return me to my horse this instant. I'm not a child, and I willna be treated like one."

He tightened his hold and turned his horse to face the rest of the group catching up to them. "Sutherland—place the boy on Isobel's mount. She'll be riding the rest of the way with me."

"I will not!"

"Aye." Alasdair yanked her back. "Ye will."

Sutherland followed orders without a word, his mouth clamped in a flat line but amusement dancing in his eyes.

Connor grinned and squared his shoulders, taking up the reins. "This be fine, indeed. Thank ye, Mama!"

"Aye, Connor. Be mindful, son." Isobel bounced backward with a hard jerk. The back of her head cracked against Alasdair's chin, and her elbow jabbed him solid in the stomach. If the man intended to treat her like a disobedient child, she would act it and make his journey miserable.

Sutherland and Ian took the lead as they followed the dirt path lacing through the center of the village and crossed the wooden bridge spanning a stream splitting the community in two. Connor and Yeva rode next in line, and Alasdair kept to the rear.

The man infuriated her even more by not reacting to anything she did other than clutching her tighter against his chest. As the men, women, and children from the dwellings gathered, she ceased her struggling. She needed allies among these people. People who would help her convince Alasdair to set aside his prideful need to confront the duke.

She was not a fool. He might say he'd send a messenger to file the papers, but deep in her heart, she knew he intended to find a way to challenge the man face to face. He might have the reputation of a calm, logical solicitor, but she knew better. Beneath his cool facade beat the heart of a raging warrior filled with bloodlust for revenge.

The grandeur of *Tor Ruadh* rose before them. The weathered, stone fortress looked impenetrable with its two guard towers, lethally defensive barbican, and iron portcullis ready to slam shut and bar entry to any intruder. Armed men scrutinized them from the battlements atop the skirting wall and arrow slits in the towers. Sutherland

MacCoinnich, brother to the chieftain, had taken the lead to ensure their entry was more a welcome than an interrogation.

Remembering what Alasdair had told her regarding the resurgence of Clan MacCoinnich, she craned her neck, staring up at the tall walls as they passed through the gate. "Ye laid siege and took this place when it belonged to Clan Neal? Just the seven of ye?"

"Aye." His tone curt, Alasdair halted his mount in the center of the bailey. Fierce scowl locked in place, he dismounted and held up his hands to her.

Isobel attempted to quell the fluttering of guilt her conscience thrust on her. She *had* treated him ill but rightly so. He should not be so stubborn. She took his hands and allowed him to lower her to the ground. "Can ye not smile? I dinna wish to meet everyone with a snarling beast at my side."

"I wouldna be a snarling beast if the woman I loved would stop behaving like a mule-headed, short-sighted—"

"Ye would be wise to stop right there, Alasdair Cameron," she warned.

His jaw, dark with several days' worth of beard, hardened, and his eyes became angry slits. Saints alive, such fierceness made him even more handsome.

She rested a hand on the center of his chest. "Forgive me," she said softly. "I should nay have been so cross and behaved so poorly. Can we not call a truce until we discuss it further? I'm certain we can work out a solution agreeable to us both."

He glared down at her, nostrils flaring like an enraged bull about to charge. His hands planted on his hips, he threw back his head and stared up at the sky, swelling with a deep breath, then snorting it out. The man was either praying for patience or trying to decide if he should turn her across his knee for a tanning.

Isobel folded her arms and lifted her chin. Let him try. She would never submit to any man's brutish behavior ever again. Her heart hitched, and her conscience kicked her. Alasdair would never mistreat her, and she wasn't being fair to even think such. Perhaps a return to kindness and wooing would bring him around. Auntie always said ye could catch more flies with honey than vinegar. "Please? I am sorry for treating ye so ill today."

He glared at her. "Ye know I love ye, aye?"

She smiled and moved to his side, sliding her arm through his. "Aye." She hugged him. "And I love ye as well."

"I like this place," Connor announced as he bounced up to them.

Yeva made her way across the cobblestones, scowling at their surroundings. "Stay close, Connor. This place very big. You get lost."

Isobel refrained from reminding Auntie that Hestlemoor had been even larger since the country estate sprawled across several counties. She pulled her son over and rested a hand on his shoulder. "Aye, lad. Stay close until we've been greeted proper and are settled in, aye?"

"Do my eyes deceive me?"

A familiar voice drew her attention to the steps in front of the entrance of the keep. A dark-haired man, braw and burly and just as handsome as Isobel remembered stood with a striking, red-haired woman at his side.

"Alexander MacCoinnich. It's good to see ye," she said as they joined the couple on the steps. Fond memories of happy times spent with Clan MacCoinnich flooded her with warm feelings.

Alexander's grin broadened, and he turned to the smiling lady at his side. "This is my wife, Catriona." He motioned toward Isobel. "Catriona, this is the Duchess of Temsworth."

Isobel flinched at the introduction. "Just Isobel. Please." She pulled Connor to stand in front of her and rested her hands atop his shoulders. "This is my son, Connor."

"Connor." Alexander gave the lad a polite nod, but Isobel didn't miss the inquisitive look he shot at Alasdair.

Connor retreated deeper into the folds of her skirts and remained silent.

Catriona bent to bring her smile even with the boy's wide-eyed stare. She tucked a coppery curl behind one ear, winked, then pointed to a pair of children waiting just inside the double doors of the keep. "My bairns, Willa and William, were about to visit the kitchen for some bread and jam. Would ye like to go with them, Connor?"

The lad didn't answer, just edged farther back against Isobel, and chewed on the side of his thumb.

"Ye like jam," Isobel urged with a gentle nudge to move him forward. "And they look to be about yer age, too."

The little boy, as coppery headed as his mother, stepped forward. "I be almost six. How old are ye?"

"Five," Connor whispered whilst still chewing on his finger.

"I be a minute older than him," said the little girl with curly locks as black as a raven's wing. She was the image of her father. She held out a chubby hand. "Come on. We gots fresh butter, jams, and honey. It be baking day, so the bread will be good and hot. Cook always gives us plenty. She likes having us underfoot. Says so all the time."

"Go on, son." Isobel gave him another gentle nudge. "It's rude to keep such a kindly host and hostess waiting."

With a worried look back at his mother, Connor took Willa's hand and trudged along behind her as she half led, half dragged the reluctant boy into the keep.

"He's not usually so shy," Isobel observed, a nagging reluctance to let her son face the fear of new friends and a new place all alone. Guilt gnawed at her for not keeping him at her side.

"They'll be thick as thieves in no time," Alexander said, then clapped a hand to Alasdair's shoulder. "Good to see ye, man. Sutherland says we have much to discuss."

"We do at that." Alasdair scooped up Isobel's hand and brushed a quick kiss to it. "Why dinna ye take Auntie inside with Catriona whilst Alexander and I talk. I'm sure ye're both weary."

She bit back that she refused to be dismissed like a child. *Nay.* She would grant him a mite more indulgence this time—at least until all in the keep knew her story. With a stiff nod to him, she took Auntie's arm, then and gave a genuine smile of gratitude to Catriona. "I thank ye for such a warm welcome. It means more to my family and me than ye could ever know."

"Think nothing of it." Catriona waved them forward. "I'm sure ye're tired and wouldna mind a crust of bread and jam yerselves—and maybe a bit of wine? Or whisky." She laughed. "Or both." She leaned closer as they made their way into the keep. "We'll let the men fill themselves with their own importance and have their talk whilst we come up with a better plan for whatever's troubling ye, aye?"

"I do have a plan," Isobel confessed.

They entered the great hall and made their way to a circling of pillowed chairs flanking a hearth with just enough fire to knock the chill and dampness from the high-ceilinged room. Catriona's manner put her to ease. The woman wore kindness and thoughtfulness like a regal mantle. Isobel felt an immediate trust for her. She released a dismal sigh as she sank into one of the chairs. "I fear convincing Alasdair to heed my plan is the problem."

Catriona drew the attention of one of the young, white-capped lasses wiping down the row of long tables running down the center of the room. "Please fetch us some hot broth, wine, and whisky, aye? Thank ye, Anne."

The girl bobbed a curtsy, then scurried toward the back archway to the left of the room.

"Oh, Anne!" Catriona called out. "Forgive me. Before ye tear off to the kitchen, would ye run to the solar and fetch Gretna and Mercy? I'm sure they'd love to meet our guests, too."

"Aye, m'lady." Anne switched directions, heading to the stone staircase to the right of the chieftain's table at the head of the room.

Catriona seated herself opposite Isobel and Yeva. "Mercy is Graham's wife, and Gretna is her companion."

Companion? How odd. Especially here in the Highlands. Of course, Alasdair had said Mercy was goddaughter to the king. Perhaps, since she ranked high in the peerage, she had brought her ways to Scotland. The thought made her uneasy. England's peerage had brought her nothing but danger and pain.

Not wishing to seem rude by remaining silent overlong, she forced a smile. "How is Graham? I was pleased to learn that all the MacCoinnich brothers had survived the sickness that wiped out so many."

"Graham is well. Proud father to wee Ramsay and another bairn soon to join us. Full moon's a coming." Catriona rested her hand on the slight swell of her stomach that the folds of her loose overdress had hidden before. "Alexander and I will also be blessed with another child before winter sets in." Her bubbling laughter echoed through the hall. "Alexander prays it's not another set of twins."

A pang of longing and a twinge of jealousy twitched through Isobel. She brushed aside the feelings. "Congratulations! I'm so pleased *Tor Ruadh* is bursting at the seams with blessings."

Soft murmuring accompanied by a steady tapping from the direction of the staircase, drew her attention. A curvy young lass with hair as shiny and bright as newly forged copper walked beside a statuesque woman of about the same age, but that's where the resemblance stopped.

Heavily pregnant, the tall lass, dark-haired and possessing a serene beauty, walked with an ornate staff, carved and painted like a work of art. As Isobel studied the pair, she realized the woman didn't use the staff as a means of support or decoration but rather as a way to know where to place her steps. The lady was blind.

Her cane lightly brushed against the tables and benches. Head held high and free hand resting on the large mound of her rounded stomach, she gracefully navigated the room. The lass at her side, occasionally steered her by the arm whenever the staff happened to miss an obstacle.

Catriona rose as the pair reached the sitting area. "Gretna, Mercy, this is her grace, the Duchess of Temsworth, and her Aunt Yeva. Yer Grace, this is my cousin, Gretna Neal, and my sister-in-law, Graham's wife, Lady Mercy."

Gretna, the lass with the coppery hair even the Goddess Brid would envy, rushed forward, curtsied, then gave a friendly squeeze to both Isobel and Auntie's hands. "A pleasure to meet ye both. Welcome to *Tor Ruadh*."

"Thank ye," murmured Isobel, wishing she had managed to escape her title as she had escaped the duke. Before she could utter another word, Lady Mercy responded with a dignified curtsy, but her smile was most definitely strained. A leeriness tightened across her face. "Your Grace."

A heaviness settled in Isobel's heart. Graham's wife knew about Temsworth. She could see it in her face. "Please, I must insist, everyone call me Isobel. I finally escaped the tyrant I was forced to wed, and I'd just as soon return to my maiden name, Isobel Mac-Naughton."

Lady Mercy's tensed demeanor melted away. With assistance from Gretna, she found Isobel's hand and gave it a squeeze. "It is truly my pleasure to meet you, Isobel—and please, call me Mercy. I, too, have cast aside my title. My father was the Duke of Edsbury. I believe he and your husband traveled in the same circles, so I am more than glad you were able to escape such a dark world."

"Yer words are a balm to my ears," Isobel said as she returned to her seat, admiring the ease with which Mercy moved among the chairs, selected one, and lowered herself into the cushions with a weary huff and a rubbing of her swollen middle.

"She can see light and dark. Sometimes even colors and shapes if the day is bright enough," Catriona said with an understanding smile.

"Forgive me. I didna mean to stare." Isobel flinched as Auntie pinched the tender skin under her arm. The age-old reprimand to mind her manners stung just as badly now as it had when she was a lass.

Gretna giggled as she rose and inspected the overflowing tray of treats Anne had set on a nearby table. "My mam used to pinch my arm when she felt I wasna behaving proper." She poured steaming cups of broth and passed them among the ladies. "And I must admit, I've done the same to my wee'uns." She glanced at Isobel as she filled a small plate with dried fruit and bits of cheese. "If ye dinna mind me asking, do ye have any children?"

"Aye. A son. Connor." Isobel accepted the cup of broth but waved aside the plate of food. She couldn't eat. Too much was going on, and too much was at risk.

"Were you able to get him away from the duke?" Mercy asked as she balanced her cup on the ledge of her rounded stomach.

"Aye." Isobel leaned forward and slid her drink to the low wooden table in front of her. She reached out and squeezed Auntie's hand before continuing. "Connor, Auntie Yeva, and I escaped to Edinburgh but then found ourselves in dire straits." She wouldn't mention all the details. The women seemed understanding enough, but she didn't wish to strain the delicate weave of these newfound friendships with information about the brothel.

"What happened?" Catriona asked. Kindness and genuine concern flowed from her.

"Alasdair saved us." Isobel smiled, unable to stop joyful tears as they spilled over. "I had thought him dead. Been told that many a time. But he found me in Edinburgh, and now I have hope for a new life." She swiped at the tears. "Forgive me."

"Nothing to forgive, lass," Gretna soothed, holding out a glass of port. "Here. Ye need this more than broth."

"Ye are too kind. All of ye." She accepted it and took a quick sip.

"We were rescued by our men, too," Catriona said with a nod

toward Mercy. "We understand."

"That we do," Mercy said, lifting her cup in a toast. She turned her head as though searching. "Gretna, would you be so kind as to fix me a plate overflowing with food? I fear I'm ravenous…again."

"Allow me," Isobel said. She handed her port to Auntie, knowing full well the feisty old woman would empty the glass before she returned to her seat.

"While ye're at that," Catriona said and settled more comfortably back in her chair. "Ye said ye already had a plan but couldna get Alasdair to see sense. Tell us. Maybe, we can help."

"Alasdair plans to file divorce papers for me. He swears he'll use a messenger to contact the duke, but I know better." She selected a bit of each treat from the tray. An expectant mother needed plentiful sustenance. "I canna get him to understand that the duke will stop at nothing. I fear for Alasdair's life." She carried the overflowing plate to Mercy and placed it in her hands. "This may shock all of ye, but I told Alasdair we could live as man and wife without the divorce." She stood in the center of the group, praying they'd agree. "Ten years ago, before my father sold me to Temsworth, Alasdair and I pledged our troth in a cave on the Isle of Skye. That makes us husband and wife and my marriage to Temsworth void." She swallowed hard and stared at her feet. She couldn't bear facing these women and what their eyes might show. "Since we had no witnesses, Alasdair insists on handling this terrible mess his way. I fear he'll be lost to me if he does so—dead for certain this time."

Catriona rose and took hold of Isobel's hands; Gretna did the same.

"What is happening?" Mercy asked, carefully setting her plate on the seat beside her.

"Join us," Gretna answered. "Three paces forward. Ye canna miss us."

Mercy smiled as she stood and moved forward, holding out both hands. "We shall help you any way we can."

"Aye," Catriona said. "Ye're not alone in this, Isobel. We understand fully and will do whatever we can to help."

"Yes," Mercy said as she found their hands and rested hers atop them. "Men are slaves to their fury. It is our duty to be the voices of reason."

"Aye," Gretna said. "And to shake them 'til their teeth rattle when they dinna listen to us."

Overwhelmed by their unquestioned acceptance, a happy sob escaped her as Auntie pushed her way in and latched her hands onto the pile.

"We make them listen," the wise elder stated with a jerking nod.

Catriona nodded, then bellowed, "Anne!"

"Aye, m'lady?"

"Drams all around, and pour a generous one for yerself as well."

"Aye, m'lady," Anne said and hurried to comply.

CHAPTER FOURTEEN

THE GARDEN BEHIND the keep teemed with children. Their excited squeals and laughter filled the air as they raced after each other among the mazes of trees, bushes, and squared off plots of freshly turned earth planted with herbs and vegetables. Auntie Yeva sat on a bench in the middle of the fray, focused on a pile of mending in her lap as she minded the children.

Alasdair leaned against the newly built stone archway of the covered walkway, amused by the bairns' boisterous game of seize the castle. *Aye.* They'd all be fine warriors someday. He rubbed his back against the rough edge of the chiseled wall, scratching an itch he couldn't reach. The fortified walkway hemmed in the garden from the rest of the keep's busy courtyard, a futile attempt at keeping the young ones penned.

Willa's furious shriek as she charged at the boys with wooden sword raised gave him a smile but also weighed heavy on his heart. The wee lass reminded him of Isobel when they had played together all those years ago. He longed for the ten years wasted all because of fate's cruelty. His own wee ones might have been at play today if not for that lost time. He shook away the thought. 'Twas futile to think of such. The past could neither be changed nor recovered.

"Willa may be the only girl, but I believe she'll be the fiercest of them all." Isobel appeared at his side, wiping her hands on her apron.

"She reminds me of ye. The way ye used to boss us about whilst we played." Alasdair pulled her close and kissed her temple. He closed his eyes and breathed in her scent, realizing at once that to do so was a mistake. His body roared to life, indignant and suffering because he'd not relented and returned to her bed since they had arrived at *Tor Ruadh*.

He kissed her again, then shifted away. "Ye smell of lavender and rosemary," he said with a slight cough as he yanked at the drape of his kilt. She didn't need any further proof of the power she held over him. He sniffed again, noticing the apron around her waist. "Sweet butter and honey, too. What have ye been about? Have ye treats for me, perhaps?" His stomach growled at the prospect.

"Aye, I have treats." She gave him a teasing look and stepped closer. "The ladies and I have been busy making soaps and lotions," she informed him in a seductive whisper. "If ye'd care to join me in a walk down to the stream beside the caves, I'd be more than happy to give ye a hearty sampling." She took hold of his shoulder and leaned in until her breasts pressed against him. Her breath tickled across his ear. "We could wash each other like husbands and wives are known to do. Think about it."

Alasdair clenched his teeth to keep from groaning. *Nay*. He'd sworn he would not lie with her again until she was his wife for true. It wouldn't be fair to do such here at the keep. Not with so many people about. He refused to sully his dear one's good name. "Once we are husband and wife, legally, I shall hold ye to that, *mo chridhe*."

Her eyes narrowed, and he could tell by the set of her jaw that if she had young Willa's wooden sword, she would most certainly club him with it. She stepped away, putting an arm's length of distance between them. "Is there any word on yer futile attempt to address Temsworth with civility? Ye do realize doing such will just reveal that ye are now a part of my escape? He will use that to his advantage."

The garden gate to the left of them squeaked, then swung shut with a clatter, interrupting Isobel's tirade and announcing the arrival of company. Alasdair turned, thankful for the reprieve. Whilst he admired her stubbornness, the woman needed to leave off and accept his decision to handle the matter as he saw fit. His spirits perked as he laid eyes on the newcomer to the garden. "Thomas Abernathy."

The short man had a pair of wire-rimmed spectacles pinched in one hand, and a thick parchment packet clenched in the other, and he hurried across the garden toward them. Perspiration shone on his pale, wrinkled forehead as he balanced his glasses on the bridge of his nose and squinted through them as though in pain. "Master Cameron. At last."

A sense of doom filled Alasdair. Thomas Abernathy was not the sort of man to travel far from the comforts of London, Edinburgh, or anywhere else that could not be accessed via enclosed carriage. He feared his own shadow and was besieged with sneezing fits at the slightest hint of a blooming flower, and had been known to walk for days to avoid riding a horse. His being at *Tor Ruadh* was either very good or very bad, and Alasdair feared it to be the latter. "I would say I'm pleased to see ye, Thomas, but I fear ye bear bad news."

Thomas bobbed his weak chin in rapid agreement. "Yer fears be valid, sir." He squinted in Isobel's direction, then made a prim, jerking bow. "Forgive me, m'lady. I didna see ye there. Thomas Abernathy, at yer service."

Alasdair stepped forward, instinctively shielding Isobel from whatever ill tidings Thomas bore. "This is Isobel, the *former* Duchess of Temsworth."

Thomas's watery eyes flared. "I s-see." He jerked his gaze back to Alasdair. "Uhm...perhaps, we might speak in private, sir?" He forced a smile and made another stiff attempt at a polite bow in Isobel's direction. "I wouldna wish to upset Her Grace."

"*Her Grace,*" Isobel said as she stepped around Alasdair and took a stance at his side. "Is directly involved in whatever tidings ye bear, and I would hear them whether they're upsetting or not." She straightened her shoulders. "I promise ye, sir, I can handle whatever ye say."

The man clamped his mouth shut and returned his attention to Alasdair.

Alasdair nodded. "Go ahead, man. What news have ye?"

Again, Thomas straightened his spectacles more firmly on the bridge of his nose. He unfolded the parchment and held it out to Alasdair, the paper rattling in his trembling hands. "As of the date on this notice, ye have been formally charged with the abduction of Her Grace, her son, and aunt. There are also whispers of forthcoming charges of treason due to the duke's fabrication of yer involvement in organizing another Jacobite uprising against the crown. Those charges, however, have not been fully realized nor placed as yet. Yer estate in Edinburgh has been seized, and the courts have suspended yer right to represent anyone as a solicitor in Scotland or England. Clans Mackenzie and MacCoinnich have been advised to find a suitable replacement to handle their affairs." He gave a half-hearted shrug and retreated a step. "And to protect my office, I have been advised to sever any connections with ye, as well."

Alasdair ignored Isobel's sharp intake of breath. She squeezed his forearm and moved in closer, peering around him at the paper. He scanned the notice, reading down the list of accusations and lies spelled out in creative detail. He had expected such, prayed against it for Isobel's sake, but expected it just the same. "Any word from the palace? Was Lady Mercy's letter delivered to the king?"

Thomas nodded. "Aye. I am afraid so, sir." He pulled a small paper from an inner pocket of his jacket. The note was folded in two and bore the king's seal, but the wax imprint of His Majesty's insignia was clearly broken. "Forgive me, but I felt it prudent to read the missive before I set off on my journey here. I wished t'be fully informed, ye understand."

Alasdair hurried to open the paper and read the words scrawled in what he could only assume was the king's own hand. The flowery writing resembled every example of His Majesty's signature Alasdair had ever seen. Mercy would know for certain, but Alasdair felt the message was legitimate.

"What does it say?" Isobel leaned even closer, stretching to see the contents.

"He refuses to become *embroiled* in a dispute between a Scot and a high-ranking member of court." Alasdair passed the paper to Isobel. He had hoped for better. "He sends his regrets to Lady Mercy but unquestionably refuses."

"It is said His Majesty is not the same man since the death of Queen Mary four years ago." Thomas shrugged again and shook his head. "It appears the late queen nurtured the king's ability for compassion, and without her, he has all but lost his sensitivities to anyone's plights but his own."

"And now ye are a wanted man because of me." Isobel shoved the paper back into his hands, righteous fire flashing in her eyes. "I told ye this would happen." Her voice broke as she yanked her apron off, balled it up, and shook it at him. "What is yer plan now, Alasdair? Which country do ye think will give us sanctuary since we'll not be safe anywhere in Scotland or England?"

"I have not been charged with treason yet," he said. "Just kidnapping." He had expected worse, although he had hoped for more from the king.

He had drawn first blood by filing the divorce papers and demanding full and unequivocal custody of Connor. This was but the first minor skirmish in the war to free Isobel and the lad. He took both the note from the king and the notice of the formal charges and tucked them inside his waistcoat. With a grateful resignation, he clapped a hand on Thomas's shoulder. "I thank ye for taking the risk of bringing me the news."

"I could nay entrust it to anyone else, sir. I feared they'd reveal where ye were." He nodded toward the papers peeping out of Alasdair's clothing. "The reward being offered is quite substantial. Greed causes folk to do many a terrible thing." His perspiring brow creased with a worried scowl, and he stole another nervous glance at Isobel. "And as far as the divorce filing…"

"Aye?" Alasdair wrapped an arm around Isobel's waist and steadied her.

"The duke states he will agree to yer terms, as well as drop all charges against ye, if ye return his son to him by Whitsun—in other words, a fortnight from now."

Isobel's trembling vibrated into Alasdair, stirring his rage even more. He gritted his teeth, struggling to remain logical. "That is not acceptable. My filing clearly stated the duke was to rescind all ties to the boy on the grounds of cruelty. Both the boy and mother fully relinquish any and all inheritance and titles if he agrees to such."

Thomas shook his head as he tucked his glasses into his breast pocket. "He doesna agree to do so and states he never will. Every public house I entered is abuzz with betting on who shall kill ye first. The Brits by stretching yer neck or the duke by hunting ye down and using whatever method tickles his fancy at the time."

"The bastards will find I'm not such an easy kill." He hugged Isobel tighter, forcing another reassuring smile for her benefit. "'Twill be all right, love. I expected this." He turned back to the solicitor. "Again. I thank ye for the risk ye took in coming here."

Thomas gave a sad dip of his chin, then resettled his jacket with a fidgeting tug. "I be off to Fort William now. That is where I told everyone I was headed." He jerked a thumb back toward the main courtyard. "Brought some fluffed-up papers to file with the commander's office. Silly notices and such to verify the trip." He yanked at his jacket again and stood taller. "Please know ye shall both be in my prayers. I bid ye Godspeed and the Almighty's blessings in this battle."

Alasdair took hold of the man's forearm and clapped his other hand on the man's thin shoulder. "God watch over ye and protect ye as well, man. Safe travels to ye."

Thomas nodded, gave Isobel a formal bow, then turned and scurried back the way he had come.

Alasdair watched him go, regret knotting his gut at involving the poor solicitor in this deadly game.

"France."

He turned to Isobel, the sight of her tear-filled eyes and clenched jaw filling him with even more angry determination. "What?"

"We shall go to France." Her voice broke as she nodded. "Aye. France should be safe enough. As far as I know, Temsworth has no connections there."

"I refuse to allow that bastard to chase me from my homeland." He braced himself. It was time to advise Isobel of the next step in this treacherous gauntlet, and she wasn't going to like it. "Sutherland has agreed to take ye, Yeva, and Connor to the Mackenzies at Cape Wrath. Matheson, the chieftain there, expects ye and assures yer safety. It's more remote, and the duke willna expect ye to seek sanctuary that far north. Nor will the British."

He fully expected Lord Crestshire, accompanied by his guard, to arrive any day at *Tor Ruadh* to search the place. Crestshire had warned him that if they ever named Alasdair as guilty, the man would have to follow orders and take him in. Charges now explicitly named him. He felt sure Crestshire would stall as long as possible to give him time to escape, but he had no idea how long that might be. He had to leave at once and put his plan into play.

"Why Sutherland?" Isobel's glare cut through him. "Why not yerself?"

"Ian and I shall travel south." He waited for the gist of his statement to sink in, girding himself for the forthcoming battle sure to ensue.

"Ye mean to challenge him." She moved until they stood toe to toe. "This is what ye've planned all along. A face to face challenge. A duel." She bared her teeth, hissing out the accusation. "Isn't it? Isn't that what ye mean?"

"It's high time for the man to reap what he has sown."

She thumped her fist against his chest. "Ye are a damned fool, Alasdair! Ye canna do this!" She opened her hand and slammed it into him. "If by some miraculous blessing from God above, ye do succeed in killing the devil, they'll hunt ye down and hang ye for murder. Even though he be a despicable man, the courts will never side with a Scot. Ye know that as well as I." She grabbed hold of his jacket lapels and did her best to shake him, tears streaming down her face. "Why would ye do this? Why do ye insist on leaving me alone when we've just now found each other after all this time?" She shook her head, trembling with silent sobs as she crumpled against him. "I beg ye—dinna do this. Please. If ye have a scrap of love left for me, please, dinna do this. We can start anew in France."

He wrapped his arms around her, cradling her as though she were an overwrought child. "It is because I love ye that I must do this, *a thasgaidh*."

"Ye call me *my darling*, yet ye insist on making me a lonely widow." She shook in his arms. "How could ye be so cruel? I can bear anything in this world, but I canna bear losing ye. Not again."

He held her tighter. "This is not the first time I've hunted down a wretch and ousted them from this world. I know what I'm doing. Ye have but to trust me, aye?" Would that he could shield her from her fears, but it had to be done. They would never know peace as long as the duke lived.

She lifted her head, flattening both hands against his chest as she pierced him with a teary-eyed stare. "Then at least give me yer child first."

"What?" Alasdair blinked and searched her face for affirmation of her meaning.

"Give me yer child."

"Isobel—"

"At least if I lose ye, I'll have yer child to console me." She stared at him. Defiant. Determined. Unyielding. "If ye love me, truly love me with all yer heart, ye willna deny me this small comfort."

Her request astounded him as well as touched his heart. A bairn. His bairn. With the woman he'd always loved. If only he could fulfill her request so easily. He cradled her face in one hand, brushing his thumb across the shimmering trails of her tears. "I canna delay my leaving for the time it might take to seed a bairn, my dearest love. I must leave tonight—or by morn at the latest."

"Then lay with me before ye go," she begged in a hitching whisper. "At least attempt to give me yer child one last time before I lose ye forever."

"Ye'll nay lose me, love. I swear it." Alasdair wished he could make her understand. "Trust me, *mo chridhe*, believe in me." He brushed a kiss across each of her teary eyes. "Dinna weep anymore. Hear me when I say, all will be well."

"Give me yer child, and I will try," she said in a desperate whisper. "Please. Cease making me beg."

Her words cut him. If only she would believe him capable of making their dream real. But she wouldn't. Her eyes never lied. Isobel had resigned herself to losing everything.

Very well. So be it.

He took her hand and led her to the back stair. Neither of them spoke as they climbed to the suite of rooms Isobel shared with Yeva and Connor. Alasdair paused in the sitting room, unsure which of the doors led to her bedchamber.

Without a word, she led him through the door farthest to the left. She closed it behind them, threw the bolt, and even lowered the beam, settling the bar firmly across it. Head bowed, she went still, both hands resting atop it. "I beg ye not to leave me, Alasdair. Please. Let us make our escape to France. Together. Aunty speaks French, and Connor will learn soon enough."

"A life of running is no life at all." Alasdair removed his waistcoat and tossed it across the cushioned bench at the foot of the bed. "I intend to free us, love. They will not deter me."

"Verra well." Fingers flying, she freed her bodice of its ties and shrugged the garment to the floor. The embroidered stomacher fell with it. Her skirt came next, followed by the padded roll tied just above her hips. She bent and unlaced her boots, then kicked them aside. Her hands stilled as she straightened, standing in nothing but her chemise and stockings, staring at him with such despair, it killed him.

"Isobel...please trust me."

She shook her head. "I fear I cannot. Demons stole ye from me once, and now they've come to steal ye from me again." She slid her chemise off over her head, then made to remove her stockings.

The sight of her stole his breath. Her fierce beauty owned him. He rushed to stop her, dropping to his knees at her feet. "Then let me worship ye as ye deserve."

She stared down at him, tears abated, but her dark lashes and cheeks were still wet. She trailed her fingers along his jawline, then buried them in his hair. With a shuddering sigh, she stepped closer and closed her eyes.

Brushing his lips across the silk of her thighs, he untied the ribbons above each of her knees while reveling in her maddening scent. He pushed her stockings down to her ankles and slid his palms up the backs of her legs. Holding her steady, a groan escaped him as he kneaded her fine, round arse. She scrubbed her feet together and rid herself of the hosiery. He couldn't wait any longer. He needed to taste her, hungered for the sound of her cries as she found her pleasure.

She fisted her hands in his hair, pulling him harder into the juncture between her thighs. With a gentle nudge, he pushed her legs farther apart, diving deeper. The longer he quenched his thirst for what only she could provide, the more she swayed from side to side, her legs trembling.

Alasdair lowered her to the floor, thankful for the tapestry carpet beneath them. As he stretched across her and sated his need for her kisses, she yanked his tunic upward. He rose long enough to rip off his shirt and toss belt and kilt aside. He covered her with his body again, flinching with an appreciative groan as she reached down between them, wrapped her fingers around the base of his cock, and pulled hard on the length of it.

"Take me," she ordered, guiding him as she arched to meet him.

"As ye wish." He plunged inside, cradling her shoulders as he withdrew and dove back in again and again.

She met him thrust for thrust, raking her nails down his back and digging them into his buttocks as she urged him to pound harder. Head thrown back, body flexing, she cried out. Her blissful wetness clutched around him.

He remained buried and held fast, determined to bring her more pleasure before spilling himself inside. As her throes calmed, he took up the dance again, holding her steady as he hammered harder and brought her to her release twice more.

Isobel bucked beneath him, hugging him with her legs as she cried out again. Her pounding rhythm as she scratched her fingernails down his sides drove him insane. He could delay no longer. A rumbling roar tore from him as he drove into her, his bollocks clenching as he emptied inside her. Somewhere deep within the ecstatic daze, he committed the feel of her pounding heart forever in his memories. This was how they were meant to be. One instead of two.

"I love ye," he rasped as soon as he could draw a steady breath. "Ye are my heart and soul forevermore."

"And I love ye more," she whispered against his cheek, her gasping breaths tickling his jaw. "Please, dinna leave me. I beg ye."

"I must, Isobel." Reluctantly, he rolled to the side, then stretched out on his back beside her. "I do it for us. For Connor. For our future." He turned his head and watched her, willing her to understand.

She stared up at the ceiling. Renewed tears, silent tears, seeped from the corners of her eyes. She laced her fingers together and slid them across her stomach, settling them over her womb. "Then give me a child to ease my suffering when ye are lost to me."

He blew out a desolate sigh. "I will stay with ye until the candle burns out and pray with all my heart that a bairn takes seed from our loving." He raised up, propping on an elbow as he brushed aside a tear from her temple before it disappeared into her curls. "But then, I must go, aye?"

"Aye," she whispered as she reached out and ran a finger down the center of his chest and into the thatch of dark hair swirling across his belly.

With a gentle shove, she pushed him to his back and straddled him. She rested her head atop his chest. As she lay there, she smoothed her hands up and down his sides and clenched her thighs tight around him, moving with a gentle rocking until he hardened once more. She rose and slid down his shaft, seating him deep inside her. "I love ye," she said as she closed her eyes and increased the speed of her ride.

Alasdair gripped her by the waist, rising to thrust deeper with every rock of her hips. "I love ye in this life and the next," he groaned. Eyes closed, he forced the melancholy of his leaving aside and concentrated on planting a small part of himself deep inside this woman he loved more than life itself.

CHAPTER FIFTEEN

I SOBEL PRESSED A hand to her middle, praying God had blessed her with a child as the infuriating, bullheaded man she loved rode out the gate.

"Keep him safe. I beg ye," she whispered, thankful for the brightness of the moonlit night. She pulled her *arisaid* close, breathing in his scent lingering in its folds. She had wrapped it around him earlier as he dozed, knowing it would bring her small comfort, but she cherished it just the same. It strengthened her, brought him close.

"Best get some sleep if ye can, m'lady. We leave at first light." Sutherland stood beside her, watching Alasdair and Ian ride away.

"I would just as soon leave now." She tore her gaze away from the men before they disappeared past the first rise in the hilly landscape of the glen. Ill luck, it was, to watch a loved one's leaving 'til they rode out of view. It dared the fates to prevent their return. "Both Connor and Auntie have slept a bit. They'll be fine. All we must do is wake them."

"Ye dinna need more time to gather yer things?" Sutherland offered his arm as they strolled across the curtain wall toward the stone steps leading down to the bailey.

"I feel certain Auntie has us ready. I warned her earlier." She swallowed hard, eyes gritty and throat sore from all the tears she had shed.

And all in vain. Nothing had swayed Alasdair. Her headstrong warrior was damned and determined to mete out justice, whether it meant his own demise or not.

As they descended the steps, Sutherland nodded. "Verra well then. I shall see to the horses and have them waiting in the courtyard whilst ye gather the others." His mouth tightened as he cast a sideways glance at her. "Ye dinna wish to wait 'til morning so ye might bid everyone farewell? They care about ye, m'lady. Care about yer plight."

"Farewells are not one of my strengths." She clutched her wrap, fighting the forlorn sense of loss about to crush her. "I wrote out notes while Alasdair slept. One for each of them." At least she'd managed to delay his leaving 'til well after the candle had snuffed itself out. They'd loved away the day, and exhaustion had briefly closed his eyes. But when the moon rose, he awoke, and she lost him.

"I understand," Sutherland said quietly.

She released his arm as they rounded the corner of the keep. Auntie Yeva and Connor stood in the courtyard between the main building and the stable, bundles clutched in their arms.

"I knew you would want to leave as soon as he left," Auntie explained. "We are ready."

Connor yawned, then resettled his bundle against his chest. "I get my own horse, aye?"

"Aye, lad." Sutherland held out a hand. "Come. It'll take us no time to saddle him."

Auntie hitched her way over to Isobel's side. "You know this place we go to? Know of the people? Their ways?"

Isobel shook her head. "All I know is it's the northernmost tip of Scotland, and they are expecting us."

"Hmpf." Her aunt pursed her lips, scowling at the stable. "I did not have time to read the stars. Not sure about this journey without being prepared."

"At this point, I would just as soon not know, Auntie." Isobel took one of the bundles from her and stepped forward as Sutherland led a horse to stand in front of her.

"Needless to say, we shall skirt Fort William and get as far beyond it as we can before daylight." Sutherland helped her mount.

"We shall travel until ye decide to stop. Alasdair has left us at yer mercy." She settled into the saddle and took up the reins as she waited for the others. She had always liked Sutherland, but at the moment, he felt more like a guard than a friend.

"Aye. That he did." Sutherland gave a resigned groan as he mounted his horse. He took the lead, and they exited *Tor Ruadh*, turning east to head higher up the mountain. "Stay close, and call out if ye see anything concerning, aye?"

"Like what?" Connor asked.

"Soldiers. Strangers. Wild animals." Sutherland scowled at the surrounding landscape. "Anything ye fear could cause us trouble."

Isobel knew her son. Sutherland would regret arming his imagination with such possibilities. She straightened in the saddle, a desolate weariness and complete loss of caring rooting deep in her soul. She warred with the dark feeling. There was still her son to protect. *And hopefully, another*, she silently added.

"Connor—keep yer horse beside Sutherland's, aye?" She and Auntie rode close behind, the terrain growing more treacherous as they climbed the mountain and accessed one of the passes. "And hang on tight to the saddle as the land grows steeper."

Connor rode well for a lad, sat a horse like one who had ridden for years. But he looked so small on his horse.

Isobel relaxed somewhat as they reached the pass, and the land leveled out. Crags and cliffs rose high on either side of them, shading the trail from the light of the moon. Their pace slowed as they entrusted the horses with finding the way.

They rode for what felt like hours. Sutherland finally took the reins of Connor's horse and tied it to his, as the boy draped himself across the beast's neck and slept. Isobel kept her gaze locked on her son. If he slid out of the saddle, he'd surely break his neck. They kept well east of Fort William, and Isobel was relieved when Sutherland held up his hand to stop for a rest along the shores of Loch Lochy.

Dawn's light glittered across the rippling waters. The sight increased her weariness. She yawned as she squatted behind a cluster of bushes to relieve herself, then blinked against the tired, scratchiness of her eyes. Best get used to the feeling. According to Sutherland, it would take them near a week to reach Cape Wrath. Once she finished, she joined the others.

Sutherland and Connor stood at the water's edge. Auntie knelt beside it, wetting her face and wiping it dry with the extra kerchief she always kept tucked in her sleeve. Isobel held out a hand to Sutherland. "Give me yer pistol. Connor and I shall stand watch whilst Auntie and ye take yer rest."

Sutherland stared at her as if she'd lost her senses. "It is I who is to protect ye, m'lady."

"Ye canna remain alert if ye dinna sleep at least a few hours between here and Wrath." She pointed at the gun stuck in his belt. "I'm as good a shot as I ever was, and since Connor is quite refreshed from his nap, I assure ye, I willna sleep until ye relieve me. My son will keep me awake."

Connor bobbed his head, then lobbed a stone across the water. "I shall help Mama stand guard and keep ye all safe. Promise."

Auntie had already curled up on a grassy area at the base of a tree. Sutherland scowled at the land, scanning their surroundings with a critical eye. "It appears quiet enough."

"It will be fine." Isobel held her hand higher. "I promise to wake ye in a few hours."

"I dinna like this," Sutherland said as he grudgingly handed over his pistol. He turned in a circle, checking the area one last time. "Call out at the sight of anything, aye? Absolutely anything."

"Aye." She nodded.

His scowl twitched a notch tighter, then Sutherland joined Auntie at the base of the tree. He sat beside her and folded his arms across his chest.

"Are ye not going to lie down?" Connor called out.

Sutherland shooed away the boy's concern and leaned more comfortably against the trunk and closed his eyes. "I be fine. Go help yer mother. It be a braw day for walking the shoreline."

"Can we, Mama?"

"Aye, lad, come along." Isobel hurried him forward. Poor Sutherland would get no rest if she didn't get the child out of earshot.

The lad found a suitable walking stick of driftwood. He stabbed the mud, overturned rocks, and poked any dead fish they passed as they strolled along. Isobel trailed along behind him.

The shoreline rose, then dipped low behind an embankment riddled with washed-out holes, ridges, and piles of rocks. She cast a casual glance around now and then. The loch held a comforting quiet she could not enjoy without Alasdair at her side.

She hurried on as Connor disappeared around a bend. Peaceful or not, she didn't want the boy out sight. "Connor! Slow down, aye? Stay where I can see ye."

He didn't answer. Only the sound of sliding rocks and the endless shushing of the waves against the shore filled the air.

"Connor?" She silently cursed the rocks slowing her down as she scrambled around an uprooted tree. Her heart beat faster. "Answer me, son."

A strong hand clamped around her wrist and snapped the pistol out of her hand. The man rose from the shadows behind the fallen tree like a wraith rising from the grave. "Not a word, or yer son will be the worse for it." The burly fiend, all in black from his greasy hair down to the tips of his boots, twisted her arm around to her back and shoved her high enough over the embankment where she could see three more men standing over Sutherland and Auntie.

"Where is my son? What have ye done with him?" She fought to turn and search the shoreline.

"The young marquess?" the blackguard asked as he twisted her arm harder, sending an excruciating burn through her shoulder. "Why…we done trussed the lad up and thrown him o'er a saddle, o' course."

With a shove of his knee into the small of her back, the man knocked her to her knees, then yanked her back to her feet. "His da paid us good money in advance. Good money." He let out a cruel laugh. He knotted a fist in her hair and jerked her around to face him. "Said he'd pay us even more when we return the boy alive." He wheezed just inches from her face, the stench of his breath nearly gagging her as his spittle showered across her. "And promised extra coin for us to kill ye and the old witch. Told us to end ye slow and ugly. Said he'd pay extra for proof ye suffered before ye left this world."

She had to save Connor or die trying. With a feigned cry, she closed her eyes and went limp, sagging to the ground. Her free hand hit a good-sized shard of rock, and she surged upward with the jagged edge and smashed the brute's face.

The lout roared with pain, letting loose of her arm. Yanking her skirts out of the way, she scrambled back to where she had lost the gun. She found the pistol, dropped to her stomach, took aim, and fired.

"Kill them!" yelled the enraged kidnapper, blood streaming from the cut on his face. He stumbled forward, one hand clamped to his upper arm. "Kill every last one of'm! Now!"

Isobel pushed herself to her feet, then lobbed the spent pistol at the vile devil's head. Without looking back, she clawed her way up the embankment. Spotting another rock, she scooped up the fist-sized stone, turned, and fired it at the man as he gave chase. Movement to the left caught her eye. The horses. The bastard had said they'd already tied Connor to one. Clutching her skirts up to her knees, she raced across the rough landscape. "Connor!"

Gagged and a rope wound around his body, her son lay draped belly first over a horse. His muffled cries ripped through her heart.

"I'm here, son." She shoved her foot into the stirrup and latched hold of the rear lip of the saddle. A sob escaped her as she fought to launch herself upward. Auntie. Sutherland. How could she leave them behind? But how could she not? She could only save Connor. Her grip on the saddle slipped, and she fell back to the ground, stirring the horses into stomping around her. Rolling, she clambered to her feet and lunged for the stirrup again.

"Ye're not headed anywhere, m'lady." Fingers dug into her hair and yanked her back. A different man, one side of his face marred with a scar that engulfed the entire side of his head, clamped his other hand around her throat and shook her. "That boy be pure gold to us."

Isobel wheezed in as much air as would pass through the tightening grip around her throat and jabbed her elbows into the demon's gut. She struggled to hit him even lower, praying to connect with his man parts.

The bastard laughed and dragged her away from the horses, plowing through the clumps of primrose riddled with clusters of wild grasses. He bounced her across the rocky outcroppings of limestone and threw her down between Sutherland and her aunt.

Auntie grappled toward her, pressing tight against her. The pitiful old woman trembled and clutched at Isobel, as though she couldn't find her. Her mouth opened and closed, but no sounds came out. Blood streamed from her nose and the corners of her mouth. Her eyes looked glazed.

A bloody and beaten Sutherland made a futile attempt at dragging himself in front of them. His right arm hung limp and useless, and one of his eyes had already swollen shut. "Forgive me for failing ye," he gasped.

"Forgive *me*," Isobel answered in a croaking whisper as she squeezed Sutherland's shoulder and clutched an arm around Auntie. How could she have missed the approach of these devils? How had they taken her unawares?

"Kill'm slow, he said." The scarred man sauntered back and forth at their feet, peering down at them with his one good eye like a scavenger sizing up fresh carrion. The man gave the perception of being the leader. He possessed an air of cruel authority.

The man Isobel had shot pointed in her direction. "I got a few things in mind for that one right there."

The shortest of the four men jerked his head toward the horses. "We shouldna drag this out. Too close to Fort William. Could be soldiers about. Duke said we might run across soldiers since he filed them charges to make it look all proper and such."

"Could just shoot'm and make up some story about a slow kill to get the extra gold," said the fourth man. He scratched a hand across his belly. "Save us time and trouble. I mean to be eating soon, so let's be quick about, aye?"

The scarred man stepped closer and kicked Auntie's foot. She had gone still and remained motionless. "This one's near dead anyhow. Gone before sunset, I'd wager. I seen that look before, and she's older than dirt anyway."

Isobel clenched her teeth to keep from screaming, praying the cruel bastard had no idea of what he spoke. She hugged Auntie tighter. "Leave her alone!"

The bloody cutthroat, still clutching his wounded arm, jerked his chin toward Isobel again. "That one is mine. Do what ye will to the others. Just gimme a bit a time wif her."

The short man waddled forward, pulling his dirk from its sheath. "No more shots. Like I said. Troops o' redcoats could be about, and there be a few crofts not so far from here. We passed'm, 'member?" He pointed the lethal tip of his long dagger toward Isobel. "That cow done fired one shot what echoed across the loch. Three more shots would draw somebody's attention sure enough."

The wounded fiend eyed Isobel and grabbed his crotch. "The shot I gots for her willna draw attention. I'll gag her so she canna manage naught but a whimper." He shoved his way between her and Auntie Yeva, kicked the old woman aside, and grabbed Isobel up by the hair.

Sutherland lunged toward the devil, but the youngest of the four yanked him back, and the man with the dirk sank the knife deep into Sutherland's side. "On yer way to meet yer Maker, my fine friend," the blackguard said as they shoved Sutherland back to the base of the tree.

The villain with his hand fisted in Isobel's hair dragged her less than a pace away. "Well done! Ye can stick this fine partridge wif anything ye want when I'm done sticking her wif me tadger."

She rolled, curled around his leg, and bit into his thigh, grinding her teeth as hard as she could through the threadbare weave of the man's filthy trews. The heartless monster might succeed in whatever he planned, but he'd do so with a great deal of pain. She'd not go easily.

He howled and stumbled backward, tangled in her skirts. His fists rained down on her as he kicked and flailed to beat her off his leg.

Isobel ignored the pain and bit harder, blindly groping upward to grab a handful of the crotch the man seemed so eager to share. Bollocks well in hand, she squeezed, digging in her nails as she twisted.

The man screamed louder, thrashing and rolling from side to side to free himself.

The coppery taste of blood spurred her on. She held fast and ground her teeth until a slamming kick into her ribcage knocked the wind from her. Tumbling aside, she clutched her middle, gasping for air.

"Enough!"

Still fighting to breathe, Isobel stole a glance sideways. Which of the hired monsters had saved her?

The disfigured assassin pulled his pistol and aimed it at the man she had bitten. "Go! Fetch the horses whilst the rest of us finish this." He shifted the aim of the pistol to her. "You! Get o'er there wif the others."

She dragged herself back to Auntie and Sutherland, gathering the unconscious old woman into her arms. If they were to die, at least they would die together. The agony of leaving Connor vulnerable and alone in the cold, cruel world tortured her worse than anything else ever could. She didn't fear death nor anything else these men might do to her. All she feared was leaving her son. And Alasdair. Her precious Alasdair. A defeated sob escaped her as she pressed her cheek to the top of Auntie Yeva's kerchiefed head. She had failed them all so miserably.

The brute with the pistol jabbed the gun at the man with the dirk. "Finish'm, then catch up. We got miles to make before nightfall. Done wif this waste o' time."

"Hold up now and wait for me," the man with the dagger said as he grabbed a handful of Sutherland's hair and pulled back his head to bare his throat. "This willna take long. I'll slice open all their gullets quick as a minute."

Gunfire split the air, and the man about to cut Sutherland's throat fell face forward across him.

"Christ Almighty!" The youngest of the group crouched low and jerked about, searching for the source of the shot. He took off in a long-legged lope for the horses.

"Aye! Outta here now!" The scarred man followed close behind.

As both men ran to meet the horses the third man had gathered, another shot rang out. One of the men yelped but didn't go to the ground. They launched themselves onto their mounts and spurred the beasts onward, disappearing over a nearby ridge. The leader had latched on to the reins of Connor's horse and pulled him along behind.

As gentle as she could, Isobel lowered her aunt to the ground and forced herself first to her knees and then to her feet. She staggered to Sutherland and latched hold of the dead man sagged across him. With a fervent prayer that Sutherland still lived, she pulled as hard as she could. The brute didn't budge. The devil weighed too much for her to move. She fell back to the ground, praying whoever her savior had been would indeed be an ally and not a British soldier. They sorely needed a bit of good fortune.

She crawled back to Auntie. Her aunt's motionless form ground salt into her already raw emotions. Auntie couldn't die. Not like this. She scooped up her limp hand and pressed it to her cheek. "I am so sorry, Auntie. Please...please dinna die."

Footsteps. Crunching louder. Closer. She lifted her head to face whatever fate had seen fit to plague her with next.

A tall, young lad, face still smooth with the soft fuzziness of a boy not yet grown into a man, marched toward her. He held a flintlock rifle in one hand and a glinting dirk in the other. He wore a woven sack slung across his body, and a brown knitted tam covered most of his rusty curls. Thankfully, he also wore a kilt. At least he appeared to be a Scot, but she decided it better to be wary just in case. Alasdair's associate had mentioned a hefty reward. She didn't know who she could trust.

"I thank ye for saving us from those scoundrels," she rasped out.

The boy edged closer. He moved carefully. His soft brown eyes studied her as he sheathed the dirk, took hold of the dead man across Sutherland, and yanked him aside. Gaze still watchful and tapping Isobel with repeated glances, the boy rolled Sutherland to his back. With a light touch to each of the man's wounds, the lad frowned, then straightened, gave Isobel a wide berth, and crouched down beside Auntie Yeva.

"My name is Ailsa MacNaughton," she said. It wasn't entirely a lie. She had been christened Isobel Ailsa Lileas MacNaughton. "I thank ye and am in yer debt."

Her champion remained silent, touching a finger to the sticky blood at the corner of her aunt's mouth. If possible, his severe frown deepened with even more concern.

"What is yer name?" she asked, tension returning, threatening to steal away what little sanity she still possessed. She needed to know where this man-child's alliances lay.

Without a word, the lad stood, drew his dirk, then flipped it, and held it out to Isobel, haft first. He fixed her with an intense look as though willing her to understand as he motioned first to his own chest, then pointed back in the direction which he had come. He nodded at Isobel and repeated the motion along with some additional hand gestures she didn't understand. He peered at her, bending closer and fixing her with an expectant, unblinking stare.

"Please be saying ye mean to fetch us some help." Isobel balanced the dirk across her knees and folded her hands as though pleading in prayer.

The lad smiled and gave her a slow, exaggerated nod as though she were a simpleton. She felt like one. She felt a complete idiot, but at least God, in His blessed benevolence, had sent her this silent guardian angel. "God bless ye, boy. Please hurry. Fetch help as fast as ye can."

CHAPTER SIXTEEN

ALASDAIR HUNCHED OVER his ale, the slant of his tam pulled
forward to keep his face in the shadows. He scratched through
his beard and stole a glance around the pub. Not a soul paid him any
mind. *Good.* He'd bide some time in this dimly lit corner whilst Ian
confirmed the information they had ferreted out in Kinlochmore. A
rumor. But rumors sometimes held precious kernels of truth. According to what they'd learned, the duke had taken up temporary residence
in Scotland and was looking to hire a few men for an undisclosed task.
Edinburgh had been named as the place where the man would be until
he'd settled certain affairs.

Settled certain affairs. Alasdair blew out a disgusted breath, then
washed away the foul taste of the matter with a deep draught from his
tankard. He thunked the vessel back to the table and motioned for
another. The weary barmaid nodded, then strolled back to the bar at a
snail's pace to fetch it.

He'd settle Temsworth's affairs for him. The only question at
present was how to accomplish the task. A duel would be the most
honorable but also carried considerable risk. If caught, imprisonment
and then hanged for murder. And since the duke had named him in
the charges of kidnapping as well as possible charges of treason, if he
killed the bastard and didn't make it look like an accident, he'd most

assuredly be the first suspect accused.

The scowling barmaid sloshed two tankards down on the table. "I brought ye two. Ye be running me ragged."

He didn't make eye contact with the cross wench, just tossed three coins instead of two on the table. "For yer troubles."

"Hmpf." She slapped a hand atop the coins and slid them off into her hand. Without another word, she sauntered away with a happier sway in her step.

Ian appeared, pulled out a chair, and settled into it with a satisfied grunt. "He's here, all right. Not even staying at the inn. Rented a place and staffed it like he intends to live there a while."

"Interesting." Alasdair shoved one of the full tankards toward Ian so he wouldn't have to wait for the lazy barmaid to take notice of him. "He plots something besides the trumped-up charges against me. Why else would he be in Edinburgh and send out word for hired men?" An uneasiness churned within him. He should have sent more than just Sutherland to escort his precious Isobel to Cape Wrath. Sutherland was a fearsome warrior, but could one man overcome an attack of several?

"We'll have to find a rougher pub than this to discover any darker plans the duke may have." Ian took a long, slow drink, then frowned down at the dented pewter mug as he lowered it. "If he's already hired the men—we'll not find out a thing and just stir suspicions with our questions." He stole a covert glance about the room. "Do ye really wish to chance such a waste of time?"

His brother's impatience with this sorry business matched his own. Again, Alasdair scrubbed his fingertips through the wiry curls of his beard. "Nay." He pulled in a deep breath and allowed it to hiss out between clenched teeth. "Where is this residence he's rented?"

Ian gave him a lopsided grin. "Not that far from yer own here in Edinburgh. Remember Kincaid Place?"

He returned Ian's grin. *Aye.* He remembered Kincaid Place well.

The house and grounds abutted his own estate to the east. It was as large as his own, taking up the remaining parcel between his land and Caldtoun. He'd never been inside the place but knew the lay of the land well enough. He'd ridden past there many a time. "Reckon the man's still hiring?"

Ian shrugged. "There's but one way to find out."

A familiar red flashed to his left. Alasdair hazarded a side-eyed glance in that direction. Redcoats. A pair of them. He kept his gaze lowered and tapped the table once.

Ian hunched over his own tankard, even going so far as to prop his elbow on the table and rest his fist against his cheek as he shifted to sit with his back to the soldiers. "I see them," he said in a low murmur.

"Soon as they light somewhere, we'll leave." Alasdair watched the pair with stolen looks from behind his mug.

"Just say the word, brother." Ian bowed his head, pretending to doze off.

The pair of soldiers seemed more intent on finding a place to sit rather than checking out the other patrons. They settled on a bench across the room and pounded their fists on the table for service. As soon as the buxom waitress strolled over to the Englishmen and blocked their view with her generous girth, Alasdair rose and headed for the door. Ian followed.

Once outside, he hurried away with long strides, putting as much distance between himself and the pub as possible. Ian strode along beside him, occasionally tossing a cautious glance behind them.

Focus locked on the ground, Alasdair ignored passersby. Time to finish this sorry business and return to his precious Isobel.

"To the horses then?" Ian asked as they turned down a side street toward the stables.

"Aye." Alasdair slowed his charging pace and attempted to appear more casual. "And then to Kincaid Place to seek employment." His squint tightened as he formulated the plan. "The man should have need for a pair of experts to manage his horses, aye?"

"If he doesna know this yet, I'm sure we can convince either him or his man of such." Ian dipped his chin in approval.

They gathered their horses and headed southward, selecting a roundabout route to Kincaid Place. "I dinna think it prudent to ride past my property or Château Delatate. Even with the beard, I could still be recognized."

"Aye," Ian said. "This isna the best way to carry out an assassination, but I reckon we must work with what we're given." He shrugged as they neared their destination. "At least when ye lived here, ye kept to yerself when ye were nay in the courtroom. Not so many folks got close enough to recognize ye with the beard."

They slowed, then dismounted, casually walking their horses around the walled-in perimeter of Kincaid Place. Alasdair memorized every detail. Stone block wall. Judging by its height, the barrier had been built more for decoration than keeping out intruders. There was a fancy iron gate at the front of the sprawling house and a wood gate at the rear. This was the entrance they sought. The gate meant for servants and deliveries.

He lifted the latch and pushed, fully expecting the attention of a guard at any moment. None came. The gate swung inward, revealing a cobblestone courtyard that reminded him of his own. He took the lead, pulling his horse along behind him. Ian followed.

Alasdair stopped and looked around, easing farther into the deserted area between the main house and the stable. He couldn't believe they still hadn't been met by anyone asking them their business at the estate. He shook his head and cocked a brow at Ian. Uneasiness raked cold claws down his spine. "This isna right. No member of the aristocracy, especially a duke, would leave his home so unguarded."

"You are right, my good man," remarked a voice from the shadowed doorway of the stable. "I thought you would never get here. I say, what kept you?" A tall man, slender but muscular and sleek as a feline, stepped forward. "Alasdair Cameron, I presume?"

"James Gordon," Alasdair lied. He'd not reveal his hand so easily. Instead, he shared his seldom-used middle names. "And yerself, sir?" Alasdair knew damned good and well the man in front of him was Temsworth. He recognized him from ten years ago when he'd gone to London and made the sorry decision to leave Isobel in the bastard's clutches. The duke had not aged well.

Faded blonde hair, thinning and slicked back in a ratty excuse for a queue, accentuated the man's overlarge red ears.

The duke carried a black walking stick topped with a highly pol-ished golden ball for the handle. His pale brows, wilder and bushier than any clump of sedge, inched higher on his wide forehead. "Now, now, Master Cameron. Let us not start our acquaintance with laughable lies. You know very well who I am, as I have most assuredly identified you." He turned and held out a ring-laden hand toward the doorway he had just vacated. "Come forward, Hugh. Do you not wish to greet your former master and thank him for his benevolence?" Temsworth shook with a high-pitched laugh. "Without him, you would not have found yourself in possession of more gold than you could ever hope to earn in your lifetime."

Hugh, one of the servants who had worked at Alasdair's estate, stepped out of the stable and faced him. "I had no choice. Got mouths to feed at home, and 'cause a ye, I lost me job. All 'cause of a bit of skirt. All 'cause that whore ye took off with!"

Alasdair held himself back from lunging forward and snapping the wee traitor's neck. "Ye wasted no time in turning on me, Hugh. We arrived in Edinburgh just today."

"Wanted to make sure I's first to get here so's to get the money." Hugh gave him a curt bob of his head. "Runned over here soon's I spotted ye at the pub."

Temsworth waved the young man away with a fluttering of his fingers. "That you did, boy. Now, be gone. You have your payment, and I find your stench most unpleasant. Do not return here. Ever."

Hugh gave Alasdair and Ian a wide berth as he scuttled out the gate.

Greedy little turncoat. Alasdair turned his attention back to Temsworth. There was no sense in dancing around the subject any longer. "I give ye one last chance, Temsworth."

"One last chance?" the duke repeated with another laugh. He held up a finger, flicking his hand until the lace edging around his cuff settled across his jacket sleeve in a manner that suited him. He cleared his throat and shifted with a haughty sniff. "You have my terms, sir. Return my son. Keep the bitch." All humor left him. "Simple. Yes? And my terms are never negotiable." A sinister smile curled one corner of his mouth. "You will find I always get what I want, Master Cameron. One way or the other."

"Man the gate, Ian," Alasdair murmured in a low, deadly tone his brother would recognize as a call to arms.

"Speak up, man." Temsworth sauntered a step closer. "I have a devil of a time understanding you insufferable Scots. Isobel's indecipherable babbling bruised my ears to no end."

Alasdair drew both pistol and sword. The sincere desire to christen each of them with the duke's blood raged through him with a vengeance. "I shall allow these to speak for me, aye? I'm sure ye'll understand them."

The self-assured man rested both hands atop the golden ball of his cane and swayed back and forth as though enjoying a tune. "The first rule of all battles is to understand your opponent." He shook his head. "You, Master Cameron, clearly did not prepare properly." He made an annoying clucking sound and shook his head again. "Underestimation loses many a war, my dear man."

Soldiers filled the courtyard, charging out of the stable, out from behind buildings, and the house. The area bled with redcoats.

"Halt!" one of the men shouted, aiming his rifle at the gate.

Alasdair braced himself for the shot. Ian wouldn't halt. He sent up a prayer of Godspeed and safe journey to his brother.

"That one is of no consequence," the duke announced, holding up a hand. He jabbed a finger in Alasdair's direction as he turned toward the house. "That one. Alasdair Cameron. Kidnapper and attempted murderer." He turned back and cast a benevolent smile in Alasdair's direction. "Lady Temsworth will be so disappointed she missed you. Rest assured, I shall give her your regards and describe your hanging to her in *intimate* detail. Repeatedly."

By God above, if he was to be hanged, they would hang him for something a damned sight better than lies. Alasdair took quick aim, shot, then rolled behind the one tree in the entire clearing that didn't have a soldier beside it.

Multiple shots rang out, splintering bark from the broad oak at his back and chipping chunks from the stone wall in front of him. He pulled free his second pistol, hunkered down lower, then peeped around the tree and fired his last shot. Tossing the pistol aside, he drew his dirk, then settled the hafts of both sword and dagger more comfortably in his hands. If he had to die, he'd be taking a few with him. He sprang to his feet and charged out from behind the tree, roaring out his rage.

Two of the closest men fired, their bullets skimming past him. A trio farther away set the butt of their rifles to their shoulders and took aim.

"Hold fire," screamed the duke from where he sagged across the stable steps. "I want him alive and properly tortured before hanging! Take that man! Now!"

The sight of Temsworth with both hands clamped high on his blood-soaked thigh did Alasdair a world of good. The man would need that damned cane for walking now rather than decoration. Soldiers marched toward him with a wariness, rifles aimed, and bayonets ready to skewer him.

"To the Tolbooth with you," growled one of the redcoats as they swarmed him from all sides and wrenched his weapons from his hands.

Alasdair head-butted the closest, struggling against their hold.

The man cursed and fell back a step, clutching his face as blood spurted from his nose.

Three of the burliest managed to force his hands behind his back and shackle him. One of them clamped hold of his hair while two others took hold of his arms. They dragged him across the courtyard, then shoved him inside a wagon fitted with a cage so cramped, he had to kneel. He hit the barricade and tested its strength. The effort disappointed him. Iron bars formed the box, and it was made well. But at least he had the enjoyable view of the duke writhing in pain as his men carried him into the house.

The wagon clattered onto the street at a good clip. Alasdair crouched like a caged animal, watching Edinburgh stream past as they headed for the prison. He knew the place well—but as a solicitor and not an inmate. The jail was renowned for its inhumane conditions, but he didn't lose hope.

The establishment had also experienced a great many escapes. His spirits lifted even more as the memory of one of his clients pushed to the forefront of his thoughts. Daegus Fitzgibbons, pickpocket extraordinaire, had escaped the Tolbooth three times. The eccentric old man, a knighted warrior who had even achieved the elevated status of an earl for his service to the crown, considered picking pockets the best sort of amusement and escaping the Tolbooth even more entertaining. The last Alasdair had heard, Daegus's adventures had slowed. The sly rascal now ruled Edinburgh's underground. If he could get a message to Daegus—

The wagon came to an abrupt halt, bouncing Alasdair against the bars. He peered around, perplexed. This wasn't High Street. They were nowhere near St. Giles or the jail.

"Clear the road! We've a prisoner to deliver!" shouted one of the soldiers driving the wagon.

The solid headboard of the wagon prevented Alasdair from catching sight of whatever blocked the road up ahead. He crouched lower at the sight of a gathering crowd on either side of the wagon. Some had been known to pelt prisoners with whatever they happened to have on hand.

A young lad sidled up close, glancing around as he crept nearer. The boy was tall enough to be a man, but the fuzziness of his face revealed his young age. "Ye be Cameron?" he asked in a hushed tone as he kept looking toward the front of the wagon.

"Aye."

"Yer bruvver means to get ye out. Be ready, he says," the lad whispered.

The wagon shook from side to side as the soldier's clambered down. "All the barrels," one of them shouted. "You missed these crates over here," the other one growled as they stomped out of sight toward whatever was blocking the roadway.

Alasdair took full advantage of the opportunity. "Daegus Fitzgibbons," he said in a loud whisper to the boy. "Tell my brother to find Daegus Fitzgibbons." Alasdair paused and strained to see if the soldiers were returning. He still had time. "Fitzgibbons is a good friend, and he'll help me. Tell him to look for Fitzgibbons in—"

"I know well enough where Daegus Fitzgibbons is," the boy said with a grin. "He's me grandsire." He peered at Alasdair with newfound admiration. "I'll take yer bruvver to him. If ye be a friend of me grandda's, ye be a friend a mine."

"Good lad." Alasdair breathed easier. "I'll pay ye for yer troubles once I'm free, aye?"

The boy winked, then melted back into the crowd.

One of the soldiers returned, grumbling as he dusted off his hands and climbed back aboard the wagon. "Bloody Scots. Drunken fools, the lot of them."

Alasdair slouched back against the bars. With any luck, Ian and Daegus would act in haste. He had no doubt the duke would demand a speedy session of torture and execution to get him out of the way. A chuckle escaped him. Of course, the man might be a bit waylaid by his unfortunate injury. His only regret was that the shot had hit so low. He'd aimed for a shot to the duke's gut. An injury such as that would have guaranteed a slow, painful death.

After a while, the wagon stopped again. Alasdair braced himself. They had arrived. The redcoat unlocked the cage and jerked a thumb for him to slide toward the opening. The stone-faced man yanked him forward. Accompanied by two of the Tollbooth's guards, they dragged and shoved him down the dingy halls. When they reached his cell, they removed his chains and kicked him inside. The door clanged shut behind him.

It took a moment for his eyes to adjust to the dim interior of what amounted to little more than a narrow stone corridor barely big enough to hold a full-grown man. He crooked an elbow over his nose to filter every breath. The stench of the place burned his eyes. He made his way across the short expanse to the small window cut high in the back wall and thanked God above for the blessing. Not all cells at the Tolbooth had windows.

He backed into the corner closest to the window and scraped his boot across the floor from side to side, kicking aside accumulated filth he'd just as soon not identify. Back against the wall, he lowered his arse to the ground. The damp sliminess lent a bone-chilling feel to the room. He adjusted his kilt, bringing it up over his head and gathering it close about his shoulders. At least it was late spring. Winter in this wee box would not be pleasant.

Keys rattled in the door. He didn't bother rising.

The iron portal swung open to reveal a pair of men, both so huge and fat, they had to squeeze sideways to enter the chamber. "Time for a bit of fun," the bald one in the front said with a toothless smirk. He clapped a hand to the back of Alasdair's neck and yanked him to his feet as though he weighed less than a sack of flour. With a shove, he pushed him into the waiting arms of his partner. "We've nay skinned one in a while. What's yer pleasure today, Beardie?"

True to his name, the bearded man shook his shaggy head. "Nay, Baldie. They mean to hang him day after tomorrow. Couldna drag the skinning out for several days as is proper." He gave Alasdair a demonic smirk. "I'm thinking we'll start with the lash 'til he drops to his knees. I like it when the big ones fall and go to crying like bairns howling for their mam's tit. What say ye?"

Alasdair clenched his teeth to keep from responding. The bastards wanted a reaction. He'd be damned if he gave it to them. They'd only use whatever he did to make the torture worse.

They shoved him down the corridor, bouncing him off the walls and guffawing whenever he tripped and fell to his knees.

They shackled his wrists to the iron ring atop a pole in one corner of a cell. The bald-headed man yanked away his kilt with a laugh. "Dinna want to get blood on such a fine bit a weave." He shoved his face close and mopped the sweat from his bald head with the wadded kilt. "I'll be keeping this. I be needing meself a new plaid." He chuckled again. "Anyway—'twill only catch fire once ye land in hell."

"Gimme his shirt," the other guard ordered. "Once we get done wif him, he'll nay want nothing touching his back no ways."

Baldie took out a knife and raked it down Alasdair's back and arms. He ripped the léine aside and tossed it to his friend. "Get Maggie to mend it. I didna want to bovver wif taking it off proper."

Arms stretched over his head, Alasdair dug his nails into the post, bracing himself for whatever came next. He'd tasted the lash before. Staring down at the stained floor, he focused on Isobel. Whatever he had to endure was worth it. He had to survive for her.

"How 'bouts we beat him a bit first? Soften him up, aye?" Beardie landed a hard punch into his ribs, knocking the wind from him.

Then he trailed the handle of the whip down Alasdair's arm and bounced it across his shoulders. "Shame he's so muscled. Yanking bones from the sockets is me favorite play. Doesna work so well when they're muscled." He clubbed the handle hard against Alasdair's face. A warm wetness trickled down his cheek and dripped off his jaw.

Beardie laughed. "Will ye look at that? Free bleeder, this one is." He slammed his fist into Alasdair's other side. "Damned lot o' trouble, ye bleeders. Gotta take care to keep ye alive for the gallows."

Alasdair sucked in a breath, wincing at the raw scraping pain when the air flowed into his lungs. He recognized the familiar jagged burn. Broken ribs. He ground his teeth tighter, sending up a prayer for strength. He had to get through this to see his Isobel again.

"He ought to hold his blood for twenty lashes. Ye think?" asked Baldie as he shuffled out of Alasdair's view.

"Aye," agreed Beardie. "Ten for me. Ten for yerself, aye?"

"Aye," said Baldie as he split Alasdair's back with the first burning bite of the cat-o'-nine-tails. "There be one o' mine."

Thankfully, he lost count of the cruel, flesh-eating lashes somewhere after six when blessed darkness closed in around him.

CHAPTER SEVENTEEN

"Here. A wee cup of broth for ye."

Isobel shook her head, never taking her gaze from her aunt's still form. She pushed up from the short stool beside the makeshift cot. Hands shaking, she wrung out the cloth in the wood basin of water laced with healing herbs. Auntie couldn't die this way.

Please dinna take her, she prayed, then daubed the cool rag across the dear woman's brow. Breath held, she watched for a twitch of an eyelid, a jerk of a finger, or a deeper intake of breath. No response. Auntie Yeva, beaten and bruised, was one whose soul had already departed, and her body had yet to realize it.

"If ye dinna mind yer own strength, how will ye help the two of them?" Euna Ranald, self-proclaimed white witch and healer of Loch Lochy, the kindly soul who had taken them in, pushed the steaming cup toward her again. "Drink this, and I'll leave ye be." The crone's dark eyes flashed and crinkled even more with her toothless smile. "Well...I'll leave ye be until the breads done a baking, and then I'll be nagging yer thin arse about eating a crust or two a that."

"Thank ye." Isobel accepted the cup, more to silence Euna than anything else. She sipped at the rich, hearty broth as she looked across the small, dirt-floored dwelling at Sutherland.

She feared for the man. Even with his upper body propped high on his pallet beside the hearth, his pained wheezing still rasped through the room like tree limbs rattling across the roof. He had coughed up blood repeatedly, and rising fever rendered him fiery to the touch. But he had managed to whisper for her not to worry, assuring he had survived worse than this. As far as she was concerned, there could be no *worse*. Connor had been wrenched from her side. Both Auntie and Sutherland were at death's door, and who knew if her beloved Alasdair was still alive or had already fallen to Temsworth.

Connor. She almost choked on the aching knot in her throat. Her dear, sweet laddie. He had to be terrified. She covered her mouth to staunch a sob and shut her eyes tight against another onslaught of tears. She had to recover her baby. Somehow. Some way.

A gentle touch patted her arm. She opened her eyes to Morley's sympathetic face. Morley Ranald, Euna's mute grandson and the guardian angel who had fired on the blackguards and saved her and the others from certain death.

With a shy smile, Morley held out a bunch of cheery, yellow cowslips.

"Lady's Keys," Euna said. She patted Morley on the shoulder. "Verra nice, Morley. Kind of ye to bring Mistress Ailsa such a lovely posy of flowers to brighten her spirits."

Isobel blinked. She still struggled to answer to the name she had told them. Ailsa MacNaughton. "Aye, Morley. I thank ye for attempting to better my day. Ye are a dear lad, for certain."

Morley ducked his head with a shy smile, then pointed to a wooden cup of water waiting on the small table.

"Ye've thought of everything," she said with a forced smile. "They'll last quite the while in the water."

Morley hurried to place the flowers in the tall cup, then slid it to the center of the table. He smiled down at them as a beam of sunlight lit the yellow of their blooms even brighter.

"Run and fetch more wood, Morley," Euna said in an affectionate tone. "Then find us some meat to add to the broth for our supper, aye?"

The boy bobbed his head and headed outside, only to burst back through the door with an alarmed look.

"What is it, lad?" Euna rushed to the window beside the table and searched for whatever had startled him.

Isobel hurried to the only other window in the thatch-roofed house and scanned the area. Redcoats in the distance. An entire unit of some twenty or so men. Headed directly for them. If the soldiers identified her, they'd return her to the duke for certain. The idea of turning herself in tempted her. If she returned to Temsworth, maybe she could steal back Connor. Instinct and experience churned through her. *Nay.* Temsworth was not a fool. He'd never make the mistake of allowing her near Connor again. In fact, if she ever returned, she felt clear to her bones that the devil would torture her until she died. She would have to recover her precious son with a great deal more wiliness and stealth.

She pushed away from the window. "They must not find me here."

Euna wrung her knobby hands, darting a panicked glance about the room. She pointed at the corner past the table. "Me weaving pile. Poor folk trade their rags for me potions. I tear the rags into strips and weave them into blankets. Curl up on the floor, and I'll cover ye." She stole another look out the window. "Make haste! They're almost upon us."

Isobel dug the rag pile out of the way, then curled into a tight ball with her spine pressed into the corner. Euna and Morley threw the musty clothes atop her. She eased a few of the scraps aside and peeped through them as a firm pounding rattled the door.

"Morley! Away from there. Stand over there," Euna said in a loud whisper as she scuttled back across the room and pulled the door open a crack. "Aye?"

Isobel strained to hear the conversation.

"Good day to you, madam. Might we have a word?"

As soon as the man spoke, Isobel recognized the voice. Alarm charged through her like a raging fire. The redcoat was Alasdair's Lord Crestshire. She flinched and closed her eyes. What would happen if Crestshire discovered Sutherland?

"What is it? I've chores to be about," Euna replied. The old woman's tone made it clear she didn't think much of the visitors or their interruption.

Isobel held her breath, praying Euna would not be forced to grant them entry.

"Has anyone passed through here of late? Specifically, a tall, comely woman with dark hair and dark eyes. Traveling with a young boy of about five years of age."

Euna kept the door open the tiniest bit. "Nay. Only boy I seen is me Morley, and he be ten and six." She laughed. "Looks younger 'cause he canna grow a beard to save his soul, but he be sixteen summers for true. Seventeen here in a fortnight or so."

"I see. But no one else has traveled through this area recently?"

Euna paused for effect as though searching her memory. She shifted in place but didn't open the door any wider. "Nay. No one else comes ta mind."

Isobel breathed easier and thanked God above that Crestshire appeared to be a decent sort who wouldn't use his authority to force his way into someone's home.

A deep, rasping groan rose from the other side of the room. Isobel tensed. Sutherland couldn't have chosen a worse time to rail with fever.

The door swung open wide, and three pairs of black boots rushed inside as Euna stumbled back from the threshold.

"Sutherland!" Crestshire knelt at Sutherland's side. "Good God, man. What happened to you?"

Isobel struggled to control her breathing, pulling in as little air as possible to keep the rags from shifting. Her jaws ached from clenching her teeth as she prayed Sutherland's raging fever would render him too addled to answer. It would be a miracle if Crestshire didn't hear the hammering of her heart.

She couldn't make out what Sutherland said. His whisper was soft and weak.

Crestshire stood, leaving only his boots in Isobel's view. "Fetch a wagon. I want them both transported to Fort William. Send a messenger to *Tor Ruadh*. Notify Chieftain MacCoinnich his brother is in a dire state. Bid him come at once."

"Yes, sir," barked one of the soldiers, then both hurried out the door.

Crestshire faced Euna. "You lied to me, madam." The man's tone was cold and deadly.

"What of it?" Euna snarled. "It was a pair such as yerself that killed my daughter and her man, leaving my poor wee Morley mute and with only me to care for him."

"Where is the woman?" Crestshire asked, ignoring Euna's excuse. "And her boy?"

His stance shifted. Isobel cringed. Crestshire appeared to be facing the corner that held Auntie's cot. "That is the Duchess of Temsworth's aunt. You can either tell me where the duchess and her son are hiding, or I can have your home searched. Thoroughly. The choice is yours."

"Search all ye want." Euna said. "Morley found these two beside the loch. Near dead. Brought them here so I could try and help them." Her worn skirts swayed as she moved about the small room. "Look at this place and tell me where a woman, a tall one such as ye described, and a boy could hide without yer notice."

Silence met Euna's challenge, then Crestshire dropped to his knees and searched under Auntie's cot. He returned to his feet and circled the room, his boots drawing precariously close to the pile of rags.

Isobel held her breath and refused to allow herself to tremble.

"I saw three horses and a donkey outside. The horses are obviously from *Tor Ruadh's* stables. The bloodline is unmistakable," Crestshire said. "Where is she? Where is the boy?"

"Ye see everyone and everything right here," Euna replied, her voice strong and unwavering. "That woman will nay survive the journey to Fort William. If ye take her from here, I wash me hands of it. Her death be on yerself."

Isobel resisted the urge to spring up from her hiding place and throw herself across Auntie to protect her. Common sense told her Auntie would be gone soon enough whether they moved her to Fort William or not. It was best to stay hidden. She swallowed hard and closed her eyes. Burning tears still seeped through. *God bless ye and keep ye, Auntie. I love ye. Go in peace.*

"I shall return with the wagon. Both will be transferred," Crestshire stated, then marched out the door and slammed it.

Isobel waited until the thundering of the horses' hooves faded away. She waited longer still, watching Euna's skirts standing in front of the window.

Euna's worn boots padded closer to the rag pile. "It be safe, lass."

She emerged from the nest of discarded bits of cloth and pulled Euna into a fierce hug. "I'm indebted to ye forever and a day." Tears broke free as she stepped back and squeezed the woman's shoulders. "There are no words I could say to thank ye enough."

Euna's smile trembled, and her eyes glistened with tears. "Ye know ye must go." She hitched in a sniff. "That commander is nay the fool. He knows ye be here. I saw it in his eyes."

Isobel nodded, then she reached up and yanked the ties from her hair, releasing her waist-length braid. She'd formed a plan whilst hiding among the rags, and now was the time to put it in motion. "Cut my hair. Same as Morley's."

"What?" Euna frowned. "Why?"

"I'll need some of his clothes, too. I think they'll fit. He and I are near the same height." Isobel scooped up a knife from the top of the cupboard and held it out. "I'll send ye money for the clothes soon as I can."

Mouth clamped shut in a tight scowl, Euna agreed with a single nod. She took the knife, took hold of Isobel's long, thick braid, and started to sawing. "Ye'll send no money," she said curtly as she cut away the hair. "I dinna know yer full story, lass, but the shadows in yer eyes tell me it's not been an easy one."

"If Auntie happens to wake before she dies, please tell her I love her, and that I've gone to fetch Connor." Isobel swiped the tears from her cheeks, finding herself dizzy with a sudden feeling of light-headedness. She caught herself on the edge of the table, then reached up to touch her hair, once well past her waist but now barely brushing her shoulders. "I didna realize it weighed so much."

"Sit so's I can even it up," Euna instructed as she pulled out a chair. She tossed the braid on the table.

"Do ye have any weapons ye can spare?" Isobel eyed Morley's rifle propped beside the door.

Morley picked up her discarded braid, then tapped a finger on the table to get her attention. He patted his chest, then pointed at her.

"Nay, Morley." She rose from the chair. "Ye canna come where I must go." She turned and rested a hand on Euna's shoulder. "I need ye to stay here and protect this fine woman from the soldiers. Please?"

Morley shook his head, thumped his chest, then pointed to her again. He glared at her, his dark brows knotted, willing her to accept him. Against his chest, he formed a heart with his hands, then maintaining the shape, he stepped forward and held it out to her. Pure adoration shone in his face.

Euna eased her way between them and took hold of her grandson's hands. "Her heart belongs to another, lad," she said with a gentle pat.

"How did ye know?" Isobel clutched her fists to her chest, wishing for a way to keep from causing this dear sweet boy any pain.

Euna smiled. "Ye called out his name whenever ye dozed off, lass. Yer Alasdair is a part of ye."

"Aye," she whispered. "He is a part of me. I pray I see him again someday."

⟫⟫⟩⟨⟪⟪

THANK GOD THEY planned to hang him tomorrow. or those two cruel bastards would have tortured him longer. One eye swelled shut, and the other closed from weariness and pain, Alasdair lay on the cold floor of his cell. He didn't fear death. Death promised relief. But, damn it all to hell, admitting defeat galled him. The thought of never seeing Isobel again hurt worse than the bite of the cat-o'-nine-tails.

He didn't have a clue how long he had been in this hell. All he knew for certain was that apparently, Ian and Fitzgibbons had not been able to come up with a successful plan for freeing him.

"Forgive me, Isobel," he whispered into the darkness. The thought of her living on without him filled him with a choking mixture of injustice and resignation. His true love regained only to be ripped away again. But at least she lived. Her and Connor. Safe at Cape Wrath. Both the MacCoinnichs and the Mackenzies had sworn to protect her if anything happened to him. Isobel and Connor's safety brought him solace.

Keys rattling on the other side of the door jerked him back to awareness. His empty gut clenched. Beardie and Baldie had promised no more cruelties since he was headed to the gallows at dawn. "I'm a damned fool," he whispered without opening his eye or lifting his head. Hopes and lies were just as effective a means of torture as the bite of the lash or the burn of the branding irons. By saints, if they intended to abuse him more, they could damn well carry him down to their room of suffering. He'd not walk for them no matter what they did.

"Thank ye, my son."

Breath held, he tensed still as stone. If possible, he'd stop the beating of his heart to listen harder. He knew that voice. It was Ian. *Please, let it be so.* He feared to look, feared he'd gone mad.

Light flickered through the dank space. "Christ Almighty," Ian murmured, his voice muffled as though his mouth was covered by some sort of cloth.

"Aye," said another voice. "Ye never quite get used to that smell."

Alasdair swallowed hard and hazarded forcing his good eye open to better see them. "Daegus Fitzgibbons," he rasped, then he squinted harder at the two men dressed in the humble brown robes of Franciscan friars. "Ian? Pray, tell me it's ye, and I've not lost my mind."

"It is me, brother." Ian crouched beside him. The dingy lantern he held high revealed the revulsion in his eyes that Alasdair heard in his voice. "Damnation." He lifted the lantern higher. His horrified scowl swept up and down Alasdair's form. "Can ye walk?"

Daegus squatted beside Ian, pulled a flask from the folds of his robe, and held it to Alasdair's lips. "*Uisge beatha*, lad. Strength for the journey, aye?" A few drops at a time, the man carefully funneled the whisky into Alasdair's mouth until a comforting warm glow trailed from his tongue clear to his toes. The old warrior frowned at Alasdair's raw shoulders and bloody back. "Beardie and Baldie appear to have grown a mite crueler with time." He shook his head. "Can ye bear the touch of a robe until we be shed of this place?"

"I can bear anything if it means I leave this hell behind." Alasdair struggled to push himself up from the floor. Arms trembling, gut spasming with the whisky, he drew on sheer desperation alone to force his body in motion.

"There's a good lad," Daegus said as he and Ian took hold and helped him rise. The man untied the rope belted around his waist and withdrew a bundle that had served well as the plump, round belly of a well-fed brother of the order. "Deep breath, aye?" he advised as he shook out the robe and held it ready to pull down over Alasdair's head.

Alasdair braced himself, wincing. He forced his arms upward and widened his stance to keep from collapsing.

Ian and Daegus hurried the garment down in place and pulled the hood over Alasdair's head, yanking it as far forward as it would go to keep his face well shadowed.

"How will this ever work?" Alasdair bit back a groan as Ian supported him on one side, and Daegus held tight to his other arm. "They admitted two friars, and yet three leave?"

"Both guards should be rendered quite harmless by now with the *special* flasks of whisky yer friend Daegus here was good enough to provide," Ian said as he angled around, eased open the cell door, and stole a cautious glance up and down the corridor.

"Aye," Daegus bobbed his grizzled chin, his scarred cheeks plumping with a proud smile. "Still for days, they'll be." He gave a wink. "Mayhap even longer if my dear, sweet Ellie, got a bit heavy-handed with the nightshade."

Deadly nightshade. Alasdair let out a pained chuckle, flinching as he forced one foot in front of the other and down the dark hallway. "I'm glad to call ye friend and not enemy."

"Aye, well." Daegus tucked his shoulder up under Alasdair's and wrapped an arm around his lower back. "I wish we couldha got here yesterday, so ye would nay have suffered so." The aged warrior, still stout as a Highland bull, jerked his own hood up over his head. "But when I discovered they kept ye in purgatory, it took a bit more planning to free ye."

"I've lost track of how long I've been here." He stifled another groan as they helped him climb the stone steps to the next level. Every step, every move, every shifting of the robe across his body tortured him with as much cruelty as Baldie and Beardie had administered.

"This be the second night of yer stay," Ian supplied. "Although from the looks of ye, I'm sure it felt an eternity."

The close spacing of the torches along the wall gave the corridor an eerie glow. Their dancing flames hissed and popped with the movement of fresh air wafting through the wider hall.

He lifted his face to the cool night air as it swirled past him. Most scents escaped his swollen nose, but the caress of the wind held the exhilarating touch of freedom. He stumbled a bit as Daegus brought them to an abrupt halt.

"Up ahead lies the exit from the tower and beyond that, our wagon," Daegus said. "Whilst the two guarding the door should nay be a problem, we dinna know who else might happen upon us as we leave." He drew his face close to Alasdair's, peering into his eyes with an intense look. "We canna support ye as ye walk to the wagon. It would give us away for certain. Ye must make it on yer own, lad. Yer life—our lives, as well—depend on it, aye?"

"Aye." Alasdair drew his arms down from around Daegus and Ian's shoulders. He could do this. He *would* do this. Entire body trembling, he folded his arms across his front and tucked his hands up inside his sleeves as he'd seen friars do on their way to prayers. He bowed his head low, ducking deeper into his hood as he shuffled forward.

Ian walked ahead of him. He focused on the hem of Ian's robe, concentrating on the sway of his brother's slow, cautious steps to keep moving forward.

They passed the guard table. Two men sat slumped across the small bit of furniture, their eyes open wide in the glassy-eyed stare of the dead. The nightshade had done its job well.

They exited the tower without incident. As they neared the wagon, a shout rang out.

"Halt!"

Alasdair swayed to a stop behind Ian. He dug his fingers into his forearms and gritted his teeth. He had to stop this infernal trembling.

With a hard, dry swallow, he turned in sync with Ian and Daegus.

A British soldier, his firearm held casually across his body, hurried up to them. "Sirs," he said with a polite bow as he came to a halt in front of them. "While I do not share your faith, I would ask your help. Would you be willing to oblige me?"

Daegus stepped forward, blocking Alasdair from view. "What is it, my son?" he responded in a pious tone that Alasdair would have found quite humorous were the situation not so dire.

The redcoat moved a step closer. "I am new to Edinburgh, and my orders here will be complete upon the hanging tomorrow, but I must say, both my heart and mind are elsewhere. Back in London. With my wife."

Lord Almighty. Get to the point, boy. I'm near to dropping. Alasdair pulled in as deep a breath as his broken ribs allowed and held it, praying for the strength to stand in place a bit longer.

"What is yer request, my son?" Daegus nudged, his tone laced with the same impatience coursing through Alasdair.

"Aye, my son," Ian chimed in, urging the long-winded fool along. "How may we help?"

"I beg your prayers for my Lucy," the boy said, his voice dropping to a reverent whisper. "She carries our first child and has grown weaker with each passing month." He shifted with a despondent sigh. "She's always been a frail little thing. I fear I shall lose both her and the babe." He set the butt of the rifle on the ground, leaned it against his leg, and clasped his hands tightly "I beg you, sirs, please remember Lucy and my unborn child in your prayers? Pray for their comfort and safety?"

"We shall keep yer wife and bairn in our prayers, lad. I swear it," Ian said, and Alasdair could tell by his brother's tone he meant every word. Ian had lost his own wife and unborn child. He knew this young man's potential darkness. "We shall light candles for them both."

"Thank you, sirs. I am most grateful," the soldier said as he snatched up his rifle and nodded. "Most grateful indeed."

"Think nothing of it, my son," Daegus replied as he made the sign of the cross in midair in front of the lad. "God bless ye and keep ye in perfect peace."

The young redcoat gave them another smiling nod, then turned and ambled away.

"I hope she fairs well," Ian muttered as he and Daegus heaved Alasdair up into the back of the wagon.

"Aye," Alasdair said as he collapsed into the hay. He rolled to his side, thankful to have made it.

Daegus threw a blanket over him. "Get us moving, Ian, and be quick about it. Go back the way we came, aye?"

Alasdair closed his eyes, relaxing with the thought that after a few days of healing, he'd join his dear love in Cape Wrath. There, they would decide their next move. France, maybe. A smile twitched his sore mouth. *Aye.* Isobel had mentioned settling in France. He could tolerate that for a while if he must. At least he would be with Isobel and Connor.

He risked a deeper breath, flinching with the effort. A home in Scotland would come to pass, eventually. He blew out the air and relaxed even more. He owed Temsworth a great debt, and he'd see it paid if it was the last thing he did. A peaceful drowsiness overtook him. *Aye.* He owed the duke a lion's share of pain before he snapped the man's neck, and he intended to see it served in full.

CHAPTER EIGHTEEN

I SOBEL BROKE OFF a small chunk from one of the oatcakes Euna had sent along for the journey. She savored the dense crumble of oats, herbs, and coarse flour held together by rich goose fat. Euna didn't have much, but the kindly old woman had shared all she had, and she loved her for it. Euna had also promised to see to a proper burial for Auntie Yeva when the time came. A peaceful place close to the loch where Auntie could spend eternity looking out across the water. Isobel's throat tightened with the need to cry, but she daren't give in to it. She didn't have time to mourn. Not yet.

Alert to her surroundings, she knelt upstream from her horse and refilled her waterskin. A handful of the clear water washed the bite of oatcake down. She had to portion out the food with care to make it last. There wasn't time to set a snare and hunt, and she wouldn't waste ammunition in search of meat. Euna had packed dried meat along with the oatcakes. She'd be able to find spring greens and edible roots as well.

God willing, maybe she'd find nesting birds. Eggs would be a welcome treat. She stood and stretched away the stiffness of hours in the saddle. Connor loved oatcakes. She would eat as few of those as possible and still be fine without hunting. The lead and powder she carried were reserved for the men who had stolen her son.

"Best be on our way." She scratched her horse's whiskery nose, then saddled up, thankful for the freedom of Morley's borrowed clothing and the loss of her long, cumbersome braid. Short hair, wild and curly, barely brushed across the tops of her shoulders. A threadbare jacket over a worn shirt. Faded plaid. Patched trews beneath her kilt to hide her feminine legs. Scuffed boots. Hat pulled low over her eyes. She'd even gone so far as to keep her face as dirty as possible to hide her lack of a beard. She looked a thin, vagrant man, or so Euna had promised. *Good.* All the better to find Connor without giving away her identity.

The way she figured it, the ruffians would think her too afraid to follow them. That played in her favor. She snorted out a bitter laugh. Fools. They had no idea of the strength and determination of a mother's love.

With an inkling that Temsworth would more than likely order Connor taken to Hestlemoor rather than London, she had headed in that direction. Instinct had rewarded her. While working for a night of shelter from the incessant rainy weather and a hot meal from an elderly pair of crofters, she had learned of a trio of men traveling with a young boy who they had claimed was deaf and dumb. Two of the men had been wounded. Said they had been shot by highwaymen. It had to be the scoundrels she sought. She had shot the one man, and Morley had wounded the other. Her rage burned at a constant, low simmer. She'd ensure the next wounds she meted out were fatal.

She spurred her horse to a faster trot. Daylight slipped away too fast. By her reckoning, the men had a two-day lead—or at least they had at the time they had stopped and paid for a meal from the same pair of crofters who had fed her. She prayed the rains had slowed them. If they hadn't chosen the longer but easier route, then crossing the belly of the glen would delay them. The land had become a marshy muck of treachery that made the act of moving forward a chore. She had to close the distance between them. It would be much easier to spirit Connor away if she reached him before they imprisoned him in Hestlemoor.

The lingering soreness of the beating she'd taken at the hands of the miscreants kept her weariness at bay. She only stopped long enough to rest the horse. If not for the beast needing a bit of ease, she'd ride nonstop until she reached her son. She kept one hand across the pair of pistols tucked into the front of her belt. The weapons had belonged to Morley's father, but the kind lad had silently insisted she take them. Three men and two pistols. The thought forced her to clench her teeth against such misgivings. It didn't matter. That merely meant she would have to kill the third bastard with Euna's butcher knife she carried inside her boot.

The faintest whiff of burning wood floated on the wind. She brought her mount to a halt, lifted her nose, and sniffed the air again whilst turning in a slow circle. There. Past the burn gurgling along the edge of the woods, deeper in the valley below. A wispy tendril of smoke rose from the stand of trees like a spirit rising from the grave.

She resettled herself in the saddle, studying the smoke as it disappeared across the horizon. Someone had made camp for the night. Could she be so blessed as to have found those she sought?

Urging her mount forward, she took in the lay of the land, noting all its secrets and possibilities. Outcroppings of limestone pushed up through the greening of the glen. Thick clusters of pine and oak sprouted here and there across the way. No caves, and no place to hide. If the camp up ahead held Connor, she would have to steal him away and ride hard.

"So be it," she affirmed as she dismounted. She daren't ride any closer. Whoever camped could have guards about. A sheltered mound of stones beside the stream provided a place for her horse. After tethering him loose enough so he could pull away if she failed to return, she hugged his shaggy neck. "Ye are a good lad, and I love ye for helping me." In a short amount of time, Thunder had become a fine, loyal friend who wouldn't leave her unless he found himself abandoned.

Pistol drawn, she eased into the woods as silent and soft-footed as a cat on the hunt. A childhood spent running with the lads when she should have been improving her stitchery, and music skills aided her now. The mouthwatering scent of roasting meat teased across her nose.

The flicker of firelight from between the trees waved her forward. A murmuring of voices spiked with an occasional deep laugh. Several voices. Over three. Her hopes faltered, but she hurried to shore them up. Maybe Temsworth had sent reinforcements to help the trio kidnapping Connor. That would explain the extra men. She drew up behind the broad trunk of a sprawling oak and peeked around it. Her heart fell. This was a small encampment of soldiers—not the blackguards and Connor.

Her stomach rumbled out a loud, long angry growl. The sound echoed through the quiet wood.

The men closest to her froze. The man directly in front of her hiding place turned and stared into the trees, squinting as he peered into the shadows. "Did the lieutenant not say he would stand first watch? What sort of beast might that be? God help us if anything ill happens to him." The redcoat eased down sideways and picked up his long rifle without taking his eyes off the woods.

A stick snapped behind her. The fine hairs on the back of her neck tingled with the realization someone was there. She eased back the hammer of her pistol.

"I do not recommend that, sir," the stern voice behind her warned.

At least the soldier thought her a man. Isobel disarmed the weapon and lifted it into the air. "Precautions, ye know?" she said in the deepest voice she could manage without sounding the fool. The old crofters had believed her to be male when she spoke. Hopefully, this Sassenach would as well.

"Into the camp," the man said as he snatched the pistol out of her hand, then reached around her and yanked the other one out of her belt. "Move." The soldier nudged her in the middle of her back with the end of his weapon.

She didn't have time for this. Both hands held aloft but head slightly bowed, she strode into the camp with the swaying gait of a man and kept her gaze locked on the fire. Her mouth started watering again. The spitted rabbits propped at an angle over the flames looked well-roasted and ready to eat.

Her captor stepped around her, positioning himself between her and the fire, blocking her view of the succulent rabbits. "Who are you, and what is your business here?"

The best way to tell the most convincing lie was to weave it as close to the truth as possible. It was a lot easier to keep the facts straight that way, too. "Name's Jamie Ferguson, and I be looking for that missing duchess and her boy," she said. "Lots a gold to be had for the man that finds them." She jerked a thumb toward the fire. "Smelled yer smoke and thought might be them that stole her and her bairn away."

Eyes narrowed and lips pursed, her interrogator studied her.

With stolen glances out from under the ragged brim of her hat, Isobel studied him right back.

He wasn't overly young, but neither was he old. Average height and build. Judging by the immaculate state of his dress and the general softness and pallor about him, the man had spent little time out of doors. This redcoat wouldn't survive a day in the Highlands were he not surrounded by troops to provide for him.

"How long has it been since you last ate, sir?" the Englishman asked.

Isobel made a derisive shrug as though she couldn't care less if she ever ate again. A Scot had pride, after all. A man would admit no weakness—especially to an English. "Ate a bit of oatcake today."

"Fields, fix the gentleman a plate." Her captor gave a polite nod and returned her weapons. "Lieutenant Frances Pewterton, at your service, sir." He motioned toward the fire. "It appears we both seek the same thing from this savage land. Perhaps we might join forces since I am quite sure you know this uncivilized country a great deal better than I or any here in my detachment."

She cast a sideways glance at the lieutenant as she accepted the small pewter plate of roasted meat steaming alongside a crust of bread. What the lieutenant suggested might work to her benefit if she played this just right. The soldiers could overcome the trio of blackguards, and she could get Connor away before the lieutenant, or his men were any the wiser. She swallowed hard to control her excitement at the possibility and the fortuitous turn of events.

Struggling to remain calm, she chose her words carefully. If she were a poor Scot on the hunt for reward, that would be her primary concern. "Say I do agree ta help ye," she said around an overlarge bite of meat and bread. "What of the gold?"

Lieutenant Pewterton waved away her question as he accepted his own plate of food and selected a delicate morsel with his little finger held up in a dainty pose. "The reward would still belong to you, my good man. My men and I operate under His Majesty's orders and are therefore not eligible to benefit from the duke's generosity."

Isobel nearly gagged. *The duke's generosity.* Indeed. She shoved the last of her bread into her mouth to keep from saying something that might give her away.

"So, what say you, sir? Do we have an arrangement?" The lieutenant withdrew a small flat-shaped bottle from inside his partially unbuttoned coat, removed the cork, and held it out. "Shall we drink on it?"

She could use a drink. Isobel agreed with a downward jerk of her chin. "Aye." She accepted the bottle, expecting whisky. Instead, a fruity, cloyingly sweet liquid assaulted her tongue. She wiped her mouth on her sleeve and handed back the bottle. "What be that stuff?"

"My family's finest brandy," the lieutenant said, preening with pride. He held out the bottle again. "Would you care for another taste?"

She held up a hand and shook her head. "Nay." She motioned in the direction from which she had just come, then rubbed her belly. "I'll be fetching me horse and taking a shite before I settle for the night."

The refined Englishman rewarded her with the taken aback look she sought. The British thought Scots to be crude, uncivilized brutes. To maintain her hidden identity, she fully intended to act the part.

"I shall walk with you," Pewterton said, passing the bottle of brandy to the nearest soldier and brushing his fingertips as though he'd somehow soiled them. He jerked as though startled and turned back to her with a wide-eyed stare. "Of course, I shall give you the privacy you require to attend to your necessities. You have my word."

While the man was polite to a ridiculous fault, he was not stupid. He didn't trust her yet. Isobel shrugged and motioned for Pewterton to follow. She tromped back through the woods, her long-legged stride outpacing his with little effort. She waited beside her horse for the man to catch up.

"Egads, what a beast," Pewterton said with a hand pressed to his chest. Mouth ajar, he approached the animal as though he'd never seen a horse before. "Wherever did you obtain such a sturdy monstrosity?"

Sturdy monstrosity? She glanced at the black, white-socked shire, wondrous in his stature and great hairy feet. How dare the redcoat call Thunder something as insulting as a *sturdy monstrosity*. She turned back to the lieutenant, not about to tell him her horse had been given to her at *Tor Ruadh*. "Sold me land and bought him for me quest. Named him Thunder. Fine warhorse, he is."

"Your quest?" A confused look puckered the man's pale brow.

"The woman and the boy? The gold?" Maybe partnering with this redcoat had not been so wise after all. The man now seemed a bit the dullard. She decided to test the waters further to get Pewterton's mind off the horse. "I talked with crofters north a here, and they said three ruffians came through naught but two days ago. Had a boy with them. A boy fitting the description of the missing lad."

"Do tell." Pewterton stepped closer, arching his sparse brows as though excited to learn a grand secret.

"Aye." She nodded. "Said the boy didna talk at all. Seemed sore afraid, too. Does that no' sound like a lad that's been stolen away?"

"But what of his mother? The duchess?" Eyes wide, the lieutenant clasped his hands in front of his chest. "Did they mention the young man's mother?"

She looked around as though fearing to be overheard. "Crofters said they heard them men talking like they'd done the poor woman in." That little white lie might help in protecting her identity.

"The scoundrels!" Pewterton fisted his hands and stood taller. "Pray tell me the crofters could tell you what direction those black-guards took."

"Headed for Foxshire Pier. Place is notorious for wicked doings. South edge of the bay, west a Gretna Green." Isobel prayed the fictitious destination would take them close enough to Hestlemoor to head off the fiends and retrieve Connor. "Mean to sell him to pirates, me thinks. Bastards of the sea always looking for innocent, young cabin boys. If ye ken my meanin'?"

Horror registered on the man's face. "How dreadful." He swallowed hard, and his stunned gaze settled on the ground. "And the ill-fated duchess. Who can say what horrible demise that poor delicate creature met with?" He shook his head as his voice dropped to a whisper. "And we may never find her remains to see the dear lady properly laid to rest."

Poor, delicate creature? She had never heard herself described in quite that way, but at least that meant the esteemed Lieutenant Frances Pewterton didn't have a clue as to her identity.

"Aye," she agreed, struggling to sound as sympathetic to the duchess's fabricated plight as much as possible. She bowed her head. "God rest her soul." She crossed herself and blew out a heavy sigh.

Pewterton stomped his foot. "We must ride forthwith. That poor, motherless child must be recovered without delay."

She couldn't agree more but turned away to hide her excitement. She busied herself with untethering her horse from the bush. While she wished they could ride hard and fast through the darkness, she knew the animal needed at least a few hours rest. "I agree with ye, but me horse is weary from a long day's ride. He needs rest before we set out."

"Yes, yes, of course." The lieutenant's attention returned to her mount. He risked a step closer, his head tilting to one side as he studied the animal. "He is a fine specimen now that I look closer." He brushed his fingertips across his chin, his forefinger tapping thoughtfully. "Perhaps, some of our horses' feed might help strengthen him for the journey." He turned to her with a benevolent smile. "When we return to camp, I shall have Atchison see that he's well-fed."

"Thank ye." She gave the reins a gentle tug and headed into the trees. Lieutenant Pewterton was most certainly the oddest Englishman she had ever met. Generous. Concerned about others. Worked hard to do the proper thing. She smiled. The man should have become a priest rather than a soldier.

Pewterton cleared his throat and lengthened his stride to hurry ahead of her. "I shall return to camp now whilst you take care of your other matters." He tripped over a small rotted log but righted himself before he hit the ground. With a sheepish smile, he held out a hand. "Shall I take your horse for you?"

"Nay. I thank ye." Isobel granted the man a less stern scowl. "The urge has left me." She shook her head and rubbed her stomach as she continued walking with a manly swagger. "Happens every time I go without me parritch for a while."

"Very well, then." He made a mannerly bow. "I shall hurry on ahead anyway and send Atchison back to help with your horse."

She didn't answer, just watched the unusual man head off through the woods at a stumbling run. "I hope the rest are fiercer, or I may have to protect them," she muttered under her breath.

Her horse grumbled as though he doubted the capabilities of the redcoats as much as she.

She spotted the tall soldier she had originally startled with her growling stomach. The man strode toward her at a plodding pace. He looked more the fighting type. An older soldier. Older than the lieutenant. This man had a weariness about him, a weariness that had nothing to do with age. Instinct warned her she best be on her guard with this one. "Atchison?"

"Yes." The man's weariness fell away when his gaze settled on her mount. "*This* is your horse?"

Isobel rested a hand on the beast's neck. "Aye. Thunder's his name. The young son of the man I bought him from couldna pronounce *Thunder* and said it was the sound this horse made whenever he galloped." It was a partial truth. Graham and Mercy MacCoinnich's four-year-old son Ramsay had christened the horse *Thunder*, and the gentle beast wouldn't respond to anything else.

"Thunder suits him," Atchison said as he ran his hands along the horse. "Exemplary horse, indeed."

"That he is." She studied him. This one appeared sharper for certain. Mayhap Atchison would give her some insight into Lieutenant Pewterton and the abilities of the rest of the group. She didn't have the time to risk a foolhardy plan. Too much was at stake. Connor needed her now.

She wished Alasdair was here. He possessed the gift of dancing with words and would have gleaned all she needed to know about this group of Englishmen within a blink of an eye. Saints alive, she missed him and prayed she'd someday see him again. Her throat constricted with a stronger threat of tears. By all the saints, she hoped he was still alive.

Head ducked as though concentrating on her footing, and she scolded herself. Alasdair wasn't here. It was up to her to discover all she needed to know. "That Lieutenant Pewterton," she said, then paused and sucked in a deep breath only to huff it out. "The man seems a bit...soft." She shook her head. "I be grateful for the meal and all, but I dinna relish throwing in with a man who might risk my chance at lining me pockets wif gold." There. That sounded greedy enough for the part she played but still respectful.

Atchison halted, his scowl locked on her mount as though trying to read the horse's mind. "Lieutenant Pewterton is a good man," he said, never taking his gaze from the horse.

"Aye," Isobel agreed, mulling over her next words and choosing them with care. "But if ye dinna mind me saying so, he seems more suited for the priesthood rather than an officer's commission in His Majesty's army."

Atchison snorted out a laugh and managed a genuine smile for the first time. "He does at that." He scrubbed a hand across his mouth, all the while staring at her. With a glance upward, he shook his head as though in conference with the Almighty. Hand rubbing the back of his neck, he returned his attention to her. "The man lost his wife and daughters to a fever this past winter." He paused, glanced toward the camp as though listening, then turned back to Isobel. "Pewterton felt it was his fault the four of them died, while he survived. God's punishment for his sins, he says."

The man's smile turned to a bitter frown in the moonlight. He rubbed the horse's nose and scratched the beast behind the ears. "He decided joining the military was the only thing left to him. I think he felt it the surest way to kill himself by someone else's hand."

Isobel struggled not to show too much compassion—after all, her male identity forbade it. But her heart went out to poor Lieutenant Pewterton for the loss of his family. She crossed herself and shook her head. "God bless the poor man. A wonder he's sane as he is."

Atchison agreed as he waved her to the right of the camp where shifting shadows among the trees pinpointed the location of the brigade's horses. "I assure you, Lieutenant Pewterton will not hesitate to charge into any fray—no matter the danger. The gold you seek is as good as in your pocket."

CHAPTER NINETEEN

"**H**OLD STILL NOW!" Ellie scolded. "Yer back is nay healed enough to go without the salve."

Alasdair gritted his teeth. Daegus's wife might be a grand healer, but the woman did a fair share of bullheaded nagging along with it. After eight days of her ranting, he'd had enough. "Are ye near done? I need to be on my way before the sun sets."

Ellie cuffed the back of his head as though he were her child. "Ye will be on yer way when I say ye be ready and not a moment before." The old woman slathered another generous handful of the ill-smelling grease across his shoulders and down his arms. "This salve healed ye days faster than if ye'd not had it. Ye should be thanking me rather than complaining about getting out the door."

Aye. Ellie was right. After all, she and Daegus had saved his life. "Ye speak true, m'lady. Forgive my rudeness. It's but anxiousness to see my dear one that makes me forget my manners."

"Are ye not done with him yet, Ellie?" Daegus strode into the room, his scowl softening as soon as he looked upon his wife. "I'm thinking ye like the lad better than me." He thumped a gnarled fist against his chest. "Dinna think of putting this old bull out to pasture." He rubbed a hand back across his silvery hair and winked. "A bit a snow on the roof doesna mean there's not a roaring fire still in the hearth."

Ellie winked back at him. "I know that fire well enough, my fine man. What say we stoke it once this laddie be on his way?"

Daegus came up behind her, wrapped his arms around her middle, and rumbled out a playful growl as he nuzzled her neck.

Alasdair jumped to his feet and snatched up his shirt. A man could only take so much. He yanked his tunic on and eased it over his sore, greasy back. *God's beard.* First order of business was a good scrubbing in the loch to rid himself of that odor. He didn't know what Ellie put in her salve, but it smelled like shite and rotted eggs.

"Ye didna let me wrap yer ribs," Ellie scolded. She pulled free of Daegus's hold and snatched up a handful of linen strips. "Take off that shirt and let me cinch them up good and tight for the ride. Ye'll thank me when ye're breathing easier with every jolt of the horse's step."

Alasdair shook his head as he pulled on his waistcoat and buttoned it. "The clothes Ian found for me are plenty snug. My ribs will be just fine, thank ye." He donned his jacket and neckcloth before she could argue. His ribs ached and burned with every breath and movement, whether wrapped or not. He'd broken ribs before. All a man could do was bear the pain until it left him in peace. Once he held Isobel again, all pain would be forgotten.

"Are we leaving today or no'?" Ian appeared in the doorway.

"Ye packed the herbs and salves?" Ellie asked, giving Ian a look that said if he valued his arse, he better answer wisely.

"Aye." Ian nodded. "Herbs. Salves. Potions. Every last bit of yer witchery is safe in a bag tied to his saddle."

"Hmpf." Ellie glared at Ian as though contemplating whether or not to cuff him.

Time to end this and go. Alasdair grabbed hold of Ellie by the shoulders and kissed her soundly on the mouth. He smiled down at the woman, finally silent for the first time since he'd met her. "I thank ye for all ye did, m'lady. I owe ye my life." He released her and turned to

Daegus before Ellie regained her ability to speak. "Thank ye, my friend. I'm indebted to ye."

Daegus took hold of Alasdair's forearm and squeezed. "Glad I could be of help, lad. Safe journey to ye, and may God bless ye and yer lady with many healthy sons."

Alasdair accepted the blessing with a nod, released Daegus's arm, then followed Ian to the horses. He pulled himself up into the saddle, expelling a grunt as his body reminded him none too gently that he wasn't completely healed.

"Keep to the alleyways until ye reach Landis Fields. From there, ye should be safe from discovery," Daegus said as he lifted a hand in farewell.

"Dinna forget to apply the salve," Ellie called out. "Twice a day. Morning and night. Ye best heed me, lad."

Alasdair held up a hand as he turned his horse. "God bless ye both and keep ye in perfect peace."

"Not too perfect," Daegus retorted with a roguish grin. "Too much peace makes a man lazy!"

Alasdair smiled, then followed Ian out of Daegus's close and the safety of Edinburgh's underground. They wove their way through the silent alleyways as the night slipped away, and the sun crept higher in the sky. He breathed easier once the city lay well behind them. The Highlands offered safety for a while until he and Isobel made their way to France. He gripped the reins tighter. Once he had Isobel, Connor, and Auntie Yeva safe and settled in France, he would return to pay his debt to Temsworth, and this time, he wouldn't fail.

They rode for days, pushing the limits of the horses and them-selves, but Alasdair couldn't wait to hold Isobel in his arms again. *Tor Ruadh* would provide fresh horses to take them the rest of the way to Cape Wrath and his lady love. His weariness and pain seemed more bearable as the majestic Ben Nevis filled the sky, and *Tor Ruadh* came into view. The first arduous half of their journey was finally behind them.

Alexander and Graham met them in the bailey. The coldness of their faces struck fear to the depths of Alasdair's soul. "What is it?" He needed them to say Isobel was safe, and it was some other dire circumstance casting shadows across them. "Tell me it's nay Isobel."

"I wish I could, cousin," Alexander said, taking hold of his arm. Urgency vibrated in the man's grip. "Come."

Graham motioned for a man in the yard to see to their horses. "Sutherland hovers at death's door," he warned as the four of them stormed into the keep.

"Sutherland?" Alarm charged through Alasdair, lengthening his stride. A surge of bloodlust fired through his veins. "And Isobel?" The sight of one end of the great hall transformed into a familiar sickroom sent his senses reeling.

Where was Isobel? Gretna and Mercy sat at one table grinding herbs and folding bandages while Catriona stood beside Sutherland's makeshift bed, pressing a damp cloth across his brow. "And Isobel?" he repeated.

"Best let Sutherland tell him," Graham advised. "Mercy said he's been more alert today."

At the sound of her name, Mercy turned her head in their direction. "Who is here, my love?"

"Alasdair and Ian," Graham said, taking a stance behind her and resting a hand on her shoulder. "Ye should be resting. The bairn could come at any time."

Mercy reached up and rested her fingers atop Graham's but turned toward the men. The sorrow in her sightless eyes broke Alasdair's heart in two. "I am so sorry, Alasdair."

He shook with anger, struggling to keep from throwing back his head and roaring until the stones of *Tor Ruadh* toppled all around him. "Tell me!" he ordered.

"Come close," Catriona called out from Sutherland's side. "He's awake and wishes to speak with ye."

He hurried to Sutherland, his turmoil mounting at the sight of his cousin's condition.

The man seemed almost lifeless. Hair, damp with sweat, body mottled with bruises, his right arm lay atop the blankets, bandaged to a board from the tips of his fingers to well past the elbow. His eyelids fluttered open as Alasdair drew closer. He lifted the fingers of his left hand. "Forgive me, cousin," he whispered.

Alasdair drew up a stool beside the sickbed and struggled to remain calm until he'd heard all his cousin had the strength to say. "What happened, man?"

Sutherland took a deep breath, eased it out, then forced a swallow. His eyelids fluttered shut for a brief moment, then he pulled them back open. "Four men. Temsworth's men." A rattling breath escaped him. Alasdair feared him dead until the man pulled in another shallow breath. "Took the boy." He wet his cracked lips. "Said they were told to kill the rest of us. Slow. Torture. Beat us. Stabbed. One pulled Isobel aside." His face crumpled, and he turned away. "Forgive me, cousin. I beg ye."

Alasdair bowed his head. He would find those men. If it was the last thing he did before he died, he'd find those four black-hearted curs along with the duke and send them all straight to hell. "What else?" he forced out. He needed to hear it all. "Tell me the rest."

"I canna," Sutherland whispered. "I've told ye all I remember."

A tug on Alasdair's sleeve drew his attention.

"Come. Walk with me," Alexander said. "I shall tell ye what Crestshire relayed about what he found when he discovered Sutherland."

It was all Alasdair could do to maintain control. Vengeance demanded he destroy anything and everything in his path until he had his hands wrapped around the duke's throat. He forced himself up from the stool and followed Alexander up the spiral staircase at the back of the room and out to the curtain wall. "Does she live or not?"

"We dinna know for certain," Alexander said with a weariness that twisted Alasdair's heart. "Crestshire found them in a crofter's house near Loch Lochy. An old woman and her mute grandson, tending them."

"Them?" His ire burned even hotter. "Ye are telling me Crestshire returned Isobel to the duke?" If Lord Crestshire had done such a heinous deed, his name would join the others doomed to die by his hand.

"Nay." Alexander shook his head, then flinched. "He said Isobel nor the boy were there. He found only Sutherland and Isobel's aunt."

"Where is Yeva? Mayhap she can tell me more to help me find Isobel." Alasdair pushed away from the wall. His physical pain couldn't compare to the fear crushing his heart.

Alexander crossed himself. "Isobel's aunt is buried on a hillside overlooking Loch Lochy."

"She died from what they did to her?" He stared at Alexander, willing his cousin to retract his words and say he had misspoken.

"Aye," Alexander confirmed. "Crestshire said she looked to have taken quite the beating."

"Heartless bastards." Alasdair raked a hand through his hair, sick at the thought of what the poor old woman had endured. "And no sign of my Isobel?"

The chieftain shook his head. "But Crestshire did say the crone tending them was nay all that forthcoming with information. She wouldna admit to Isobel ever being under her roof."

"Would nay admit it, or was Isobel stolen away by the four that took Connor?"

The man shrugged. "I dinna ken. It's what Crestshire said when he brought Sutherland to us."

"How long ago?" Alasdair asked as he strode across the curtain wall to the outer steps leading down to the bailey.

"Near on a sennight now." Alexander hurried after him. "I know what ye're thinking, cousin. Ye canna leave for Loch Lochy, then on to who knows where without a bit of rest and a meal. Look at yerself."

Alasdair came to a dead stop, then turned and faced Alexander. "I'll accept a meal and tarry here the time it takes to pull together supplies and ready a fresh horse. No longer."

"Dinna act the fool, man. Ye're no good to her dead." Alexander latched hold of Alasdair's arm and held fast. "Wait at least a day or so. Ye need sleep. Lord Almighty, man, ye look near dead."

He yanked his arm free of his cousin's hold, then shoved his face within a hair's breadth of the chieftain's nose. "Think back, cousin. Did ye *rest* and wait a day or so when it came time to save Catriona?"

Alexander's nostrils flared, and his jaw tightened. He huffed out a growl and took a step back. "How many men do ye wish to take with ye? The MacCoinnich forces are yers for the asking."

His cousin's generous offer eased Alasdair's pounding bloodlust down to a controlled thundering. "Nay. 'Twill just be Ian and me." He yanked his neckcloth away and bared his chest. There, just below his collarbone, scabbed over but still an angry red was the brand Baldie had burned into his flesh. A sign for all to see while he hanged, the cruel bastard had said. The brand of a traitor. "I'll not endanger Clan MacCoinnich by using yer warriors."

Alexander clapped a hand to Alasdair's shoulder. "Whatever else ye need ye shall have, and we'll do whatever it takes to ensure Fort William doesna hear of yer passing through the area."

"Ye understand they'll be watching *Tor Ruadh*." He turned and bolted down the stairs, waiting for Alexander to catch up. "Another reason my stay here must be brief."

Ian appeared in the keep's doorway, both hands clutching several steaming bannocks. He took a bite out of one as he trotted down the front steps and met them in front of the stable. Two lads followed close behind him, both of them laden with rolled blankets, bulging cloth sacks, and waterskins so tight and full, the leather glistened. He offered a handful of the bannocks to Alasdair. "Fresh from Cook's oven, and the lads here bear all we'll need for the journey."

Alasdair accepted two of the bannocks, bit off a chunk of the crusty bread, then managed a smile. "I'd be lost without ye, brother."

Ian shrugged away the compliment. "Where to next? London? Back to Edinburgh?"

"Loch Lochy," Alasdair replied between bites. He gave Alexander a solemn nod. "We need to pay our respects to Yeva's grave, then speak to the woman and boy who helped Sutherland. I'm thinking her respectful care of Yeva was not just because she thought she should. I'm wagering she promised Isobel. It's my hope she can tell us what's become of her and whether she left of her own accord."

"Godspeed to ye, cousin." Alexander took hold of his shoulder and squeezed. "Yer wisdom and level head have always taken care of others, make sure ye use them this time to care for yerself, aye?"

Alasdair snorted out a humorless laugh. "My heart and my rage lead this campaign. I can promise nothing more."

Alexander nodded and allowed his hand to drop away. "I understand."

"To the horses, aye?" Alasdair said to Ian and shoved the last of the bannock in his mouth.

The two saddled up and were on their way. Alasdair paused after passing beneath the portcullis and cast a glance up at the curtain wall. Alexander stood watching, one hand raised in farewell.

Alasdair thumped a fist to his chest, lifted it to Alexander, then spurred his mount into a ground-eating trot. Loch Lochy was not that far. Northeast a bit. But Fort William lay close to the west. Troops would be about—searching for him and Isobel both. He glanced down at the rifle and swords sheathed at the fresh horse's side. Ian had thought of everything.

Neither he nor his brother spoke, just covered ground and watched for signs of anyone else in the area. He rubbed a hand along his still tender jaw and cheek. Baldie and Beardie had burned away his beard and blistered his flesh in the process. The scarring didn't appear severe, thanks to Ellie's stinking salve, but the healing itched like a fiend, and he doubted he'd ever be able to grow a beard again.

A flash of movement to the left made him draw his pistol.

"Naught but sheep," Ian called out. He motioned down the hillside with the barrel of his pistol. "More of the herd and the dog are just over there. See them?"

A bright glinting in the distance caught Alasdair's attention as he watched the dog working the herd. It was the sun's rays bouncing across waters farther to the east. Loch Lochy. The journey had passed quicker than Alasdair expected. It had taken half a day, but with the longer light of the summer days, they still had a few hours of daylight left before the sun sank below the horizon. *Good.* The old woman they sought might be more comfortable speaking to strange men at her door if she could see their faces.

"Catriona told me Crestshire placed the croft but a short distance from the westernmost tip of the loch." Ian pointed to the left. "The waters spill into the rivers there." He drew an invisible line to the right. "I say we head that direction. What say ye?"

"Aye." Alasdair fought against the urge to spur his horse into a full gallop. It would be unwise. Might scare the poor woman and make her withhold valuable information.

"Just there. See it?" Ian pointed toward a tiny, thatch-roofed dwelling with an even smaller building, a stable perhaps, to the back of it. Both squatted on a small rise of land overlooking the loch. A donkey meandered about in a small fenced-in area. A pair of goats, a sheep, and three chickens wandered around the perimeter of the white-washed house.

Alasdair slowed his horse, and Ian did the same. Within a stone's throw of the cottage, they both dismounted and walked their horses the rest of the way.

"Ye can stop right there, the both of ye, and state yer business," called out a voice from the center window of the place. The barrel of a rifle peeped out from between a crack in the closed shutters.

Alasdair kept his hands where the woman could see them and assumed as non-threatening stance. "Be ye the woman who assisted a wounded man and an old woman?" he bit back the words *and a beautiful lass*. While he champed at the bit to hear all the woman could tell him about Isobel, he had to win her trust first.

"If I am?"

He chanced a glance in Ian's direction, then returned his focus to the tip of the gun barrel aimed at them. "We be cousins to the man ye saved and close friends to the old woman. We come to thank ye and pay our respects. It's our understanding our dear friend died."

"Yer names?" The tip of the gun barrel didn't waver. The old woman was relentless and unyielding.

"Alasdair Cameron, and this is my brother, Ian."

The gun slid out of sight, disappearing into the shutters. A thumping behind the door told him the bar across the threshold had been lifted and set aside. With a groaning squeak, the door opened with a slow, cautious swing.

"Ye be him?" asked the raggedy old woman standing in the doorway. "Ye be her man?" Her eyes narrowed as she studied him. "Come inside. Ye're looking a mite peely-wally 'cept for that burn on yer face. Be ye injured elsewhere?"

"My heart," Alasdair managed to rasp out as he hitched his way forward. He found himself suddenly weak, drained with the relief that mayhap he'd finally learn of his dear love's whereabouts. "Tell me, I beg ye, tell me she lives."

The kindly old crone reassured him with a smile and waved him forward. "Aye, she lives," she said soft and low as she stole a glance around. "Come inside. Morley will see to yer horses."

A young lad, a scythe clutched in his hands, stepped out from around the corner of the house.

"It's all right, Morley," the woman said. "Take their horses in the shed and get them some feed and water, aye?"

The boy gave an obedient nod, leaned the blade's long wooden handle against the wall, and hurried to gather the horses.

"Come." She stepped aside and held out a hand.

Alasdair ducked to enter the home, and Ian followed.

"I be Euna Ranald." She shuffled around them and pointed to the only two chairs in the room. "Sit. The both of ye."

"Where is she? Where is my Isobel?" He couldn't bear waiting any longer.

"Isobel," Euna repeated with a thoughtful smile. "Aye. That name suits her better." She plunked two wooden cups on the table in front of them and hurried over to the cupboard beside the hearth and fetched a bottle. As she filled each of the cups, she nodded. "She told us her name was Ailsa MacNaughton in order to protect her son." She motioned toward the cups. "Drink. It's not the whisky ye look like ye need, but it's nay so bad. Brewed it m'self."

Ian scooped up the cup, took a hearty swig, then thumped his chest and wheezed out a coughing fit. Face red and forehead peppered with sweat, he slid the cup back to the table with a shake of his head.

"It's not all that bad," Euna scolded, then turned to Alasdair. "Wee sips, aye?"

"After ye tell me about my Isobel." He leaned forward, his fist resting on the table beside the cup.

The woman's smile turned sour, and she blew out a heavy sigh. "She went to get her son back from those men that stole him away."

"By herself?" He launched to his feet, willing the woman to eat her words, and tell him the truth.

Euna backed up a step, hands held high as though to fend him off. "I told her it was ill-advised, but she wouldna listen. Especially, after the soldiers came here searching for her and the boy, and one of them recognized yer kin."

"Lord Almighty," Ian said. "Would she truly do such a foolhardy thing?"

"Aye. She would," Alasdair said. He sank back into the chair and dropped his head into his hands. The thought of her out there all alone—defenseless, vulnerable, helpless—the thought crazed him. He lifted his head and looked Euna in the eyes. "Do ye know which direction she went? Did she say where she believed the men would take the boy?"

Euna puckered her mouth and drew her brows together. Tapping a finger against her chin, she paced around the small room. "South for certain, but she named a place, as well." She scowled harder, eyes narrowing. "What did she say?" she muttered to herself.

Alasdair chanced a drink of Euna's deadly brew. The fiery liquid hit his tongue and burned a trail clear to his gut. He breathed in a hot breath and blew it out. He'd had worse but *damnation*. Strengthened by the cup of dragon's blood, he glared at the pacing crone. "Think, woman! Isobel's life depends on my finding her."

Euna shot him a fierce look and waved his words away just as Morley entered the room.

"Morley!" She whirled about. "The place Ailsa named. The place where her son might be?"

The boy made a hissing sound along with some odd motions with his fingers and hands.

"That's it!" Triumphant finger in the air, Euna faced Alasdair. "Hestlemoor. She said that was where that bastard would lock up her son. It was where he held her prisoner all those years."

England. Alasdair's heart fell, but his anger and determination strengthened. He didn't know England as well as he knew Scotland, but he had heard of Hestlemoor. It was the wicked duke's summer home that sat on the shores to the west of the Lake District. Rumors abounded about the place and all that went on there.

He turned to Ian. "Four days' ride. Maybe three if we push hard."

"Then push hard, we will," Ian said as he rose to his feet.

Morley tapped Euna's shoulder, made several more curious gyrations with his hands, then hurried to a cot in the corner. The boy pulled back the blanket and gathered something to his chest. Face solemn and eyes filled with sorrow, he came to Alasdair and held out a thick braid of hair.

"It's hers," Euna explained. "She bade me cut her hair, and then she dressed as a man." With a reassuring squeeze of her grandson's shoulder, she nodded toward the hank of hair the lad held between his hands. "He thinks ye should have it since ye be the man of her heart."

Alasdair accepted the silky tress. He stared down at its glossy blackness. She had cut her hair and dressed as man. How could she hope to succeed at such a thing? Jaw tightening, he tucked the braid inside his shirt, close to his heart. "I have to find her before she gets herself killed."

CHAPTER TWENTY

"I SAY, FERGUSON," Lieutenant Pewterton said. "I do believe you are the finest tracker I have ever known. We could use a man like you in His Majesty's army. Have you ever considered it?"

Isobel bit back a scathing retort. Instead, she nudged an elbow hard into Pewterton's side, then placed a finger across her lips.

The lieutenant's eyes rounded, and he gave a quick, apologetic nod.

She shook her head and glanced to her right, Atchison and Fields both shrugged. The four of them lay on their bellies atop the rocky crag overlooking the camp of the three men who held Connor captive. The remainder of Pewterton's squad waited behind them, at the base of the rugged cliff.

Her heart twisted, and she nearly sobbed aloud at the sight of dear sweet Connor huddled in the firelight. So forlorn. So lost. Her poor wee lad cowered at the base of a tree, his knees drawn to his chest, and his arms clutched around them. He looked so pale.

She motioned for them to slide back from the ledge. She had a plan, but she would need the soldiers' cooperation. Partway down the rocky hillside, she held up a hand and stopped them. Waving them in close, she spoke in a low, gruff whisper, "If we charge'm, they might hurt the boy to save themselves. I wouldna put anything past ruffians such as them." She watched the trio of Englishmen, letting her words sink in and doing her best to seem more like a bounty hunter than an anxious mother about to reclaim her child. "If the boy gets hurt, there'll be no gold for me, and ye're sure to get a reprimand for failing in yer orders."

Atchison and Fields both gave slow nods of agreement. The lieutenant scowled back at her, pursing his lips.

"What do you suggest?" Atchison asked.

"Three men. Three shots. Clean and simple." She glanced back up the hillside. "They're within range from up there. Pick'm off like fine fat birds on a limb, aye? Then hie down to their camp and gather up the lad."

"You mean to kill them?" Pewterton stared at her in horror. "Without proper trial or even hearing a word of their defense?"

"Ye saw the boy. His condition." She clenched her fists to keep from clubbing him with the butt of her pistol to knock some sense into his thick skull. Over the past few days, she had gotten to know the British soldiers. Several were not so bad. She might even say she liked Pewterton, Atchison, and Fields. But if Pewterton didn't pull his head out of his arse, she'd quickly change her opinion. "Ye doubt their abuse of the lad? Open yer eyes, man. Ye saw how he looked."

The lieutenant stared downward, pulling at his chin as he appeared to ponder her words and war with his conscience. He shook his head, fixing her with a troubled look. "I am not comfortable acting as both judge and executioner. We should merely capture them and ensure they go to trial. Let the court decide their fates."

They were but a day's ride from Hestlemoor. In fact, they stood on Hestlemoor land right now. She recognized the landscape. One way or another, she had to recover Connor tonight. Once behind Hestlemoor's iron gates, getting him back might prove impossible. And the kidnappers had to die—quickly. If any lived, they might make out who she was and give away her identity.

It would be difficult enough keeping Connor from recognizing her. A son would know his mother. As much as she hated the thought of it, the only way she could keep her identity safe was by keeping her distance once they rescued him until it came time to spirit him away.

But now, she had to play on Pewterton's weaknesses to get the indecisive fool to act. "I canna believe ye would choose to defend those heartless curs over that poor innocent lad's welfare. Ye willna condemn them to die, but ye'll risk a wee bairn's life? God forgive ye. God forgive ye for denying the lad the rescue he needs."

"God does pay particular attention to the innocents, does he not?" the lieutenant said as though in a daze. He glanced back up the mountain, frowning at the ledge. "He watches over them?"

"Aye," Isobel affirmed, allowing her argument to take root and grow in the troubled man's mind. She struggled to remain calm. It was all she could do to control the raging desire to dash into the camp and snatch Connor up by herself. They needed to get on with it while the current situation remained in their favor. "What say ye, man?"

"Count me in," Atchison said.

"I, as well," Fields chimed in, clutching his rifle in both hands. "Although I be a better cook than a marksman."

She patted the rifle hanging from her shoulder. The soldiers had been good enough to loan it to her since all she possessed were the two pistols that had once belonged to Morley's father. "A blackguard for each of us, then." She turned to Pewterton and nodded to the rifle slung across his back. "If any of us should miss, ye can finish the job we started, aye?"

He pulled his rifle into both hands, stared down at it, then looked up and nodded.

"I shall take the man in black." She had promised herself to finish that particular rogue off. Tonight, vengeance belonged to her.

"The scarred man will be my target," Atchison volunteered.

Fields let out a frustrated huff. "That means I get the skinny one."

He scowled at Isobel and Atchison both. "I told you my aim is poor, and yet you give me the thinnest target?"

Atchison shook his head and rolled his eyes. "The scarred man is fatter. You take him. I'll take the thin one."

"Might we just get on with it? I still have an ill-feeling about this whole affair, and my nerves can bear no more." Pewterton swiped the back of one hand across his forehead. He looked ready to faint.

Isobel nodded and led the way back to their perch on the ledge. Dearest Connor still crouched at the base of the tree, staring into the flames. Her target sat with his back to her, poking branches into the crackling fire. Both the scarred leader and the thin man with the cold, dead eyes stood opposite him but still well within range.

"On my word," she whispered. All of them readied their rifles and took aim. She leveled her sights on the center of the man's back, right between his shoulder blades. She eased in a deep breath, then blew it out. "Now." She squeezed the trigger.

Three shots exploded, followed by a fourth shot moments later. Connor scrambled to his feet and darted behind the tree. His pitiful wails echoed through the night. "Mama! Mama!"

Isobel swallowed hard and forced herself not to react. Instead, she stood, slung the rifle to her shoulder, and brushed off her hands. "Well done, lads."

"I shall run and get the poor child," Lieutenant Pewterton announced, then scurried down the rocky slope and around the base of the cliff to the dead men's camp.

She watched from the ledge as he bent down and talked to Connor for a long while, then lifted the boy into his arms and carried him back to where the troops waited. Struggling to calm her pounding heart, she pulled in deep breaths. Connor was safe, and their final escape was at last within reach. Hovering at a safe distance, she basked in the view of her beloved son. The soldiers stood a few feet away around Connor, chatting with the lad, and attempting to put him at ease.

"My time will come," she whispered. As soon as her new English friends drifted off to sleep, she and Connor would steal away and not stop until they reached the sanctuary of *Tor Ruadh*.

"Ferguson!" Pewterton called out as he waved. "Come down, man. Lord Temsworth wishes to meet the man responsible for his rescue."

"I must be strong." She hitched her thumb up under the strap of her rifle and trod down the hillside. When she reached the base of the hill, she stood a few feet away, kept her head bowed, and touched the brim of her hat. "Lord Temsworth." A knot tightened in her throat as Connor peered up at her. Eyes narrowing, he studied her entirely too long for comfort. Thank the saints for the cover of the night.

"Think ye can find my mama like ye found me?" Connor finally asked.

She ached to sob out her love for him. Her knees shook with the need to fall to the ground, but she managed to hold firm. "Where did ye last see her, m'lord?" she asked.

"Back in Scotland. By the water where those men grabbed me up and stole me away."

"I'll do what I can," she promised, all the while keeping her head ducked and her face in the shadows. She prayed for clouds to cover the sky and block what little light there was coming from the waning moon and the stars winking around it.

"We shall make camp at once," Pewterton announced with a pleased-with-himself smile. He bent and brought his face close to Connor's. "Fields shall cook you a fine meal, my lord, and then you may sleep to be well-rested when we return you to your father tomorrow."

Connor backed up a step, a horrified look on his face. "Nay! Ye canna take me back to him. Father's a terrible, mean man. A cruel, heartless bastard! Auntie Yeva said so, and I say it, too."

Isobel bit the inside of her cheek to keep from cheering.

Lieutenant Pewterton's jaw dropped. He slowly straightened and stared down at the lad. "Oh, dear." He bent, returning to Connor's level. "Lord Temsworth, how could you say such a thing? Did those miscreants torture you? Who is this Auntie Yeva? Who filled your head with such slander about your father?"

The boy frowned and stared at the lieutenant as though he thought him addled. "I dinna know what slander means or mis-cer…miscre…whatever that other word was." His look grew more thoughtful. "All I know is I want ye to take me back to Scotland to my real da. He'll find my mama. He can do everything. I think he's in Edinburgh now."

"Your *real* da," the lieutenant repeated with some difficulty. "Is the Duke of Temsworth."

"Nay." Connor shook his head. "Temsurth is the mean bastard." He crossed his arms over his chest and lifted his chin. "Alasdair Cameron is my *real* da."

Pewterton made a sad clucking sound as he clasped a hand over his mouth and studied the boy. "Poor mite," he said in a lowered voice. "Confused due to the trauma he's experienced." He snapped his fingers toward one of his lower-ranking men. "See to the burial of those criminals at once. Perhaps that will ease his lordship's mind."

The foot soldier paired off with another and took off.

"Search them first," the lieutenant called out after them. "I should like to know whether they did this of their own volition or if someone hired them to torment his lordship."

Isobel tensed. Surely, the criminals would not have anything on them that pointed to an association with the duke. She cleared her throat. "Best make camp and get the lad's belly filled and then to bed. Looks worn out." The quicker the entire camp slept, the quicker she and Connor could make their escape. Then she'd find Alasdair and get word to him. They'd be together again. Finally. *Please keep Alasdair safe.* She pointed at the lad. "Look at them shadows under his eyes."

"I agree. Lord Temsworth does look in dire need of rest." Lieutenant Pewterton took hold of Connor's shoulders and gently steered him toward Fields. "Fields here is a fine cook. If you would be so good as to go with him, your lordship, I feel certain he can find you something delicious to enjoy until your dinner is fully prepared."

Connor glanced up at the lieutenant. Eyes narrowing, he cocked his head. "Ye seem nice, but Auntie Yeva told me all redcoats are liars and cheats, so ye best know I'll be on my guard wif ye."

Pewterton pressed a hand to his chest, astonishment filling his face. "Have you ever heard of such?" He turned to Isobel, eyes wide.

She shrugged. "Sounds like the lad has been through a lot. I wouldna pay it much mind."

"Perhaps you are right." Pewterton turned and watched the boy toddling off alongside Fields. "I am truly glad we recovered the young marquess, and as soon as we return to London, I shall see you justly rewarded."

The only reward she needed now was reuniting herself and Connor with Alasdair. She gave a slow nod and touched the brim of her hat.

"Lieutenant Pewterton!" The call rang out from the direction of the deceased men's camp.

The hairs rose on the back of her neck. An ominous tingle shivered all the way down her spine. What now?

"What is it, Ladney?" Pewterton turned and waited like a hunting dog about to flush a pheasant.

"Something you should see, sir."

"Excuse me." Pewterton jerked with a polite bow and strode off toward the kidnappers' camp.

Instinct told her to grab Connor and run. She turned and spotted the whereabouts of the horses. Her mount stood tethered among the others already settled for the evening. She hurried over and pulled him free, then led him a few paces away from where the remaining soldiers were setting up camp.

"Stay here, lad. Wait for me, aye?" Isobel rubbed the horse's nose, then pressed her cheek to his muzzle.

Keeping watch for Pewterton's return, she hurried over to the wagon where Fields and Connor stood perusing the offerings for the evening's meal. She pulled her hat lower and kept her chin tucked.

"Stew, I think, your lordship. Would that be to your liking?" Fields held up a chunk of dried meat in one hand and a handful of root vegetables in the other, waiting for the boy's decision.

"Aye." Connor tiptoed to see into the back of the wagon. "I like me some carrots."

"How 'bout we fetch the water?" Isobel offered, scooping the pot out of the back of the wagon before Fields could argue. "Come along, lad. A stretch of yer legs will do ye good. Sharpen yer appetite."

He eyed her for a long moment, munching on bites of the dried fruit he clutched in one hand. "How come ye're wif them?" he asked, pointing a chunk of dried date in Fields's direction, then aiming it at her. "Ye be a Scot. Not an English."

"Aye, that I am." She waved him forward, willing him to cooperate before it was too late. She couldn't reveal herself in front of Fields. She had to get Connor in private. "Come along, and I'll explain it best I can."

The boy shrugged and followed her, pausing to call back to Fields. "We be back in a bit wif yer water."

"Thank you, my lord," Fields responded without looking up from the carrots he had spread across his chopping board.

Isobel headed toward the place she had left Thunder waiting.

As soon as Connor spotted the horse, he halted and fixed her with an icy glare. "That's my mama's horse." He threw down his treats, grabbed up a nearby stick, and struck her across the shins. "What have ye done wif my mama?" he growled.

Legs stinging, she bit her lip to keep from crying out as she dropped to her knees. "Connor!" she whispered, whipping off her hat and rubbing away the sooty grime from her face with a swipe of her sleeve. "It's me, son."

Connor launched into her arms, knocking her to the ground. "Mama!" he sobbed against her neck as he burrowed into her embrace. "Mama!" he cried out again, hugging her tight.

"Shh! Quiet now. Quiet." Arms wrapped around him, she rolled and staggered to her feet. She pushed him up into the saddle, then stuck her foot in the stirrup, and struggled to launch herself up behind him.

"Mama, look out!"

A hard yank on her coattails knocked her off balance. She fell back to the ground and found herself staring up into Pewterton's bright red face.

"You lied to me, madam! Played me for the fool." Sputtering and spitting with indignation, he jabbed a finger against a small tattered piece of parchment bearing a broken wax seal. "Never did I imagine you to be anything other than what you appeared until the child claimed you as his mother." He shook the document in Isobel's face. "And you had me assist in the murder of three innocent men. Your husband hired those men to recover his son!"

"He is *my* son!" she roared, every last shred of her control snapping. "You have no idea what a monster that man is. Connor is *my* son, and I mean to see him safe from that evil bastard." She scrambled to her feet, crouching low as she pulled the butcher knife from her boot and backed toward the horse. "And those men were far from innocent. They murdered my aunt by beating her to death. They tied my son like a felled deer, threw him across a horse, and rode away. Does that sound like innocent men to ye?"

"Your husband is the Duke of Temsworth, and the marquess is his son!" Pewterton shook as though beset with a fit of tremors. "Every word you have spoken since we met has been a lie, and yet now you expect me to believe these horrid tales you spew? Disgraceful." He shook his head and smoothed a hand back across his hair. "I refuse to listen to any more lies. Save yer breath, madam."

"My mama doesna lie!" Connor shouted. "Father used to beat her all the time and lock her away in a box. She almost died lots of times and wouldha if not for Auntie Yeva helping her get better. Father laughed whenever she'd scream, then he'd hurt her even more. Said he liked it when she screamed. He told me when I got to be seven, he'd make me be the one to kill her or he'd hurt me 'til I screamed, too."

The knife dropped from her hand as she turned and stared up at Connor. Revulsion and hatred for both Temsworth and her own cowardice buckled her knees. Why had she not left with Connor years ago and shielded him from that demented monster? She'd had no idea Temsworth had tormented the boy in such a way. She'd thought him safe—at least until the duke had openly threatened the boy's well-being to her. Then she had run away with him. She covered her face with her hands, sobs escaping her. How had she allowed her son to be treated so?

A soft patting and tiny arms around her neck made her weep all the harder. "I am so sorry, Connor. I'm so verra sorry," she whispered.

"It's okay, Mama." Connor hugged her tighter. "Ye didna know, and I couldna tell ye 'cause he said he'd hurt Auntie if I did."

She gathered Connor into her lap and rocked from side to side. With a glance up at Pewterton and the other soldiers who had gathered around, she pleaded, "Please. I beg ye. Let us go our way. I swear, I willna tell a soul about ye."

The lieutenant glared at her, fists trembling at his sides. He spun about, gave her his back, and strode a few steps away. "Place her in irons, Atchison. Tether the boy to her, as well. We shall deliver both the duchess and the marquess to His Grace at Hestlemoor tomorrow. I refuse to be played the fool again. The Duke of Temsworth can deal with them as he sees fit."

"Please show mercy." Isobel eased Connor out of her lap and clambered to her feet. "Return me if ye must, but I beg ye, protect my son. Please take him somewhere safe. Please. I swear I willna betray ye no matter what Temsworth does to me. I promise. Please keep my son safe, and I shall die with the secret of how ye helped me."

Pewterton kept walking, then disappeared from view.

"Forgive me," Atchison mumbled as he clamped the shackles around her wrists and ankles.

"Leave her be!" Connor shouted, launching himself at the man, kicking and biting as soon as he made contact.

"Leave off, boy!" Atchison snatched hold of Connor and held him at arm's length while Ladney tied a rope around the lad's waist, then tied the other end to the chains between Isobel's wrists.

"Please, let us go," she begged in a desperate whisper. "Ye know I'm not lying about Temsworth. I can see it in yer eyes. Ye've heard of his cruelty. Please—dinna condemn us to him."

"I know you speak the truth, Your Grace," Atchison said. "But I cannot help you. The duke is too powerful, and I've a wife and children."

"Ye send us to our deaths then." Isobel sank to her knees. "Ye understand that well enough, do ye not?"

"Yes, Your Grace." Atchison turned away and bowed his head. "I *understand* it all too well." He took a step away and paused, head still lowered. "And again—I beg your forgiveness." He hurried away.

CHAPTER TWENTY-ONE

A LASDAIR HELD UP a hand and reined in his horse. He concentrated on sifting through the sound of leaves fluttering in the breeze, birdsong, and what he thought he'd heard—a sound that didn't belong in the woods.

Ian did the same, remaining silent with his gaze locked on Alasdair.

There. Alasdair nodded and motioned to the left as he mouthed, *"Men."*

Ian gave an assenting dip of his chin.

They dismounted, tethered their horses to a tangle of rowan saplings, and eased deeper into the trees, their steps as silent as if they were a part of the land.

Up ahead, several men were deep in conversation. Alasdair paused, taking in every word.

"Just the few of us now. Think them others'll report him mad once they reach the garrison?" The man talked in a low, cautious tone. "Surely, they'll not. Most of'm like the lieutenant. Don't they?" Shuffling leaves and a chorus of low-pitched grumbling responded. "I know," the original speaker said. "Most of'm know his story. I hope they keep it in mind."

Alasdair eased to one side and peered around a trio of trees. Three men sat on boulders and stumps at the edge of a clearing. A smoldering fire crackled and popped in front of them. Alasdair scanned the area further, counting six more men scattered across the way, cleaning their weapons, napping, talking—redcoats, the lot of them.

Pistol drawn, Ian appeared, nudged him, and cocked a brow. "Poor odds," he mouthed.

With a shake of his head, Alasdair held up a finger, pointed to the men, then touched his ear. He wanted to hear more of what the soldiers had to say.

"You seen him today? He looks poorly. The man needs rest. And he hasn't eaten in days near as I can tell." The soldier in the center of the trio shifted with a sad shake of his head. "He's stood watch over that road ever since we took her and the boy in there."

Alasdair tensed even more. A dangerous combination of rage and the need for vengeance surged hot and fierce. *She and the boy.*

"He feels guilty, he does," said the Englishman to the left. He paused in his whittling and shook the carved stick at the other two. "He knows of the duke's evil ways. He knows the duchess and the boy spoke true about that soulless devil."

Clenching his teeth to keep from roaring, Alasdair struggled to hold fast.

Ian's eyes widened. He took hold of Alasdair's arm and squeezed.

"Then why did he turn them over?" the redcoat on the far right asked.

"Pride," said the man in the middle with a disgusted snort. "Hurt his pride that she tricked him." The soldier shrugged. "Dunno why. She tricked all of us. I thought Ferguson a man. Didn't you?"

The other men agreed.

Enough. Alasdair crashed through the trees. He aimed his gun at the nearest man's head. "What did ye do with my Isobel?"

"You do realize you are gravely outnumbered, sir?" A tenth man, one Alasdair had not seen in his assessment of the camp, stepped into view. The bedraggled soldier, a lieutenant from the insignia on his smudged and wrinkled coat, held up a trembling hand toward the other soldiers. "Hold fire. Understood?"

The men lowered their weapons but stood at the ready.

Alasdair scanned the odd assortment of redcoats, then disarmed his pistol, and shoved it into his belt. "Ian," he said over his shoulder before turning back to address the lieutenant. "I may be sorely outnumbered, but it seems to me, the lot of ye are not all that fierce."

The man bowed his head and swiped a hand across his brow. "You are correct, sir. I fear we are beleaguered. I've no one to blame but myself." With a heavy sigh, he raised his gaze to Alasdair's. "I am Lieutenant Frances Pewterton. I assume you must be Alasdair Cameron?"

"Aye." Alasdair studied the troubled man. "Would ye mind telling me how ye came to know my name?"

Pewterton took on a thoughtful, pained look. "The young marquess informed us you were his true father." He shook with a humorless laugh. "His *da*, I believe was how the boy phrased it."

Pride warmed Alasdair, filling him near to bursting. *Aye.* He loved Connor like a son. The lad had spoken true. Remembering the conversation he'd just overheard, the warm feeling left as swiftly as it came. "What did ye do with them?" He took a step forward, flexing his fingers. The man's answer determined whether or not he allowed him to live.

The lieutenant stared at him. Silent. Sorrowful. He closed his eyes, and his chin dropped. Hands lifted as though awaiting judgment, he heaved out another great sigh. "We took them to Hestlemoor. Four days ago." He lifted his head, looking as though ready to weep. "Forgive me. My foolish pride took hold and held fast until it was too late."

"But the duke isn't there yet," volunteered one of the original trio of men. "We've stood watch over the road. According to the duke's man at Hestlemoor, he's due to arrive any day."

"Depending on where they've put her, we might be able to get her and Connor out at nightfall," Ian suggested as he moved to Alasdair's side. He spared a narrow-eyed glance at the gathered redcoats. "If they feel as bad as they say, they could help."

Ian's proposal galled him. Whether or not the English helped, he'd see to Isobel and Connor's freedom this day or die in the trying. He gave each of the men a long, hard look. "How much do ye regret condemning an innocent woman and child to certain torture and death?"

"More than you shall ever know, sir," the lieutenant answered for the men as he stepped forward. "I claim full responsibility and shall assist you in any way possible." He held his head higher and addressed the soldiers. "Those of you who wish to leave may do so without fear of reprisal. I do, however, implore you to remain silent until such a time as Master Cameron and his associate are well on their way to safety with the duchess and the marquess. I feel it the least we can do to reverse my grave error in judgment."

"I'll stay and help," a soldier said. "Name is Atchison." He thumped a fist to his chest. "At your service, sir."

"I as well," said another as he stood alongside Atchison. "I be Fields. Not the best shot, but I can brawl good enough."

"Ladney." The third redcoat took his place next to the other two. He grinned. "I can shoot the wings off a midge."

One by one, the remaining six sounded off, assuring their willingness to help.

Alasdair had never thought to find himself leading a troop of redcoats, but if that's what it took to save Isobel and Connor, then so be it. Time to plan the battle. "When ye turned her over, did they allow ye inside the house? What do ye know about the grounds? The guards? The servants?"

"We saw the entry hall only, I fear." Pewterton frowned, stroking his chin as he paced in a slow circle around the campfire. "A strange arrangement with the servants." He stopped his meandering. "Not a woman among them. At least, none that we saw. And the interior of the place looked more a stark prison than what one would expect of the summer home of a wealthy member of the peerage." He resumed wandering about the clearing. "The one called Hawkins did order the duchess and her son be escorted to her private wing. A trio of men laid hands upon her and the child and dragged them up the staircase to the right of the entry hall." With a frustrated shake of his head, he faced Alasdair. "I fear that's all we know."

"I need to see the place." Alasdair paused and glanced back at the lieutenant as he headed for his horse. "How far?"

Pewterton motioned toward the south. "Not far. I'll wait for you at the base of this rise while you fetch your mount. You can see Hestlemoor in the distance from there."

Alasdair and Ian hastened back through the woods.

"Should we trust them?" Ian asked as they saddled up and turned their horses southward.

"Not yet." Alasdair took the lead, noting movement through the trees to his left.

The English. On their horses. Apparently, the soldiers didn't trust them either. He motioned for Ian to follow and turned his mount to come up behind the soldiers who had decided to join their lieutenant. He kept some distance between them. Enough to watch. Enough to be ready.

"The man was right," Ian said as the thinning trees revealed a rolling green landscape ahead. He pointed toward the horizon. "If that's Hestlemoor, it's not what I expected."

Alasdair agreed. Centered on a tract of land overlooking the sea and surrounded by stone fortifications, the place looked more defensive stronghold than country estate. Pewterton had said the interior resembled a prison. The exterior looked the same. "Removing Isobel and Connor should prove interesting."

"Aye," Ian agreed as he scowled at the challenge ahead. "I wish the MacCoinnichs were here rather than all these bloody English."

Alasdair urged his mount onward at a slower pace, all the while studying the building. "Aye, brother, I as well." He halted his horse once again.

Hestlemoor faced inland, and the structures within the boundary wall laid out in the shape of an arrow. Two wings, each two-stories high, and at their apex, a hexagonal building of at least four levels. All the buildings were constructed of the same thick stone blocks as the defensive walls. "The lieutenant said they took her to the right."

"Aye." Ian pointed to the wing in question. "We need to see it from the seaside."

"I dinna see any guards walking the wall." He set his horse in motion again. The corners of the walls were rounded towers bereft of windows but fitted with arrow slits at different levels. Guards could be behind those arrow slits. Watching.

"You see what I mean, sir?" Pewterton asked as they joined him. "Not quite what one would expect when reference is made to a summer home." He frowned at the place. "And according to the nearest village, the duke is rarely seen."

"But he's due to arrive any time?" Alasdair shifted in the saddle, itching to charge into the place and tear it apart stone by stone until he recovered his precious love and the lad. "Ye discovered this, how?"

"The duke's man, Hawkins." The lieutenant cleared his throat. "I understand your distrust. I would feel the same if in your position."

Alasdair didn't reply. It took all his control to keep from throttling the man for what he'd done. If not for that sorry fool, Isobel and Connor would be safe and dispatched to France by now. A glance skyward told him they had some time before nightfall. He dismounted and yanked a pair of trews from the bag behind his saddle. His beloved kilt would betray him here. "Don yer trews and stow yer kilt. We'll ride to the sea."

Ian complied without question.

His colors folded and tucked away, he remounted and spurred his horse forward, galloping across the open landscape toward the sea. He gave Hestlemoor a wild berth but studied its barrier wall with stolen glances as he rode, Ian thundered along behind him. Pewterton and his men had the good sense to stay behind. Alasdair allowed himself a deep-throated growl. So far, the Englishmen appeared genuine, but time would tell. They halted at the cliff's edge, riding back and forth along the rim as though admiring the view.

"Whoever built this didna fear attack from the sea," Ian remarked with a glance at the skirting wall surrounding the back of the castle. "No guard tower. No arrow slits."

Alasdair drew closer to the edge and peered downward. "Look below." No wonder the builder didn't fear an enemy from the water. Dense clusters of rocks, a jagged barrier sharper than dragon's teeth, abutted the base of the cliff. Waves crashed and swirled around the deadly spikes, honed and blackened by the briny caress of the water. He retreated from the dangerous edge and faced the fortification. "This is where we shall enter."

Ian studied the wall. "The English could provide a diversion."

"Aye," Alasdair agreed. "At the front." The redcoats could draw Hawkins's attention by visiting to warn him of some such lie. He didn't care what they said as long as it kept Hawkins and the other servants occupied long enough for him and Ian to breech the wall and get inside. Damn, he wished they knew more about the inside. He gave a decisive nod. "As soon as the sun sets, we scale the wall. Those supports should give us good enough foothold."

"Aye." Ian risked riding a few yards closer. "'Twill be a chore. Especially with ye still healing."

He ignored his brother's observation. Chore or not, it would be done.

They rejoined Pewterton and his men.

"Have you formed a plan?" the lieutenant asked. The others drew closer, their eyes wide with rapt attention.

"As soon as the sun sets, ye and yer men need to visit Hawkins. Keep the man and as many of the servants occupied for as long as possible." Alasdair glared at the four men. They had to realize the importance of what he was asking. "Can ye do that?"

Pewterton reacted with a worried frown, but Atchison edged his horse closer. "What better way to keep their attention then to notify them we received a report you're in the area?"

"So ye want them to double the guard whilst we're trying to breech their enclosure?" Alasdair rubbed a hand across his brow and groaned. Fate had saddled him with a bunch of damned fools.

"Ah...yes. Well, I guess that would be ill-advised. Forgive me," Atchison retreated, his cheeks scarlet as he ducked his head.

"Tell them ye bring word the duke is injured," Ian supplied. "Carriage accident and they must come at once to fetch him and send for help. Ye said they're expecting him, aye? Such news wouldna stir suspicion."

His brother impressed him. He'd never known Ian to be such a good liar.

Pewterton brightened. The man even smiled. "Yes. We could tell them we came upon the wreck whilst returning to the garrison. There's no help nearby for the duke, and he needs them immediately."

Fields, Atchison, and Ladney nodded. "We could tell them we left half our regiment there to guard him. That way, none of them will question our fewer numbers since we all crowded into the ward before," Ladney said. "I heard'm complaining 'bout all the horse shite we was leaving in their courtyard."

"I dinna care what ye tell them as long as they believe ye, and we're granted time to find Isobel." Alasdair turned and looked back at Hestlemoor. *God grant me the patience not to kill these fools*, he prayed. *And help me get Isobel and Connor back*, he added.

>>>><<<<

"I MADE IT so easy for you. Simple as could be. All you had to do was return my son."

Wrists locked in iron shackles attached to the outer sides of the cuffs around her ankles, Isobel fisted her hands as she crouched at Temsworth's feet. She twisted, adjusting her awkward position, and leveled her glare with his, knowing how much he hated eye contact. She didn't care. If this was to be her end, she'd die fighting. "Why do ye even want him? Ye've never loved him."

The duke limped around her, the tip of his cane thumping with every step. "Wealth." He jabbed the end of the walking stick between her shoulder blades and shoved downward until her face touched the floor. "You see, to ensure I didn't squander away all he had worked so hard to acquire, my father placed a brutish provision in his will. I received a mere tenth of my inheritance upon his death. Barely enough to survive, really. Once married, I received another tenth. That was still a laughable amount. Upon the birth of my heir, another tenth. Year by year, my allotment has increased. By the time the boy reaches his seventh birthday, I shall at last come into my full inheritance."

"And then what?" She turned her head to the side and boldly stared at him as he walked past.

The cane came down hard across her shoulders. She locked her jaws. She would not cry out. Temsworth fed off the pain of his victims. "It appears you have forgotten your lessons, dear wife. You are to keep your eyes lowered unless given permission to lift your head."

"Why should I?" she dared, riveting her gaze back to him. "I know what ye've planned for me."

"My, my, haven't we become the brazen little bitch." He limped out of her range of vision. "But you are correct. You are no longer necessary." The sound of his footsteps silenced. "Of course, there was a time when you provided ample enough amusement. Several prominent members here at Hestlemoor have commented on your absence. They would be most pleased to learn of your return. Perhaps that's how I shall dispose of you. I could allow them the full rein of their passions this time."

She closed her eyes and concentrated on breathing and escaping this hell. She would not revisit those terrible memories no matter what the bastard said.

A creaking whined to her left, then a gust of air blew across her. Briny. Damp. Cold. Waves crashed in the distance, mixed with the low rumbling of thunder. Temsworth had opened a window.

"Mama!"

Connor's faint call reached her, followed by the duke's cruel chuckle. "The lads are amusing themselves with the boy this evening. They must've told him you were in the garden maze. Have no worry, though. They did provide him with a lantern."

"Mama!"

"Rather sounds like the bleating of a lamb, don't you think?" the devil observed. "He's quite persistent. His little light bounces up and down the path as he searches."

"They've sent him out in the rain? In the dead of night?" She strained against the restraints. She wanted to keen out her sorrow but refused to give him the satisfaction. Connor's cries ripped through her. "If he catches his death from being soaked to the skin, ye'll fall short of yer inheritance, will ye not? He's but five, remember?"

"Quite true." Temsworth rapped his cane hard against the window facing. "Hawkins! Inside with him. Immediately. Get him dry and locked in his room." Temsworth's hitching step drew closer. His shadow danced across the rough wood of the floor biting into her knees. "And regarding your question as to what happens to the boy once he comes of age, never fear. Hawkins sees to the disposal of all unwanted litters here at Hestlemoor."

"I will find a way to kill ye," she warned through clenched teeth. "I swear it."

"Ha!" Temsworth grabbed her by the hair and jerked her face upward. "You amaze me, wife. Cut your hair and dress you as a man, and suddenly, you display a bravado I've never seen in you before." He twisted his hand tighter against her skull and brought his sneering face closer. "Whatever shall I do with you?"

Isobel spit in his face. He struck her hard enough to make her see flashes of light. It was worth it. The man's look of shock was priceless.

"Whatever ye do, I grant ye, it willna be easy. Ye willna break me this time." Too much was at stake. She had to save Connor. And now that she knew a promising future awaited, a life with Alasdair rather than isolation and thinking all she had ever loved was dead and gone, she'd fight to overcome anything that dared get in her way.

Temsworth's glare hardened as he pulled a square of lace-edged linen from his sleeve and wiped her spittle from his face. "We shall see." His head tilted as he studied her. "I have always relished a challenge."

He thumped his way to the door. Or at least in that direction. She couldn't tell for certain. Hinges gave a rusty groan. Good. He was leaving. "Until tomorrow, dear wife."

She sagged forward, resting her cheek on the floor. She had to overcome this, but how? With hands bound to her feet, she had few options. But Connor. She swallowed hard, his pitiful cries replaying through her mind. Her son needed her. She had to save him. If only Alasdair was here. But Alasdair thought her and Connor safe at the northernmost tip of Scotland. A cold, choking bleakness filled her as a gust of wind sputtered the lantern out, leaving her in darkness. Lightning flashed, and thunder rumbled like horses galloping across the sky.

She would not give up. Knees scraping against the floor, she pushed with her legs and pulled her arms, doing her best to wrench her hands free of the cuffs. The rough ironwork chewed into her flesh, and a warm wetness trickled into her palms. She paid it no mind. Maybe the blood would help her slip free.

Her aching muscles rebelled against the awkward positioning. Legs and shoulders knotted and cramped. The pain forced her to gasp. "God, please help me," she pleaded in a whisper. "Help me save Connor." She paused in her struggling and drew in several deep breaths and blew them out. "I can do this." Maybe if she rolled to her back. Perhaps that would be easier.

She twisted to her back, scolding herself as she stared up into the darkness. If she'd thought of this before the lantern blew out, she could've examined the shackles and better seen what she fought.

She narrowed her hands as much as possible and worked against the metal with a slow hard pull. Blood trickled faster up her arms as she lay with her feet and hands in the air. Her less dominant hand, the left, slid free, bloody and throbbing. Her left foot hit the floor. "Now the right," she encouraged, panting from the pain.

She folded her fingers tighter together, pushing with her left hand while she pulled the right. With a sickening, sucking sound, she yanked free. Her right heel bounced down to the wood beside her left. She stayed there for a long moment, scraped and bleeding hands clutched to her chest, breathing hard as she flexed her aching legs.

At least Temsworth's cruel form of shackles had no chains between them. Now that her hands were free of her feet, she could move about with ease. She crawled to the window and stiffly pulled herself upright, holding fast to the ledge as the strength returned to her limbs. Thank goodness, she'd only been bound a few hours. Much longer and she'd be sore pressed to walk at all.

She peered out the window, attempting to gather her bearings. Hawkins had called the place the temperance building. Said it lessened the rigor of even the most stubborn. She'd never been here before.

Apparently, her obedience when she had thought her situation hopeless, had spared her from even more cruelty. She hung out the window, craning her neck and squinting to see through the murky night. From what she could tell, she was on the second floor of the squat round tower in the center of the courtyard behind the main keep. Interesting.

She'd always believed the odd structure to be a dovecote. She could just make out the outline of the south wing to her left and the north wing to her right. Connor's suite was in the north wing. Or at least it had been before their escape. Her rooms had been connected to his.

Fingers spread, Isobel patted around the dark room, searching for anything that might be useful. The place was bare as old bones. She'd nearly decided to jump from the window and risk a broken leg when she brushed across something hanging on the wall. Leather whips. An entire rack of them hanging beside the door. She ran the braided leather through her fingers. The cording seemed seasoned. Supple. Strong. If she could tie some of the whips together and wedge them in the window hinge, she could get close enough to the ground to jump without injury.

Rain splattering against stone raised such a din, she could no longer hear the sea beating against the cliffs. *Good.* The night and the storm would hide her. She dumped an armload of the whips beside the window and knotted them together, discovering that some had razor-sharp barbs woven into their strips. By the time she finished, her fingers were as raw and bloody as her wrists.

She climbed onto the window ledge and jammed the whip with the knobbiest handle into the space between the window casing and the wall—forcing it open. "God be with me," she whispered as she eased out the window, hanging tight to the braided leather.

Thank goodness she wasn't any higher. Her strength would never hold. Trembling overtook her as she worked her way downward, biting her lip to keep from crying out when barbs she'd overlooked sliced into her palms. She peered downward but couldn't tell how close the ground might be. *I dinna care. God be with me.* She pushed away from the wall and let go, landing not on soggy ground but on top of a very solid person. A hard, muscular shoulder caught her in the ribs.

"Holy Mother of God!" someone cursed. A comfortingly familiar sound.

She struggled to catch her wind, holding her side as she rolled away from whoever she had hit. *Nay.* It couldn't be Alasdair. He'd gone to Edinburgh, maybe even London. Her panicked state must have rendered her addled.

A hand closed around her ankle, yanked her back, then jerked her to her feet. Another hand clamped across her mouth.

"Make a sound, and it'll be yer last," her assailant warned in a low, deadly tone.

Isobel closed her eyes and sagged into her captor's embrace, relief sapping her ability to stand. It was Alasdair. Thank God in heaven above.

"What the hell are ye playing at?" whispered another familiar voice.

Her heart sang. Ian was here, too.

"Kill whoever it is and toss them aside," he hissed.

"They hit me from above," Alasdair defended. "It's as though they were trying to escape. They could be an ally." One hand locked around her throat, and the other pressed across her mouth, he gave her a hard shake. "I'm going to give ye the chance to speak. Cry out for help, and I'll snap yer neck. Understand?"

She nodded, unable to hold back relieved tears.

Alasdair's hand slid away, but his grip on her throat remained.

"It is me, dear husband," she whispered, struggling not to sob.

The strong hands spun her about. Hard fingers dug into her shoulders. "Isobel? Speak again, so I'll know my ears didna deceive me."

"It is me," she said, struggling not to keen out her joy and alert all in the stronghold.

"Praise God in heaven above." Alasdair crushed her to his chest, raining kisses across her upturned face. "Thank God Almighty."

"We need to move," Ian interrupted, urgency ringing in his voice.

Ian was right. She forced herself free of Alasdair's beloved embrace. "I was headed to the north wing. Connor's rooms used to be there." Squinting against the pelting rain, she motioned toward the farthest window on the second floor. Her heart ached. The window was dark. She always kept a candle lit for Connor. "That would be his window, but I dinna ken if they're keeping him there or not."

"They separated ye?" Alasdair asked as they pressed their backs against the rounded wall of the torture building.

"Aye." She peered around the wall, glancing beyond it to the main building of the keep. All appeared quiet. "Temsworth no longer needs me, and he said he'd only allow Connor to live to his seventh birthday." Cold hard rage filled her, fueling every ounce of resolve she needed to finish this battle. "I mean to kill the bastard." She held out a hand. "Spare me yer knife, aye?"

"He's here?"

"Aye. Arrived today. Now give me yer dirk."

"Pewterton," Ian said in a tone that gave her chills.

"Aye," Alasdair agreed. "As soon he tells the lie to Hawkins, we're discovered."

"What lie?" Isobel asked. Ian and Alasdair weren't making sense.

"There's nay time to explain," Alasdair said, then bounded out of the shadows toward the north wing. He waved for them to follow. "We must make haste and find Connor."

CHAPTER TWENTY-TWO

T HE KNOWLEDGE THAT at any moment the alarm would sound tempered his joy at reuniting with Isobel. Once the warning rang out, Connor's recovery and their escape would become a greater challenge. Alasdair palmed a pistol in each hand as they crept along the wall. So far, all was quiet. He prayed they'd reach the lad before all hell broke loose. So much at risk, but so close. They couldn't fail now.

"This way," she whispered, pushing past him to take the lead. "There's a side door Connor and I always used to reach the gardens." She hefted his short sword in her right hand and his dirk in her left.

He hated the sight of her wading into the fray. But there was naught to be done about it. She stood the best chance of leading them to Connor, and they would not be leaving here without him. As they slipped in the side door, the alarm bell sounded, clanging long and loud through the stormy night. Determination pounded harder through his veins.

They hurried down a dimly lit passage, coming up short as doors slammed farther up the way. The clattering of boots against the stone floor thundered toward them. Wide hearths burned at each end of the wing, casting enough light that they risked being spotted. Isobel yanked hold of his arm and pointed in the opposite direction. "The garderobe. Back there. Hurry!"

The curtained-off alcove took them away from their destination, but there was no helping it. Alasdair stood in the center behind the curtain, pistols raised and ready in case any of Temsworth's men had noticed them seeking a place to hide. He'd shoot them right between the eyes if any dared pull the curtain aside. Ian stood to his left, pistol in one hand, sword in the other. Isobel pressed against the wall to his right with his dagger raised.

An unknown number of guards stormed past. The curtains swayed with the wind the group stirred. He held his breath, shifting his weight from one foot to the other, tensed and ready. The area grew quiet.

He slid the barrel of his pistol between the heavy curtains and peered out, glancing first one way, then the other. The hall was empty. "Looks to be safe," he said as he stepped out and took a better look around. Nerves on edge, he waved the others forward. "Best make haste. I fear they may try to take the lad somewhere more secure."

"Up those stairs," Isobel said, pointing her sword at a dimly lit archway at the far end of the hall. She took the lead at a dead run, charging up the narrow steps two at a time. Sconces fitted with hanging lanterns lit their way.

"Wait." He grabbed hold of her and pulled her back as they reached the arched opening of the second floor. He held a finger to his lips and tilted his head toward the hallway, listening. It was time to take greater care. The duke knew he'd come for Isobel and her son. All was silent. He eased out into the corridor, keeping Isobel tucked behind him.

"The door at the end," she whispered as gunfire popped somewhere off in the distance.

"Pewterton must be fighting back," Ian observed as they rushed down the hallway to Connor's room.

"Good," Alasdair said as they reached the door. "God be with them."

Isobel tried the latch, frowning when the door clicked and opened with no issue. "It's not locked," she said.

Heightened apprehension made him gently set her aside. He pulled her hand away from the latch. "I'll be going first, m'love. I smell a trap."

Thankfully, she didn't argue. Gunfire sounded again. Closer this time.

Alasdair eased through the door, pausing to allow his eyes to adjust to the darkened room. He would've thought there'd be at least a candle burning since the place appeared to be a nursery. Perhaps they'd imprisoned Connor elsewhere or, as he feared, already moved the lad somewhere more secure.

"There," Ian whispered, directing them to a faint light flickering under one of the three doors on the far wall.

"His room?" He looked at Isobel, the concern on her face stoking his readiness even more.

She shook her head and tapped her chest. *"Mine,"* she mouthed.

"Pray he's there." *Alone,* he silently added. He didn't fear a fight but didn't wish the child endangered. He motioned for them to stand to the right of the door as he eased it open.

"It appears the Tollbooth has grown lax," Temsworth observed in a sneering drawl. "You look entirely too hardy for a man who should've been properly tortured and hanged by now."

"Revenge does a lot to keep a man strong." Alasdair stepped forward, assessing the room while keeping Connor in his sights. Five men, including Temsworth. One of the wretches held a hand across Connor's mouth and a knife to the boy's throat. The other three flanked the duke with short swords and cudgels at the ready.

"Ahh, I see you brought your pet," The duke's gaze shifted to Alasdair's left. His mouth curled to one side as he pointed his cane at Isobel. "Since I'm feeling so magnanimous upon the return of my son, I am prepared to offer you a deal, Master Cameron. Leave now and take the bitch with you. I shall allow you and your men safe passage."

Alasdair risked another step forward, coming up short as the man holding Connor tightened the knife against the wide-eyed lad's throat. "Ye know that's not acceptable," he said with a tilting of his head toward the boy. "I willna leave without Connor. He is *my* son now."

"Then it appears we have a dilemma." Temsworth spared a glance at the lad. "Surrender your weapons, or the boy dies."

"He willna kill him," Isobel said as she moved to Alasdair's side. "He needs him alive until he's seven years old to get the rest of his inheritance."

Temsworth's mouth tightened, and his left eye twitched. He sidled over and positioned himself behind the man holding Connor. "Kill them," he ordered. "All except her. I shall see to her demise personally."

Alasdair aimed both pistols and fired. Neither went off, just popped as the hammers hit the caps. Damned wet powder.

The duke laughed, sounding like a hissing snake. "Oh, joy! Unexpected entertainment for the evening. Kill them now!"

"Here!" Isobel tossed him the short sword and switched his dirk to her right hand.

Three to three. Even odds. Somewhat. Isobel had always held her own with the lads when they were naught more than bairns. Hopefully, she'd nay forgotten the skills she'd learned as a wee lass. Alasdair knew the duke didn't possess the courage nor the skill to fight, and the one bastard could do nothing more than maintain his hold on Connor.

"Dinna let them near the door," Alasdair shouted to Ian as he surged forward.

Steel to steel clashed. Blades slid together, then hilt locked with hilt. He roared as he shoved the brute back to the wall. Arms locked, he buried his blade up beneath the man's ribcage and gutted him. He whipped his sword free and turned just as Isobel dropped and rolled hard against her approaching assailant's shins, tripping the man. Alasdair smiled. She had used that tactic often when they were children. She turned and jumped on the rogue's back, held fast, and slashed the long, lethal dagger across the man's throat.

Ian took out the third man but received an ugly slash across his chest in the process.

Alasdair stalked forward, pointing his sword at the man holding Connor. "I've a choice for ye, man. Release the boy, and I'll allow ye to see if ye can get past my brother."

"Do it and die," Temsworth growled, drawing his ornate small sword from his side and setting it against the man's neck.

Connor chose that moment to go limp, then bounced back up and slammed the back of his head against his captor's man parts.

The man choked out a pained grunt, struggling to maintain his hold. The duke slashed his throat, then lurched to grab hold of Connor's collar.

Before Alasdair could charge forward, Isobel stormed past him, screaming like an angry wraith.

Shock, then fear, registered on Temsworth's face, but it was quickly replaced by rage. He raised his sword to meet Isobel's onslaught, whilst struggling to maintain his hold on his son's shirt.

Connor twisted free, but rather than run, he snatched up Temsworth's cane and cracked the gold ball of the handle hard across the man's knees.

Thrown off balance, the duke staggered, twisting his weak leg. Isobel tackled him to the floor.

Alasdair waded in and wrenched the man's sword away as Isobel drove her dagger up into the soft underside of his chin.

"To the hottest parts of hell with ye," she screamed as she pulled the blade free and stabbed him again. "To hell!" she yelled, lifting the knife for another strike.

Alasdair caught hold of her wrist and pulled her away. "It's over, love," he assured as he held her until she stopped struggling. "Ye killed the bastard. He'll never trouble ye again."

"Mama!" Connor latched hold of them, wrapping his arms around them both.

Isobel's hiccupping sobs changed to joyous laughter. "My dear son," she hitched out as she wrapped an arm around him.

Connor lifted his tear-stained face to Alasdair. "Ye came for us. Ye came for both of us."

"'Course I came for ye." Alasdair patted the lad's back whilst still holding one arm tight around Isobel. "I would never leave my wife and son to such a terrible fate." He smiled down at him. "And I'm proud of ye for the way ye fought to protect yer mother."

"I was brave, aye?" Connor hugged himself tighter against them, pressing his face to Isobel's leg.

"That ye are, lad, that ye are." Alasdair cast a look about the room, the realization of what they'd accomplished, and the ramifications, hitting him full force. They had killed a duke. Not a particularly well-liked man, but a powerful man just the same. And several of his men. France as sanctuary was now their only choice—for an indefinite period. He squeezed Isobel in another hug and kissed the top of her head. It mattered not. At least they were reunited. "Time to go. Quickly now, aye?"

Ian spoke Alasdair's thoughts aloud. "*Tor Ruadh* first and then France, or straight to the port?"

"My gold is with Alexander for safekeeping. We'll need it to settle in France." Alasdair stepped back and touched a hand to Isobel's roughly cropped hair. "But if we travel as three men and a boy, we should make it to *Tor Ruadh* with no trouble." Ian's bloody chest concerned him. "How bad?"

"Naught but a wee scratch." His brother strode to the bed, ripped away a wide strip from the bedclothes, and shoved it into the front of his shirt to staunch the bleeding. He held his arms aloft and smiled. "Bandaged and ready for travel."

Isobel looked around the room, a strange expression on her face.

"This isna finished yet."

Gunfire and shouts within the keep sounded closer.

Alasdair took hold of her hand, fearing the entire ordeal had pushed his dear one's mind off-kilter. "Come, *mo chridhe*. We must make haste."

"Nay." She strode across the room, picked up the lantern burning brightly on the table, and tossed it to the center of the bed. "This place has been hell on earth. Time to purge it with fire." As flames took slow hold across the linens and blankets, she yanked the bed curtains from the rods and shoved one end of them into the hearth. The glowing hot coals ignited the cloth, and fire licked its way across the folds. Smoke filled the air.

"That should do it, lass." Alasdair took a firm hold of Isobel's arm and pulled. "Come. We need to go. Now." He understood her need for vengeance, but Temsworth's guards would be upon them soon.

Connor pulled at her other hand. "Come, Mama."

Her troubled brow smoothed, and she smiled. "Aye. Good enough, I reckon." She pulled away from Alasdair and retrieved his dirk from the floor. The weapon in her right hand, Connor's hand in her left, she nodded to Alasdair. "If we leave the way we came, we should miss everyone."

Ian lifted a burning candle from the sconce beside the door, then opened it. He glanced about, then turned to Alasdair and smiled. "Canny woman ye have there, brother. Fire is a fine distraction, and we've plenty of sconces to leave the place in ashes."

"Lead on, brother." Alasdair left the door to the blazing bedroom open, so the fire could spread easier.

The hall was still empty of guards, and the gunfire and shouts had died away. At each of the sconces along the walls, Alasdair lifted Connor so the boy could remove the lit candle or tin of oil. The rooms in the wing were sparse, but each had enough furniture to fuel a healthy flame that would soon reach the wooden rafters and bring down the roof.

Alasdair glanced back as they headed down the stairs. Smoke rolled from all the rooms, hanging low in the damp air. Satisfaction filled him and hope for the future as well. France would nay be so bad. Especially with Isobel and Connor at his side.

"Soldiers!" she hissed as they reached the base of the stairs. "I saw the red of their uniforms when they passed in front of the hearth." She stole a frantic glance in the other direction of the hall. Smoke already filled the tower housing the spiral stairs behind them. "Someone approaches from both sides. We're trapped."

Alasdair pushed around her. "Keep close behind me," he ordered. "And Connor—hold tight to yer mother."

Ian took his place at Alasdair's side, nudging his shoulder against him. "Now what?" he asked, strain clear in his tone.

"We shall see," Alasdair said as he swiped sweat and grime from his burning eyes. The smoke and heat had grown fierce, and the flames crackling on the floor above had set to roaring. It wouldn't be long before everything caught, and the wing came down around their ears.

A redcoat stepped out from behind a column, shoving the tip of his musket in Alasdair's face. The man's eyes rounded, and a smile flickered across his grimy face. "Master Cameron!" He lowered his gun, and his smile grew as he peered from side to side and took in Ian, Isobel, and Connor.

Atchison. Alasdair exhaled and lowered his sword. "I never thought to be so relieved to come face to face with an Englishman."

Isobel peeped around Alasdair's arm. "I owe that man a good hard kick in the bollocks."

Atchison's gaze fell to his feet. "Please forgive me, Your Grace, and believe me when I say, I am truly glad to see you safe and leaving this place." He lifted his head and fixed a startled glance at the staircase behind them. "The smoke is coming from the second floor."

Alasdair scooped up Connor in one arm, looped the other around Isobel, and pushed past Atchison. "Aye, the place is afire, and we intend to let it burn."

"We've overcome the duke's people." Atchison rushed forward and waved for them to follow. As they trotted toward the part of the wing connected to the tall main building of the keep, he shook his head. "Strange lot. Many died defending the place. More devoted to the duke than any servants I've ever seen."

"I want the entire place in ashes," Isobel said as she pulled away. She took hold of an iron rod beside the hearth and raked the burning logs and roiling coals out onto the floor. She ran to a long bench, latched hold of the armrest, and strained to move it. It didn't budge.

Alasdair blew out a frustrated growl. The place and the terrible memories it held had taken hold of his love and held her prisoner. He set Connor to his feet, strode to her side, and hefted the bench over to the fire. As she ran past him to fetch another chair, he snatched hold of her arm and brought his face close to hers. "Enough, Isobel. The devil bastard is dead, and his hell is on fire. We must go now, love. We're still at risk."

The glow of the fire flickered across her filthy, blood-spattered face, the demons she fought reflected in her dark eyes. "He really is dead?" she whispered, casting a fearful gaze back at the stairs.

"Aye, *mo ghràdh*." Alasdair eased his fingers to her smudged jaw and barely touched her face. "I swear the bastard's dead and already burning in the hottest part of hell."

She launched herself against his chest and wrapped her arms around him. "Thank God Almighty," she said. "And thank God for ye."

As much as he wanted to hold her and never let her go, they had to get to safety. Alasdair turned her in the direction they needed to go. "Come, love. This place will soon be down around our ears."

Her smile widened. "Aye. That it will, and glad I am of it."

A loud rumbling followed by timbers splitting affirmed their words.

The lad in one arm, Alasdair took hold of Isobel's hand, and they ran, following Atchison and Ian through the wide archway leading to the center building of the stronghold. Congregated in the entry hall at the foot of the double set of stairs, weapons held at the ready, stood Lieutenant Pewterton and several of his men.

As soon as the man spotted Alasdair with Connor and Isobel in tow, his scowl melted away, replaced by a relieved smile. "Praise be, you recovered them."

"Aye." Now wasn't the time to celebrate. Alasdair headed toward the main doors. "Ye cleared the way?" he shouted back.

Isobel hefted the dirk higher as she hurried along beside him. "I'm nay so sure I trust that man."

"Yer job is to watch for the enemy, aye?" Alasdair said to Connor as he hitched him higher on his hip and unsheathed his sword.

Connor responded with a solemn nod, looking all around as they rushed down the steps flanking the main entrance.

With Ian to his left and Isobel to his right, Alasdair hazarded a glance back. Pewterton and his men followed close behind, silhouetted by the orange glow of the blazing north wing and the flickering of the fire in the other windows as the fire spread. The shell of the place might be stone, but there was enough wood inside to fuel quite the blaze. Once the rest of the roof caught, the entire stronghold would meet its end.

Just as they cleared the gate and reached the horses, a shot rang out. Alasdair shoved Connor into Isobel's arms and pushed them both to the other side of the animals. "Ride away as fast as ye can. I'll meet ye in yon woods." He motioned toward the forest at the top of the rise and turned to go.

Isobel grabbed his arm. "Nay! I will not leave ye again."

"Do as I say, woman." Alasdair jerked his arm away. He'd not tolerate argument this time. "For Connor's sake, aye?"

He didn't wait for an answer as he crept back around the beast, scanning the area. A grim sight met his gaze. Pewterton was down. Lifeless. The one called Ladney stepped forward, musket raised and trained on Alasdair. "I've got him in my sights, Jones," he called with a toss of his head to a man behind him.

A younger soldier, one who had never said much, stepped alongside Ladney, his rifle aimed and ready. "In light of our lieutenant's diminished mental capacity and his series of poor judgments, Ladney and I are taking control of what remains of our brigade. You are under arrest, sir, for the murder of His Grace, the Duke of Temsworth, for your escape from prison, and for whatever other charges were previously filed against you." He nodded toward a point beyond Alasdair. "And I assure you, the duchess and her son will soon join you with like charges filed against them."

Alasdair stared at the scrawny bastard daring to step in the way of all his hopes and dreams. He'd be damned if he allowed all he had fought for to slip away now. There was but three broad strides between them. Good enough. Decision made, he bowed his head. A bone-shaking roar ripped from his throat as he charged forward with sword raised.

Gunfire boomed as Alasdair tore his blade down across Jones, splitting him from gullet to gut. The man remained upright for a moment, a look of shock on his face, his mouth opening and closing, but no sound coming out. His weapon bounced to the ground as he sagged to his knees, then collapsed across his gun.

Sword readied, Alasdair turned.

Ladney, the other traitor to Pewterton, lay dead beside the lieutenant. Fields stepped over Ladney and kicked the man away from the lieutenant's body. He scowled at the remaining six men. "We gave him our word. Each of us swore we'd stand at his side." He switched his rifle to his left hand and pulled his pistol from his belt. "Who else wants to die for breaking their word to that fine man who suffered so and did his best to do right by us?"

None of the men answered, just shuffled from side to side and slung their rifles back to their shoulders. Atchison walked over to the lieutenant and stared down at him.

Alasdair studied the man. He realized the Englishman looked happy for the first time since they'd met. "Put him on a horse," Alasdair ordered. "We'll give him a decent burial in the woods."

"We should bury him with his family," one of Pewterton's men volunteered. "He'd wish to be with his wife and daughters."

"We'll take him to them," Atchison said, still staring down at the lieutenant with a sad look on his face. With a deep sigh, he finally pulled his gaze up to Alasdair. "We'll say he died trying to save the duke from the fire." He glanced back at the burning estate lighting up the night. "Lieutenant ought to be known as a man who died a hero." He shifted his attention to Ladney and then Jones. "Not a man shot in the back by a pair of liars."

"And them?" Alasdair pointed his sword at the traitors' bodies.

"Them two." Atchison turned and looked at the sea. "Got too close to the edge of the cliff. Shame their bodies got swallowed up by the sea."

As far as Alasdair was concerned, even that was too good for the pair. He wiped his sword on his trews, sheathed it, then held out his hand. "I thank ye, Atchison. For everything."

Atchison gripped his hand hard and strong. "Godspeed to you, man."

Alasdair turned to Fields and shook his hand. "Ye are good men, and I'm grateful to ye."

Fields nodded. "The report shall read we spotted the fire and did what we could, but all inside died. Far as I know, we got them every last one. God go with you wherever you end up, sir."

With a nod, Alasdair left them, joining his brother, who stood a few steps away, waiting beside their horses. "She didna listen," Ian said as they settled into their saddles.

Alasdair scanned the hillside. Isobel and Connor, astride their horse several yards away, were silhouetted against the sky growing lighter behind them.

"Aye, well," Alasdair said. "I didna expect she would." They'd be having a long talk about her stubbornness. He pulled in a deep breath and rolled the tension from his shoulders. When they came up even with Isobel and Connor, he pointed to the horizon. "Shall we ride a while and put a bit a distance betwixt us and England?"

"Aye," said Isobel, Connor, and Ian in unison.

Chapter Twenty-Three

THE WIDE STRIPE of black, blue, and sickly purple across Isobel's back stirred the remnants of Alasdair's rage and deepened his remorse. He lightly caressed the ridge of her shoulders, each dark with additional bruises, as well as the raw flesh around her wrists and hands, and her scraped palms and fingers. She still bore the shackles around her ankles. It would take a blacksmith to free her of them.

He closed his eyes and buried his face in her short curly hair. "I am so verra sorry, my love," he whispered.

Isobel turned and faced him, the water in the pool swirling as she moved. She passed her hand over the angry red brand on his chest, then reached up to touch the partially healed burns along his jawline and cheek. A sad smile played across her lips. "These scars show our love and devotion to one another. Dinna be sorry. I bear mine with pride."

"I love ye, my heart." He dipped his head and kissed her. He'd never get enough of this precious woman. Not ever. They'd just made love beside the peaceful waters they had found hidden in the woods, but he already wanted her again. A faint huff of amusement escaped him.

"Ye find my kisses entertaining, do ye?"

Dribbling water across her shoulders, he smiled. "We just made love, and I already want ye again." Walking backward, he drew them closer to the embankment. He settled his arse on a rock beneath the water's surface, then guided her into his lap. "Even the cold water canna sway me."

She settled on top of him and slid against his chest, leaning into him with a promising wiggle.

"Are ye all right, love?" he asked.

"Aye." She reached down between them and stroked him. "Just a bit stiff and sore in places from our wee adventure. I think both our bodies could use a bit a healing." She nibbled along his bottom lip as she pushed herself upward, then settled him deep inside her warmth. "Healing together as one. Do ye not agree?"

"Aye, love. Most certainly." Hands filled with her slick arse, Alasdair squeezed as she rocked back and forth atop him.

She buried her fingers in his hair and arched, bringing her breasts close enough for tasting. Her cool flesh warmed in his mouth, and another gasp escaped her. Alasdair smiled, then returned to suckling her nipple. That gasp had been one of pleasure, not pain.

She clutched his head closer and rode faster, letting out a cry as she peaked. He rose from his watery seat, remaining inside her and rested her back against the bank of moss beside the stones. Then he thrust deeper until a roaring release rendered him incapable of anything other than gasping for breath.

He collapsed across her, burying his face in the curve of her neck. Her hands smoothed up and down his back with a gentleness that filled his heart even more. "Ye amaze me, woman," he said between hard breaths.

She shook beneath him. "How so?"

"Each day." He kissed her collarbone. "Each day, I love ye more, and I dinna know how ye manage it."

Isobel sighed. "I think ye were right. Our souls were stitched together before we were born." She kissed his shoulder. "We were never meant to be apart. Now, we're finally back together. Whole again."

"Mama!" The long, demanding wail that only a child can manage shattered the serenity of the woods.

"It appears our solitude is over," Alasdair chuckled as he righted Isobel and helped her climb the bank.

"Ian can only do so much with the lad." She shook out her clothes and donned them. "He's as sore and battle-weary as we are."

"Aye," Alasdair said as he belted his kilt and pulled on his boots. He rose and offered her his arm. "But Ian has always loved a challenge."

"Connor can be a challenge, all right." She hugged his arm close as they wound their way through the trees, toward the sound of Connor's call.

"Mama! Da! Where are ye?"

"We're coming, son," Alasdair called out. *Da*. He liked the sound of that. Connor might not be blood, but the lad was most certainly the son of his heart.

"We caught fishes!" The boy stormed through the trees, meeting them halfway to the clearing. He held up two fingers with one hand and three with the other. "This many, and they're fine, fat ones. Found some mushrooms, too. A bit of garlic and greens. Ian said we'll eat like kings this day!"

"Well done!" Alasdair tousled Connor's hair. "Shall I help ye gut the fish for cooking?"

"Nay." He shook his head, then turned and started gathering sticks. "Ian's doing that. I'm 'posed to be getting more wood for the fire." He glanced back at them with a grin as he trotted off. "I like living in the woods."

"Perhaps we should settle in the countryside in France rather than the city," Alasdair mused as they strolled toward camp.

"Even with Temsworth dead, we still must leave Scotland?"

"Aye." The prospect pained him as well, but there was no escaping grim reality. Alasdair scooped up a good-sized log for the fire and tossed it onto Connor's pile as they entered the clearing. "I'm still a wanted man from the charges he filed and the prison break." He dusted off his hands. "I'm sure I'll be blamed for the man's death, as well. No matter what Fields reports."

Isobel seated herself on a rock near the fire and set to stripping away the loose bark and tiny offshoots from the sticks intended to skewer the fish. She propped a flat edge of a rock over the flames and pushed a pile of the hottest coals beneath it. The Highlands had provided them with quite the skillet. She shook her head. "I'm not sure where Connor and I stand in all this. I might be Temsworth's widow, but many knew I'd find a way to leave him before he died."

Ian and Connor returned to the clearing, Connor clutching an armload of wood and Ian holding the fish. Ian's pallor concerned Alasdair. Isobel had cleaned the cut across his chest, and while it was true, the wound wasn't deep, his brother had still lost quite a bit of blood. Alasdair hoped the man's stubbornness pulled him through. He didn't want to ponder a life without his brother.

With a weary smile, Ian held up the largest of the fish. "Look at the size of this one. Nearly big as the lad."

"Well done the both of ye." Isobel patted another flat stone beside the fire. "Place them here, and I'll set them to cooking."

Connor dumped the armload of wood in the pile but kept one of the heftier sticks tight in his hand. He brandished the branch like a sword and pointed to the side of the area rising with a gentle slope. "I'll take first watch. I saw a fine rock up yonder that looks out across the glen." He widened his stance. "Aye, Da?"

They'd had no trouble, and with them within a day's ride of *Tor Ruadh*, Alasdair didn't see the harm in letting the boy feel courageous. "Aye, lad. Remember how I showed ye to move through the trees? Canny as a wee fox. Stealth, ye ken?"

Connor gave a curt nod. His gaze shifted to his mother. "Dinna fear, Mama. I'll warn ye in plenty of time if anyone draws near."

Isobel smiled as she brushed the dirt away from the mushrooms and mixed them with the greens and garlic atop the rock heating over the coals. "I know ye will, son."

"That's a good lad, right there," Ian said as he flopped the fish down on the stone.

"He is that," she said with a proud smile as she set to cooking their meal.

Alasdair leaned back against the tree, a feeling of contentment easing through him as he watched Isobel. All was as it should be. Nearly. Once they reached *Tor Ruadh*, Father William could hear their vows and pronounce them married for true. Then they'd leave for France and start their lives together. Eyelids heavy, he found it impossible to stay awake. Maybe he'd indulge in a wee nap before supper. He drew in a deep breath and settled more comfortably against the tree.

A skittering through the leaves in the direction Connor had gone jolted Alasdair. The boy exploded into the clearing. "Soldiers!" he hissed. He pointed in the direction of the glen. "A good-sized army of'm!"

"Douse the fire," Alasdair ordered. He unsheathed his sword and rushed to Connor's side. "Show me."

Connor led him up the hillside to the lookout post. The boy was right. An entire regiment of redcoats rode through the valley at a slow pace. Some were fanning out as though in search of a place to make camp. Fort William was a day and a half away, well past *Tor Ruadh* and Ben Nevis. If headed to Fort William, the British would travel the same direction as they intended to take.

"At least we're hidden in the woods," Connor whispered, his focus locked on the men below.

"Aye." Alasdair blew out a hard breath.

Now they had no choice but to move. To where, he hadn't a clue.

They couldn't risk a night so close to the British. The trees surrounding their clearing was small, barely spanning the side of the steep rise. The area where they'd made camp could be easily found—especially if the soldiers decided to hunt for food or water. But if they left the cover of the place now, they'd surely be spotted. He gazed overhead. The sun hung low over the horizon. An hour or two until nightfall. He tapped Connor's shoulder. "Back to camp. We'll slip away when the sun sets and the fog rises, aye?"

The lad cast a worried glance back to the glen. "I thought us finally safe." He slipped his hand into Alasdair's.

"I know, lad." He gave Connor's fingers a reassuring squeeze. He felt the boy's disappointment as keenly as he did his own. "I did, too."

"How many?" Ian asked as they entered the clearing.

"A large detachment. Looks to be searching for a place to camp for the night." Alasdair frowned at the fish among a generous pile of chanterelles, greens, and wild garlic sizzling on the rock over the hot coals of what had been the fire. The pungent aroma of cooking was unmistakable. "Did I not say douse the fire?"

"I did," Isobel defended. "But the rock had already heated through, and the coals have yet to die. I didna want to waste such a bounty, and Ian agreed."

Ian pointed at the tops of the trees swaying in the wind. "We're downwind from the glen. All should be well."

"Ye'd risk our lives for a bit a fish and mushrooms?" Alasdair pointed toward the horses. "We need to hie ourselves out of here as soon as darkness covers us." Had his brother lost his senses?

"I'm hungry. I'm tired. And ye know as well as I that a troop of bloody Sassenachs canna find the warts on their own arses." Ian glared at him. "We shouldna panic and run like grouse flushed from the thicket." He jerked a thumb toward the glen. "Put out the fire? Aye. For certain. Then bed down. If we leave this grove, be it night or day, I say we risk discovery. It's too open through here and too far a ride to the mountain pass leading to the glen at the base of Ben Nevis." He swiped a forearm across his forehead, then strode back to the fire, squatted down, and plucked up a steaming mushroom and popped it in his mouth.

Tension knotting his gut, Alasdair studied his brother. Ian had seen a good many more battles than he had and survived. Perhaps he was right. Above all, they couldn't lose their heads. Not when they were so close to regaining their hopes and dreams.

Isobel piled chunks of fish, mushrooms, and garlic on a length of bark. She rose from the fire and held it out to Alasdair. "Here. Ian's right. Eat. The fish is done, and the sooner we eat, the sooner the smell goes away."

"Might there be enough for another?" Lord Crestshire stepped into the clearing and gave Ian a smug look. "Couldn't find the warts on our own asses, eh? Who's the ass now, my friend?"

Crestshire would be the only Sassenach who could track them. The cunning rascal knew a Highlander's ways as well as any Scot.

"Depends. What do ye mean to do?" Alasdair asked, seating himself atop a downed tree. He might as well enjoy his meal if he was bound back to the gallows.

Crestshire shrugged. "I intend to enjoy the food, if Her Grace has enough."

"There is always room at my table," Isobel said as she thrust the rustic plate of food into his hands. "But dinna bite the hand that feeds ye, for its mate could verra well hold a knife."

"So noted, Your Grace." Crestshire gave a gallant nod. He took a seat on the log beside Alasdair, then dug into the food like a man starved. "You understand you are a wanted man," he noted between mouthfuls.

"Aye." Alasdair finished his meal and tossed the bark aside, waiting. He wouldn't kill Crestshire, but he wasn't past tying him to a tree. He could always send word of where they'd left him to Fort William.

"And ye understand, ye're outnumbered in this camp, aye?"

Crestshire grinned as he ate the last of his fish. "Yes. I am quite aware, I assure you." He rubbed his stomach, belched as big and loud as any Scot, and smiled at Isobel. "A fine meal, Your Grace. I thank you. I wasn't relishing eating in my tent since my former cook was replaced by an incompetent man who I'm certain is trying to poison me."

Isobel answered with a glare as cold as death.

"I see." Crestshire turned back to Alasdair. "You know it is my duty to arrest you. You also know how I feel about duty."

Alasdair tensed, resettling his feet and propping his hands atop his knees. If Crestshire moved, he'd take him to the ground. Ian edged closer, ready to help with the task. "And ye understand I willna allow ye to do so."

All humor left Crestshire as he pulled in a deep breath and stared down at the ground. "You and I have been friends a long time, Alasdair."

"Aye."

Crestshire stood, careful to move away from Alasdair as he walked. He clasped his hands to the small of his back. "I received word of the duke's demise and the unfortunate fire." He settled a thoughtful gaze on Alasdair, studying him for a long while. "I've just come from London. It is my understanding no one mourns the man. In fact, his debtors are searching for Temsworth's heirs to beg leniency regarding their notes. Last I heard, there was quite the celebration as a result of his death. It appears His Grace had a great deal more enemies than friends."

"Of that, I have no doubt," Alasdair said as he rose. "Yer point?"

"If the charges against you were appealed..." Crestshire paused, rubbing a finger across his chin as he aimed a faint grin in Alasdair's direction.

"If Temsworth's heirs didna fight the appeal and, in fact, dropped the charges," Alasdair finished, a blinding sense of realization jolting through him.

"We are Temsworth's only heirs," Isobel offered, rushing to Alasdair's side.

"I'm surprised you didn't think of that before now." Crestshire strolled over to the fire, plucked the last mushroom off the cooking stone, and ate it. He glanced back at Alasdair. "Finest solicitor in all of Scotland? Ha! Your wiles are slipping you, old man."

"I've been a mite distracted." Alasdair waited for Crestshire's next move. The charges still stood for now, and he'd be damned if he returned to the hellish Tollbooth for the time it took to get them overturned.

Crestshire dusted off his hands. "Alexander informed me of the reprehensible treatment you endured at the Tollbooth." His face tightened into a disgusted scowl. "My sense of duty to king and country is strong, but not so strong as my abhorrence for such deeds— especially in regard to a friend." He strode to the edge of the clearing, pausing just before stepping into the trees. Without looking back, he lifted a hand. "I found enough mushrooms and berries in the woods to help me endure whatever disgusting meal has been prepared for me this evening. Godspeed to you and yours, my friend."

Then he strode away before Alasdair could reply.

CHAPTER TWENTY-FOUR

STRONG ARMS ENCIRCLED her waist, and a mouth possessing the power to weaken her knees nibbled a burning trail from her nape to the sensitive skin just behind her ear. "I thought I'd never find ye, *wife*," Alasdair grumbled as he snuggled close.

"Wife," she repeated as she hugged him. "I love it when ye call me wife." A soft laugh escaped her. "Except when ye're scolding me, of course."

"If ye'd behave, I wouldna have to scold ye," he teased as he rested his chin atop her shoulder and tightened his embrace. "I worried when I couldna find ye. Especially when Mercy and Catriona had no idea where ye'd gone off to. I know yesterday's visit to Yeva's grave was hard."

Isobel didn't comment, just returned her attention to the sprawling glen below. She'd sought solitude atop the skirting wall, hoping the land's rugged beauty might calm her troubled mind. She'd been wrong. The deep, verdant stretch of green dotted with dwellings and divided by a ribbon of water snaking across it fueled her dread even more. They had been here a month. A wonderful month that felt like a different lifetime. *Tor Ruadh* and the MacCoinnich lands felt like home now, and she loved the place. But if they didn't soon receive word of the charges against Alasdair being successfully reversed, to France they had to go.

"I dinna wish to leave here," she whispered. A heavy sigh escaped her. "I dinna wish to leave Scotland."

He shifted to stand at her side, slid his hand beneath hers, then lifted it for a kiss. "I know, lass. Neither do I." He gave her an apologetic smile, then turned and gazed out across the glen. "It's my hope we'll only be in France a little while."

"How much longer dare we wait before we leave?" She knew the answer. Dreaded it. But prayed he had changed his mind.

"One more sennight. No more."

She leaned against the rough, cool stone of the battlement, staring down at the road connecting *Tor Ruadh* to the village and then beyond. Just seven more days. Connor would be just as heartbroken as her. Everyone had grown so close—Alasdair's family had welcomed her and Connor as one of their own.

"A rider." Alasdair stepped closer to the wall and pointed toward the horizon. "Just there."

Her hopes soared as she squinted at the dark dot making its way toward them. "I see. They're traveling at a good trot."

The rider disappeared from view, hidden by the cluster of dwellings in the more populated part of the village. Isobel held her breath. *Please...* She excitedly patted the top of the battlement as the rider reappeared, heading toward the stronghold. "They're coming here."

"It's Abernathy." Alasdair smiled. "I'm certain of it." He offered his arm. "Come. Let us meet the man and hear what he has to say."

They hurried down to the bailey. Isobel focused on the gate, clenching her hands so tight, her nails dug into her palms. Her heartbeat thundered as Thomas Abernathy rode into view. God bless the man. He sat a horse so poorly, clutching the reins and the front of the saddle as though he feared his mount would throw him at any moment.

"Stop now, horse." Abernathy made a nervous yank on the reins.

"Halt this instant, I say."

Alasdair stepped forward and took hold of the animal's bridle as Abernathy made an awkward dismount.

Isobel pressed her fingers to her mouth to keep from smiling. How had he managed the trip all the way from Edinburgh without breaking his neck or losing his mount? His wee mare had to have the temperament of a saint.

"Good heavens," Abernathy huffed as he brushed off his clothes, then fished around in the breast pocket of his jacket. He withdrew his spectacles and wiped them with a square of linen. After wedging them on the bridge of his nose, he turned to Alasdair with a sheepish smile. "I wouldna risk such a wild beast for anyone but ye, Master Cameron."

"I'm well aware of that," Alasdair said as he shook the man's hand. "I pray ye bear good news?"

"I do, sir." Abernathy sidled back to the mare and pulled a packet from the pouch hanging from the saddle. He placed the packet in Alasdair's hands. "See for yerself."

Isobel couldn't contain herself any longer. She rushed to Alasdair's side, took hold of his arm, and squeezed. "Alasdair's name is finally cleared?"

Abernathy gave a startled hop to one side. "Yes, Yer Grace. Name cleared. Properties released. And he's fully reinstated to represent clients in any courtroom he sees fit to enter." He turned back to Alasdair. "Ye can return to Edinburgh whenever ye wish, sir. Yer residence is fully staffed and waiting. I saw to it m'self."

"At last," she sobbed. "We can claim our happiness!" She pressed a hand to her chest and snatched hold of Alasdair's sleeve, dizzy with the sheer joy of it.

He caught her to his side and steadied her. "Are ye all right, love?"

"More than all right, my dearest one." She held tight to him, closing her eyes as she rested her cheek on his chest.

Abernathy excitedly patted his hands together again. "And I've even more grand news. The young marquess, or perhaps I should say, the young *Duke* of Temsworth's inheritance is now his without claim or issue. The will also granted a generous stipend for the duchess." He cocked a brow. "Quite surprising but fully verified by the estate's solicitor." He took a step closer and gave a knowing nod. "I'm sure the provision was made to satisfy terms in the late duke's father's will."

"Of that, I'm sure," Isobel agreed.

"Lady Bel! Lady Bel!" Little Willa's piercing shout of the name all the children called Isobel shot through the courtyard.

Momentarily pulled from the joy of her hard-won freedom, Isobel waved the little girl down. "Here, child!"

Eyes wide and cheeks aglow, Willa scurried to Isobel's side and latched hold of her hand. "Mama says come quick. The bairn's coming. Aunt Mercy's bairn's a comin' fast!"

Isobel squeezed Alasdair's arm. "A blessed day, indeed. Freedom and a new babe."

"Aye, love," he laughed. "On wi' ye now. We'll celebrate as soon as the bairn and Mercy be safe."

"Aye." Isobel gathered her skirts in both hands and hurried after Willa up the steps. She halted at the sight of four MacCoinnich warriors, standing side by side across the end of the hall.

They stood in front of the chieftain's table with arms stretched skyward, each of them clutching the corners of a tapestry and holding it aloft like a curtain behind their backs. They had the expressions of men waiting at the gallows to be hanged. Red-faced. Uncomfortable. Pained. The discomfited men effectively walled off the head of the hall from view. A cry sounded from the hidden part of the hall.

Willa waved her forward. "Hurry. Aunt Mercy couldna even make it to her rooms."

Isobel rushed past the men. "God bless ye," slipped from her lips.

Mercy half stood, half squatted in front of the chieftain's chair, hands gripping the wooden armrests so tightly, her knuckles glowed white. Catriona and Gretna stood on either side of her. Catriona rubbed her lower back while Gretna dabbed a cloth across her brow.

Catriona acknowledged Isobel with an upward jerk of her chin. "Wee Ramsay was the same. Came hard and fast when he decided to finally enter the world, but at least he gave us time to send for the midwife. Only problem was he came feet first. We fear this one's the same, and there be no time to send to the village for old Elena."

Isobel swallowed hard. Such births often ended badly. Many a time, the child couldn't be born. "Not today," Isobel swore as she rolled her sleeves up above her elbows.

"Willa—run and fetch more linens, aye?" Isobel squeezed Mercy's shoulder. "Do ye feel as if the wee dear is ready for me to catch?"

Mercy bared her teeth, bore down into a deeper squat. "I don't know. Just pull the child out of me! I beg you!"

At Catriona and Gretna's nod, Isobel lifted Mercy's skirts. "Help her stand," Isobel ordered, remembering Auntie Yeva's teachings and her own experience of giving birth to Connor the same way. "We've got a bum peering out at us."

"Not again," Mercy sobbed. "Ramsay nearly died, and so did I."

"None a that, now," Isobel reassured. "We're all here, and ye'll be holding this fine babe to yer breast in no time."

"Aye," Gretna agreed. "We're stronger than any warriors, aye?"

"Aye," Catriona joined in. "Fight with us, lass. Fight to bring yer precious bairn into this world."

Isobel worked her fingers up around the babe, gently maneuvering and pulling as Mercy pushed. With Mercy's pains and long, steady pushing, Isobel untangled first one leg and then freed the other. She supported the wee one's body in her palm and held out a hand for linen. "A cloth, Willa. Hand me a cloth."

Willa complied, wide-eyed and uncharacteristically quiet.

Isobel wrapped the cloth around the bairn's slick body. "'Tis a lassie!" she laughed. "What be her name, Mercy?" Mercy's strength was waning fast. The poor woman needed something to bolster her.

"Effie Marsalla Jeanette," Mercy said, sounding stronger. "A daughter? I have a sweet daughter?"

"Aye, a precious one," Isobel said as she finished cleaning the babe.

Little Effie's cries informed all and sundry she had arrived into the world.

"Praise, God," Mercy gasped as Catriona and Gretna eased her down to her knees, then helped her lie back on the pile of pillows on the pallet they'd hastily assembled. A weary smile set her face aglow. "She sounds fierce and strong."

"Aye, she is all that and more. Praise, God, indeed." Isobel smiled down at the squalling, red-faced babe in her arms. Such a joy-filled day. The perfect day to share the secret she'd been dying to tell Alasdair. *Aye.* It was time. She felt certain of it now. She lowered Effie into her mother's outstretched arms.

As she moved away, Mercy snagged her arm. "Thank you, Isobel. Thank you for helping get my darling Effie here safe and sound. There was no time to fetch old Elena from the village, and poor Gretna was so afraid because she'd never delivered such a bairn before."

"I feel blessed to have been a part of Effie's arrival." Isobel cupped the child's head. The wee one's dark hair was quickly drying and growing silky as thistle flower. "Now Willa and I shall fetch Graham whilst Catriona and Gretna get Effie and yerself better settled."

Willa took hold of Isobel's hand, bouncing along beside her as they rounded the wall of warriors. Isobel grinned at the poor man on the end, sweating but maintaining the position of the makeshift wall. "Ye can rest soon. It will nay take them long to get her sorted."

"Thank ye, m'lady," the polite man said with a strained smile.

"Can I be the one to fetch Uncle Graham?" Willa asked as they exited the keep.

"Aye. Run and fetch him." Isobel shielded her eyes from the brightness of the wonderful day, searching the bailey for Alasdair. She spotted him near the guard tower, chatting with Alexander. Both men looked toward her at the sound of her approach.

She smiled and made the announcement before they even asked. "A healthy wee lassie. Both Effie and mother are doing well."

"Effie," Alasdair repeated with a pleased nod. "A fine name."

"Aye," Alexander agreed. "Graham will be beside himself."

"Willa's gone in search of him. Yer daughter was a great help in getting the babe here." Isobel looped her arm through Alasdair's, wishing Alexander would leave. "Ye should praise her greatly when next ye see her."

Alexander shook his head. "Six years old and already midwifing. The child never ceases to amaze me." He smiled as Graham loped past them, vaulted the steps leading up to the keep, and disappeared inside. "I best go pay my respect to my new niece."

"I as well," Alasdair chuckled.

"Ye may go in a moment," Isobel said as she pulled back on his arm.

Alexander paused and gave them both a puzzled look, then shrugged and left when Isobel nodded and waved him on.

"What is it, love?" Alasdair took hold of both her hands, concern wiping the happiness from his face.

"Has Mr. Abernathy already left?"

"Aye."

"But he did say yer home in Edinburgh is ready as soon as ye care to return?" Isobel pulled her hands free of his, clasping them across her middle.

"Aye, but there's nay reason to hurry if ye wish to stay here and help Mercy with the babe." Alasdair gave a faint smile. "I know how women are with bairns."

"Do ye now?" Isobel lifted her chin. "And how are *ye* with bairns?"

Alasdair shrugged. "All right, I reckon. Although I prefer the older ones." He grinned. "Connor is the perfect age."

"I see." Isobel put on as serious a face as she could manage. "Perhaps we best stay here a while so ye can practice with wee Effie."

"Practice?" A more confused look on her beloved man's face she'd never seen.

Isobel nodded. "Aye. Practice." She took a step closer, tilted her head, and smiled. "Tiny Effie is good practice for ye holding yer own wee one come late next summer."

Alasdair's jaw dropped. "A child?"

"*Our* child," Isobel corrected.

"Our child!" Alasdair roared as he grabbed her up into his arms and spun her about. "Our child," he repeated as he stopped spinning, set her on her feet, and gazed into her eyes. "Finally," he whispered. "Our dreams…"

"Aye, m'love." Isobel stretched for a kiss, then pulled back and smiled. "All our dreams have at last come true."

EPILOGUE

Three years later…
Edinburgh, Scotland
Late summer 1701

"B ARELY TWO YEARS old and already sitting a horse."

"Aye." Alasdair smiled. A mix of love, pride, and content-ment filled him as he leaned against the paddock fence and watched Connor walking the docile mare that had once been his. Upon picking out his own much larger horse from *Tor Ruadh*'s stables, the eight-year-old hadn't hesitated in passing along the smaller mount to his wee sister.

"Faster!" the little girl ordered. She squirmed and bounced, thump-ing her tiny heels against the saddle's sides. "Faster, bruvver!"

"'Tis fast enough, Keavy," Connor scolded, although he relented and increased his pace a bit. "Sit ye still this instant, or I'll be gettin' ye down from there."

Haggis gave a sharp bark, as if adding his opinion. The black dog trotted back and forth beside Connor, ever vigilant to his master's every move.

"Ye're a fine, patient brother, Connor," Ian said. He turned to Alasdair with a grin. "We never had a sister, but I remember Isobel was quite the chore when we were all bairns."

"I'm still quite the chore," Isobel stated as she waddled toward them with one hand pressed to the small of her back and the other propped atop her rounded stomach.

"A beloved chore," Alasdair corrected as he pressed a kiss to her temple." If possible, he loved her more every day, and the sight of her swollen with his second child still undid him. "Ye're supposed to be abed. Resting."

Isobel shook her head. "A terrible craving came upon me for Auntie's fried bread, so I greased up her griddle and made some. I made plenty for all." She gave a weary sigh as she patted her swollen middle. "Besides, yer child is nay in the mood for resting. The wee beastie is all pokes and prods today. I swear there's an entire clan at war in there. I dinna remember Connor nor Keavy thrashing about so."

"Ye do look larger this time, sister," Ian noted with a wicked grin.

Alasdair cringed. His brother was a dead man.

Isobel locked a fierce scowl upon him. "Why, thank ye, Ian. With so much charm about ye, how is it we've nay married ye off to some poor, unsuspecting lass?"

"I meant 'lovelier'," Ian hurried to amend with a hopeful smile. "Ye look even lovelier than last I saw ye." He shifted, a pleading gaze aimed at Alasdair.

Alasdair shook his head. "Nay, brother. Ye dug this pit yerself, and now it's up to ye to find yer way out of it."

"I'm certain Ian is truly sorry for his ill-timed jest at the expense of a woman heavy with child," Isobel said. "Are ye not, Ian?"

Alasdair took a step back and watched. His brother might as well commit his soul to Almighty God because Isobel was about to have his arse.

"Aye, dear sister," Ian said, assuming a mournful look. "I truly am. How can I make amends for my thoughtless jest?"

"Make amends?" Isobel's head tilted the slightest bit, and her expression became thoughtful.

If Alasdair didn't know better, he'd say she was preparing to fire a kill shot.

"Aye, sweet sister." Ian's smile stretched wider. "Name my penance, and it shall be done. I swear it."

Alasdair scrubbed a hand across his mouth, clenching his teeth to keep from laughing. He knew without a doubt what Ian's penance would be. Isobel had been pestering him about that very subject for the past three weeks. Better Ian hear it from Isobel since she, along with Catriona and Mercy, had already decided his poor brother's fate. Whenever those three women set their minds on something, it was done. God help Ian. His poor brother didn't stand a chance.

"Winter at *Tor Ruadh*," she said.

"Winter at *Tor Ruadh*?" Ian repeated. Brow furrowed, he shrugged. "Easy enough, even though I thought to winter here in Edinburgh with all of ye."

"Ye are needed at *Tor Ruadh*," Isobel stated with the curtness of a military commander. "Gretna Neal needs a man's assistance with her sons, and ye're most definitely the man suited for the task."

Realization and pure fear flashed across Ian's face. He shook his head while retreating a few steps. "Nay, Isobel. I know now what ye be about. I'm nay the man to wed Gretna Neal and take over the taming of those three demons a hers." He shook his head faster. "I'm cursed, remember? Any woman I take dies. Would ye truly wish such a fate on yer friend? Why...what would Mercy do without her dear Gretna?"

"Ye are nay cursed." Alasdair rested his arm around Isobel's shoulders. "And she's nay asking ye to marry the lass. The woman merely needs help training up her bairns. Widowed now all these years. Two husbands dead. She couldna even bury the last one and have a grave to cry over. They never found the man's body." He gave Ian a hard look. "Come now, man. Are ye so hard-hearted that ye'd refuse a poor widow yer help?"

Isobel leaned against him. *Good.* His dear wife was pleased with his words. Mayhap now she'd leave off nettling his arse about Gretna Neal needing a father for those three terrors of hers—the wildest, unruliest trio of children he'd ever seen.

"If ye dinna agree to winter at *Tor Ruadh,* ye'll not be wintering here either." Isobel lifted her chin. "I dinna mean to seem stern, but 'tis yer Christian duty, and yer honor as a Highlander to care for poor widows and their children. I know how yer mother raised ye. What would she say about ye refusing to help?"

Jaw tight, Ian shot a simmering look at Alasdair.

"Come on, man. No one's saying ye have to marry the woman. Just help her tame those hellions. It's just one winter. Come spring, ye can be on yer way." Alasdair grinned. "Ye always were the best at breaking horses, surely three lads willna be such a chore for ye."

"Ye're a cold-hearted man, brother," Ian growled, then jerked a thumb in Isobel's direction. "And ye're married to an even colder-hearted woman." He stomped to the stable, coming to a halt in front of the wide, double doors to shake a finger at the both of them. "I dinna know where I'm headed. Maybe *Tor Ruadh.* Maybe not. I'll see the two of ye come spring—if I've forgiven ye by then." With a growl, he disappeared into the building.

"He'll winter at *Tor Ruadh,*" Alasdair assured as he pulled Isobel into his arms. He brushed a kiss across her forehead and smiled down at her. "Happy now?"

"Nay," she replied with a mischievous look.

"Nay?"

"Nay," she whispered as she pressed as close as she could get so her lips were within a hair's breadth of his. "I'll nay be happy until I receive a proper kiss."

"Gladly, m'love." Alasdair leaned into the task. *Happily.*

If you enjoyed The Judge, please consider spreading the word about it by leaving a review on the site where you purchased your copy, or on a reader site such as Goodreads or BookBub. Reviews help authors more than you know and they are SO appreciated. Your review could help another reader decide if they'd like to meet Alasdair and Isobel.

I always love hearing from readers so drop me a line at maevegreyson@gmail.com

OR visit me on Facebook: facebook.com/AuthorMaeveGreyson

Maeve's Corner is my private Facebook Group. It's about books, life, Scotland, dragons, dreams and wishes too! Kindness rules there. Smiles, laughter, hugs, and hearts are always welcome!

You can find out more about the group here: facebook.com/groups/MaevesCorner

I'm also on Instagram: maevegreyson and authormaevegreyson It's a long story how I ended up with two accounts. Suffice it to say, I'm a newbie to the "gram".

Twitter: @maevegreyson

Visit my website: maevegreyson.com

If you'd like to receive my occasional and very sporadic newsletter, please sign up at: maevegreyson.com/contact.html#newsletter

Follow me on these sites to get notifications about new releases, sales, and special deals:
Amazon: amazon.com/Maeve-Greyson/e/B004PE9T9U
BookBub: bookbub.com/authors/maeve-greyson

My best to you, and may your life always be filled with wonderful stories!
Maeve

About the Author

"No one has the power to shatter your dreams unless you give it to them." That's Maeve Greyson's mantra. She and her husband of almost forty years traveled around the world while in the U.S. Air Force. Now, they're settled in rural Kentucky where Maeve writes about her beloved Highlanders and the fearless women who tame them. When she's not plotting her next romantic Scottish tale, she can be found herding cats, grandchildren, and her husband—not necessarily in that order.

SOCIAL MEDIA LINKS:
Website: maevegreyson.com
Facebook Page: AuthorMaeveGreyson
Facebook Group: Maeve's Corner
facebook.com/groups/MaevesCorner
Twitter: @maevegreyson
Instagram: @maevegreyson
Amazon Author Page: amazon.com/Maeve-Greyson/e/B004PE9T9U
BookBub: bookbub.com/authors/maeve-greyson